Tattoos & Tans

Jason P. Reed

Published by New Bayou Books, LLC.

NewBayouBooks.com

Publisher's Note

This is a work of fiction. Names, characters, places and incidents either are the product of the author's imagination or are used fictitiously, and any resemblance to actual persons, living or dead, business establishments, events, or locales is coincidental.

Jason P. Reed

Tattoos and Tans/Jason P. Reed

ISBN 978-1-7374528-1-2

For Toby, for reasons that need not be explained here.

The world needs more Louisiana literature!

If you dig this book, please review it, join the mailing list at newbayoubooks.com, and help spread the word.

Table of Contents

Episode One
Walking to New Orleans

❀

Curtis Laroux arrives in New Orleans just ahead of a package of steroids he had shipped to his unwitting friend, Jacque Duchaney. Later, with the steroids in hand and a trunk full of weapons and surveillance equipment, Curtis heads to his hometown of Eunice, deep in the Cajun Prairie. There he will help his best friend, a tattoo artist named JD, settle a dispute that threatens to undermine his new business, the town's very first tattoo shop.

"If you get caught, just do that trick where you turn yourself into steam and escape through the vent." — Jacque Duchaney

By the time he touched down in New Orleans, Curtis

Laroux was pretty sure one of two things was gonna happen in the next hour. If the authorities were already on to the box of steroids he had shipped from China to the local address of his old Air Force buddy, a dude named Jacque, they would be there waiting for him. And his Louisiana adventure would end right then and there, long before he ever got to Eunice.

Instead of doing what he came down to do, he'd be busy facing an international drug trafficking charge, finding a lawyer, getting fired from his job at a certain three-letter intelligence agency in DC, having his security clearance revoked, and losing whatever kind of professional credibility he had after fifteen years in the business. All this while trying to avoid being beaten and/or sodomized in a local New Orleans jail. It wasn't how he wanted to spend a random Tuesday in January.

The second potential outcome Curtis was worried about—and it seemed more likely in that moment, taxiing into the gate at Louis Armstrong International with nothing to do but wait and breathe—was the package arriving on Jacque's doorstep before he got there and had a chance to explain.

If that happened, he might avoid jail, but there was a good chance Jacque would button up his little fortress of a house in Metairie there by the big Walgreens, and Curtis would lose a box of steroids and one of the two friends he had left in the world. And his plan would be fucked, to boot.

He had tried to reach out ahead of time, but Jacque wasn't the kind of dude who answered his phone or put his current email address out on Facebook or something for any fool to find. So Curtis had sent a letter a few days ago, old school, and hoped for the best. If he wanted to have any chance at handling the real business of his trip back home, he needed to beat the package to Jacque's place.

He had come back to Louisiana to help the second of his two friends, a dude named JD Dugas, un-fuck a situation in their hometown of Eunice. It was something Curtis could never have predicted. Not because of the trouble itself—JD mixed up in some kind of drug shit was hardly headline news—but because of where it was all going down.

JD had earned himself a reputation as a pretty badass tattoo artist over the past ten years or so, mostly in Texas, but for some reason he'd decided he needed to move back to Eunice and open the town's first-ever tattoo shop.

Why he would want to do such a thing was one of the first questions Curtis was looking forward to asking. His second, when and if they got a chance to talk face-to-face, assuming he wasn't about to get arrested at Jacque's house, was why the fuck JD had decided to rent a storefront in downtown Eunice from one of the biggest pricks in town. Lenny Prichard.

When the name bubbled up in his head, Curtis couldn't help but spit it out like he would hawk a loogie at the back of his throat. Lenny fucking Prichard. Curt had done a little homework on the dude he remembered all too well from high school baseball, one of the kids from the private school across town that Curtis and the rest of the team from Eunice High inevitably met in the all-parish tournament every year. The adult version of Lenny wasn't so different from the younger prick that Curtis remembered growing up. If ever there was a person you didn't want to be doing business with, it was Lenny fucking Prichard.

So there was that. And there was going back to Eunice, a place he generally avoided, not just in real terms, but even in his mind. Over the dozen or so years he'd been working for the government, first as an enlisted Air Force man, and then, for the last six years, as a civilian in the Department of Defense, Curtis had trained himself to put Eunice out of his mind.

His mom and his brother still lived there, but that was a whole 'nother story. He spoke to his mom on the phone a few times a year, and he'd sneaked into Eunice twice over the last decade, just to keep things on something like an even keel. But that was before she'd moved into his brother's house. There were some thresholds Curt just couldn't cross.

On top of it all, Curtis was an intel analyst, not an operator. He didn't kick doors in. His job was to identify the right door from a comfortable spot set far from the real action. He was not cut out to come swooping in to save the day.

He spent most of his time in a quiet cubicle in D.C. reading detailed reports, considering the new sources of intelligence that had come in overnight, and synthesizing a wide swath of information to try and piece together what country or bad guy X was most likely going to do. That was his whole gig, and he was good at it.

What he *wasn't* good at—what he had no real experience to speak of—was *acting* on the intelligence reports he created. The meatheads who did the dirty work did not look like Curtis. They tossed around kettlebells that looked like they belonged on pirate ships. They carried gallon jugs of water with them to the gym, where they lifted whole racks of weights at a time. They had neck tattoos and dead eyes. They subscribed to magazines about guns and had closets full of "tactical" gear.

Curtis was in a different class entirely. He wasn't a nerd, exactly. He'd been in the service too, after all, and all told, he had a little more than two years' worth of deployment time to his credit, including some months in some pretty austere, forward operating environments. And he kept himself fit. He also paid very close attention to what was happening around him, and he prided himself on his ability to outthink a lot of the folks in D.C. with much fancier educations. But at the end of the day, he was a support guy. An analyst.

But when the seatbelt light dinged at the gate, Curtis took a deep breath and tried to reprogram himself with a new affirmation he was trying out. *You will win because they will not see you coming.* Whatever he'd done or not done in his past, the fact was he was there in New Orleans, about to disembark, and when he stepped off the plane, like it or not—experienced or not—he would be the operator, because that's what JD needed. And of course he didn't intend to kick in any doors, but if it came to that, he would do his very best.

The first step was simple: get to Jacque's place before the FedEx package did. Curtis showing up at Jacque's door was enough of a surprise, maybe even a pleasant one. But if the package beat him to the house, there wouldn't be anything pleasant about it. Jacque was not a man to tolerate such things.

To say Jacque "Tick-Tock" Duchaney was a man who didn't like surprises was like saying they do things different in Louisiana. You weren't saying anything at all. He was a very cautious dude. Paranoid, to put a finer point on it. Jacque propped up his sanity on a framework of prescription pills, cannabis, and a layered home security system that only a military man could conceive of.

With those elements of mental and physical security dialed in, he could approximate normal life. At least what passed for normal around New Orleans. But his whole world was a delicate balance. An unsolicited box of steroids from the Far East showing up on his doorstep would not just tip the scales. It would catapult his life into chaos.

The authorities might already be at Jacque's place before Curtis even got there. He would have no way of knowing until it was too late. Everything would look totally normal, until it wasn't. But maybe things were normal, but there was only one way to find out. Curt took a deep breath and pictured his old friend Jacque, standing slim and proud, if a little out of place, in his Air Force uniform.

He checked his phone. The package still showed *out for delivery*. As people started flowing out of the front of the plane, he called the number he had for Jacque. It had been something like three years since they last spoke. And knowing Jacque like Curtis did—there was little chance he'd grown *less* paranoid—it was unlikely he'd pick up for a strange number. When the anonymous voice mail prompt came on Curtis kept it brief.

"Hey, buddy. It's your old pal Curt. Did you get my letter? I'm in town. Heading over to your place now. Keep a look out, okay? I'll be the good-looking white dude pulling up in the cab." When he ended the call the lady next to him chuckled at his little joke, not so much eavesdropping as overhearing. He kept his head down and repeated another little reminder to himself. *Stay invisible. You were never here.*

Curtis had been vague with his supervisor back in D.C. about why he suddenly needed two weeks of personal leave. Even something as simple as that, a little white lie, was enough to get him in hot water. When you hold a top secret security clearance, the government owns your ass. They have a right to know where you are pretty much at all times.

As far as red flags go, telling your boss you were going to New Orleans for some R and R when in reality you planned to drive into the interior of the state, off the radar, was barely even pink. Nobody was gonna raise an eyebrow at that, especially with Curtis. He was good at his job, he was responsible, and he was well-liked. But if he was honest with himself, he'd also have to admit he was bored as shit. In that light, the emergency call from JD had almost been a blessing.

He'd done two deployments as a civilian in the six years since he traded in his uniform for an oxford shirt and a tie, but even those experiences paled to the kinds of shit he got up to in Air Force intel. And even if the civilian deployments that kept him pretty far in the rear had been a kind of half-dose rush compared to his uniformed escapades, any residual high from those experiences was long gone.

Not that he was putting his whole career on the line to fly down to Louisiana just for kicks. He wasn't crazy. The emergency was legitimate, and JD was the one person in Louisiana who could call him at any time and the answer would always be yes. The only other person on that list was Jacque Duchaney, but Jacque wasn't so much the type to call for help as he was to just ratchet one in the chamber and take his chances.

Ostensibly, Curtis was here to visit Jacque and as far as the electronic record was concerned, that's how it would be. His digital trail would never leave New Orleans. Curtis would leave his phone with Jacque and maneuver off the radar—for the whole two weeks if necessary. Though he hoped it wouldn't take that long. He'd almost rather be in jail than spend two whole weeks in Eunice. But it wasn't up to him. He still didn't know how deep this hole was that JD had gotten himself pushed into.

Curtis double-checked his phone. The tracking still showed the package *out for delivery*. As the rest of the passengers stood unnecessarily, Curtis took a few deep breaths—60 seconds of meditation that might be the last mindfulness he experienced as a free man if he wasn't careful. But the thought of going back to Eunice was somehow just as nerve-racking as his rendezvous with the steroids–and maybe the cops—at Jacque's house. *Fuck*, he thought. *I'm going back to Eunice.*

The name of his hometown held a special, sour place in Curt's mind. *Eunice.* It was embarrassing, like a bad tattoo. Ever fading, but persistent. There when you stripped everything else away. And for Curtis, when you stripped away the last twelve years of language, tactics, and tradecraft honed in training and applied in analytic-support roles in Afghanistan, Iraq, West Africa, all he had learned and achieved, you ended up with Eunice. Countryfied, backwards-ass Eunice. A name right out of a fucking Hee Haw skit. He tried not to hate it, but he did.

When the passengers in the seats in front of him started to exit, Curtis worked his military-style CamelBak out from under the seat. He refused to call it his "go-bag," but the big black pack was nevertheless always ready with cash, prepaid credit cards, and a dozen or so ziplock bags with underwear and socks, toiletries, caffeine in gum and pill form, nootropics, melatonin, vitamins, and a sanitized laptop.

A year ago when he got the pack he now thought of as his *EverReady*, he'd brought it to his local dry cleaners and asked the Vietnamese lady there to sew on a handful of decidedly non-military patches, hoping to give the bag a friendly look. National Geographic, Telluride, Acadia National Park, the Louisiana Black Pot Festival and Cook-off. The patched-up EverReady suggested its owner was a harmless hippie traveler. Curtis liked to believe that wasn't too far from the truth.

When he stepped out at the taxi stand at Louis Armstrong International, the warm winter sun of Louisiana in January was like a hug from an old friend. For an instant he imagined a different set of circumstances, where maybe he could just be chilling at Audubon park at that one spot by the bend in the river, watching barges slide by on the muddy Mississippi. Maybe join in an ultimate frisbee game, drink a beer.

But the package was *out for delivery,* and if Jacque hadn't received or opened his letter he wouldn't even be expecting Curtis. It was no time to daydream. He had to move. There was a line at the taxi stand but Curtis walked a few cars up towards a group of drivers and made eye contact with a youngish Rasta guy with a beanie and dreads. "I'm in a hurry," he said, and the driver nodded towards a Crown Vic further back in the line and pivoted towards it. He could hear the other drivers grumbling behind him, but Curtis and the driver kept walking.

As soon as they got moving, the driver made eye contact in the rearview mirror and said "I can't sell you no weed, but I'll tell you the table at the French Market to get it. Just tell 'em Solomon sent you." Curtis was happy to be mistaken for that kind of tourist—maybe the patches on his bag and his casual clothes were projecting the right image—so he accepted the tip, pulled out his phone, and dropped a pin on the map. Maybe Jacque could use another source.

The windows were down in the old cab and Curtis sat back, enjoying the cool afternoon breeze and hoping the driver wasn't in a mood to talk. The car radio was tuned to WWOZ, the old-school New Orleans music station that had been around forever. Curtis didn't recognize the band, which was no surprise. He dug the Big Easy and the universe of music and culture it produced, but his ear had always leaned towards the grittier stuff that came out of South Louisiana, whether it was Sonny Landreth's electric slide guitar or the new Cajun and zydeco styles that bands like the Red Stick Ramblers and the Revelers breathed life into.

The band on the radio was in the middle of an extended, funky jam with all kinds of percussion and horns that was perfect for the ride because it gave Curtis a chance to think. He watched the flat, suburban scenery scroll by through the window and rehearsed what he'd say to Jacque. *I'm here to help a friend in trouble. I need your help.* The old cab had pulled onto Airline Drive by the time the band broke back into the chorus—another New Orleans party anthem for a city of party bands and their party songs. By then Curtis had tuned the music out almost entirely. He focused on his breathing, meditating with his eyes open and working hard to manifest a positive kind of energy he hoped Jacque would respond to.

One deployment had proven to be exactly enough for a troubled motherfucker like Jacque. He came out of it with all kinds of commendations, and his Air Force future would've been bright. But there were discipline issues. Fights over stupid stuff, schoolyard stuff. And in another service that probably would've been just fine. But when he developed a fixation on how IEDs worked and started building miniature ones in his tent, that got leadership's attention. The psych eval revealed a whole range of issues Jacque already knew he had. They let him finish the deployment, gave him a medical discharge, and within a few weeks of getting back stateside he was a civilian again.

Jacque had moved back in with his elderly mother, to the little house he grew up in—the same house Curtis was on his way to now. Curtis had only been there once before, for a weekend trip when he was still in uniform, maybe a year or so after Jacque had been discharged, but just a few weeks after Jacque's mom had passed. He had been supporting the brass at a war gaming exercise at Maxwell Air Force base in Montgomery, and so decided to drive down for the weekend. It wasn't like he had anything else to do in Alabama. Jacque had already begun to transform the house by then, purging his mom's conventional idea of domestic order to make room for his own needs—fixing clocks, smoking weed, listening to WWOZ, making his little gadgets.

In the cab, Curtis thought about calling Jacque again as they made their way from one traffic light to the next on Airline Drive. But he knew it would be a waste, so he checked the package tracker real quick and, relieved it still showed *out for delivery*, he breathed and spoke silently to himself about the outcome he was trying to engineer. *I'm here to help JD. Jacque will help me because he is my brother. I will fly under the radar.*

After a while the driver eased into the turning lane and Curtis recognized the big Walgreens on the corner near Jacque's house. You could almost smell the Mississippi River from here, just a few blocks across River Road. The neighborhoods back here were solid working class. Neat little wooden houses that had probably been all white back in the day but were very much mixed up now. Kids were playing in yards and on the sidewalks. A couple dudes worked on a truck. Some windows were barred, but not many.

Curtis passed two twenties to the driver when they stopped in front of Jacque's nondescript little house on Magnolia Street with the fenced-in yard, and he was relieved there weren't any packages sitting on the front porch. He glanced at his phone: still *out for delivery*. He thought about giving the driver a little speech about anonymity, but the words were too corny to utter. Instead, he just took a couple seconds to watch the windows of the house. If Jacque was home, he'd be watching. If he wasn't, Curtis was sure he'd trip some kind of alarm on his way to the front porch. What would happen after that was an open question.

Jacque's powder blue VW Bug rested like a still life under the carport. It had been his mom's. Curtis visualized the various gun compartments in the vehicle he knew for sure were there— the slider under the dashboard, the Saturday Night Special locked against a magnet on the radiator. There was a "Beware" sign on the gate in the chain-link fence. The thing it cautioned against was Jacque's .44 Magnum. Curtis lifted the latch and stepped into the yard, his hands visible. The house came alive with noise and light before he took his third step.

There was yapping from inside the house and scratching at the front door as he neared the porch. A red light flashed across the blinds. Curtis called out "Yo, Tick-Tock! Tick-Tock Jacque!

It's me, Curt!" he was smiling broadly like a dumbass, his hands visible, certain Jacque was watching him now or would watch him later on video. "I'm coming up brother and I can't remember if we have a secret code or not." He stood there on the steps to the porch wondering if maybe Jacque wasn't home after all, but then the dog abruptly stopped barking and Curtis knew he'd cleared the first hurdle. He wasn't prepared for what came next.

The door swung open and there stood a very pissed-off looking black man with a wifebeater stretched taut against his potbelly, a cigarette dangling from his mouth, and a sawed-off pump shotgun hanging at his side. Jacque just stood there with a practiced glare, not saying a damn thing. The cigarette burned. The little spotted dog, some kind of terrier, stood obediently at his side.

Curt was still trying to think of something clever to say when Jacque's stare began to break down. "I'm sorry," Curtis said. "My friend Jacque used to live here. Did you, maybe, eat him or something?" Jacque's face broke into a broad grin and he put the shotgun on an inside table before stepping onto the porch to grab Curtis in a bear hug. He picked Curtis up, EverReady and all, demonstrating he still had his strength. Jacque put him down and grasped Curt's head in both hands. "Damn nigga. You got a lot of balls just walking in the yard like that. That's a good way to get electrocuted."

"You didn't get my letter?" Curt asked. "Wait, electrocuted?"

"Of course, I got it," Jacque said, scanning the block in both directions. "But I don't necessarily believe everything I read. And the porch is wired with a few thousand volts. Now get your ass in here."

The suburbs of New Orleans vanished when the door closed and Curtis found himself standing in a house transformed, less a domicile than a physical reflection of Jacque's mind. They stood in the living room on polished pine floors reflecting light and sound from dozens of rescued clocks, old brass fans, and little motorized LED lights and gadgets, all humming with motion. The fans washed the room with warm air and pushed tiny dust particles through shafts of sunlight from the kitchen at the back of the house. Above the sink a *feng shui* crystal hung at the window, reflecting little rainbows around the room.

The kitchen was small and neat. Antique appliances, checkered floor, and a classic diner-style Formica table. Curtis noticed the birds then for the first time. Three of them, in cages. Finches, it looked like. The mutt terrier's name was MaMutt, Jacque-speak for "my mutt." The place was busy but immaculate. Some low funk from the same WWOZ programming the cab driver was jamming to filled the space from everywhere at once. There were vintage stereo speakers, many of them removed from their cabinets and ingeniously hidden in found objects throughout the house.

Curtis took it all in. "Holy shit, Tick-Tock," he said. "So, um, do you happen to have the time?"

By that afternoon Curtis had settled in and all indications were Jacque was enjoying a calm and rational day. The package was still *out for delivery*. They both drank "Jachimo Specials"– tap water, ice, and big chunks of frozen lemon from the backyard tree sweetened with sugar cane that Jacque traded for. Curtis took his time bringing him up to speed, drawing out the details to paint the full picture for Jacque, figuring the more context he offered, the easier he'd accept either the cops or the FedEx package showing on his doorstep.

Curt started with the call he'd received from his mother. Just the fact of her calling was enough to signal an emergency. "JD stopped by today," she'd said. "It's probably for the best that Bobby was at Wal-Mart because you know he doesn't like all those tattoos and stuff." As if Curtis, or JD for that matter, gave a fuck what his brother Bobby thought of anything. "He visited for a little while," she had continued. "He said he's trying to open a tattoo shop in Eunice, and I should tell you 'one hand washes the other' and if I could give you his number." She had paused, amusement laced with the worry of a mother's intuition. "He was real specific I tell it to you exactly like that."

"What's that from?" Jacque interrupted to ask. "I feel like I know that line."

"It's from *Fear and Loathing*. When we lived in Houston, me and JD spent a lot of nights with a big ass bottle of rum, some coke, and that book. Reading out loud."

"Yeah, I get it," Jacque said. "The Hunter Thompson rite of passage. All you white dudes go through it." Curtis couldn't argue with that.

"Right. He could've just said 'tell Curt to call me,' but what can I say, the man has a flair for the dramatic. You should meet him, actually. You two have a lot in common."

"Hey, let me ask you," Jacque said. "Did you put down on your security paperwork with the agency how you and your old buddy JD liked to stay up doing blow and reading Hunter Thompson?" Curtis practiced one of his deadpan looks on Jacque.

"I'm sure the agency doesn't care about my reading habits," he said, skirting the question about as elegantly as he knew how. "But the coke thing kind of relates to why I'm here. So let me tell you about Houston." Curtis settled in at the kitchen table and relayed the relevant parts of his history with JD.

Curt and JD had first met sophomore year at Eunice High School and they pretty much hated each other from the start. To be more specific, JD hated the preppy baseball player with glasses that his friends called Curt and he hated all the other carbon copies of Curtis the school was full of. JD—who everyone had called by his given name, Jack, up until that year—had showed up to school on the first day of 10th grade with long, black and red-streaked hair, earrings and chains and a volatile gleam in his eye that he must've worked on all summer. He was no longer Jack Dugas. He was JD, a teenager transformed. Not quite a confident adult yet, but definitely not a kid anymore.

And from that moment forward JD was the rock and roll badass at Eunice High, a self-created island unto himself within the teenage caste system he despised. The country boys, the jocks, the preppie kids, and the nerds all had their friends. JD just had JD, and that was the way he wanted it.

If he hadn't been so talented, high school might've been hard. But he could draw, he could play guitar, and since he was from the country and he had older brothers, he could fight. And so the island of JD actually worked out pretty good for him. He was a singular thing at school, and he imposed a cost on anyone who fucked with him–whether it was a teacher telling him to tuck in his shirt, some jock mistaking his earrings for weakness, or another asshole who didn't know better. When you engaged

JD, you had to put some skin in the game.

JD did his own thing. He drew, in notebooks, on walls, on his clothes, on his skin with ballpoint pens. He started playing guitar in his older brother's Cajun band. By junior year he had a rock band of his own with some older kids from the area, and they started gigging around at house parties and low-grade bars. He started painting too, at first small renaissance-type pieces, but the subjects soon turned dark and the canvases grew, and it wasn't long before every new portrait was beautiful and equally shocking. Exactly what JD was aiming for, of course.

Curtis, meanwhile, had started to read and think about politics more than was socially acceptable for a ballplayer. He got hooked on CSPAN, drawn by the intellectual discourse that was so different from the way people talked and thought in Eunice, his teachers included. He borrowed a copy of *War and Peace* from the school library, drawn by its size and figuring it must be a political book, and he labored through it for most of the school year.

One day as Curt sat in the hallway reading *Animal Farm*, JD made a joke about the title and Curtis told him it was an allegory about communism and the bourgeoisie, still not entirely sure what those words meant. But it was enough to get them talking, and it turned out they had some things in common, mainly a shared interest in the larger world and an intense desire to get the fuck out of Eunice.

A few days later Curtis showed up at school with a brick of blank 90-minute cassette tapes, asking JD to record some music for him. To return the favor Curtis would preview any book rumored to be edgy—by Henry Miller, Timothy Leary, Kurt Vonnegut, Wolfe, Kerouac—and if he could make sense of them, he would read the best passages aloud while JD soaked it up.

Something solidified between them the day Curtis came to school with a copy of *On the Road* and showed JD where their town of Eunice was mentioned. It was nothing, just a list of towns along Highway 190 in the middle of a long Kerouac riff, but somehow it meant everything to them. Neither of them knew it at the time, but this brief period of discovery and innocence wouldn't last for long for either of them. Within a year, without warning, both JD and Curtis would lose their fathers.

It happened to JD first. His old man was a master welder, respected for his skill with metal and his work ethic. He spent twelve hours a day in a shop he ran with one of JD's uncles, and the only other thing they did with as much gusto was drink beer after work. Since it was a single-vehicle accident—the truck flipped upside down on the wrong side of a curved embankment less than a mile from their house—the coroner called it a massive heart attack, allowing the family to save face and maybe do better with the life insurance, if there was any.

JD missed a couple weeks of school, and when he came back, it was just to clean out his locker. He told Curtis he was gonna get his GED and move to Houston. He had an aunt who lived in Baytown, a suburb set among the chemical refineries of the eastern edge of the sprawling city. And Curtis didn't hear from JD again until the next year, when his own father died.

It was his senior year, and baseball season was just ramping up. Curt would always remember the sinking feeling in his gut when his older brother showed up at the practice field. He didn't need to be told something was very wrong, and Bobby had never been one to mince words, but the shock of hearing the words "Dad's dead" before he'd even reached the car stayed with him for a long time.

It was an offshore accident. Curt's dad had worked on the oil rigs in the gulf for more than 20 years and on that random Wednesday morning, a pipe wrench fell from a hundred feet up and killed him dead, hard hat and all. Just like that.

JD had called the house a few days after the funeral and he and Curtis caught up for a couple hours, talking around the grief they both felt, but connecting through it at the same time. And just like that, their casual friendship took on a spiritual kind of symmetry and weight that was more profound than anything either of them had expected. By the time Curtis graduated from Eunice High, it just made sense to move to Houston, and the two of them found a cheap apartment right in the heart of the city. They were finally ready to have the kinds of experiences they'd both dreamed about back in Eunice.

The next few years were intense. Still only 19, JD had landed a job drawing concert posters and working everything but the bar at the *Roadhouse on Montrose*, the rowdiest music venue in the city. From there, the whole world seemed to open up to him. The three-story complex could hold a thousand people, and it wasn't long at all before JD seemed to know everyone who passed through. On any given week he spent his time drawing, fucking, and partying, and the next week he did it all over again, and again.

Curtis was far too timid to follow suit. He got a job delivering packages for DHL, and for the most part kept his nose clean. He experimented a little, but the death of his father still weighed heavily on him, and in those key moments with a girl he didn't know or a pile of drugs on the table, he imagined his dad looking down on him. He couldn't shake it.

One day a few months after they had settled into their cheap apartment, a package arrived in the mail. His mom had sent some old papers of his dad's along with a little note, and there among random grade school report cards, insurance forms, and other pieces of his dad's life, Curtis unfolded a photocopy of a DD 214. Army discharge papers. He hadn't even known his dad had served.

The seed started to germinate in Curt's mind then. And if it hadn't quite matured by that second summer in Houston, his first and only brush with the law forced the issue. He had cashed an overtime check for an extra shift he'd worked, and it was Friday and there was a show that night they drove over in Curt's little truck to the upscale shopping district where a lady JD knew was happy to sell coke to friends of friends for a twenty percent markup. They got an eight-ball. They didn't need that much coke, but Curtis had the money.

When the police lights flashed behind him and suddenly there was a real-life cop in the rearview mirror, it felt to Curt like a dream. Which quickly transitioned into a nightmare. In the driver's seat, Curt had pulled the baggie from his pocket and jammed it between the seat cushions of his little Toyota. But he couldn't stay cool, despite JD's soothing reassurances from the passenger's seat as the cop approached. Curt panicked. He was barely able to croak out his name when the cop started questioning him.

It unraveled quickly. The cop jerked him out of the vehicle and searched the truck over JD's furious protests. And when he found the fat baggie of coke, JD blurted out "That's mine! It's my blow!" JD was so animated—enraged, really—cursing the cop and the justice system and everything else, the cop turned his attention to JD and somehow, Curt became a bystander in the incident. For his part, Curtis felt relieved. He couldn't help it. But once the cop put the handcuffs on JD and led him away, he was deeply ashamed. Fifteen years removed from the incident, Curt still carried the guilt with him.

Jacque gestured with a heavy old cleaver he was using to chop sugar cane on a hickory board. "Now that's a friend right there," he said. "That's a real muthafuckin' friend."

"It's why I'm here," Curtis said. "Simple as that. Whatever JD needs from me . . .man, I can't repay that debt. *Everything* would be different if he hadn't stepped in that day. They probably wouldn't have let me in the Air Force, which means no cush civilian gig, no fucking *life* man."

Jacque looked back from the counter and gave him a look. "That's uh, what they call it? Hyperbolic. Yeah, you slinging that *hyper-bolic-ness* and shit. Just get back to the story and tell me what happened."

"He got arrested. Right then and there. But then the public defender got him off for illegal search and seizure."

Jacque stopped working the cleaver and pivoted to give Curtis another look. "Okay, good. He got off. But, actually, what I meant was, what happened with his tattoo shop, in your shitty hometown. What's it called?"

"Eunice."

"Right. So what happened in Eunice with the tattoo shop? Skip to the present, my brother. Why are you *here*?"

Curtis checked his phone. The package was still out for delivery, but surely he was running out of time. He took a deep breath.

"Okay, I was just getting to that anyway. But let me just finish giving you the context and then there's, um, a development I need to tell you about." Jacque eyed him, skeptical, but didn't say anything.

"Well get to it then, bruh. I can't smoke for another hour and you trying my patience."

JD was out of jail the next day, and they ended up getting all the charges dropped. But things were never the same for him in Houston after the incident. Whether it was karma or plain bad luck, or if he'd been tagged by the local cops, whatever the reason, all of a sudden he started running into cops everywhere. He'd get stopped in his little Nissan and made to turn out his pockets, and even when they didn't find anything, the cops would still make him sit there for an hour while they ran his plates, ran his license, studied the inside of his car with their flashlights. JD even swore one cop had checked his license for coke residue during one stop.

When he got stopped walking on the sidewalk near the club one afternoon, just minding his own business, JD considered it a sign he needed to get out of town. So that's what he did. He'd already grown infatuated with the tattoo trade, and he knew plenty of dudes who worked in shops around Houston. On the strength of the concert posters he'd drawn for the *Roadhouse on Montrose,* somebody made a call for him and he got hooked up with an apprenticeship in Killeen, outside Fort Hood.

The whole incident had a similarly dramatic effect on

Curtis. JD never made him feel bad about what happened, and when Curtis brought it up JD just shrugged it off. He hated cops and the motherfucker had been wrong to start leaning on Curt in the first place. But Curtis still had trouble looking his friend in the eye. He felt like a coward. And more to the point, maybe the whole incident was a wake-up call.

A few days later he walked into an Air Force recruiting center and they gobbled him up. Curtis was smart. He spoke some French, and he had absolutely no criminal record. He was enlisted in a matter of days. And when he got his orders for boot camp in San Antonio, he took them to the landlord and got them out of their lease. Curt gave JD his half of the cash from their security deposit, and JD left for Kileen, where he'd learn to tattoo on soldiers bound for Iraq and Afghanistan. In a way, they were both enlisting. It would be years before he and Curtis crossed paths again.

JD learned his new trade quickly and for the next ten years or so he built a reputation as one of the steadiest hands on the southwest tattoo circuit. He never totally abandoned his extracurricular drug habits, but by the time he hit thirty, the party lifestyle that had been the centerpiece of his earlier existence started to lose its luster. After starting over in a dozen different towns across three states, people started to look the same to him. He wanted more. At some point, he'd had enough of working for other people, and he wanted to be close to his family again, so he decided to open his own place. He moved back to Eunice.

"Why are you telling me this man's life story?" Jacque demanded. He had finished chopping the sugar cane and returned to the kitchen table with a few chunks of it on the flat part of the cleaver. He placed it on the table between them as he sat down. "Here. Suck on this." Jacque grabbed a chunk of sugar cane and popped it in his mouth. "And hurry the fuck up, please."

When he returned to Eunice, JD had rented a storefront that had once been a flower shop. It was on 2nd Street, the main drag in tiny downtown Eunice. He'd just been walking by and the place looked perfect—right across from the library, and next to the famous Liberty Theater—so he called the number posted in the window. And the agent, a good-looking woman he couldn't quite place, had dropped everything to come right then and there to show him the shop.

The woman's name was Jackie. She had a blue streak in her hair and a figure that was hard to miss. They flirted a little bit. When he offered fifty bucks less per month, she said she was seeing a guy who was looking to break into the business; maybe JD would consider taking him on as an apprentice? By then, he was dead set on the location, and he figured he'd need some kind of assistant anyway. JD accepted her offer.

"So that afternoon JD files for his license at the courthouse, does his paperwork online to schedule the health inspection. He's in business. Psyched about this place, you know?"

"Yeah, sounds perfect," Jacque grabbed both their empty glasses–old pickle jars–and went to the counter to refill them with ice cubes and lemon wedges from the fridge. Curtis continued.

"The next day he gets the keys and it's all good. He starts setting up the place. It's a simple shop, the way I understand it. Basically just a big rectangle with a glass storefront that looks out onto 2nd Street, which is like the main drag in the little downtown. It's the one nice commercial street in Eunice. The rest of the town is pretty drab. There's a bunch of big box stores and such along 190, which is the main east-west highway that runs through town. But 2nd Street downtown is nice. Classy even. It's like Decatur street in the quarter."

"Or maybe St. Charles, it sounds like," Jacque said. "Streetcars, Spanish moss, white mansions with columns and shit. Old white money." He came back to the kitchen table with the glasses and dropped a couple chunks of sugar cane from the cleaver into his glass. Curtis followed suit.

"Yeah, actually. You're right. It's like St. Charles. Classic. Classy. White too, for sure. But, well, his perfect location doesn't last long. So what happened was—and this is where it just gets stupid—Eunice stupid. So, JD's checking out his new place, imagining how he's gonna set it up, you know, and he goes into the bathroom. I'm telling you, man, you have to meet JD. He has a sixth sense. Anyway, in the bathroom he notices one of the ceiling tiles—it's a, what do you call it? a drop ceiling—well, it's all smudged in the corner, like."

"Like something's hidden up there," Jacque said, right on cue.

"Yeah, exactly!" Curtis got up and walked over to the EverReady against the wall and pulled out his laptop. "What's the Wi-Fi password?" he asked. Jacque just stared at him. "I'm using a VPN, don't worry," Curt said.

Jacque got up from the kitchen table, silent, and walked down the tiny hall to a back bedroom. He came back with a small leather notebook already open to the right page and held it out for Curtis. There was a long list of previous passwords he'd used, each redacted with a permanent marker. It looked like he was changing them once a week. As an intel man, Curtis could appreciate his careful security practices. As a friend, it seemed excessive.

Once he connected, Curtis tunneled into his encrypted files where he was storing all the intelligence for this Louisiana excursion, to a folder he'd named *Tattoos and Tans*. He typed in his password and pulled up a series of photos. The first one was a priority mailbox lodged in the ceiling, ringed fingers holding up the tile to expose the standard USPS white, red and blue box. In the next one, the hand was holding the flaps of the box open, and inside were the silver tops of neat rows of vials. Curtis told Jacque there were fifty of them.

"So, that's your man JD holding the box open."

"You noticed the knuckles?"

"Yeah. White dudes love to tattoo their knuckles. Shit, we have the same initials! Maybe I should get mine done." Jacque studied his fist for a second, then leaned forward, squinting at the photo. "What's that, steroids or something? What kind of dumb muthafucka stores drugs in a rental property?"

Curtis considered the question. "The kind of dumb motherfucker who doesn't expect the place to be rented." Jacque put his hand to his chin, considering the scenario.

"So, then what happened?" he asked.

"So then, JD took this picture and went to confront the dude who owns the property. And—so this is where it starts to get more complicated—the cat who owns it is named Lenny. Lenny

Prichard, and he's a royal fucking meathead prick that I know because of baseball. Or used to know, anyway."

"Oh yeah? So what? They fight?"

"No. But apparently Lenny had a pistol when JD went in there—he owns a tanning salon, of all things." Jacque made a disapproving noise. "And basically, Lenny just told him it's none of his business, that whatever was there when he moved in better be there when he moves out, or else."

"Moves out?"

"Well, yeah, that's the crux of it. So the next day JD goes into the shop and the box of steroids is missing. And right about the time he's thanking his lucky stars for *that*, the real estate lady calls him and says they're cancelling the deal. He needs to vacate. She gave him 15 days."

"Muthafucka!" Jacque was shaking his head. "That's cold, man."

Just then a high-pitched beeping at full volume changed everything. By the time the third beep sounded and Curtis was becoming aware that it was an alarm—the front door, the delivery, he realized at the same instant—Jacque was emerging from the broom closet with the sawed-off shotgun. MaMutt went apeshit. The alarm stopped and Jacque glided to the front door in a practiced movement, which Curtis saw now was reinforced with steel plating. He held his body in profile to present a smaller target. The special ops mantra *slow is smooth and smooth is fast* came to Curtis in that moment. Jacque slid to his right to the corner of the living room to look through a peephole drilled through the wall there.

Curtis got up silently and walked to the broom closet, and he wasn't surprised at all to see a whole array of tiny screens showing the entire perimeter of the house. Some of the monitors were from the 80s and 90s. Some were modern tablets. A FedEx driver was standing at the door with a package. There didn't appear to be anyone else on the street. The FedEx guy knocked, and Curt's heart pounded. He padded quietly up to where Jacque was near the front door and whispered, "It's my package. I was just about to tell you it was coming."

The look that Jacque gave him made Curtis queasy, but he managed to maintain eye contact and control his breathing. After a few seconds he could see Jacque starting to ebb, and he squinted into the peephole once more, then walked back towards the broom closet to return the shotgun. Jacque was grumbling loud enough for Curt's benefit. "Twice in one day. I'll kill a muthafucka for less than that."

Curtis just stood there for a minute. Jacque had retrieved a pint jar full of shapely cannabis buds from above the stove, and he sat at the table with a plate, breaking down the weed. "Go on then, hotshot. Go get your package, then," he said.

His phrasing worried Curtis enough to ask. "Hotshot?"

Jacque smiled.

"No, bruh, I'm not gonna electrocute you just yet." Then he looked up at Curtis. "But If that's what I think it is on the porch you better go get it before I change my mind."

Later that evening, they were sitting in the grotto Jacque had created under the big oak tree that dominated his backyard. The little oasis had a similar vibe to the interior of the house. A couple old traffic lights fixed with purple and green LEDs hung from boughs of the tree, casting multi-colored light down on them. All around there were ingenious little solar-powered LEDs glittering. Underfoot was a patchwork of paving stones—red brick, cement pavers, and wine and beer bottles all sunk into the earth and overgrown with grass.

Jacque had lit a half dozen sticks of incense, and music from WWOZ—an extended reggae jam at this hour—was still surrounding them. Curtis had spent five minutes trying to locate a speaker he was sure was up in the tree, but he never could find it. Jacque had opened an antique Coca-Cola fridge under the carport, the kind where the bottles hang upright from their necks and used the built-in opener to open what looked like an old Heineken bottle. Jacque handed Curtis the bottle and when he raised an inquisitive eyebrow, well aware that bad things happened when Jacque drank, his friend said, "Tea. I bottled it myself." They clinked bottles and sat in silence for a moment.

"So, thanks for the items." Curtis began.

"You gonna remember how to use all that stuff?" Jacque gave Curt a sideways look. "No offense, my brother, but I don't remember you as a technician. Damn sure not an operator."

"None taken," Curtis said. "I'm out of my element, for sure. But I gotta get this done, so I will."

"Just keep the hard drive with you," Jacque said. "That's the most important thing. When you get to the motel or whatever, just connect it to the tablet and leave it plugged in, like I showed you. That'll run your trackers, your encryption, all that shit. Hit me up on the channel I showed you if you need anything."

"I appreciate it," Curtis said.

Jacque gave him a look of warning, a fresh blunt—tobacco and weed—pinched in his fingers. "Don't need anything. Now here, hit this, and let's talk about your car." Jacque produced a tin of Altoids from his pocket and handed it across to Curtis. "Give this to Moe. The man's gonna sell you a car for seven bills. You got that, right?" Curtis nodded. "Now, he said it wasn't stolen. But he said it like four times, so that means it just might be. But he does have a bill of sale he's gonna sign over." Jacque turned one of his practiced glares at Curtis. "Whatever shit you get into on the road is on you, you hear? You don't mention Moe's name, and you damn sure don't utter mine. But I assume you know that."

"Yep. Got it." Curtis said, a little uncomfortable despite the fact that he'd been anticipating some kind of speech along those lines. "So, LaPlace, right? It's just that one exit?" Jacque was already cracking a smile. He was always going on about the stupid names people assigned to things. "LaPlace," French for "the place," was near the top of that list for him.

LaPlace wasn't much more than a little piece of land, a peninsula between the massive Lake Pontchartrain and the Mississippi River. It was basically a boat launch and a bait stand surrounded by brackish water and the elevated bridge that was Interstate 10. About twenty miles from the New Orleans city limits.

"That's right," Jacque said, drawing on the blunt he had insisted they smoke together. "LaPlace is the place . . .no more, no less."

"Got it," Curtis said, playing along, a little high now, having fun. "So when I get to the right place, I'll be in LaPlace?" Curtis asked. Jacque gave him a knowing look.

"Yeah, bruh, when you get to LaPlace, you'll be in the right place. And if Moe's there and he has a car for you, it's for sure you're in the right place."

"Which is . . .correct me if I'm wrong." Curtis said, struggling to contain his laughter, "LaPlace?" Maybe it was the weed, or maybe it was stress. Or just the moment. Whatever it was, Curtis started laughing first. Jacque gave Curt a hard look, eyeballing him while he took a long swallow of tea from the old Heinekin bottle, but he couldn't hold the pose, and when he started laughing a spray of tea erupting from his mouth hit Curtis in the eye. And they laughed like schoolboys, MaMutt sitting up at Jacque's feet just staring up, wondering what he was doing.

The next morning, just before 8 a.m., Curtis left his smartphone at Jacque's and set out in a cab for the hamlet of LaPlace. It was just a twenty-minute ride from the western suburbs of New Orleans, but things changed dramatically once you left the city limits. New Orleans was undeniably beautiful; it had that Old World European charm thing going for it. The wetlands on the other side of the drab western suburbs of Metairie and Kenner, where Curtis had spent the night, had its own kind of stark beauty.

As the cab ascended the elevated section of I-10, Curtis allowed himself a few moments to enjoy the view. The vast expanse of Lake Pontchartrain to his right and the Mississippi River off in the middle distance to his left. The sun reflected off the massive lake, and he could see pelicans standing on cypress knees a couple feet off the water. Fishermen standing in their boats, casting their lines. There was a beauty here that, when he thought about Louisiana, was easy to forget. Curtis was always quick to dismiss his home state, but it truly was a special place. More dumbasses per capita, but still, it had its charms.

Moe's place was very much like Jacque had described it, and Curtis could see their domiciles had a lot in common. The little ramshackle complex that was Moe's empire sat on a minuscule piece of *terra firma* almost surrounded by brackish water. It was right under the elevated freeway, protected by erosion barriers. The little finger of land was just enough for an extended neon sign advertising overpriced gas, a hairpin exit ramp, and Moe's Bait, Tackle, Launch & Salvage. Though the urban sprawl of New Orleans made this former outpost far more accessible these days, the place still looked like a kind of living postcard, a glimpse into the past.

The gas pumps were of a certain age but had been retrofitted with a credit card payment system for nights and afternoons when Moe wasn't around or was hiding out on the little screened porch facing the waterfront. The boat launch was a self-service one where only the occasional tourist bothered to fold their bills and slot them into the padlocked collection box. Moe kept a modest inventory of gas-station snacks and canned beer in the old shack. There was a ragtag collection of old junk cars scattered around the property.

He wasn't so much a businessman as he was a survivor and a scraper, a self-professed "junkman," kindred spirit of Jacque and others like him. The rotating collection of rusted-out chassis, engine blocks, and irregular rims he held were just trading pieces, little artifacts that might prove valuable to the right man who happened along. But every now and then, a complete set of wheels came his way, usually with a dubious origin story Moe didn't want to know about. It was just luck that Jacque had called when he did.

The cab pulled away and Curtis was left standing on the gravel lot of the weathered little network of buildings, the EverReady on his shoulder and, in his hand, a laundry bag with the box of steroids and some old clothes on top. He scanned the property. Old junk cars and equipment were scattered around. He immediately regretted leaving his smartphone in the city. He was sure he'd be stranded there. But after taking a moment to survey the little compound he took a measured breath and walked around to look for Moe.

Who, as it turned out, could've been Jacque's granddad or great-uncle. He beamed with a familial kind of pride when Curtis said Jacque's name and led the way to a heap covered in a blue FEMA tarp. Curt was not optimistic. So when Moe pulled back the tarp to reveal a road-worthy, badly oxidized early 90s Mazda coupe, he felt an overwhelming sense of relief.

"There she is. Seven hundred for a friend of my boy Jacque's." Curtis handed over the bills without preamble, no need to kick the tires. Moe thumbed through the notes like a veteran backwater entrepreneur and then pocketed the money, and just stood there waiting. Curtis responded to Moe's nonverbal cue, fishing the Altoids tin from his pocket and handing it over. Moe accepted the offering without comment, cracked the lid slightly, and held it to his nose to inhale the deep floral aroma of the cannabis Jacque had packed inside. Curtis had already popped the trunk to load the EverReady and the laundry bag with the concealed steroids.

Moe gave him the paperwork and showed him where to sign his name. Curtis signed it with his real name, though he made sure it looked different from his real signature and was impossible to read. What good that would do, he didn't have a clue. He put the forms in the glove box, glanced with suspicion at the freshly vacuumed back seat, took a long, deep breath, and turned the key. It cranked the first time, and then Curtis was off.

The old Japanese four-cylinder did what it had to do. He managed to get it just north of sixty miles an hour and tried the cruise control, which no longer worked. Likewise for the little oscillating feature on the air conditioning vents, which must have been a big deal back in the day. There was a sunroof, too, but when he hit the button on the ceiling, nothing happened. The radio worked, so Curtis tuned it to 90.7, WWOZ and let the New Orleans music ground him for twenty minutes or so before it went to static.

The interstate was elevated here over the swampland that bled into Lake Maurepas, which flowed into the expanse of Lake Pontchartrain—technically two bodies of water that were indistinguishable from this vantage point. Curtis kept the front windows down despite the morning chill so he could smell the salty air coming off the water.

After twenty minutes of driving, the wetlands gave way to grass and the elevated section of I-10 transitioned to level ground near the outskirts of Baton Rouge. The state capitol had grown a lot in the years after Hurricane Katrina, and Curtis had to admit he felt a certain sense of awe as he crested the big bridge over the Mississippi—the river easily a mile across at that point—and saw the capital city below. But Baton Rouge would never be anything more to Curtis than the city you had to pass through to get to New Orleans or Lafayette. He'd never known it to have a soul.

He debated whether to exit the interstate outside of Baton

Rouge to pick up Highway 190, the two-lane state road that ran parallel to I-10, or to stay on the interstate. He could slow the Mazda down and take 190 all the way into Eunice, hitting every traffic light in every little town for the ninety miles it took to get there. But he decided it was safer to stay on the interstate. There were speed traps all along 190, from Livonia to Port Barre and beyond. If there was a positive side to his only previous experience traveling with drugs in the car, it was that Curtis assumed the local cops along the state highway were more inclined to illegal search and seizure than state troopers who patrolled the interstate would be. So he stayed on I-10, hugging the right lane between sixty and sixty-five. The actual limit was seventy for most of this stretch, but he didn't want to push the old coupe any more than he had to.

Traveling west on I-10 from New Orleans you hit Baton Rouge, then Lafayette, then Lake Charles, and—getting into Texas—Beaumont, then Houston, all in pretty much one-hour increments. The hour between Baton Rouge and Lafayette included fifty miles or so of elevated road over the Atchafalaya Basin, which Curtis always told people was the largest contiguous wetlands area in the continental U.S. Accurate or not, it felt true from up there, just two lanes of the interstate positioned something like fifty feet above the water with nothing but a low guard rail separating drivers from the swamp water below.

It was dangerous. Any accident could be fatal, cars getting pushed over the edge. Not that anyone seemed to drive more carefully here, from what he could tell. There was an anxious beauty here—white-knuckled driving on the elevated concrete track, stealing glimpses of the expansive natural beauty of the wetlands below.

He was relieved to finally come off the bridge outside Lafayette, a town he knew well. If Baton Rouge was the cultural purgatory separating the urban lure of New Orleans from the rest of the state, then Lafayette was the Cajun refuge on the other side. A place where Cajun culture existed uncoupled from the tourist dollar. It was a good size city, home to a couple hundred thousand folks with names like Arceneaux, Babineaux, Doucet, Fontenot, Gautreaux, on through the alphabet all the way to Zaunbrauker, one of a dozen or so German clans sprinkled in and assimilated into the Cajun family stew of Acadiana.

The city was home to the University of Louisiana at Lafayette. It was respectable, affordable, and drew a diverse faculty that helped to balance the more tribal elements of broader Cajun culture in Acadiana. Baton Rouge had sports and all its associated fanaticism. Lafayette had vibrant living that was somehow more grounded in authentic cultural roots. French and zydeco music, real Cajun food that didn't need to be advertised as such—people here had a way of living, a *joie de vivre* that was just damn hard not to like. It had always appealed to Curtis.

In another life he might have decided to put down roots in Lafayette, maybe get a degree in poli-sci, learn to manipulate the public for their own good—but in this life he was just passing through. Feeling less tense to be on familiar ground now, he watched the five exits that comprised the city tick by: airport, university, downtown, commercial district, and just before the exit for the Cajun Dome, he saw a billboard advertising the state's largest gun show. He decided to check it out. He had a nice off-brand 9-millimeter in the EverReady that Jacque had given him, but there were a few other tools that would be useful to have. Ammunition he could trust, for one thing. Plus, he needed to take a dump, and he figured the bathrooms would be cleaner there.

In the parking lot of the Cajundome, he began to worry about the car. Something about the bargain basement price and the fresh vacuum job in the little Mazda made Curt suspicious, and he thought long and hard, sitting there among the pickup trucks in the vast parking lot, about switching the plates with some unsuspecting citizen. The car was hot, he was sure. But in the end, he didn't. Curt already felt like a criminal, but there was a moral necessity to what he was up to, and that seemed important. Lifting license plates was petty, and it smacked of guilt and a certain kind of desperation he wasn't ready to embrace.

Instead, he readied himself for any potential discussion about how he came to own the car, just in case. He had a bill of sale. And it was cheaper than a rental if he decided to stick around for a while. Every operator needed a legend, and the car story was part of his now. He went over it a couple times in his head as he walked to the entrance, rehearsing. *To tell the truth officer, I figured it's cheaper than a rental, you know?*

At the Cajundome, the same sports arena where his older brother Bobby had brought him to see Def Leppard as a kid, it was like the concert was still going on. Here it was more than twenty years later, the very next time he stepped into the venue, and they were blasting the same music. Guns and Roses, AC/DC, Bon Jovi, the Steve Miller Band. The whole arena had a festive atmosphere; the phrase *redneck convention* flashed through Curt's head as he stood there taking in the booths spread across what would ordinarily be the home court of the

Ragin' Cajuns basketball team.

He knew the average Louisiana male well. Hell, despite his faded accent and his DC facade, he *was* one. So he wasn't especially concerned about walking into a gun show, even though it would be a first for him. Curtis knew what to expect. In fact, the music and the festive atmosphere made it kind of fun.

He wasn't a gun guy, but he knew how they worked and had plenty of experience with them. He had weapons training in the Air Force, and if the qualifying range wasn't enough to gain real proficiency, a dozen deployments in six years offered lots of idle time with people who definitely were gun guys, though some of them had actually been women. Curtis had fired all kinds of guns, from rocket-propelled grenades, both U.S. and Russian made, to all manner of machine guns and an array of handguns of small and larger calibers. They basically all worked the same.

The main differences, at least as far as Curt was concerned—especially in a *domestic* context—were noise and the size of the hole the bullet made. In a military context—in a war on foreign soil with combatants, objectives, tactics—so much relied on having the right weapons available to complete the mission. But in a civilian context, in ordinary, polite American society, the *fact of* a weapon makes all the difference. The shock of the sudden appearance of a pistol serves the purpose. For his purposes in Louisiana, at least, Curtis had chosen a pistol based on the noise it made when fired.

A lot of people underestimated the sound a gun makes when it fires, especially in an enclosed place. Curt knew from experience that it was hard as fuck to concentrate with guns popping off around you. So when Jacque gave him the choice between the 45 and the 9-millimeter, he'd chosen the nine-mil, in large part because it was relatively quiet. Relative being the operative word.

Curtis emerged from the gun show with a certain peace of mind, more confident now that he was at least prepared for the potential sticky outcomes of his trip to Eunice. He opened the trunk of the Mazda and got himself organized. He didn't waste time with his new all-in-one Leatherman tool, making a series of discrete slits in the bald spare tire to stow the ammo and pistol, secured now in a new belt-clip holster he'd just bought.

The spare tire was an obvious hiding place, but he didn't have the time or tools to start creating false panels or chambers here in the parking lot. It was still better than in his backpack. Curtis put one can of police-grade pepper spray he'd bought in the EverReady and then locked the bag in the trunk. The second can he kept with him, along with a camouflage ball cap he'd picked up at the gun show. It was a promotional thing from a local company that provided "mud"—lubricant—to the oil rigs in the Gulf. It said "CAJUN MUD" in block letters, and Curtis picked it up on impulse, not so much out of necessity as he just liked the two words together.

Combined with the equipment Jacque had given him, he felt as ready as he ever would be. Curt was prepared to set foot in Eunice. Now he just had to get there with a car full of contraband.

From Lafayette he tracked north on I-49 for a half hour and picked up Highway 190 near Evangeline Downs in the city of Opelousas, just about twenty miles from Eunice now. Opelousas was known as a black city. As Curtis rolled through town, he was tickled by a childhood memory of his older brother Bobby railing on about race, infuriated by the new St. Landry Parish phone book he'd held in his hand.

Both Eunice and Opelousas, the only two proper cities in the area, fell inside the parish. There were five or six average citizens on the yellow cover of the new phonebook—circa nineteen ninety-something—and only one of them was white. It was a reflection of the power balance in the larger city of Opelousas. Eunice was still majority white, but Opelousas had the numbers. Bobby had been furious to see so many blacks on the cover.

Curtis realized now as he reflected on the incident for the first time since it happened that this was an early wedge between him and his brother that would only get deeper as the years passed. He wondered if he and Bobby could ever close the distance, get close again, or if it was already over for them.

It was almost twilight by the time he came through Opelousas into the flat, expansive Cajun Prairie. Fields that would soon be flooded and dotted with the white tops of crawfish traps stood empty and dry in the setting sun. Highway 190 cut a straight line through the prairie here, direct to Eunice. Curtis switched over to AM and found the local Eunice station.

On Friday nights you'd get the local high school football games. On Saturdays, old men spoke French between Cajun and zydeco tunes that tended to all sound the same if you didn't have an ear for it. At that moment when Curtis tuned in, it was a full five minutes of paid, prerecorded advertisements for local businesses: Ace Auto, for all your auto needs, drive-through drinks at the Daiquiri Hut, a nightclub called the Purple Parrot, where every Tuesday had been ladies' night since Curt was still in high school . . . and at the end of the string of advertisements, a pitch for the semi annual fundraiser for St. Edmund Catholic Booster Club.

Curtis wondered if Lenny Prichard would be writing a check for the cause. The childhood bully Curt had grown up with was now a local business owner. On paper, he seemed legitimate enough, but Curtis knew better. To Curt's government-trained eye at least, Lenny Prichard's public record screamed out shady. There was no doubt his bias played a part in the judgment, but Curtis was sure even the most detached auditor would see a similar pattern. He thought about it as he passed through the hamlet of Lawtell, on the eastern edge of Eunice.

Lenny owned two LLCs, each with cheesy names that echoed the much larger and more successful local institution his late father had established in the eighties. Curtis had done his research, and there did not appear to be a legal connection between the market-dominating Sun-*N*-Sports Academy that Lester Prichard had established, and the two much smaller enterprises Lenny created, Sun-*N*-Tans and Sun-*Y*-Realty.

Lenny was the sole owner of both the tanning salon and the real estate business, but the financial records Curt got his hands on showed that Ely Prichard, the brother of Lenny's now-deceased father, had provided the seed money. Ely Prichard was the patriarch of the family and a name everybody in Eunice knew. People around town called him "Uncle Ely," even people who didn't know the man. The elder Prichard man didn't have that much wealth on paper, but Curtis knew better. And he also knew that Lenny was joined at the hip to his successful uncle.

Curtis was thinking back to high school, about watching from a lawn chair in the bed of a truck beyond the outfield fence as Lenny and his St. Ed's teammates won their first state championship. It would have been 2004, both Lenny and Curtis juniors—Curtis at Eunice High and Lenny at St. Eds—enjoying yet another stellar year on the field. St. Eds was always a collection of well-trained rich kids and working-class ringers on scholarship.

However they were formed, St. Eds had a damn good baseball team. Curtis could still remember the pile up on the mound after Lenny caught a weak line drive for the last out and St. Eds clinched the state championship that year, the bile of deep jealousy that sat in his stomach as he watched the celebration, he and his teammates from Eunice High sitting beyond the outfield fence. Some of them had applauded. Others, like Curtis, had cursed and added another few splashes of Old Charter whiskey to their Cokes.

In the Mazda, just beyond the Eunice city limits, Curtis passed the Regency Motel and didn't realize until he was watching the long rectangle of the building slip by that he'd missed the turn. He was tired from a day of traveling. He drifted into the left lane of the divided highway to double back towards the place people probably still called the "Roach Motel" that would serve as his headquarters for as long as he was in town.

The car stalled out as he came to a stop in the median, the engine falling silent. Curt checked his mirrors, put the coupe in park, and took a deep breath before turning the key. Nothing happened. The situation was too new to make him nervous—he could walk to the motel if he had to—but that changed quickly when the unmarked police car pulled up behind him. A heavy bead of sweat appeared on his forehead instantly as Curtis registered the car in the rearview. All of a sudden, he was back in his little Toyota on the shoulder of Westheimer Avenue in Houston with a pocket full of coke, panicking as the cop approached. Except this cop was in plain clothes.

Curtis registered this fact and did what he could to center himself. He sat up straight and breathed deeply through his nose, eyes open, watching the cop approach, feeling air pass over the hair follicles in his nostrils, his usual technique. It took just two seconds. As he watched a somewhat familiar figure approach in the side mirror, he told himself *you are in control.* He opened the door of the Mazda and slowly emerged, smiling with his hands out in front of him in a casual way intended to suggest that the sudden appearance of this cop was a welcome intervention.

"Back in the car!" the cop barked, his hand moving reflexively to his gun. Curtis complied, dropped his butt down into the bucket seat, and fought the fear rising from his stomach. He sat with his feet on the pavement, hands out. Steroids in the trunk. A concealed and unregistered handgun. A car of dubious origins. He willed himself to avoid dwelling on these things. *You are in control,* he told himself. But the officer standing in front of him in standard-issue narc uniform—jeans, open collar, badge around the neck—suggested otherwise.

Episode Two
Hometown Blues

———— ✿ ————

Curtis has a nervous encounter with local Eunice cop and former high school acquaintance Levi "Tac" Youngblood. Anxious and overwhelmed to be back in town, Curtis tries to make the most of his association with Tac. Meanwhile, the situation with the missing steroids is more perilous than Curtis ever realized.

"I hitched to Texas when the sun was beating down . . . won't nothing bring you down like your hometown" — Steve Earle

It was a crisp sixty degrees outside, but the window of his motel room didn't open, so Curtis used the room's copy of the New Testament to prop the door open for fresh air. To mitigate the security risk, and just because he wanted to test it out, he ran one of Jacque's little cameras under the door so he could monitor the walkway from the feed on his computer. Curt had three more such devices in his EverReady, all Frankenstein creations that combined the essential parts of doorbell cameras with flexible cables and hooks for easy mounting. Jacque was a genius.

Curtis sat on the edge of the bed with his laptop, the Wi-Fi spotty as hell. He was reviewing his *Tattoos and Tans* folder of intelligence he'd collected over the past week, refreshing himself on the overall situation, hazy as it was, and the information on Lenny he'd pulled together. Literally everything Curt knew about what he was getting into had come from a singular discussion with JD seven days prior. Most of what he had was background. It was useful as context, but he wasn't here to write a paper. He was here to *act*.

There was so much he didn't know, but the central fact of the situation—the one thing Curtis *did* know—was a box of steroids with a street value of something like twenty thousand dollars was missing. And right or wrong, Lenny Prichard would blame JD. *People get killed for a whole lot less than that*, he thought to himself, not for the first time. Especially when the guy who got shorted is an unstable motherfucker like Lenny Prichard. Curtis still couldn't believe it. Of all the assholes in town to be tangled up with.

On paper at least, Lenny looked like a model citizen. Curt had gained mostly public records stuff, but also some financial documents he'd received from a nice lady at the statehouse in Baton Rouge who somehow got the impression he was an IRS auditor. Lenny's records showed just the one arrest for public intoxication in Charleston, South Carolina. Nothing at all in the state of Louisiana, a fact which stank to high heaven. You didn't spend your teens and twenties running around with the privileged kids of the asshole men who owned practically everything in Eunice and never get in a fight, or wreck a car, or get busted for stealing street signs or egging somebody's house or some other juvenile nonsense. It just didn't happen. Around Eunice, pretty much everybody has a jail story.

More to the point, Curtis had first-hand knowledge of the kind of person Lenny Prichard was. He could still remember the incident behind the concession stand after a late game in Pony League—they must've been seventeen by then—when a Little Leaguer who couldn't have been more than twelve made the mistake of saying "good game" to Lenny. His parents owned everything at the ballpark, so he was just walking in the back door of the concession to grab what he wanted. Curtis had been on the opposing team and had watched Lenny grow more enraged as his team won despite him going zero for four on the night, throwing tantrums in the dugout as the game wore on and he couldn't get a hit to save his life.

The kid had no idea. He never saw the punch to the gut coming. Neither did Curtis. By the time he realized what had happened the kid was doubled over, half-gasping, half-sobbing, and Lenny had disappeared into the concession stand. The little guy had limped away silently when Curtis went over to help.

A guy who pulled that kind of shit at seventeen wasn't likely to grow more compassionate as he grew up and life got harder. Curtis had studied people enough to know that.

Curt pulled up his online map of Eunice. He'd paid extra for the premium package of the software, which gave him all kinds of layers he could add and subtract from the base map. He'd already customized his map of Eunice, pinned with points of interest, including the Prichard businesses, JD's tattoo shop, and Lenny's home out near the enclave of Mowata, off of Highway 13, which ran north to south through Eunice. Highway 190 ran east to west and served as the main thoroughfare for business and traffic. The downtown part of 2nd Street was a one-way, south-bound, just a handful of winding blocks of wide sidewalks, shade trees, and commercial awnings of old money businesses. It was on this nice stretch of downtown that the original location of JD's tattoo shop would have been. Just looking at the map, even without the clusterfuck of the hidden steroids, Curt could see this location would have been a disaster.

The new spot—out in the Old-East Shopping Center on the eastern edge of town—made more sense, to Curtis at least. He figured JD would have more freedom in setting up in this older, somewhat dilapidated strip mall. The new place was easy to find, but out of the way. Not the thumb in the nose to the Eunice establishment that the 2nd Street location would've been.

Back in the day, when the town was much smaller, the Old-East Shopping Center had been a commercial hub, home to Sears, Western Auto, and a handful of little restaurants. But as the town grew, extending west along Highway 190 with newer, big-box stores, the commercial center lost its luster.

Lenny's tanning salon—Curtis could barely say the name of the place, even to himself, without wincing in embarrassment—was on the west side, where Walmart, Winn-Dixie, and the newer shopping centers were located. Taco Bell, Popeyes, McDonald's, Pizza Hut, all that stuff was right there by Sun-*N*-Tans. It was no coincidence that for the most part, black families were clustered in neighborhoods on the east side, while the better-off white families anchored the west side.

Curtis dropped a pin on the location not far from the hotel where Tac Youngblood had stopped him earlier. It wasn't necessary, just a habit the intel-analyst in him did automatically. He reminded himself he hadn't technically been *stopped* or *pulled over*. The Mazda had already crapped out on Curtis. And he'd certainly made the best of it, but it was a rocky start to be sure. The cop, whose actual name was Levi but who had gone by "Tac" for as long as Curtis had known him, actually recognized Curt first.

"Curtis Laroux! What the hell are you doing in town? Shit, bruh! I was about to practice my choke hold on you!" he'd said.

Once Curt had registered the smile, everything about Tac Youngblood—nerd with a firearms fetish—rushed back into his head. He was instantly scheming on how to best leverage this new development. Of course Tac was a cop now! The lanky kid he had known in high school had bulked up some. He had his sleeves rolled up, and there was a fresh tattoo on his forearm. He had the cop swagger. Curtis had done his best to turn on his Eunice charm.

"Tac? Hey man! I figured you'd be on a peak somewhere in Afghanistan with a long gun. Different uniform, I guess. What a surprise! I didn't realize I was gonna get a police escort coming back to town."

"In that hooptie? Shit man, you don't need an escort, you need a tow!" They shook hands, and Curtis was encouraged that Tac didn't go for the macho death grip. It suggested he didn't have anything to prove, was comfortable in his own skin. Curtis let the implied question about the car hang in the air and redirected with an appeal to nostalgia.

"It must be, what, graduation, the last time we saw each other?"

"Tac rubbed at the tattoo on his forearm—an eagle swooping down, claws extended—giving the question some thought. Yeah, must be. You pretty much disappeared after that." Curtis leaned into the car to pop the hood, curious if the action would make Tac nervous at all, but the cop just kept on talking. "I figured the next time you rolled into town it'd be in an Escalade or something. Presidential motorcade kinda shit."

They both walked around to peer at the engine. Curtis didn't quite know where this was going, but he was relieved the conversation had taken a friendlier tone. "Why's that?" he asked.

"Your brother told me you were working for the Pentagon or something." Curtis studied the mass of cables, dust, and grease of the engine block, willing himself to stay calm while a wave of anger passed over him. He must've asked Bobby a hundred times to stop telling people he worked for the Pentagon. Curtis had stopped asking because somewhere in early 2017 they'd just stopped talking altogether. It was better that way. But it was funny how his brother could still get to him.

"Well," Curtis said, "I try not to talk bad about my brother, but he's a fucking idiot."

Tac laughed. "There's your problem right there," he said, and Curtis was confused for an instant, thinking he was talking about Bobby. But Tac was pointing at the battery, the cable all corroded and nearly detached from the post. "You got jumper cables? Pop the trunk and I'll check." Tac was already in motion before he could protest.

Another wave of heat rolled over Curtis and he found himself reaching down with the bandana from his back pocket to grab the battery cable and twist it down hard onto the post. He wiped some of the little barnacles of corrosion away. When he looked up, Tac—was walking towards the back of the Mazda. "I'm pretty sure I don't have any. But let's try to crank it again first, just in case." Curtis said, hoping fear had not crept back into his voice. And at that, Tac pivoted and plopped himself in the driver's seat of the Mazda, one foot still on the pavement.

"Try it now?" he asked. And miraculously, the engine had cranked.

Curtis had given up on the concept of God not long after his dad died, but that moment had felt like divine intervention. Later, In his motel room, remembering the incident, he made a mental note to swap out the battery, and maybe have a mechanic inspect the car. Even if it was the hand of God this time, surely He wouldn't always be so generous.

Curt and Tac had stood there for a few more minutes talking while the car idled—no way he was turning it off—and it was clear to Curtis there was a kind of mutual admiration between them. They'd both gone into defense, Curtis at the national level, Tac at the local level, where the rubber meets the road. It was something he might be able to work with.

Their graduating class at Eunice High was around a hundred students , so everybody pretty much knew everybody. Tac tended to be in the advanced classes—calculus, chemistry, physics—all of which Curtis avoided to free as much time as possible for baseball and books. But they had been in English together for a couple years, and they'd even hung out socially on a few occasions. Around the time Curtis was getting into the rebellious fiction that offered a glimpse into the wild possibilities that life outside Eunice offered, Tac was absorbed in paperbacks with titles like *Marine Sniper*, *Killing Zone*, and *Shoot to Kill*.

But it was their mutual association with JD, then and now, that had prompted Curtis to push it a bit further, thinking he might be able to cultivate Tac as a human intelligence source for Operation Tattoos and Tans. He was hardly an expert, but it was clear the tattoo on Tac's arm was fresh—he could see some flaking that must've itched because every so often Tac would give it a slap—so Curtis asked about it. Pride showed on Tac's face.

"This? You remember JD, right? He did this for me week before last. He brought his stuff over to my house."

"Really? That's cool." Curt said. "That's actually why I'm in town. To help JD get his shop set up." Curtis could see the tattoo more clearly now, an eagle with a writhing fish—a bass, it looked like—in its talons, and some kind of Latin script beneath it. Tac looked up.

"Yeah? That's cool. I didn't realize you were still in touch.

He's gonna be over on 2nd Street, right? The old flower shop."

"Actually, that fell through," Curtis said. "He signed a new lease on a place in the Old-East Shopping Center. Supposed to be right next to Sugar Ray's Bakery. Say, what's that Latin inscription?" Curtis was watching Tac closely, learning all he could from his body language. Tac raised his eyes skyward, thinking.

"You know," Tac said after a beat. "That's a better spot for him. That old guard around the City Hall and the fucking Chamber of Commerce would've gave him fits, I'm sure. Eunice still might not be ready for its first tattoo shop." Tac looked at Curtis then. "It's good you're here to help him. Remember, just 'cause people are friendly at City Hall and around town, it don't necessarily mean they want him around." Just then, the walkie-talkie at his hip squawked to life.

"Yeah, I hear you," Curtis said. He pulled out his flip phone to get Tac's number. "Hey, give me your cell. So we can catch up."

Tac eyed the burner phone and Curtis knew he'd made a mistake. But it was too late. Curt hastily prepared an answer in case he asked. He'd left his phone on the plane, and so had to get the burner—no, not *burner*—this *temporary* phone till he could make a claim with his insurance. But Tac didn't ask. He just recited the number and watched Curtis punch it into the phone. He didn't say anything, but something new was suddenly hanging in the air. "You remember Rudy's Cafe, right?" Tac asked.

Curtis said yes, of course, and as Tac leveled an interrogator's look at him, he lurched into the silence and asked again, just to have something to say: "So what about the Latin? What's it say?"

"It says 'Don't fuck with me.'" Tac said, stone cold. And then, "Let's meet at Rudy's tomorrow morning. 08:30." At that, he pivoted to walk back to his unmarked car, speaking into his walkie-talkie as he did.

Curtis couldn't bear to think about it now. What he needed right now was to talk to JD, face-to-face, and maybe have a couple drinks to unwind. After the day he'd had, he deserved it. He opened a new tab on the laptop to access the text messages for his flip phone. He felt more at home managing everything from the laptop, where he could save, sort, and organize the intelligence. And it was easier to type out texts on the computer. He felt a pang of regret for leaving his smartphone in New Orleans as he navigated the menu to the contact list that now included two numbers for the EPD—the public number and Tac's personal cell. He started a new text to JD.

I'm at the Regency. Room 10. Come pick me up when you're ready.

And then he got up from the bed and nudged the Bible out of the way with his foot to close the door to the room, sliding the chain into place. He did a quick 80 push-ups before his shower. Five-plus years removed from annual PT tests, Curtis still maintained his regimen of calisthenics and running. Eighty push-ups in under two minutes got you a max score on the Air Force test.

The motel room was Spartan. He'd had better shower experiences in Afghanistan. When he emerged from the tiny bathroom with a scratchy towel around his waist, there was a reply from JD waiting for him.

On my way, bubba! Should I bring hookers, or just the blow?

Curtis replied.

Your mom's always welcome.

He peeked outside to check the Mazda. He'd backed it up to the room, no more than five feet from the door. He didn't like leaving the steroids in the trunk, but he was going out, and he liked the idea of leaving them in an empty motel room even less. There was no telling how many keys were floating around St. Landry Parish. Besides, he did have some additional security measures in place.

He walked back to the laptop open at the edge of the bed and on his map of Eunice, activated the layer with one of Jacque's RFID tags he'd embedded in the box of steroids. The Radio Frequency Identification tags Jacque had given him were about the size of a Mardi Gras doubloon, but a bit thicker. They sent a GPS signal back to the hard drive connected to the tablet that, per instructions, Curtis had set up and plugged in as soon as he got into the room.

The RFID flashed on the map on Curt's computer, showing it was right outside his room along the front of the motel. Like the flexible cameras Jacque had sent him to Eunice with, the RFID tags were modified with extra power and features you couldn't get on the open market. The tag Curtis had installed in the steroids to keep track of them at all times wasn't totally invisible, but it might as well be. It was nestled between the folds of the box and you would never know it was there unless you took the box apart.

He pulled on a pair of jockeys and spent a few minutes familiarizing himself with the new tools he'd acquired from Jacque and at the gun show. He disassembled the pistol, checked the firing mechanism, the slide, and the safety, and then logged the serial number into his encrypted notes file. Just in case. For tonight, the loaded pistol would stay tucked deep in the EverReady in the trunk of the Mazda.

He pulled on his jeans and clipped the police-grade canister of mace inside his front pocket and slid the Leatherman tool through his belt. Standing in front of the mirror, he felt like a dork with the all-in-one tool on his belt. He may as well have a fucking cell phone holster. He breathed deeply and tried to center himself, couldn't help but flex a bit in the mirror. You couldn't tell from the way he dressed, but Curt was rock solid. He wasn't a fighter, but he was fit and would be ready, he told himself as he stood in the mirror, to do what was necessary to protect JD and his business.

A sudden pounding at the door blasted him out of his reverie. It was enough to make him move towards the pistol in the EverReady despite himself. But then he heard rings raking against the door and he realized it was JD. He crossed the room and opened the door with the chain still on, bracing it with his shoe. Two closed fists came through the opening, "J-D" inked across the middle knuckles of the right hand.

"Pick a hand," the voice behind the door said. Curtis reached out and gave the top one a hard slap, and after some cursing JD's hand opened to reveal two small round pills. "Here," he said, "save these for later, so you can sleep." Curtis reared back to slap the second hand but JD pulled it back in time, then brought it back, palm up, to reveal a small vial of white powder. Curtis grabbed the vial from JD's open palm and closed the door, presumably to release the chain.

"Thanks very much, bubba," he called from behind the locked door. "I'm just gonna drive back to New Orleans now. I'll see you next time."

JD was laughing on the other side of the door. "Shit, Laroux!" he called. "I didn't realize you were such a cheap date." Curtis took one more beat to open the door. He didn't want to look at the drugs in his hand, and a part of him didn't want to give them back.

JD was leaning against the trunk of the Mazda, lighting a cigarette from a cupped Zippo when Curtis opened the door. In no rush at all. The only thing about JD that had changed was the depth of his cool. Where the edginess had once been, there was now just confidence. The current of anger in the way he carried himself a decade prior had evolved into something like wisdom. There was less original skin on his arms now.

What looked like the tail of some kind of creature poked out from his collarbone onto his neck, but otherwise it was the classic JD Dugas who stood before him. Faded jeans, boots, a black tee shirt—this one with "Black Jack Tattoo" in orange sort of Headbanger's Ball lettering—and a whole variety of silver jewelry and chains. His hair was close-cropped on the sides and spiked up top, emphasizing his angular features. It was hard to not feel something when you were in his presence.

He stepped through the door and embraced Curtis in a long, heartfelt hug, cigarette clenched between his teeth. Something in Curt's bones changed in the embrace with his best friend. Much later, as he reflected on the three spiraling days he'd spent in Eunice, Curtis realized this was the first real hug he'd had in several years. For all the camaraderie military life offered, it had brought him so incrementally into detachment and isolation that he never realized it was happening. And as a civilian working in a military world, that sense of detachment was all the more pronounced. Emotional detachment made you good at your job. It also tended to make you lonely as fuck.

JD pulled back, flicked his cigarette out through the open door, and gave Curtis a long appraising look.

"What's up, faggot?" he said, looking into his friend's eyes with nothing but brotherly love. "I missed you!" Curtis gave him a final squeeze, then detached. He held up the little bottle of coke.

"I don't really do this stuff anymore, you know."

JD paused.

"No, I didn't know. But I hear you. I imagine they piss-test you pretty regular?" Curtis gave him a noncommittal look.

"Really it's weed you have to worry about," Curtis said. "Crazy as it sounds. The THC sticks to the lipids in your urine and it can show up even thirty days later. But coke . . . it actually flushes through pretty quick. Two days. Three tops, depending."

"And how long are you in town for?" JD was looking around the room. "Back in the day, you could always use the top of the TV," he lamented.

Curtis wasn't proud of what had happened next. He hadn't put his life on hold and his career in jeopardy for a couple lines that JD got from who knows where.

Sometime after, he found himself in the passenger seat of an eighties-era Astro van that had seen better decades. He was hyperalert. JD at the wheel. It was a short drive to his new shop in the Old-East Shopping Center, next to Sugar Ray's Bakery. Which was good because Curtis was in no mood to sit still, especially in this van.

It wasn't that it was disgusting. It was just sort of *lived in*. Empty cigarette packs and various food and drink wrappers littered the floor. There was a bench seat behind Curtis that was mostly duct tape, from what he could tell. Behind that, it was just open storage space that reminded Curtis in his amped-up state of the old R.E.M. music video for "It's the End of the World As We Know It," the one where the kid spends the whole video rummaging around in an old abandoned house full of random artifacts and junk.

The backseat was stacked with a variety of cardboard boxes. Some of them had clothes spilling out. Others had art supplies—acrylic paints, spray cans, gesso, brushes, and smeared bottles of solvent. A printer paper box contained "Black Jack Tattoo" tee shirts like the one JD was wearing. Another had stickers—silver on black—with the name of the shop and, just above the 337 phone number, and the slogan "Welcome to Your New Addiction!" Curtis reached back and grabbed a tee shirt for himself and a few stickers.

"You always had a way with words," Curt said. JD just gave him a knowing look and smiled.

"You like that?" It wasn't really a question. The translation was more like "badass, right?" And it was, though maybe it cut a little close to the bone.

The shopping center itself was fairly dilapidated. Curtis took it all in as they approached. There was a Dollar Tree in the biggest store on the lot that Curtis thought had probably been the Sears store when he was a kid. At the other end, nearest Highway 190, there was a chicken joint called Kluckie's in the old A-frame building that had been a hamburger place of some kind back in the day. A couple storefronts down from that was Sugar Ray's Bakery, the longest-running business in the center.

Sugar Ray's was the one bright spot in the shopping center. On weekends, especially Sundays, there were almost certainly still lines of well-dressed penitents out the door for donuts. It had a warm dough smell that was magnetic. It was one of the few places in town where you saw black and white folks intermingling without a hint of tension.

"They still line up for donuts at Sugar Ray's?" Curtis asked.

"Shit, bubba, I couldn't tell you," JD said. "It's been a *looong* time since I been up that early. Plus, I heard they sell Krispy Kremes at the Conoco station now." They'd pulled up in front of JD's shop, between the chicken place and the bakery. Curtis studied it carefully with a growing sense of disappointment.

Aside from the chicken place, the forthcoming Black Jack Tattoo was the only other business with the lights on at just after 8:30 on this January evening. In Eunice. Suddenly the simple absurd fact that Curtis was standing here in Eunice, a man with a good paying government job, turned criminal—a simple criminal in the eyes of the law—dawned on him. A primitive part of his brain demanded *what are you doing here? Get out!*

But he couldn't listen because he had already committed to the act. He was here, standing in front of JD's bare-bones tattoo shop in Eunice, Louisiana, ready to figure out how to deliver the illegal steroids in the trunk of his new seven-hundred-dollar car to Lenny Prichard and square accounts so JD could have a fighting chance of making it work. If it weren't so reckless, it would have been funny. Or maybe absurd was the right word. What had he got himself into?

Retail space was plentiful in the Old-East Shopping Center. Only half the stores were filled, and most of those had a desperate look to them. Curtis could see the black outline of "Black Jack" on the window at the front of the shop, done in the same style as the lettering on the shirt and bumper stickers. The lights were on in the shop and he could see someone inside in a ball cap, brim flat as a frisbee, hunched over a notebook and nodding his head to a beat they could hear in the parking lot.

The inside of the place didn't look much different than the Astro van. Boxes, debris, stuff stacked on every available surface. Yellowed cinder block walls and once-white drop ceiling tiles to match. As JD opened the door the music, an intricate rap over a dense beat, assaulted them both.

"It ain't much, bubba, but it's mine," JD said, walking to the back of the shop to hit the spacebar on the open laptop to stop the music. "And come next Saturday when I open this fucker, there's gonna be a line *out the door!*"

"Dat's what I'm talking 'bout boss! They gonna be *lining up,* baby!" At JD's emphasis, the young dude called out. He was half-black, maybe, or possibly Latino. Which was unexpected, Eunice still pretty much either black or white.

Curtis found himself amused—loving it, actually. Even though he didn't believe a word of it. This place was a dump. JD was gonna need some kind of reality TV overnight makeover to get it into shape. JD glanced up at Curtis standing in the doorway and a single look was all he needed.

"I know what you're thinking, bubba, but this ain't D.C. or L.A. Ink or some shit. It ain't even New Orleans or Lafayette. I could open this shop *tomorrow* and I'd have customers. Shit, bruh, I could put out some metal folding chairs and they'd still roll up their sleeves for me cause we're always gonna be cheaper than driving to Lafayette."

"And we will *never* compromise on quality!" the kid added with a tone that suggested he was mocking JD in some way.

"Yeah, makes sense," Curtis said.

"Whatever. Don't give me that shit, Laroux." JD ducked behind a Japanese-style room divider, each paper segment of which had been painted with black calligraphy-style strokes that at first glance looked like some kind of Chinese character, but when you looked closer, was actually a face. A different, stylized face in each segment of the panel. It was uncanny the way the strokes suggested calligraphy at a glance but formed a distinct, often menacing face on closer inspection. But you had to study it to really grasp the illusion.

Curtis was still marveling at it when JD came out from behind the divider with a little red Igloo Playmate ice chest, pulling a plastic folding chair into position. "By the way, this is Angel. Angel, this is Curtis Laroux, my best friend in life and death. Stand up and shake the man's hand, Fucker!"

Angel looked up with a smile that was almost a wink, like there was already a secret between him and Curtis that JD didn't know. "Oh yeah. My bad." He rose a couple inches from his chair and offered an outstretched fist, which Curt bumped. "Nice to meet you, Curtis. Boss man's been *going on* about you the last couple days! Shit, for a minute I thought he was *in love*."

"If you knew what this man was capable of, you'd be in love, too," JD said. He handed Curtis a bottle of beer from the cooler and motioned for him to come to the back of the shop. There was a massage table behind the Japanese divider, which JD had pushed to the side to make room for the plastic chairs. "Step into the piercing studio," JD said. And then to Angel: "Angel, do me a favor and go work on that window like I asked, please." He paused for a beat. "Block it out exactly like we talked about. *Exactly*."

JD changed the music on the laptop, and Curtis heard the opening notes of *Guitar Town* as Angel said something sarcastic on his way out the front door. He had a little can of paint and a brush and was untangling some earbuds to plug in his phone. JD took a chair and propped a boot on the top of the red Playmate as Steve Earle sang "Nothing ever happened around my hometown / And I ain't one to just hang around."

JD double-checked that Angel was outside. "Okay. You ready to hear the full story or you want another bump first?"

His unabridged version of events tracked pretty close to what JD had told Curtis on the phone, though the new version was much more colorful. JD was in a celebratory mood. As far as he was concerned, they were in the clear. Curtis had saved the day with the replacement box of steroids. All that was left to do was actually put them in the old shop, and that was a simple errand.

Curtis hoped he was right, but there was so much more he needed to understand. Or, wanted to, at least. By the second Bud Light, he felt like he had a firm grasp of the facts, all recorded in his pocket notebook, and the logistics of replacing the steroids seemed pretty straightforward. JD still had the keys to the old place. Tomorrow, sometime after Curtis had his breakfast at Rudy's with his new/old cop friend, Curtis would use the key JD gave him to enter the old 2nd Street shop and put the new package of steroids in the ceiling. Simple.

Then Curtis would return the key to JD, who would go immediately to the real estate office to turn it in. JD would take it from there while Curt stayed out of sight. JD would get a receipt and ask the woman—her name was Jackie—to do a walk-through right away and release his deposit. He would document everything with pictures they could use later, if necessary. All this would happen in the daytime—no sneaking around—but they would do it after Curtis had his breakfast with Tac, just in case. Curtis wasn't about to let the chance to learn a thing or two from local law enforcement slip by. When there was intelligence available, you collected.

"What if the shit you got doesn't match the steroids that were originally there?" JD had asked.

"Well, what's he gonna do?" Curt had said, having already given this problem some thought. "It's not like he can take you to court. And, you made him whole again, even though he knows damn well it wasn't you who took 'em in the first place. Either way, it's over."

Angel, the apprentice boyfriend that Jackie had not-so-gently pushed on JD, was done filling in the "Black Jack" on the window, and it looked pretty good, even backward. JD didn't come out and say it, but Curtis could tell he had a certain rapport with Angel. Angel was an outcast—JD had spotted that right off the bat—and he had not only talent but courage. And that was more than enough to allow JD to trust him. Angel looked to be in his early twenties and to Curt, he seemed to be a good guy. The way JD gave him a hard time, you could tell he certainly thought so.

But Curtis was still alarmed when Angel strolled back into the shop, no longer listening to music, and JD just kept right on talking. It was an egregious breach of security. Curtis stood up, and he didn't need to say anything for JD to understand he was alarmed by something. Curtis raised an eyebrow towards Angel and suggested they take a walk or head back to the motel or something. JD drained his beer, said "Let me just take a piss," and Curtis walked outside to check out the progress on the window and get some fresh air. He'd forgotten the way the acrid smell of cigarette smoke got into your clothes and lungs. Nobody smoked indoors on the East Coast anymore.

It was already past ten o'clock when they got back into JD's faded blue van and headed less than a mile down Highway 190 to the Daiquiri Hut, the main daiquiri place in town. Aside from maybe the Purple Parrot, this was the last place Curtis wanted to be. Mostly as a matter of courtesy, he tried to mask his skepticism. It was no use of course. JD had always been able to read him like a billboard.

"Don't sweat it, bubba," JD said, killing the ignition. "See that truck over there?" A relatively new red Ford F150 was parked on the side of the little tin building raised up on cinder blocks that was the Daiquiri Hut. "That's Tee-Bug's truck. He owns the place." JD was lecturing, and Curtis was annoyed.

"You see any *other* cars in this parking lot?"

"No, I don't."

"That's because there's no one else here. So, you don't need to worry about running into any of your brothers or your old preppy-ass friends from high school. We'll have a couple drinks, then I'll bring you back to the motel."

"Okay, fine," Curtis said. "But can you please stop giving me Bud Light? I hate that shit."

Curtis trailed JD through the gravel parking lot, up the wooden steps to the door of the Shack. JD flung it open and announced "This is my friend Curtis! He lives in Washington D.C. and he works for the government!"

The bartender—Tee-Bug, it had to be—wasn't much more than a bushy mustache and narrow eyes under the heavily rounded brim of a camouflage ball cap. Not unlike the one Curtis had picked up at the gun show, except with a lifetime of wear. The music was loud—the Eagles, it sounded like, singing about a peaceful easy feeling they had—and so Curtis was surprised when Tee Bug started in on him when he was still halfway between the door and the little four-stool bar.

"Ah, no! No, you didn't! You brought a fucking Democrat into my place, JD!" He squinted and thrust his head forward, a turtle poking out of his shell, as if he could get a better look at Curtis through his eye slits and the cigarette smoke in the dark bar. "You *got* to be kidding me!"

Curtis stopped, a fight-or-flight impulse flashing in his spine. But during the instant it took for the thought to make its way through his circuits, he took note of the fact that Tee-Bug was still behind the bar, and he was in open space with room to maneuver, if necessary. Anyway, Tee-Bug's hands were casual. This was just a man in a bar talking shit. Probably half-stoned or drunk.

"Actually, I live in Virginia," Curtis lied. "And I'm registered Independent," he lied again.

"*Actually*, I don't give a fuck who you are or what you do," Tee-Bug came back. "As long as you pay your bar tab and you don't play F2 on the jukebox." Curtis looked over then to see a 90s era CD-style jukebox next to the bathroom. He pulled out a stool next to the one JD had taken.

"What's on F2?" he asked, and JD answered for Tee-Bug.

"Tone Loc."

"Funky Cold Medina?" Curtis guessed.

"No, the other one," JD said, and did a mocking version of the big drum intro to "Wild Thing."

"I hate that fucking song!" Tee-Bug barked behind the bar, talking to himself mostly.

"Why doesn't he just take the CD out?" Curtis mouthed to JD. He answered loudly, needling Tee-Bug.

"Cause the dude he bought the jukebox from probably stole it and he didn't have the key for the part where you access the CD. Just the money part. So whatever's in there is in there for like, the fucking *duration*."

Curtis was beginning to enjoy himself. "It's like a time capsule," he observed and then asked Tee-Bug if he had Jameson. Tee-Bug just gave him a disparaging look and filled two small Styrofoam cups with ice and brought them over. He pulled a bottle of Old Charter whiskey from the well and more or less filled each cup.

"There's your Jameson, Yankee boy," he said, and walked back to the end of the bar to start fiddling with his smartphone.

Curtis hadn't seen a bottle of Old Charter since the 7th grade when he poached a pint jar's worth from his dad's liquor cabinet before a school dance. It had been his old man's favorite whiskey. But after the incident, the entire contents of the cabinet had disappeared, and Curtis didn't learn until long after he died that from then on, his mom had insisted the Old Charter stay locked in an old toolbox in his shop. Curtis made a silent toast with the cup and took a big swig, trying to appreciate the harsh burn. He turned to JD.

"So, tell me about Tac Youngblood. I had a very close encounter with him this afternoon."

JD lit a cigarette and smoked it down as Curtis told him what happened. As he finished Curtis heard the opening chords of Boston. What was the name of that song? Just as the name "More Than a Feeling" came to him, Curt realized it was actually Nirvana. JD spoke up. "Tac's a good dude. Totally by the book. I've known some crooked-ass Eunice cops in my day, but Tac's from the heart. He'll be chief of police one day, no bout a doubt it."

"Okay, two questions," Curt said. "One, how is it you've known a lot of crooked Eunice cops in your day, since you just moved back? And, two. And, please forgive me if this is obtuse, bubba. But if he's so from the heart, why didn't you just go to him about the issue with Lenny?" Curt was careful with his phrasing, aware that Tee-Bug's hearing was apparently pretty good, despite the loud music.

"I always came back through at least once a year," JD said, giving Curt a look that bordered on judgment. "You know, to see my family. Like at Christmas time and such. Like people do." Curtis didn't bite, and he continued. "And I said he was a good dude, but he's still a cop. And the thing is—remember this when you talk to him tomorrow—once you tell him something, he's gonna act on it. It's not confession, bruh. If the cops get involved this shit gets messy real quick, and Lenny Prichard is connected, man! How you think he got where he is?"

It was a good point. And a good reminder for Curtis that there was nothing casual about this situation. They damn sure weren't out of the woods yet. Curtis motioned for Tee-Bug.

"Another round of Jameson, please," he asked, just as Wayne Toups was coming on the jukebox. Curtis couldn't name the tune, but he knew it. Wayne Toups had been something of an innovator in the early 90s, pandering to a mainstream audience with a style he called "ZydeCajun" that involved wearing Day-glo headbands and singing pop-style hooks in English.

In recent years, there had been a real Cajun music revival, led by bands of young people like the Lost Bayou Ramblers, the Revelers, and too many others now to count. Curtis followed the movement from afar with fascination and something like jealousy. Even through the footage of their shows on YouTube, there was an authenticity and spirit that was palpable. He envied the way those people had embraced the best parts of Cajun culture. By the time Curtis had been able to see the beautiful aspects of South Louisiana, he was already too far removed from the place. He was an outsider now. It was too late.

"What do you know about Lenny?" he asked, plucking a cube of ice from his refreshed cup.

"Man, if I'd have known it was his place I would've just kept on walking!" JD said. "But I never even saw the dude until it was too late. I'd already fallen in love, and the real estate chick, Jackie—yeah, I'll admit she lured me in."

"She's the one who showed you the place?"

"Yeah. I was standing there outside the empty shop and I called and like five minutes later she was there. Sashaying up to me and stuff with her cleavage and that blue streak in her hair. Man, I couldn't resist!"

"Couldn't resist?"

"Nah, bruh. It's not like that." JD assured him. "I actually had Sadie with me. Did I tell you Sadie's back in town? So no, it wasn't like that. But the thing is. . ." JD looked sheepish.

"The thing is what?"

"So, if it's the Jackie I think it is, I did actually fuck her. But that was like fifteen years ago when we were still playing shows around here. I think she was a groupie! But I'm not entirely for sure."

Reflexively Curtis reached for his notebook, ever the intel analyst. He needed to remind himself to ask about Sadie. She and JD had only broken up when he moved to Houston. Curtis had heard all about their love affair when he and JD were roommates. "You don't need to write this shit down!" JD said.

Curtis closed his eyes for a couple seconds and breathed

through his nose. "Okay. So, the real estate agent you rented Lenny's place from is a groupie you had sex with in high school. And Sadie, your serious high school girlfriend—the one you would've probably married if you'd stuck around—was there with you when you rented it . . ." Curtis flipped back in his notebook to check something. "And the real estate woman, Jackie, asked you to hire her boyfriend as your apprentice. That's Angel, right?"

"Goddamn, Laroux! You make it sound so bad." JD pulled the last cigarette from his pack of American Spirits on the bar, then he asked Tee-Bug for a couple Shiner Bocks. "Look," he said, leaning into Curtis. "It's just Eunice, bruh. Everybody knows everybody. They get around. Shit, you played baseball with Lenny Prichard and you graduated with Tac! It's just the way it is around here. You think I'm not coming to grips with that myself? I mean, shit, man! You're gonna go back to D.C., but I'm trying to open a business here."

A little more than seven hours after JD dropped him off at the motel, Curtis parked the Mazda in a small parking lot behind the Liberty Theater, where Park Avenue crossed 2nd Street. This was the cultural heart of Eunice. Across from the theater was the little two-story library that hadn't changed since Curtis was a kid. And on the opposite corner was City Hall, a three-story tan brick building with flags out front and a big parking lot with marble embankments that gave the building a certain authority. Between the library and City Hall was a life-size bronze statue of Eunice, the woman the town was named after. As a work of art, Curtis thought it was a nice gesture.

He finished his Red Bull, squirted some Visine in each eye, and put his EverReady in the trunk. He felt like shit, but he was just going to have to rally. On his way up the block to Rudy's, he stopped for a second to peer into the Liberty Theater. It was nicely refurbished, with a traditional box office window and etchings on the glass that opened to the lobby. It was nice. Classy even.

From the looks of the place, tickets to the weekly *Rendez-vous des Cajuns* live music show were still selling, and the Liberty, Cajun Culture's version of the Grand Ole Opry, was going strong Right next door to the Liberty was the old flower shop that would have been Black Jack Tattoo. Curtis slowed up as he walked past to get a good look inside. It looked the same as it did in the online street view. No cover at all in the main area. Anyone inside could easily be seen from the sidewalk unless you were in the small bathroom in the back.

He turned left at Walnut and there was Tac standing two doors down in front of Rudy's Cafe, looking stoic and sharp in his plainclothes cop uniform—jeans, button shirt with the sleeves rolled up to show that fresh tattoo, gun at his hip. He turned as Curtis approached and they shook hands.

"Glad you made it," Tac said. "Your car alright?"

"Yeah. It cranked fine this morning, but I'm gonna find a place to look at it today. Any recommendations?"

Tac had his hand on the door to Rudy's. "Take it to Ace Auto." He could tell Curtis didn't know the place, so he added "across from Cecil's Bar. Look for the three-wheeler suspended fifty feet in the air." He paused and studied Curtis for a beat. "Now that the car's out of the way, I have another recommendation for you. And it's real simple. Just tell me the truth about why you're in town. That would do us both a lot of good."

Tac walked through the door without waiting for a response. Curtis just stood there for a bit too long, holding the door as Tac made his way towards a table in the corner of the cafe. He wasn't unprepared for Tac's question, given the way the cop had balked at the sight of the burner phone, but the answer that he'd prepared—the one that he'd already offered yesterday when they met on the road, that he was just in town to help JD set up shop—was so weak that Tac hadn't even bothered to wait around and hear it for a second time.

Rudy's Cafe might have been as old as the town itself. It was at least as old as Curtis. Some of the men sitting at the little five-stool counter looked like they might have been there since the day it opened. The place had the look and feel of a place for old people. The decor was standard issue Louisiana grandma: linoleum floors, wood-paneled walls, rickety spindle chairs, heavy plastic table coverings, and various paintings of wildlife, ducks and fish mostly. They had the local AM station, KEUN, on in the restaurant and the DJs were speaking French, talking about the weather.

A matronly waitress holding a pot of Community brand coffee greeted Tac. "Have a seat, Detective Youngblood. Y'all want some coffee?" Curtis nodded at Tac.

Tac said "Yes, please. And Mrs. Rhonda, when are you gonna just start calling me Tac?" She was already at the little table just as Curtis was getting settled.

"Oh, I don't suppose I'll *ever* do that," Rhonda drawled. "Before you were Detective Youngblood you were Officer Youngblood, but I sure do like calling you *Detective*. Until you make Lieutenant, of course. I can't *wait* to call you Lieutenant Youngblood. Hell, maybe I'll call you Chief or Sheriff someday . . . but no, *honey*, I don't suppose I'll ever just call you Tac." She winked at Curtis. "Welcome to Rudy's, *sugar*." Curtis almost asked her what's good, but he was already tiring of the chitchat, so he put his head down and busied himself blowing on his coffee, which he knew would taste like sticks.

Curtis was happy the place was at least loud because everyone was right on top of each other. Anything like privacy was out in a place like this. Besides the old guys at the counter, who, with their wrinkled faces and big lumpy noses, reminded Curt of alligators sitting there sipping coffee, there was a group of older men sitting at two tables that had been pushed together. They looked like regulars, the way they yucked it up, and at first glance Curtis took them to be retirees. But after another look he wasn't so sure. They were all pretty well-manicured, and they weren't wearing the uniform of men who had spent a lifetime working with their hands. No worn Dickies, work shirts, and overalls. No truckers' hats. No flannel shirts. These old cats were buttoned up in Polo shirts and slacks.

He must've looked for too long because Tac was waiting when Curtis turned his head back. "You wanna sit here?" he asked.

"Nah. I'd just as soon have my back to the room," Curtis said. "I'm not looking to get recognized." Tac laughed.

"Well then, you're probably safe here. I come in just about every day. Every day I'm working, anyway. And I'm always the youngest dude in the place."

Curtis waited a beat, then said:

"So, Detective Youngblood, huh? Nice!" The waitress appeared again, and Curtis asked for a glass of ice water, then ordered biscuits with a scoop of crawfish etouffee on top of it. Tac asked for his usual.

"Late night?" Tac asked.

"More like a long day," Curtis said. "That drive from New Orleans was tiring. Baton Rouge is a lot bigger than I remember." No way was he going to acknowledge his hangover.

"How long are you in town for?"

"I'm not sure, exactly," Curtis answered honestly. "I'd like to see the grand opening of JD's shop, but we'll see." He took a sip of coffee, surprised despite himself at the acrid bite of it. "So, I gotta tell you, man, I was surprised to see you in town. I thought you were going in the Marines?"

Something twitched in Tac and Curtis was sure he'd hit some kind of nerve.

"Shit, Curt. That's a long story," Tac said, shaking his head. "But I'll tell you the short version."

"Fuck that," Curtis interrupted. "Tell me the long version, bruh. This is important." Tac lit up. Curtis had studied and practiced enough human intelligence to know that people liked to talk about themselves. Plus, the more Tac talked about himself, the less Curtis might have to give up. Especially in this place where everybody was within earshot.

"I tell you what," Tac said. "I'll tell you the short version now and if you want, later on I can give you the blow-by-blow because there's some stuff I want to ask you—" Curtis interrupted again, taking a calculated risk.

"I'm in town to help JD. Simple as that. Now tell me. What happened to the Marines?" Tac stared at him for a couple seconds, and Curtis could see him considering his statement. At that moment, Rhonda reappeared with a steaming plate of etouffee in one hand and a simple egg sandwich on toast, cut corner to corner.

"Somebody's hungry!" she said.

When the waitress had gone, Tac told his story. "So, the short version is I got a screwdriver put through my hand in a fight with some Army dudes in Mississippi. Coming back from the senior trip after graduating high school, actually. And not only did I almost get convicted of aggravated assault, I fucked up the nerves in my hand. Tac held up his right hand for Curtis to inspect a small stigmata-type wound that had healed over pretty good. He turned his hand in profile so Curtis could see some of his digits were permanently crooked.

"But your trigger finger still works?" Curtis confirmed.

"Oh yeah. I'm fully functional now. The thing is, the Marine Corps wasn't gonna wait. Honestly, I'm lucky. That shit coulda ended up way worse. A four-on-four fight between Marines and Army? In a fucking rest stop bathroom on I-10? I don't know what possessed me to bring the screwdriver in there, but I'm lucky it didn't end up in my head."

Tac started in on his sandwich. Curtis wasn't sure his stomach could stand up to the etouffee. He was thinking he should've ordered something more basic.

"What do you mean between Marines and Army? You got

in a fight with soldiers?" Curt asked, not just because he wanted Tac to keep talking, but because he was curious.

"Army recruits. You didn't go on the senior trip, did you?"

"Nah. I booked out for Houston right after graduation." Curt said.

"That's right. I remember now. You totally skipped Panama City. So yeah, what happened was the Marine recruiter kinda put four dudes from the area together. We were all on delayed enlistment—two guys from Ville Platte and another dude from Crowley. I guess he figured we'd all keep each other out of trouble. He even gave us a little speech before we left, the way I remember. Anyway, there was a group of Army dudes in the same hotel as us, kinda doing the same thing. I think they were from Lake Charles. I can't remember. Anyway, it's not important anymore. The point is, I fucked up my chance to be a Marine—". Curtis was startled by the sound of the waitress, Rhonda, clearing her throat.

"Um. Detective Youngblood. *Language?"*

Tac raised his hand in supplication, then turned back to Curtis. "So I stayed in Eunice and became a cop." He looked down at his sandwich. "Next best thing, I guess."

Curtis watched him for a second and when Tac came back into the moment, he said "Shit, Bruh, you shoulda joined the Air Force. No *way* you'd find Air Force dudes fighting in the bathroom." Curtis gave him a big smile and Tac laughed, but he wasn't feeling it. There was real regret there, Curtis could see.

"I gotta say, Laroux, I never pegged you for a military man. Not even in the *Chair Force.*" Tac smiled at his own joke, but his smile evaporated. "Maybe you ended up having the life I thought I was gonna have," he said.

Curtis shook his head. "Nah, bruh. I'm not an operator, man. I'm a bureaucrat. I just push paper around." He pushed his fork into the etouffee to find a bite of slightly soggy biscuit. He'd start with that and maybe pick out a few pieces of crawfish.

"But you traveled, right?" Tac asked.

"Sure."

"Iraq?"

"A couple times," Curtis said.

"Afghanistan?"

"Well, yeah. Everybody went to Afghanistan." Curtis said.

"Where else?" Tac asked.

"You mean, deployment wise?" Curtis paused. "That's hard to say. Basically, all the continents." It registered to Curtis then that Tac was envious. At least on some level. He continued. "I'm not gonna lie man. The service was good to me. I got to see some interesting stuff. But always from the sidelines, you know?"

"Afghanistan's not the sidelines," Tac said. "What province were you in?"

Curtis said, "Well, several. But I spent the most time in Helmand."

"Fuck. That's in the shit!" Tac said. And then looked up to see if Rhonda had heard him curse.

"Yeah, but it's not like I was camped out on some remote peak with a bag of beef jerky and a rifle. Don't get the wrong idea. Anyway, I been a civilian for a few years now. It's a lot tamer."

"You're not still working for the Air Force?" Tac asked. Curtis got the feeling he already knew the answer. He just shook his head.

"So, what exactly do you do now?"

"Whatever they tell me," Curtis said.

"NSA?" Tac asked. Curtis knew the question was coming. He just cocked his head and gave Tac an exasperated look. A few seconds ticked by, during which Tac recognized that he'd taken it too far. He took a sip of coffee and seemed to regroup.

"Yeah, I get it, man," he said. "Maybe we can talk more later, but I understand. What I *don't* understand is why a guy like you . . . with, what, six or seven years in uniform and another, what, maybe five or so doing who knows what up in D.C. What I *don't* understand is how a guy like that can roll into town in a seven-hundred-dollar hoopty he bought from a junkman outside New Orleans and a fucking burner phone." He looked square at Curtis and those hard cop eyes were back. "That," he said, punctuating it with his finger, "is something I don't understand."

Curtis had seen this coming. He'd even told Tac about how he came to own the Mazda, though he'd left Moe's name out of it, of course. They were questions Tac would have to ask if they were ever going to get to a point where they could trust each other. Curtis hoped they could get there because Tac had much to offer. He waited, figuring Tac wasn't quite done.

"So, what I want to know is why are you here?"

Curtis breathed through his nose, then took a long drink of cold water, working his meditation technique. Then he looked at Tac and tried to convey to him that he was right. That his instincts were on the money. "The answer is just two words," he said. After a small pause, he said, "Lenny Prichard."

Tac's eyes showed panic and Curtis could have sworn the cafe went silent for an instant.

Episode Three
Heir to the Throne

———— ❀ ————

When he finds out they're both interested in Sadie Lee, Lenny Prichard decides to fuck with JD in the most cold-blooded way possible. Meanwhile, it comes to light that Angel, JD's new apprentice, is an associate of Lenny's, and it's unclear if JD and Curtis can trust him.

"Now Lemmy—he was a cool motherfucker. May he rest in peace. But *Lenny* is a whole 'nother thing. That dude's a *Meat*head, not a Motorhead." — JD

Lenny Prichard had a lot on his mind, and he hadn't had

breakfast yet unless you counted the PowerBar he had in the truck on the way to the Eunice Health Club. So he was already on edge and it was barely 7 a.m. He was thinking about Sausage McMuffins, JD Dugas, his cousin Jackie, and especially Sadie Lee. He was maybe the slightest bit hungover, so he couldn't ignore his hunger, and that got him thinking about the new girl at the drive-through he'd started flirting with.

She always gave him extra cream for his coffee. Last week, she complimented his new Toyota Tundra and he knew right then it was on. But he played it cool—just gave her a look and pulled away. He was thinking it was about time to give her a free pass to Sun-*N*-Tans. What he'd do, he'd give her the pass and write his number on the back. A lot of times that did the trick.

Not that he was too worried about it one way or the other. There were plenty of young things like her around. She or the next one like her were just there to tide him over because his eye was really on Sadie Lee. And she damn sure wasn't falling for a tanning pass. Which he'd never try anyway because it was partly that beautiful fair skin she had that got him so stirred up. What was the word? *Alabaster.* That was it. Alabaster skin. She was like no woman he had ever fantasized about.

The parking lot at the club was still empty when he backed into one of the spots reserved for staff. The club wasn't open yet, but that didn't matter. He had his own key. Lenny had insisted on getting a master key to the building as soon as Uncle Ely had signed the papers for the first fifteen percent stake in the business. Since then, Lenny had managed to get another five percent just in his name. In three years, he planned to be majority owner of the Eunice Health Club, and once he wrapped up the club he would be set.

He would have to pressure the other two owners, white-collar dudes from the 80s who never quite made it. They still had delusions of turning the place over to their kids someday or cashing out for a few hundred grand. But that wasn't gonna happen. The club had never been renovated, still sporting its original fixtures. It just wasn't worth that much, at least not in the current state. The old guys would sell, and for cheap too. They just didn't know it yet. And once he had the EHC, it would be the centerpiece of his empire.

Uncle Ely ran his businesses like a fucking clock, and he probably would keep doing exactly that until the day he died. But then Lenny would inherit Sun-*N*-Sports and probably the other off-record enterprises too. Though those other, shadier enterprises were tricky, and Lenny wasn't sure he was ready for all that. Anyway, the legitimate stuff was more than enough. Sun-*N*-Sports alone was good for at least a hundred thousand in taxable income every year, and that was just the tip of the iceberg. Of course, Uncle Ely was a tough son of a bitch and didn't show any signs of slowing down even though he was pushing seventy.

In Lenny's mind, Uncle Ely hadn't changed a bit since Tee-ball, when Lenny could first remember him sitting in his lawn chair by the dugout in his collared shirt, growling at the umpire. There was literally not a single game Lenny could remember without Uncle Ely in his usual seat.

And Lenny played *a lot* of baseball. Starting at eight years old he'd traveled every year with the all-star team. In high school, they'd gone all over the state for four years in a row, Uncle Ely trailing them everywhere in whatever Caddie he was driving then. Both years when they'd won state, Uncle Ely was the first face Lenny looked for, nothing but pure joy on his uncle's face as he stood by the dugout pumping his fist. There was something deep in the way Uncle Ely looked out for him that Lenny was only now beginning to understand, well into his thirties. Maybe it was because Uncle Ely himself never married or had kids.

Lenny's dad had coached him every year he played organized baseball, and that had been alright. His old man was a good dude. Nice, even. People around town knew Mr. Lonnie

Prichard and they weren't afraid of him like they were of Uncle Ely or even Lenny. It was like Lenny's dad just didn't get the gene. Sometimes Lenny wondered if his dad would still be alive if he had gone ahead and played junior college ball. But by then he just couldn't get his shit together, still coming to grips with the limits of his talent. Maybe the end of his baseball dream had something to do with his father's death, at least indirectly. If he had played college ball, his parents might've stayed together. If they hadn't got divorced, maybe his dad wouldn't have run himself into the ground within a year. Maybe Lenny's baseball career held some kind of innocence or purity his old man was hanging on to. It was a stupid thing to think, but sometimes that occurred to him when he was drunk and introspective.

In his mind, he didn't even think of the Eunice Health Club as *the* club anymore. To Lenny, it was *his* club and he wasn't shy about treating it that way. He came and went as he pleased, often before or after hours as a way to make a point to the chickenshit managers. This group had been there for the last ten years and didn't understand the potential they were missing by only focusing on one demographic. The days of rich families buying annual memberships were over. What's left of those people were all on the edge of town at the Eunice Golf Club, which had gone exclusive a few years ago when the businesses in town started to diversify. All those families paid dues at the golf club so they could keep wearing white and let their kids run around while they sat by the pool drinking beers and martinis and shit, or played a round of golf or tennis just to say they did something.

Lenny knew it was the younger crowd they needed to be attracting. It was just like his tanning business. You made your money from women and men in their prime, people who wanted to look good. People who were willing to pay hard-earned money to make sure they looked their best for the opposite sex. Those kinds of people didn't shell out membership dues a year at a time. They wanted to pay by the month or by the session even, and they wanted to go tan or work out whenever they felt like it. This nine-to-five bullshit just had to go.

So Lenny felt he needed to demonstrate this when he came in before the club opened. But there was no justification for why he co-opted two lockers in the little staff dressing room, or why he used three towels at a time or stored extra clothes in the storage room. That was just shit he did because he was the owner. One of them, anyway. And because sometimes it was easier to shower and change at the club than to drive all the way out to his place in the country. If anybody had the guts to say something about it to him, their days were numbered. Shit, they were probably numbered anyway.

He hopped out of his new Tundra pickup with his gym bag over his shoulder and stood back from the truck to admire it while he pulled the St. Eds lanyard from his pocket to find the fob on his key ring to lock it. It was a tough-looking ride. A full-size truck in glossy metallic black with dark tinted windows and chrome and shit. Fucker was tight, though it was already due for a wash. The license plate said Sun-*N*-1, and Lenny thought that was cool as hell. The way it referenced his other businesses and how the "one" had a double meaning.

Ever since Tee-ball he'd worn the number one, because he *was* Number One. And also, the number one on the plate made it seem like he had a whole fleet of vehicles. Lenny liked that idea a lot. Right now, it was just the new Tundra because he'd traded in his Tacoma to get it, not to mention put down ten thousand in cash right there on the desk at the dealership, but it was only a matter of time. Lenny was gonna be the king of Eunice.

And he already had his queen picked out. Sadie Lee, and even though they had just started talking, he just knew in his bones it was gonna work out the way he fantasized. He could see her in maybe a little Miata or something—a sporty little thing with a plate that said "Sun-*N*-2." Or maybe he'd get her a little SUV, like a BMW Z4 or something, a car that would really make a statement around town. A Beamer might be a stretch, but Uncle Ely would hook him up, especially if she was the one.

Lenny opened the front door to the club and started flipping on lights. It wasn't that he was scared of the dark or the quiet or anything, it was just that he didn't like either of those things. Plus, he liked the idea of casually telling the staff members when he saw them he had opened the place up. For a second, he wondered if he should try to put Pancho on staff at the club as a janitor or something. That way there would always be somebody to greet him when he came in early.

Pancho's real name was Angel, and Lenny didn't actually employ him. Not officially, at least. You might've called him an associate, and really it was pretty casual and low-key. He wasn't a racist or anything, but he damn sure wasn't gonna put some blaxican hip-hop kid from Opelousas on the payroll, even if he was dating Lenny's cousin Jackie. He would throw a few bucks Pancho's way for odd jobs, not all of which were totally legal, but that was about it.

Lenny had told Pancho to swing by the tanning shop this afternoon to give him an update on the package. He wasn't thrilled about Pancho holding onto it, but it was worth the risk. JD was probably freaking out right about now, seeing that box of steroids had disappeared and knowing he was responsible for it. The fucker deserved it. Especially after the shit he'd pulled the other day, it would serve him right. And not only that, but if he worked it right, Lenny was thinking maybe he could find a way to use the whole situation to create a wedge between this greaser and Sadie Lee. Damn, he loved the sound of her name!

Lenny stopped for a minute at the racquetball court and imagined it as a mixed martial arts fighting venue. You couldn't put an octagon in there but the beauty of it was you wouldn't have to. The room itself was a box. He'd have a mat custom made to fit the space and leave the three hard walls just like they are, to give it an extra edge. Spectators could watch through the glass at the back of the court, and he could turn the viewing area up above that looked down on the court into a VIP lounge.

Shit, he could even mount cameras in every corner and stream the fights live. He could have some kind of bout in here one night a week and start the fees at twenty-five bucks a head or something. That, plus the points on the betting would make him a couple thousand easy.

The Nautilus equipment in the main weight room had been top of the line in its day, and it was still in good working order. As a younger man, he wouldn't have bothered with them, Nautilus being for pussies, but he'd had to let that prejudice go as his joints started to stiffen and the extra weight started to creep in around his waist. He damn sure wasn't fat—not by a long shot and especially compared to most of the tub o' lards his age. But it was definitely harder these days to keep the beer and the boudin and poboys and shit from sticking to his ribs. So, he made it a point to hit the EHC at least three times a week, usually in the mornings when it was quiet.

One thing Lenny had learned about life, you could create an impression in people's minds based on the things you did and talked about, even if you weren't dedicated to those things. Go to the gym regular and people assume you're in shape. Talk about investing and they assume you're rich. Pursue a couple ladies at the same time and . . .well, you know. It wasn't like he was a phony—he *was* an athlete, he *did* have money, and he *was* a ladies' man. But you had to take care to cultivate your reputation. If there was one thing he'd learned from Uncle Ely, it was that. Reputation was everything.

Which is probably why Sadie accepted his friend request. She must've known who he was already, though she had played it coy when she responded to his first direct message, asking how they knew each other. He couldn't very well tell her he'd seen her in Sun-*N*-Sports trying on sports bras and he pulled her name from the credit card receipt. He just said he was a local business owner and a good person to know, and she answered "good to know." He just loved that, Sadie flirting with him right off the bat.

He gave it a few days and then reached out again, suggesting they get together. And so they ended up meeting for coffee at a new little place on 2nd street somebody's wife had opened up in the old Sattler building. It was kind of a faggoty joint, but Lenny played it cool and it seemed like they hit it off pretty well. She hadn't really lived in Eunice since she graduated from the nursing school at LSUE and moved away, first to New Orleans, then Atlanta, then Memphis. He could tell she had been kinda wild back in the day, just from the way she talked, but all that was behind her now. She was back home to help take care of her momma and she got her stress out by running up and down Park Avenue.

She was a runner! Lenny couldn't believe his luck. The way most of the chicks around Eunice started to blow up before they even hit thirty years old, he'd hit the jackpot with Sadie. It was a wonder she didn't have any kids or other baggage or anything. He'd just asked her about it, point-blank, five minutes into their conversation because he didn't have time to fuck around with those kinds of entanglements. And plus, he was pretty sure the answer was no, just by looking at her. He was right. She never married. No kids. She was a professional woman, a nurse, no less . . .and an athlete to boot.

He literally couldn't have asked for more. Well, she didn't exactly have any kind of family pedigree. But really that didn't matter. Lenny's own family had pulled themselves up, so that was no big deal. Plus—and he hated to be cold-blooded about it—but it sounded like it was just her mom left and she had one foot in the grave, so it's not like he'd have a big extended family on her side to worry about. Which was a bonus.

Lenny was rummaging through the stack of burned CDs next to the stereo that controlled the speakers in the weight room, looking for his mix, thinking it was about time he reached out to her again. It was time for a real date. Maybe dinner in Lafayette, something like that. Something where he could drive and have her as a captive audience for the forty minutes it took to get there. So they could really connect. He found his CD, cleaned it with his shirt, and put it in the disc carousel of the stereo system that was pretty nice when people were still using iPods and burning discs. The whole building was a lot like a museum in that way.

He started moving around the weight room, limbering up, slowly pulling himself out of his head as the song "Coming in the Air Tonight" built up. Some people thought it was lame or whatever, but nobody who'd ever heard that song blasting from the PA before a big game would say some dumb shit like that. This song always put him in the zone, the way it started out intense, even in the quiet part when Phill Collins punctuated those taglines with *Oh lawd*, and how it just boiled up from there to that eruption of drums—every time it got to that part Lenny couldn't help but rock the air drums in perfect time to the song—and he dared anybody to mock him for that. Of course, it was just him in the club still, so he could do whatever the fuck he wanted.

He was doing his squats when "Sweet Child of Mine" came on and of course he loved that song, but it fucked him all up because images of Axl Rose and Slash came into his mind, naturally. Which was fine but then he just went from there to thinking about this fucking guy, JD Dugas, maybe because of all the tattoos and stuff. Why Jackie had decided to rent the old flower shop without checking with him was something he'd never understand, and they'd damn sure had words about it. Cousin or no, he was ready to fire her ass. But the damage was already done and it had thrown everything he had going on into total disarray, to the point where the dude actually showed up in his office at Sun-*N*-Tans waving his fucking phone at him. Lenny did another rep, pushing out air through his teeth and seething with anger. He couldn't help but imagine the scene just two days ago.

Lenny had the whole building wired for video—thanks to his best friend Lefty—even the parking lot, and so he'd actually seen JD come up the steps to the commercial-size trailer that was Sun-*N*-Tans. Motherfucker walked right into the reception area and then dumb-ass Britney pointed towards Lenny's office and JD just walked right down the hall and was suddenly standing there. Lenny was caught off guard, even though he watched the dude approaching on his laptop. He just couldn't believe it. And yeah, thinking about it now while he finished his leg extensions, he was man enough to admit he was caught flat-footed, but he'd come on strong once he fully grasped the situation.

"Hey, bruh. What's the shit you got hidden in my shop?" Lenny remembered the way the guy's neck was all tense as he stood there holding out his phone, skinny but all wired up like a spring. Lenny was distracted by the fierce look in his eye and a little piece of a tattoo sticking up by his collarbone. Before he even really understood what was happening, something in Lenny's spine triggered and reflexively he reached down to pull open the top drawer of his desk. Seeing it now in his mind as he finished his squats, Lenny could tell JD had noticed the big chrome .38 in the drawer because that was the point where things seemed to change. Lenny looked at the picture on JD's phone, jutting out from his hand, and recognized his box of 'roids. Then it finally made sense, why JD was there. Lenny had felt something like relief.

He had taken another couple seconds to appraise the man in front of him. He probably had thirty pounds on JD, and he had a gun. There was a desk between them, and JD had barged into *his* place. There was nobody else there. No cops. No bikers or any kind of other greasers there backing him up. Lenny put it all together and realized the dude wasn't there to fight.

"Close that," Lenny had said, jerking his head towards the door. JD tucked his phone in his jeans and closed the door, hanging back but still standing tall. "Who else saw that?" Lenny demanded, again with a jerk of his head.

"Nobody but me, man." Even in the heat of the moment, Lenny had noticed how JD's tone got more cautious after he opened the drawer. "I took a picture because I couldn't believe my fucking eyes. I told myself there's no way this is what I think it is. No fucking way somebody's gonna be dumb enough to leave shit like this laying around. And in my shop of all places? I had to take a picture because I couldn't believe what I was seeing."

Lenny's adrenaline was leveling out.

"Look," he'd said, trying to strike a businesslike tone. "It's real simple . . .. First of all, chill. That has nothing to do with you." Here, Lenny had paused and offered something short of a smile. It was a trick he'd learned in fights in high school, to get the guy to let down his guard just before you sneaked him. Except the strike he was planning was more subtle now. "I'm not saying it has anything to do with me," he continued, "but it damn sure don't have anything to do with you. So how 'bout you don't go snooping around looking for trouble?"

"Snooping around?" JD had taken a step forward. "No, no. Hold up, bruh. I don't think we're understanding each other. It's my place. You rented it to me! You want simple? Get this shit out of my shop. How's that for simple?"

"It ain't your shop! You don't own dick. Remember that." Lenny's adrenaline was surging again. This dude had a lot of nerve.

At the health club, remembering the incident, Lenny couldn't help but tense up. "She Talks to Angels" was on, his stretching song, but now he was all tight from just thinking about JD Dugas. Especially the way the dude had managed to get the last word. "Just get the shit out of there man. I don't need the hassle," he'd said, and then had the nerve to add, "It's not too fucking much to ask."

Lenny had to give him credit. The dude had balls. And to tell the truth, he had a point. He was just trying to open a business . . . and it was a cool business, Lenny had to admit. He didn't have anything against tattoos. In fact, if Jackie hadn't fucked the thing up, he might've tried to figure a way to get in on the action. But JD Dugas was fucked now, and the funny thing was, he didn't even know what he was dealing with. The poor bastard actually thought it was about some steroids. He didn't even understand that it was really about Sadie Lee. No way anybody but Lenny was gonna be with her.

It was a complicated situation. Lenny tried to cut through it all in his mind to find the one thing he needed to do next. He moved through the club towards the locker room on autopilot, nodding to older men in tennis shorts entering his racquetball court and a fat man with a towel around his neck, hanging over his tits, on the way to the sauna.

He had used the old flower shop to temporarily store steroid shipments before. Technically, Uncle Ely owned the storefront, but it was one of a dozen commercial properties Lenny managed through Sun-*N*-Y reality, which Jackie basically ran for him. It had been empty for like two months and *nobody* was interested in it, so storing the dope there just made sense. Until

Jackie rented it and gave the guy the keys inside of twenty-four hours, it had made sense.

But then he found out from Jackie that Sadie—his Sadie, of all people—was there with JD when she first showed him the place. And then Pancho mentioned it to him, too. It wasn't enough for Jackie to rent the empty shop to this freak, but she had to get her little brown boyfriend an apprenticeship out of the deal too. So now Pancho was all *buddy-buddy* with JD and Lenny had learned that JD and Sadie used to go together. Like, seriously go together, in high school . . .and they were both back in town. Lenny was ready to kill Jackie when all this shit came out.

Of course, the only thing she had to say about it all was number one, she was the real estate agent, not him, and two, her boyfriend's name was Angel, not Pancho. As if Lenny was gonna call another man Angel . . . and anyway he was pretty sure Pancho liked his nickname Lenny had given him.

He had never understood the dudes Jackie decided to get involved with. It was just a parade of weirdos and quote-unquote artists for as long as Lenny could remember. Jackie was a few years older than him, and he could still remember how Uncle Ely and his mom and everybody were always up in arms about whatever shit she was starting at St. Eds that year (pink hair, nose rings).

Hell, one year she managed to hire a punk band for a school dance. And this was way before grunge got big. Lenny was maybe thirteen or so, but he could still remember the incident. He even remembered the name of the group: *John Doe Disciples,* the perfect name to piss off the parents at a Catholic school. You had to give Jackie credit. She did her own thing, and she didn't back down. But she had royally fucked up things for him.

It wasn't until the next morning—after JD had busted in his office waving that pic of the package at him, and after he and Jackie had it out at the real estate office—that he finally saw the opportunity in it all. This JD Dugas was at the center of all his troubles. JD stood in the way of Lenny's future wife and he knew about the steroids in the ceiling of the old flower shop. But he wasn't going to the cops; if he was gonna do that, it would've already happened. Lenny realized JD must've had everything riding on that shop, so maybe the thing to do was create some additional pressure and see if that didn't get him to back off.

Lenny told Pancho to go and pull the package from the flower shop. He already had a key—hell, Pancho was the one that stowed it up in the ceiling in the first place. He'd decided JD had to go. No way they could have a tenant-landlord relationship after what JD had done to him. So he told Pancho to move the shit outta there right away and told Jackie to wait until he said to give JD the bad news. Pancho was the first to balk. He knew this was bad for JD and he'd already started to like the guy by then, but then Lenny palmed him three hundred-dollar bills and that was that.

"Relax," Lenny had told Pancho. "I'm not gonna do anything to him. I just want to see him squirm a little. Just hang on to it for a while . . . till I say."

Jackie was next, but when she started in on how JD Dugas' money was just as green as anyone else's, he just gave her that look that let her know there were things in the mix she didn't want to know about, and she dropped it. If Ely Prichard was your uncle, you got to know that look.

Sadie Lee was dead tired, struggling to stay awake as she entered the Eunice city limits with all the windows down, the steady blast of cool air her best defense against nodding off. She had worked a twelve-hour shift at Opelousas General, about 25 miles east of Eunice, a straight shot down Highway 190. It was the closest job she could find when she moved back to Louisiana just in time for Christmas—probably her mom's last one. The nursing racket pretty much looked the same here as anywhere else—different accents maybe, better food—but basically the same. Despite this fact that she repeated to herself a few dozen times a day, she was not loving the job. It was weird being back, and she was working so much—no other choice there, the money had to come from somewhere—that she might as well still be in Memphis.

She had never intended to move back to Eunice. But then again, her mother had never planned to get cancer, so there you go. She was here and she would make the best of it. It was strange, but the thought somehow comforted her that it was ultimately a temporary arrangement. Her mom was stage four and the simple fact was she would measure the rest of her life in weeks. Months if they were lucky. This often made Sadie think about the azaleas in the yard; it would be a miracle if her mom could enjoy them one more spring before she died. April was still three months away.

Still, it wasn't too early to have some work done in the yard. Put down some mulch, clean up the edges around the flower beds, that kind of thing. She'd have to hire someone, which her mom wouldn't like, but the activity might give her something to look forward to. Something more to fight for.

It was weird being back in the house, of course, but the quality time she was getting with her mom—work or no work—was precious. Her eyes were wide open on that front. This was it. If she fancied herself as independent before, it would be a whole new level once her mother passed. At which point, it would just be Sadie. Just her.

Her brother's death had rocked her and her mother and neither one of them had ever been the same. But he was Army infantry, with more than two years in Afghanistan to his credit before he died. In a way, it was a blessing. Remi had always been something of a mama's boy and watching her die would have been too much for him. And *that* would have been too much for Sadie.

She put it all out of her mind. Sat up straighter in her seat, tapped the steering wheel, rolled her shoulders. She just needed to get home, relieve the sitter, kiss her mom, and sleep for a few hours. If she could just get a solid two hours she could be up in time to fix a late lunch and maybe sit out on the front porch with her mom in the afternoon, once it warmed up. With three days off in front of her, she'd try to power through the day to reset her circadian cycle tonight. Set a couple redundant alarms on her phone, maybe even swallow half a Vivarin before she went to sleep to help her pop up in the afternoon.

She thought of her phone then. She hadn't powered it back up since she got off shift. It drove the other techs crazy that she actually turned the thing off and left it in her locker while she was working. Their phones were like an appendage for them, even at work. But she liked to detach, and when she was at work, she was focused. And anyway, she basically had no social life, so she didn't need to be carrying her phone around, and if something came up with her mom she'd get paged immediately. Plus, the damn thing was a hassle to lug around, always turning sideways in your pocket and making a huge bump on your butt. Another thing for people to stare at.

She rummaged around in her Eastpak for it. Some women carried purses, which was fine for them, but she'd always found a backpack to be more useful. Maybe it was the leftover tomboy in her. People had always used the word to describe her growing up and she still felt that, in some ways, it still applied. She was a woman, no doubt—even in her scrubs that was obvious—but she never saw herself as overly feminine either.

She felt around in the front pocket of her trusty pack: wallet, keys, mace . . . phone. She pulled it out and turned it on. When it booted up, she held it up in front of her, just something to keep her awake more than anything. A missed call from JD, which produced a smile, and a Facebook message from Lenny, which did not. She knew it was only a matter of time before he asked her out on a real date and it looked like the time had come. But they could both wait. Unless one of them wanted to do some yard work, they were shit out of luck. The thought of it brought another smile to her face. JD in the flower beds with a hoe in his hands and a cigarette in his mouth, a good sport but handsomely inept at the task.

Just making it to the old house on 4th and Vine felt like an achievement. She aimed the tires of her champagne-colored Corolla at the parallel gravel strips that constituted the driveway and stopped a few feet from the bumper of her mom's VW Bug under the carport. The sitter was good about parking on the street. It occurred to her for the first time that she'd have to sell her mom's car, and the thought just weighed her down more. She closed her eyes for a moment and took a couple deep breaths. It was a technique she used at work to center herself, but when she opened her eyes, she didn't feel any less tired. And her feet still hurt.

She walked to the mailbox before she went inside and there was an elegantly folded piece of sketch paper that didn't come from the post office on top of the envelopes and grocery circulars. Her pulse quickened and she couldn't help but smile. The drawing on the front was too good to be anyone other than JD. It appeared to be her in silhouette, leaning against her car, stretching out before a run. There was the house, the swing, the azalea bushes. She opened it up to find a traditional "Sailor Jerry" style rose on the inside, beautifully rendered with thorns and filigree framing the petals. He had penned a little poem:

Roses are Red

Violets are Blue

I'm So Happy

You're in Eunice too.

A little stick figure below the poem, complete with an oversized red heart in his chest and spiky hair and jeans decorated the bottom portion of the little card. An arrow pointed to him with the caption: "(somewhat) attractive and available tattoo artist who's glad you're in town." Sadie couldn't help but smile as she walked back towards the house with the stack of mail in one hand and the handmade card in the other. It had been a long time since she felt this way about anyone. Instead of going right to bed, she'd ask the sitter to stick around for another half hour so she could get a quick run in down Park

Avenue.

Curtis dropped a twenty-dollar bill on the table at Rudy's and he and Tac navigated through the patchwork of tables in the small cafe. On the sidewalk, they shook hands. Tac checked his watch. His unmarked but obvious police car was parked at the curb. Tac had played it cool after what Curtis saw as initial shock at the mention of Lenny Prichard, but the whole momentum of the discussion—or maybe it was a kind of interrogation—had stalled.

"I definitely want to hear more about that, but right now I gotta start my shift," Tac had said. Curtis, for his part, was happy to get out of there. The cafe had started to feel claustrophobic and the etoufee had congealed on his plate. They'd agreed to get together again with the unspoken understanding that the next time they might both be willing to show cards you couldn't just lay down on the table at Rudy's.

Outside in the fresh morning air, Curtis was beginning to overcome his hangover from the night before. He watched Tac pull away and then decided to stretch his legs, get the blood circulating. He crossed Walnut Street right there in front of Rudy's and made his way back toward 2nd Street, where he turned left, away from the Mazda and the old flower shop, and went up the sidewalk towards where Highway 190 cut across 2nd.

Back in the day, this one-block strip on either side of 2nd street had been prime commercial real estate. For the most part, the shops that remained still had that old money vibe about them. It sort of felt to Curtis like returning to walk the halls of your elementary school; everything seemed smaller, less glamorous than he remembered. He felt like he was experiencing another blast from the past, one of many he had encountered since stepping foot in Eunice.

The display window of the "Men's Shop" had its mannequins in designer blue jeans and Ralph Lauren shirts and "Rick's on 2nd" with its naked appeal to New Orleans urban chic that just made you want to gag. It had specials written in script on a chalkboard beside uncomfortable wrought-iron chairs and wobbly tables. "Deshotels," the female version of the Men's Shop, with its red brick exterior balanced against floral wallpaper that looked expensive even from the sidewalk. It was like it had never changed since it was placed there in the 1950s.

But not all the stores were still there. Babineaux's Printing and Office Supplies, the largest space on the block, was just a shell now. Likewise for three or four of the smaller stores that had long since closed. Curtis stood at the intersection and counted the seconds till the green light turned red on Highway 190, watching vehicles, mostly pickups, roll by in either direction. He wasn't planning to cross the highway, but he was still a little surprised there wasn't a pedestrian crosswalk painted on the road. Probably something like that was just impractical. Not anymore at least. There probably weren't a lot of shoppers on foot making the rounds of 2nd Street these days.

As he stood at the corner, a long tan-colored Cadillac approached from the west and slowed to take a right onto 2nd Street. As the car passed him, Curtis observed a skinny senior citizen with close-cropped hair and what looked like a gray Members Only jacket who seemed right at home in his car. Curtis pivoted to watch him cruise down the street, and he was only half-surprised when he read the three-letter license plate—

E L Y—and watched it turn right at Walnut, towards Rudy's.

Curtis crossed to the other side of 2nd Street and doubled back towards the Mazda and the old flower shop, where he'd ultimately need to be to return the package of steroids . . . soon, before his nerves got the best of him. There didn't appear to be anyone around to observe him, but still Curtis reminded himself to keep cool, keep it casual.

He got to the intersection at 2nd and Walnut in time to see the old man, presumably the one and only Ely Prichard, enter Rudy's Cafe. Instinctively he longed to take a photo of the car and especially the plates, and again he cursed himself for leaving his smartphone in New Orleans. But in the next instant, he reminded himself that he didn't need technology to remember a three-letter license plate.

Curtis kept walking, now approaching the old flower shop on the other side of the street. The cross street here was Park Avenue, the nice oak-lined boulevard that originated at the intersection—like Capitol street in DC, starting from the Congressional Building on Capitol Hill—where probably the two most important buildings in Eunice stood on opposite corners. The Liberty Theater, next to the old flower shop, was the cultural heart of Eunice. Or at least at the heart of the tourist dollars the town could hardly do without. And catty-corner from there, City Hall, a fairly nondescript three-story tan brick building with flags outside and a modest little raised concrete public address platform where Cajun bands played and politicians spoke at festivals and holiday gatherings.

The little two-story Eunice Public Library, just as nondescript and utterly unchanged from what Curtis remembered, stood on the corner of 2nd and Park Avenue, opposite the Liberty Theater. He stood under the eave of the building, surveying the landscape with the image of Ely Prichard still very much on his mind. From the research he'd done, it was clear the elder Prichard man was the patriarch of the family and probably very wealthy—not just by local standards—but Curtis didn't know much more about him.

Here in the little plaza from where Park Avenue emerged and stretched all the way across town, tree-lined and pretty, to Eunice High School, there was a statue of the town namesake, Eunice. She was bronze, dressed in what Curtis thought might be considered a petticoat, with a big hat. He could see the statue well enough from where he was standing against the public library, but he felt like a sore thumb just standing there, so he ambled over to have a closer look. She looked like Mary Poppins. There was a little bench in front of the statue, so he took the opportunity to have a seat and update his notebook with details from his breakfast with Tac.

He did his best to remain hyperalert, taking a mental picture of the few cars and trucks that occasionally passed. It was almost 10 a.m. now and activity seemed to be picking up in the downtown area, but it was all vehicular traffic so far. He needed to take a leak and told himself he needed to get on with putting the package in the shop so he could one, clear his nerves and, two, swing by the Winn-Dixie to pick up some fruit, snacks, Red Bull, and water. If he didn't get some fiber soon, he probably wouldn't be able to shit until he got back home.

Just as he was slipping his pocket notebook back into his jacket, the sound of accelerating footsteps behind him registered a couple seconds too late and he turned to see a slim brunette— black jogging tights, midriff, sports bra, ponytail, fierce expression—pumping her arms and heading right at him. He was alarmed; she was really moving. It was only as she leapt up onto the cement platform where Curtis had been sitting in front of the Eunice statue that he realized she hadn't been locked in on him. It was the statue, she was running to Eunice.

Curtis could hear her rhythmic breathing as she rounded the back of the statue and reached out with her left hand to graze the bronze of Eunice's petticoat as she came around. She glanced at him and was gone, within a few seconds already fifteen or twenty yards down the boulevard, hugging the curb at the right side of the street but staying off the sidewalk: a serious runner, comfortable on the blacktop. Curtis pivoted in his seat, stretching out his back and checking her out as she receded down Park Avenue.

He still needed to take a leak, so he got to his feet and made his way to the library.

As Curtis was entering the Eunice Public Library through the double glass doors for the first time in maybe twenty years, Lenny stood in front of his staff locker at the health club pulling on his topsiders over sockless feet. He wore jeans and a red polo shirt, the short sleeves of which made the suede jacket he'd wear over the top of it more practical, once he got outside.

He clasped his gold chain around his neck, slid his oversized 2004 state championship ring on his finger—he kept his other championship ring from his senior year in the trophy case at home—and ran a comb through his hair while he checked himself in the mirror. A lot of dudes his age were already starting to lose their hair, but Lenny was in good shape on that front. His was still nice and thick. Satisfied that he was looking his best for that little redhead at McDonald's and whatever else the day would bring, he got ready to go. He checked his cell phone on his way out the locker room. Jackie had texted.

Good morning sunshine! Nonc Ely called. He wants to talk. Said meet him at Rudy's after your workout.

Lenny tried to take it in stride, but he couldn't help but feel a wave of something like panic, which receded just as quickly. It wasn't the first time he'd been summoned, but it didn't happen often. And it was probably *not* good news. That wasn't Uncle Ely's style. For an instant he had an impulse to ask his cousin what it was about, but he quickly dismissed the idea. He was the boss, and you didn't go asking your subordinates questions like that. Besides, Uncle Ely would never tell Jackie shit, anyway.

He wasn't sure he wanted breakfast from Rudy's; the shit they served there was so heavy and the waitresses damn sure weren't good-looking, but he'd been called so he was going. No two ways about it. The last thing he wanted to do was park himself at Rudy's and listen to a bunch of old men talk about LSU and immigrants. But he didn't have a choice. Uncle Ely had a lifetime's worth of connections around town, not to mention most of the wealth in the family. And he was good to Lenny. There was no denying that.

Lenny was no fool. He understood that things would have probably been different if his dad was still alive. At least on the business side of things. His dad might have objected to some of the shadier stuff Lenny and Uncle Ely got up to. His old man had been like that; he never had the killer instinct Lenny shared with Uncle Ely.

Lenny's success on the ball field had a lot to do with the bond he had with his uncle. The state championship especially. Even so far removed from high school, it was *still* a big deal. Lenny—and handpicked teammates like Lefty, who he'd played with since he was eight—occupied a special status with Ely Prichard. Two double-A state championships in a row put you in rarefied air with the old man.

And anyone who knew Ely Prichard knew just how big a deal that was. The bond between him and his nephew would have been strong even without his brother's death. The truth was Uncle Ely had more to do with fielding those teams than the coaches did. It was Uncle Ely and the St. Eds boosters who'd found scholarship money for the boys they recruited. Jobs for their parents in some cases. Hell, he even managed to make some legal troubles disappear for some of them, from what Lenny had heard.

And it had paid off, too. For two years they were a powerhouse, with dangerous hitters all the way through the lineup. For the most part, Lenny hit in the number seven slot—that's how good of a team they became. When you put a team of top players together and it really gels, that's how it goes. You end up with a right fielder who other teams would build their whole team around, or like in Lenny's case, a second baseman who could be playing short and hitting cleanup for the public school team across town.

That fall after graduation, Uncle Ely had pulled every string there was to pull to get him a tryout at LSU. And the fact that he made it happen was more a testament to his political juice than it was to Lenny's abilities on the field. But nothing came of it, and that was a defining moment for Lenny. It didn't take long for him to realize that every small Louisiana town had an Uncle Ely, men just powerful enough to get an unofficial, courtesy tryout for their nephews, but not nearly enough to put them on the team. The lesson Lenny took was power is strongest close to home.

Delusional as it was, it took Uncle Ely a long time to get over the fact that Lenny was never going to wear the purple and gold. And when Lenny settled back in Eunice after a couple botched junior college attempts, Uncle Ely didn't hold it against him. In fact, he set him up good.

The whole business with the old flower shop on 2nd was still doing laps around Lenny's mind. He couldn't help but worry Uncle Ely had heard something about it. Lenny would assure him the deal was dead and he had it under control. He might even throw Jackie under the bus if that's what it took, but even *having a conversation* about the feasibility of a tattoo shop downtown would weaken Lenny's position with his uncle.

For the most part, Ely liked Lenny's ideas for modernizing the enterprise, for going after the younger blood and that "trashy dollar," as he called it, with tanning salons and mixed martial arts and such. But a tattoo shop on 2nd Street would be too much. Jackie should have known better! It still chapped his ass to think about it.

Lenny made his way through the EHC, which wasn't exactly buzzing, but the activity level had picked up a little bit. Shelly, the new aerobics teacher they'd picked up basically for free because she needed the hours for her certificate at LSUE, was sitting at the front desk. She was strawberry blond, with sharp eyes and freckles. Lenny gave her a quick once-over as he walked past and started to say something clever about how she was too talented to be sitting behind the desk. But he just kept walking. He had other things on his mind all of a sudden.

The first thing Curtis noticed about the library was the smell, an antiseptic sort of mothball smell he remembered from his childhood all of a sudden. The second thing was that it was exactly the way he remembered it. The walls, carpets, and even the furniture—which would probably go for a pretty penny to vintage dealers on either coast—were done in varying shades of a sort of seventies-era green. The way it contrasted with the blonde wood of the card catalogs, the wide, empty tables, and the wooden stairs leading up to the second floor almost made it feel like a movie set. Or maybe the Brady Bunch house. Curtis couldn't help but smile as he stood there taking it all in. This was awesome. Another time-capsule moment.

The place appeared to be empty, which made him conspicuous, just like when he stood outside. But an empty library was probably better than a crowded one. At least he didn't have to worry about running into anyone he knew. Curtis walked right to the men's room, tucked beneath the stairs on one side of the little elevator that went up to the second floor. He remembered the elevator well. It was the only one he could remember in town, though there must've been one in City Hall, now that he thought about it. When he was a kid coming to check out books or later, as a young teenager when they'd spend hours skateboarding on the curbs and little embankments around 2nd Street, the tiny elevator was a novelty. When he came out of the toilet, he thought about hitting the button, just for old times' sake, but he didn't want to risk a ding resonating throughout the place. He took the stairs.

It was stuffy on the second floor, and just as quiet. A handwritten sign announced that this floor contained the Louisiana Section which, aside from a column of four large tables stretching to the back wall of the main space, pretty much made up the whole floor. Curtis made his way over and plucked up a book called *Cajun Country*, the glossy picture on the cover weird enough to give him pause. It featured a Mardi Gras rider from maybe the early eighties in full regalia—bright white handmade costume and clown paint on his face—standing on his horse with an odd, somewhat menacing expression that was probably nothing more than inebriation. But still, it was intriguing. On another day, Curtis might've sat at a table and read the whole thing, but today it was just a prop.

The whole rural Mardi Gras tradition of the Cajun Prairie was fascinating. On some level—just like the newer Cajun and zydeco stuff centered around Lafayette—Curtis regretted he'd never bothered to lean more into it when he was growing up. Mardi Gras here was totally different than the carnival, free-tits-and beer fest that was New Orleans. The tradition around here reflected the hardscrabble life that the earliest descendants in the region endured. It was a whole Catholic trip, wrapped up in poverty and revelry too.

Masked riders would head out in bands the day before Lent, making the rural circuit of their neighbors, dancing and fooling around in their costumes and screen-masks, hoping for an offering for the communal gumbo that would be the centerpiece of their last celebration before the forty days of Lent. They wore masks because they were proud. They danced because, whatever hardships they endured, they couldn't help but express a *joie de vivre* that couldn't be snuffed out. They collected ingredients for the pot because that's what Cajun people do;

they cook amazing food from whatever's around.

Curt walked over to one of two small windows that overlooked 2nd Street and peered through. He had a perfect view of the old flower shop from here. There was a table nearby positioned a few feet from the window, so Curtis found a chair and opened the book and watched and listened for a few seconds. He breathed deeply, happy for a chance to settle himself. The muted sound of a telephone ringing downstairs and being answered during the second ring reassured him in a strange way; he'd honestly begun to worry if maybe the library wasn't open yet, the place was so quiet.

He got up and tried the handle of the transom-style window and it opened with a squeak. The cold fresh air felt great, and he stood there slowly breathing it in and easing into a meditative state with his eyes open. It was hard, but not impossible to do, especially with a static scene in front of you. He had learned the technique way back at language school in Monterey. His roommate Rashad had taught him. When the members of his training unit weren't in class, they were standing in the sun at the position of parade rest. They did that for hours: feet apart, hands clasped behind the back, eyes "caged," staring straight ahead at nothing.

Rashad had an older brother who'd learned it in jail, and he himself had gotten enough practice during basic training at Lackland to not only teach Curtis what he needed to know, but to wax wise on the virtues of *conscious awareness* for the modern-day fighter. Rashad himself was *not* a fighter, but he was deep. He taught Curtis that the mind was the only weapon you carried with you into every situation.

But the mind needed to be trained, and meditation was the

key. Through breathing and mindfulness exercises, you could raise your awareness, power down and refresh your system, regulate your physiological responses in stressful situations, and give yourself an edge. Where the breath went, the body followed. *Meditation is a super-power* was Rashad's mantra. Pretty soon, Curtis started to believe it, and he relished the daily opportunity to stand at parade rest and meditate with his eyes open.

It might have been two or ten minutes later when the still-life scene down below him changed. A kid in a black hoodie pulled over his ball cap and carrying a printer box in both hands rounded the corner at the Liberty Theater and—Curtis could hardly believe it—the dude stopped in front of the old flower shop. He put the box on the ground, fished a key from the front pocket of his baggy khaki pants, and unlocked the glass door. After he'd pulled the door open and used his foot to prop it open, he looked down the length of the sidewalk and got a decent view of the guy in profile. A hot spot flashed on his neck as it registered. He was looking at Angel, from JD's shop.

Curtis watched him pick up the box and back his way into the shop, and as soon as Angel was inside, he turned away from the window to make his way downstairs, still processing what he'd just witnessed. Curt stopped cold. A small, neatly dressed older man was standing there, silently, waiting for him.

"Good morning. May I help you?"

Curtis was dumbstruck. He stood there, awkwardly coming to grips with this new person standing in front of him while he was still trying to sort out what he'd seen on the street. *Was that really Angel . . . and what was in the box?*

"Hello," Curtis said, and couldn't think of a single other thing to say to the man. He just wanted to get downstairs—for what, he wasn't entirely sure. After a second, his brain started to work again and it clicked; he needed to follow Angel. That's what he needed to do. But this little man continued to stand in front of him. Curtis needed to move. His heart raced, but when it finally occurred to him to breathe, things came back into focus. The man was probably in his seventies. A volunteer, most likely.

"I'm sorry," Curtis said. "You caught me by surprise!" He laughed and made a point of loosening his shoulders. "So quiet!"

The older man gave a polite chuckle. "Well, it is a library," he said. "And I wear these." He held up a foot to reveal a pair of New Balance with a sole at least two inches thick. "It's like walking on a pillow," the man said with a kind of conspiratorial smile.

Curtis wracked his brain for something intelligent to say in return, trying his best to mask his desperation to get out of there. Finally, he simply handed over the *Cajun Country* book to the man and said, "I'm sorry, but I have to go." Then he rushed past the old man, down the stairs, his mind already back on Angel.

When he pushed through the glass door of the library the street was quiet again. He looked right, up the street towards Rudy's and the fancy shops, then he scanned left, across the little plaza with the statue of Eunice, towards the City Hall parking lot, but there was no movement there either. As he crossed the street in front of the Liberty Theater, a dirty blue Ford Focus pulled out the lot behind the building, the same one where he'd parked the Mazda, and turned onto Park Avenue. Curt took a mental picture of the license plate and did his best to confirm it was in fact Angel as the car gained distance.

He stood near the box office counter at the Liberty watching the car recede, pulling his notebook from his pocket. And as he did so, he saw brake lights at the first intersection, 3rd Street, and realized Angel was turning right, even before the first blink of the turn signal flashed. Curtis pivoted on his heel and started walking back up 2nd Street as fast as he could, thinking maybe he'd get lucky and Angel was making the block and Curtis could confirm it was him, even though he already knew it was. But as he reached the corner of 2nd and Walnut, just a few steps from Rudy's, the stupidity of what he was doing finally occurred to Curtis. If Angel did make the block, he would pass right by and most likely recognize Curtis at the same time. Curtis stopped and hugged the brick wall at the corner, cursing himself. Dammit!

He stood with his back to the wall for a second, sticking out like a damn sore thumb, again. He quickly scanned down the block, all the way to the old flower shop and the Liberty Theater, its awning casting shade on the sidewalk, and once he confirmed it was empty, he checked the other side of the street. The old man from the library was standing out front, looking in the opposite direction. So Curtis turned the corner at Walnut to conceal himself and he had no expectation of seeing the Ford Focus again as he took a few steps towards Rudy's, where a big black Toyota pickup truck was idling on the street, blocking the view beyond.

Curtis slowed up and read the license plate as the truck pulled away: Sun-N-1. He didn't need to guess who it was, because he had the vehicle information in his files. Hell, he even had the VIN number. He stood and watched as Lenny approached the stop sign at 3rd Street, his jacketed elbow hanging out the window, and turned right. Curtis took note of the tan-colored Caddie parked directly in front of Rudy's—Ely Prichard's ride—and as he strolled past the window to the little cafe. He glanced inside and saw the man himself sitting at the head of the table of that same group of well-dressed, older geezers, animated in conversation. Curtis just kept on walking.

The old Queen Cinema, the only movie theater in Eunice, was right next to Rudy's and from the looks of the posters, all newish releases that Curt would never see, the place was still hanging on. But the old Music Central store next door had not been as lucky. The place where Curtis and everyone else in town used to get their records, tapes, CDs, and even video rentals back in the day was now a place called *Cajun Customs.* The sizable storefront on the corner of 3rd and Walnut was now full of shiny spinning rims, other gaudy vehicle accessories like fuzzy dice and dashboard figurines, and some serious car stereo equipment that Curtis could hear bumping and rattling the store windows.

As he turned left to make the full block back to the Mazda, a standard counter-surveillance move, he saw that they'd built an addition on the back of the store, a large Quonset hut structure with open bay doors at the back, through which Curtis could see a group of dudes in stylish flannel shirts preparing a little truck for painting. He got a good look at the red-brick exterior of the Acadian Cultural Center as he turned left at the sidewalk on Park Avenue. The center was new to Curtis, which only meant that it was less than fifteen years old. He walked as close to the building as he could, keeping the library doors in front of him at the end of the block out of sight, in case the old man was still there. He slipped into the little parking lot between the Liberty and the new cultural center and just sat in the front seat of the Mazda for a few minutes, slumped low in the seat, breathing deep to slow himself down. He repeated the mantra *slow is smooth and smooth is fast* to himself a few times.

When he was sure enough time had passed, Curtis slipped off his jacket and donned his Gulf Coast Mud hat, pulling it low over his eyes. He double-checked he had the key JD had given him, transferred his notebook and his flip phone from the jacket to his pants pockets. Outside, he locked the Mazda with the key and rummaged through his EverReady in the trunk for some tools and another one of Jacque's small RFID trackers. He walked around the corner, head down and scanning from beneath the brim of the hat. There was no one in front of the library and no one on the sidewalk, so Curtis simply walked up to the door of the old flower shop, put the key in the lock, and went inside.

Standing just inside with his back to the door, he surveyed the empty shop. It was entirely bare except for an empty printer paper box in the middle of the space. He pulled his bandana from his back pocket and walked directly to the little bathroom at the back of the empty shop. Inside the small space and totally concealed from anyone peeking through the windows, he studied the ceiling tiles where the steroids had once been. He raised a foot onto the edge of the sink, where there was already a footprint, braced himself against the wall, and pulled himself up. When he pushed against the ceiling tile there was resistance, but he got the tile lifted enough to work his hand inside, and eventually he maneuvered a post office box from the ceiling and set it on the back of the commode before he jumped down. The steroids were back.

Episode Four
Angel Resurrected

❦

Discovering the original box of steroids has been returned, Curtis plants a GPS tracker in the box to monitor its movements. Angel confesses his association with Lenny and that he's responsible for removing and later returning the steroids.

He drew tattoos for his friends / They'd sit around and get real stoned / And he fought with guys twice his size / So he wouldn't feel so alone
— The Iguanas, "Angel"

As Curtis stood in the bathroom of the old flower shop, staring at a priority mailbox of steroids that wasn't supposed to be there, Angel was pulling into the Old East Shopping Center in his blue Ford Focus. He had the stereo cranked to a New Order remix Jackie gave him, freestyling some rhymes on top of it. He was feeling free for the first time this week. Even though what he had to do next was gonna suck.

It seemed like every third person he got mixed up with these days was fucked up in some like, fundamental type way. He couldn't help but dwell on this theory as he pulled into the shopping center, just a few cars in the potholed parking lot, most of them clustered around Kluckie's Fried Chicken. He had been thinking about it since yesterday.

First, there was JD. JD Dugas. A cat he'd only known for about a week now but easily the coolest old head Angel had met in Eunice, ever. Dude could draw shit, just improvising, that you couldn't even come up with on a head full of acid. The man had *come back* to Eunice to open a tattoo shop. He was an expert, with experience in three other states. The thought of having that much talent, escaping not just Eunice but the whole fucking state, and then *coming back* to open the first tattoo shop in this hick town . . . like shit, man! His mind was blown. He both admired the move and at the same time didn't understand why someone would want to do that. His twenty-two-year-old ass would get the fuck out and stay out.

And then there was Jackie Guidry. Damn!. Like something out of a movie, man. She wouldn't tell him for sure, but he knew she was getting close to forty—legitimately old—but she had a blue streak in her hair and an amazing body that could still rock all night. And her music collection was dope. She had albums and tapes and CDs of crazy, off-the-wall shit she was always turning him onto. Joy Division. David Bowie. Television. That old school stuff that you needed someone to introduce you to. Sometimes she let him stay over and they'd stay up all night playing tunes and fucking. He never felt more free.

But she was Lenny Prichard's cousin, and *that* dude was trouble. Dangerous even. Being around him was like plugging into an amp that wasn't grounded. It might sound good, but sooner or later, you knew you were gonna get shocked. The dude was into all kinds of stuff and technically he was Jackie's boss, though Jackie wasn't really one to take shit from anybody. And in the nine months or so he'd been kind of working for Lenny, he'd never once heard the man say anything nice about her.

Angel had spent the last twenty-four hours thinking about it. How every third person he met seemed to be fucked up, and why he had somehow put his loyalty with the wrong one.

He'd met Jackie first. It was maybe a year ago now, at an open mic night at this little bar in Opelousas. He got on stage with a boombox his sister still had and pressed play on a tape of him beatboxing and recited some of his poetry over the top of it. People were laughing their asses off, especially when he started mixing in some lines in Spanish. That's when the racist jokes started flying. It hurt but he tried to play it off. Then Jackie came up to him afterward and started talking about Patti Smith, who he didn't know but she turned him on to later, and eventually he saw videos of Patti doing the same type of shit back in the sixties. The streak in Jackie's hair was pink that night and she was wearing suspenders that made her tits look amazing. She gave Angel her number and the rest was history.

Angel knew Lenny was trouble from the get-go, but the man could put money in your pocket. It was May and already hot as fuck, and he was totally broke. All his little hustles had dried up, to the point where he couldn't even pay his sister her hundred bucks rent or put gas in his car or even buy smokes, and Jackie had said something to Lenny. The next thing he knows, this dude named Lefty that owns a construction company—called SouthPaw Construction or some shit—called him up and offered him a job as a helper on his crew. Man, that was the *last thing* he wanted to do. But what choice did he have?

Angel lasted a week. It's not like he didn't appreciate it, especially by that Friday when Lefty laid four hundred dollars on him. But he was an artist, man! He couldn't be lugging toolboxes and pounding nails and shit in the sweltering heat. The thing nobody told you about construction was how much it made your hands ache. He could barely play guitar or draw that whole week. Angel had told Lefty right then and there, on that first Friday, that he wouldn't be back on Monday. And then he went straight to Sun-*N*-Tans and told Lenny the same thing, wanting him to hear it directly, and with the right measure of respect and appreciation.

Lenny was cool about it, sitting back in his air-conditioned office, scoping out the chicks in the tanning rooms with his secret camera feed on his computer, asking Angel if he'd maybe be up for some less regular type of work. Strictly under the table and just between the two of them.

That's how he got sucked in. By the end of the summer, he had something like seven hundred dollars stashed in his room at his sister's house, and he still had time to work on his music and draw and hang with Jackie. So he learned to live with how Lenny treated him, calling him Pancho and shit. His blood boiled a little more every time he heard that; it felt like a bruise that kept getting hit. At first, he thought the dude was joking until he realized the name-calling wasn't gonna stop. Sometimes he called Lenny *puta* under his breath.

As far as the work, he didn't have any complaints there. Half the time he was just running errands, delivering checks or invoices or inventory or what have you between one business or another, just regular gopher-type shit. And a lot of times Lenny gave him gas money on top of whatever else he got. Other times, the packages carried jail time, but Angel had a way of keeping his head cool for that stuff.

Things had changed though. Now JD Dugas was in town and Angel had a real shot at learning a trade he believed in. And he'd gone and put all that in jeopardy, maybe fucked it up beyond repair, pulling those 'roids out of the old flower shop just because Lenny thought it was funny or whatever. And this friend of JD's was in town to try and help, and it sounded like the dude did Black Ops or something. He talked real serious, in a way that made Angel nervous. He could sense shit was going to hit the fan.

Angel parked in his usual spot and turned the car off. The CD kept playing and he just closed his eyes for a few moments to listen and clear his mind. Today was a new day. He'd put the shit back in the ceiling where it belonged—and Lenny was gonna be pissed about that, for sure—but Angel was gonna do what he had to do from here on out. He wasn't done yet though. He had to get clean. It was time to start living like a man.

The sound of his brother playing accordion on the back porch, about ten feet from the little shack where JD slept, was close enough and loud enough to wake him, but still he laid there for ten minutes before he opened his eyes. He reached for his phone, which he'd thankfully thought to plug into the charger when he came in early this morning. It was 10:42. Way too fucking late. He had all kinds of shit to do.

His sinuses felt like they'd been scoured with bleach and then sandblasted for good measure. He rolled off the couch and made his way to the old refrigerator in the corner and chugged cold water from a pickle jar. Refilling the jar from the tap, JD put it back in the fridge, then grabbed the actual jar of pickles—Vlassic Dills—from the door of the fridge and took a small sip of the juice. His brother Jesse was still cranking out a familiar tune on his button accordion there on the porch. JD stepped out of the little wooden building that most Cajuns called an outdoor kitchen—shirtless, skinny, and tattooed. He squinted up at his brother.

"I guess you just *got* to practice right now, huh?"

Jesse was sitting on a kitchen chair with his accordion on his knee, still playing. A cigarette burned in an ashtray at his feet, next to a cup of coffee. JD eyeballed the steam coming off the cup. His older brother was in sweatpants and a Saints shirt that said *Qui Ça?*, Cajun French for "Who Dat"? He had the same angular features as JD except he was fleshier in the face and the belly, with dirty blond hair and a bushy mustache that made him look like an extra in an old cop show. Jesse just kept playing, a mischievous smile plastered to his face.

JD picked his way barefooted over some paving stones to the steps of the porch and went through the door into the kitchen. A squeal from his two nieces, ages four and six, erupted as he came into the kitchen. "Uncle JD! You sleepyhead!" JD pulled his hand back from the coffee pot as the two little blonde whirlwinds caught him around the legs for a big hug. He reached down for some strategic tickling that caused them both to squeal again, this time in retreat to the living room. When the coast was clear, he filled his cup and walked back out to the porch to join his brother.

Jesse had been playing traditional Cajun French music since JD was in junior high. The band he fronted, the Tell-You-

Whats, were pretty well-known around Eunice, and they even played regular gigs as far as New Orleans and Houston. If people treated local musicians like celebrities, Jesse would have been one. But instead, he ran the produce department at Winn-Dixie—five-thirty a.m. to four p.m., five days a week. He'd been there since forever. He played music for the same reasons anyone else did, because he needed it. You didn't want to meet or work with the person Jesse Dugas would become if he didn't have that outlet.

JD sat down on the steps and tried angling his naked torso to the sun to keep warm, thought better of it, darted into the outdoor kitchen, and came back wearing unlaced combat boots and a black sweatshirt. He sat back on the steps and lit a cigarette from his brother's pack of Winstons.

"And no, I don't need the practice," Jesse said, finally. "I just like fucking with you, bruh."

JD gave him a look. "Yeah, I kinda figured," he said. "Since you been playing that same fucking jig since I was fourteen, I don't guess you need no more practice."

Jesse leaned over to set his accordion down on the porch and came up with his coffee and his cigarette. The Dugas brothers stared out into the sunlight in the yard. The silence would have been awkward with either of JD's two other brothers, but the bond he had with Jesse, the oldest, had long since solidified. When JD was in town, he stayed in the outdoor kitchen. It was to the point where JD's girls called it Uncle JD's tiny house.

"Don't you got shit to do, bruh?" Jesse said eventually, more or less out of the blue. It wasn't really a question.

JD had sensed it was coming, and if it had been anyone else he'd be on his feet and cursing by now. Instead, he shook his head and worked his way through a to-do list that was getting more complicated every day. "So, the Department of Health and Hospitals has my application—they told me yesterday it's good. Now I just have to get my documents together for the inspection next week, on Wednesday, I'm pretty sure . . . yeah, Wednesday." He took a drag. "Let's see. I gotta bring my disposable needles letter to the notary to get certified ."

"Where you going for that? Robicheaux?" Jesse asked.

"The dude that did mom's divorce? Fuck no! I found a guy in Opelousas. He's not a lawyer. Just a notary. Thirty bucks."

Jesse finished his coffee. "You gonna drive all the way to Opelousas to save, what, fifteen bucks?"

"Can I finish, please?" The door opened and JD's sister-in-law, Beatrice, came out with the coffee pot. "My new assistant Angel, he's gonna drop it off for me. Anyway, then I gotta go to Eunice Memorial and get my sharps container disposal letter . . . though I'm hoping down the road I can maybe change that to Opelousas General so Angel or maybe even Sadie can drop it off for me since she works there." JD waited his turn as Beatrice filled Jesse's cup and then held out his own. "Thank you, sweetie," he said as she poured him the last of it.

"Your Sadie?" she asked.

"Well, she hasn't been *my* Sadie for a long time . . . but yeah, one and the same," JD said. "And I still got to type up my plan for aftercare instructions. I already have it written out, and I'm gonna do some little thumbnails to illustrate it, you know, for the illiterate customers." Beatrice laughed. "I just need to type it up, and then I need to get the money order for a thousand bucks for the inspector. But I'm not quite ready for that yet."

"I can type up your letter," Beatrice said. She smiled down at JD, and he reached over and gave her leg a squeeze through her sweatpants.

"Thank you, sweetie."

"If you're short for your money order you can help us set up Friday night at Cecil's Bar," Jesse said. "Shit, maybe I'll even let you sit in."

JD was seeing himself jitterbugging with Sadie around the tiny dance floor. He smiled despite his headache but still dismissed the idea. Sadie was way too fine to take to a place like Cecil's. He'd end up in a fight for sure. Plus, he didn't need Lil C, the owner, sliding up to him acting all friendly. Sadie would ask questions he didn't want to answer. "Thanks, bro," he said, and stood up. Beatrice had turned back to the house. "I'll get you that aftercare sheet," he called to her as the door shut. Jesse was looking up at him.

"How you doing with that other thing?" he asked. JD stopped, deflated that the question had even been necessary, though he'd had a feeling it was coming. He turned and met his brother's gaze.

"I'm alright," he said.

Curtis wasn't really nervous until he realized he'd forgotten his latex gloves. The first thing he did was use his blue bandana to wipe the outside of the blue and white and red priority mailer, just in case. And then he checked his watch—he would give himself ten minutes to get this done. For the third or fourth time since he arrived in Eunice, he silently regretted his decision to leave his smartphone in New Orleans, with its alarms, flashlights, camera, and GPS.

He gently pulled open the flaps of the box that had been tucked in on themselves and saw the grid of small glass vials with silver tops. They looked the same as the ones he'd ordered on the dark web, the ones that were sitting in the trunk of the Mazda right this minute, a felony waiting to happen. He did a quick count: twenty-five on top, with another square of cardboard underneath and presumably another twenty-five under that. Fifty in all. He pulled a vial with his bandana and held it to the light.

The liquid was a pale yellow. He extracted the flip phone from his pocket and spent nearly sixty precious seconds navigating to the camera, and once he did, he took a few pictures of the label. He recognized the word *Dianabol*, the brand name for the kind of steroid bodybuilders used. Same as what he'd bought.

His mind was jumping ahead. His impulse at that moment was to fall deep into the task of comparing these steroids with the ones he'd bought. He was eager to not only understand how similar they were (curious still about the now moot point of whether they would've passed muster as a one-for-one substitute) but also to see if he could figure out their origin. His love of analysis wouldn't let him stop trying to figure this shit out.

But right now, he had to be a special operator, a badass, stealthy mother fucker. *You will beat them because they will not see you coming.* He repeated one of the two mantras he'd been working in his head for the last twenty-four hours, even though he felt totally unprepared. For a brief moment, he considered taking one of the vials with him. In the next instant, he forced the thought out of his mind and returned to the task at hand. His pictures captured, he now set about emptying the box so he could plant another of Jacque's souped-up RFID trackers. Before he started, he glanced at his watch—nearly five minutes had already passed. The bad thing was he was totally blind to the outside world from there in the bathroom. The entire Eunice Police Department could be amassing outside the shop and he wouldn't know it.

And the bathroom was small, just big enough to fit a toilet and a little sink. That was it, aside from cinder block walls, the drop ceiling, and a linoleum floor. He moved the box to the toilet seat, then pulled out the first ten bottles and lined them around the sink before he ran out of room. It already felt claustrophobic in the bathroom, and this exercise wasn't helping. Now he started pulling out bottles with his bandana, pivoting, and placing them on the floor behind him. His biggest concern was breaking a vial, so he took his time and maybe three or four minutes later he was finally done, the vials arrayed all around him like an OCD alcoholic draining the hotel minibar and lining up the empties. The only spot where they weren't was the spot he was standing in.

Curtis took a few seconds to inspect the box. It was just a box. He turned it over. It was well taped on the bottom. He turned it right side up and noticed for the first time the residual evidence of postage markings. Someone had gone through the trouble of removing the shipping labels, but there was part of a purple stamp still visible. All Curtis could make out were a few faint markings: APO AE, and then the numbers 09 at what looked like the beginning of a longer sequence.

He instinctively reached for his notebook and copied what he saw, his brain already puzzling on the fact that an Army Post Office in Europe seemed to have processed this package. Or maybe it was just a random box. But he didn't have time to consider it further. He put his notebook and pen away, then removed the adhesive backing from the RFID tracker and nestled it between the folds in the bottom of the box. He placed the empty box back on the toilet seat and couldn't help but smile. He was getting good at this.

It took maybe two more minutes to return all the vials to the box, and as he completed first the bottom layer and then the top, one by one, his anxiety climbed with each vial he returned to the box. He glanced at his watch—something like thirteen minutes had gone by. It was time to get the fuck out of there.

He wiped the top of the box again with his bandana for good measure and then awkwardly positioned it underneath, between his hands and the box, his grip tenuous. He pulled his leg up onto the edge of the sink and got his weight on that side so he could get his other foot on the toilet seat. But when he put the weight of his left foot on the seat it shifted underneath, slipping off its little plastic hinge on one side. Avoiding a slip and disaster, he used his foot to lift the half-attached toilet seat all the way up and instead put his foot on the rim of the toilet bowl, and from there pushed himself up to reach for the ceiling.

Curtis considered it a minor miracle that his foot didn't fall into the toilet. His biggest problem now was time and the sudden need to piss. He looked up at the ceiling. The tile was in its place. It was smudged as hell in the corner where clearly hands had been all over it, but that was how he found it. His footprints were on the sink. He wiped it down with his bandana, tapping his foot as he did because his bladder was screaming now.

In the next few seconds, he found himself desperately whipping it out and taking a leak. There was nothing else to be done, and as he relished the sweet human relief of a draining bladder, he was pleased to note the toilet seat wasn't actually broken. It had just sort of popped out of place. There was no toilet paper, of course. Curtis had no choice but to take a deep breath and dive in with his hands on the bare toilet seat and the rim, hoping the droplets he saw and felt there were his own, and with some effort, he managed to get the seat securely back in place.

As soon as he was done, he turned the hot water on with his elbow, and though he still had one task to complete before he left and he was well over the time he'd given himself, Curtis stood there at the sink rubbing his hands together till they were pink with friction and heat. When he was done, he picked up his bandana from the back of the toilet and used it to wipe a few remaining spots on the top of the toilet and the floor, aware that his hands were again contaminated but somehow feeling far less grossed out about it. He reached down and tucked the damp bandana into his shoe and rinsed his hands again in the sink, air-drying them as best he could. Using his shirt, he turned the doorknob and peeked out into the main room and through the windows to the outside.

There was no activity. Still concealed behind the door and peering out, he counted to one hundred while he eyed the ceiling for potential spots to put one of Jacque's flexible doorbell cameras, which he carried in his jacket pocket. The corner near the door would be perfect, if only he could get up there to conceal it in the ceiling tile. But it was probably ten feet up and there wasn't a stick of furniture in the place to stand on.

As Curtis was considering this problem, a glare of sunlight on the street caught his eye and he looked up to see the glass door of the library opening. The old man exited the library doors again and stood out front in the sunlight, slowly panning up and down the street, occasionally using his hand to shield the sun glare. Curtis eased back behind the door. Fuck! It was impossible to get out without being seen.

He'd been in this bathroom going on twenty minutes now, and he was ready to get out. He took a deep breath with his eyes closed, reminding himself to slow down. He cracked the door again. There was the library, and there was the old man. Curtis had the feeling he could stand out there all day. If he hadn't decided to go to the library in the first place he wouldn't be in this situation. But then he probably wouldn't have seen Angel. The vantage point from the library window had been perfect. Just then, two related solutions occurred to him at once.

He eased the door closed again and pulled out the flip phone. He wasn't even sure if dialing information was still a thing, but he punched in 411 to find out. It started ringing and his mood lifted, then an automated voice prompted him for the city and state, and he felt like a genius. A couple seconds later, the computer voice was reciting the number for the Eunice Public Library. He would only have to remember four numbers—there was only one prefix for all of Eunice—but still, he readied his notebook and pen. He copied them down, punched in the phone number, then opened the bathroom door a little and watched. It rang six times and went to voicemail. The recording sounded like an actual answering machine. He hung up and dialed again. On the third ring the old man cocked his head and froze for an instant before he darted back into the library.

Curtis slipped the phone, still open, into his front pocket and marched to the door with the key in his hand. He got it locked and discreetly used his shirt to wipe the door handle and around the lock, for what reason he wasn't quite sure, and he didn't quite run around the corner of the Liberty Theater to where the Mazda was parked, but it damn sure wasn't a casual walk. The car cranked on the first try and he was pulling out of the little gravel lot within seconds, reaching into his pocket to pull the phone out. He could hear the old man saying *Hello?*, *Hello?*, as he closed the phone and tossed it on the front seat and made his way down Park Avenue, feeling victorious and nauseous at the same.

He'd reached the little circle park a few blocks down, situated in an expanded part of the median under a canopy of big oak trees that shaded a cracked tennis court and a little playground of bright plastic that somehow seemed depressing, when the flip phone rang. Curtis made a right turn onto 7th Street, thinking he'd jump onto Highway 190 and make his way to the western edge of town to hit the Winn-Dixie. On the third ring, he decided he wouldn't answer and he tried to put it out of his mind. By the seventh ring he realized he would still need to go back to the library. So he took a deep breath and said *I'm glad you called* to himself before he punched the green button, getting into character, and as it was ringing, the first story occurred to him: *I am a college student.*

"Hello? Yes, this is Mr. Able, from the Eunice Public

Library. I believe you just called?"

"Oh, hi, Mr. Able. My name is Curtis. We . . . uh . . . well, we just met, actually. I was up on the second floor of the library?"

"Yes, of course!" the older man said. Curtis couldn't detect any suspicion in the man's voice. "I was wondering where you went!"

Curtis offered a laugh he hoped would convey embarrassment. "Yeah, I'm very sorry about that Mr. Able. I had to . . . sorry, but there's no nice way to say it. I had to go to the bathroom." He laughed again, waiting for the inevitable question, the answer to which he was just now forming.

"I see," Mr. Able said after a pause. "There's a bathroom in the library, you know."

"I figured there was, but I don't really like to use public restrooms. It's just a kind of personal thing I have." He paused for a beat "But anyway, Mr. Able, I'd actually called to apologize for rushing out. There's a research project I'm working on, and I thought maybe you could help. What time do you close?"

"Oh. Well, believe me, I understand, young man," he said. "We close at six. What kind of research are you doing?"

"I'd be happy to tell you more about it later, Mr. Able. It involves that statue outside the library," Curtis said, totally winging it. "The one of Ms. Eunice? Can we talk more about it later?"

He hung up not feeling the least bit guilty for manipulating the goodwill of a nice, old man. Instead, Curtis was thinking about adhesive. He was gonna have to mount his little camera outside the library window some kind of way. He turned onto 190, bound for the Winn-Dixie. Hopefully they had LaCroix. And hopefully his Gulf Coast Mud hat would be enough of a disguise. The fear of running into his brother or someone he knew from high school was still way up there, just below getting caught with illegal steroids and a gun in the trunk of his car.

JD wasn't there yet, so Angel had the shop to himself. He never liked sitting around doing nothing, and the place was kind of a mess, and—truth be told—he was feeling guilty as hell, so he got to work. He pulled everything off the floor and swept and mopped the whole place, then he reorganized dozens of teetering stacks of tattoo magazines and binders of laminated pages of flash—drawings of tattoos customers could look through for inspiration—and made a home for them in a seating area in the front that he improvised with folding chairs and boxes and milk crates to serve as furniture. When he was done, it looked pretty much as good as possible. Not fancy, but clean, at least. He still needed to finish the lettering for "Black Jack Tattoo" on the window, but he decided to wait on that.

For now, the only real workstation was JD's, which basically consisted of a black hydraulic chair, the one nice piece of furniture in the shop, stacked with books and magazines on the seat of it, a Snap-on toolbox, and a big mirror propped on top of it, leaning against the wall. Angel was wary of fucking with JD's area, but the sight of the clutter got the best of him and he took a chance and cleaned and organized it too.

He wasn't a neat freak by any stretch, but a few years ago

when Angel had moved in with his sister and got his own room, he discovered his art came easier when everything was in its place. It felt good to bring some order to a space. Of course, today's activities were more about penance and self-preservation than rolling out the red carpet for the muse. He needed every advantage he could get. He also needed an outlet for his anxiety because he was kind of nervous.

When he was done with the cleaning, he changed his hip-hop playlist to a Rage Against the Machine mix and found a spot on the floor to start sketching a design that he thought up. He was sure he could find the materials he needed and put something together in a couple hours. Just as he was finishing his sketch, JD walked through the door. Angel looked up to see him silhouetted there against the light pouring in through the window.

"What's up?" JD strutted into the room. "Damn! This place is clean!"

"What up, boss?" Angel went with the sketch in his hand to the laptop to turn down the music. "I figured I'd make myself useful." He walked over towards JD with the sheet, his eyes cast down and slumping a little. "Hey, check this out," he said, handing JD the paper and pointing to an empty spot along the wall. "I think we could put a little light box there. It's just basically a frame with a piece of plexiglass and a light. I can build it." There was something in Angel's voice that JD didn't like. JD studied him for an instant.

"What's wrong?" he asked, suspicious, and in the brief silence that followed he took another look around the shop, appreciating for the first time the level of effort necessary to get the shop so organized. But it only seemed to make him more skeptical. "What'd you do?" JD demanded, and it was clear he wasn't talking about how clean the shop was.

Angel was looking sheepish, about to speak when JD's cell phone started ringing in his pocket. He pulled it out and exchanged greetings with Curtis, Angel just standing there, waiting.

"What does Angel drive?" was the first thing Curtis wanted to know. He was in the Mazda, on his way to the Winn-Dixie. JD automatically pivoted to check the parking lot, Angel still standing there in front of him with an awkward look on his face.

"That's your Ford Focus, right?" JD asked. Angel understood something was up at that moment.

"Yeah, why?" he wanted to know, but JD was no longer paying attention to him. He said the color, make, and model to whoever it was on the phone. Angel wasn't sure, but it was probably the government man, Curtis. Why was he asking about his car?

And then it dawned on him. Maybe someone saw him going into the old flower shop. The look that JD gave him at that moment was enough to confirm it.

Fuck! The timing was terrible. He blurted out "I was just about to tell you!" and JD scowled at him.

"Hold up," he said into the phone, and then pulled it away from his ear, his attention on Angel again. "What?"

"I was just about to tell you," Angel said. JD looked down at his phone and put it on speaker.

"Tell me what?" JD said, holding the phone about between

them. Angel took a deep breath. Glanced down at the phone.

"It was me," he said. "I'm the one that pulled those 'roids out of 2nd Street . . . and I'm the one that put 'em back. I did that this morning, just before I came here." JD's eyes burned holes into him, utterly silent. "Lenny Prichard's the one tole me to pull 'em outta there. To fuck with you." Angel raised his hands in something like an apology as JD started to speak, but he held back. "Now that was the day before I met you." Angel continued. "I didn't even know you, man! But now I respect you so much. I had to make it right! That's why I put 'em back, 'cause it wasn't right what Lenny was trying to do to you." He was pleading now.

To some extent, Angel was aware he was speaking to JD's man, Curtis, listening on the phone. For whatever reason, JD put a lot of stock in the dude, which was fine by Angel. It's not like he had an opinion. But this Curtis dude had the vibe of an outsider. He was hard to trust, and the fact that now Angel was somehow confessing to both of them didn't feel good.

For his part, listening in from the aisles of Winn-Dixie, the tone of Angel's voice suggested sincerity to Curtis, but whether or not Angel was laying it on a bit thick wasn't his concern. The thing that got Curt's attention was Angel's connection to Lenny. He *had* to have Lenny's trust if he had a key to that storefront and was moving steroids around for him. That was something they could use. As the pieces started to fall in place for Curtis, he remembered JD's temper.

As if on cue, JD exploded. He must've barked "Goddammit, Angel!" a dozen times or more, and then transitioned to a refrain of "It was you? *You,* of all people?" while Curtis tried to get his attention. When Angel started trying to explain himself again, Curt could feel the tension rising. He had to cut in.

"Gentlemen! Gentlemen!" and after a few seconds JD went silent. "Listen, bubba. I'm heading to the shop now. Why don't you go smoke a cigarette? Take a break and cool out. Let's all talk this through when I get there." Silence ensued, and Curtis worried he had come in at the wrong moment.

He called to JD. "Can you take me off the speaker, bubba?" And when JD did and asked what he wanted, still seething, Curtis said "Don't touch him. And don't berate him too much. Maybe there's opportunity in this situation. I know you're mad, but we can't afford for him to clam up. Just do me a favor and wait 'till I get there." JD grunted and hung up.

It took Curtis less than ten minutes to check out with his fancy water and snacks at the Winn-Dixie and make his way over to the tattoo shop in the Old East Shopping Center, which gave him time to think. There was still so much he didn't understand. He hadn't even been in Eunice twenty-four hours yet, and there was already so much going on. He still hadn't even gotten everything he needed from JD; their only conversation at this point was not much more than a few phrases voiced over loud music and around Tee-Bug's prying ears at the Daiquiri Hut.

Tac Youngblood was a total mystery—how much he knew, what he cared about, and how far he was willing to go. Curtis had no idea. He hadn't had time to process anything, much less gain the intellectual distance from it all to come to any kind of objective conclusion. The same was basically true for Lenny Prichard. Curtis had done some research, and of course he had some distant personal experience that influenced his thinking, but he didn't—couldn't—have a sense of who the man had become and what he was about. Everything he knew about Lenny was basically circumstantial.

Hell, even JD, the blood brother he was one hundred percent committed to—and it was a point Curtis hated to even consider, even in the unspoken confidence of his own mind—could be misrepresenting the reality of what had happened, deliberately or not. Friend or no, he wasn't the sanest person Curtis knew. And that fact was independent of any kind of chemical dependency, which Curtis was already suspecting might be an issue. The bottom line was he didn't know anything for sure.

Still, there was probably an opportunity here with Angel. Curtis wouldn't know for sure until they talked, and he was definitely in uncharted territory here. He'd never interrogated anyone but he had a distinct feeling this was a positive development. The game board had shifted this morning, offering advantages they might be able to leverage.

He had a second box of steroids now that he could put in play if he wanted to. And it wasn't just a kind of dirty bomb, tossed out in desperation. It was a precision weapon. He could track either of the packages of steroids, and that was powerful. And there was a second opportunity with Angel. He could never be trusted, no matter what he would say when Curtis arrived at the shop and no matter the circumstances. But Curtis didn't need to trust Angel. He just needed to understand what was motivating him. With that information, Curtis could predict his behavior, and that was perhaps more valuable than trust.

Curtis pulled into the Old East parking lot and noticed the blue Ford Focus right away. He pulled into the open spot next to it, and by the time he got out of the Mazda, JD was standing in the open door of the shop, lighting a cigarette from a butt.

Curtis hung back and JD walked over, looking none too happy.

"Ain't this a bitch?" JD said by way of opening, scanning the parking lot and dragging on his cigarette. The shopping center was dilapidated, the vaguest shadow of its former commercial glory. Even Sugar Ray's, which still did brisk business on the weekends, was a shell on weekdays.

"Did he say anything else? Curtis asked. JD shook his head, his gaze still on the mostly empty parking lot.

"Just that he's sorry and he respects me so much, that's why he put 'em back . . . et cetera, et cetera."

"Okay, that's good. That's good. Any thoughts on why he decided to confess? Does it feel like he's bullshitting you, so far?" Curtis asked.

JD looked at Curtis then. "You mean like, did Lenny or somebody put him up to coming in here and confessing?"

"Yeah. That kinda thing."

JD thought about it while he took another drag. He hit the cigarette again, made a face, and flicked it away.

"Nah. It doesn't feel like that. It feels like he's just either a dumbass or a coward or both."

"That's good," Curtis said. "Okay, so before we go in there is there anything you think I should know?"

"Other than I'm gonna kill this dude and drop his body in front of that fucking tanning salon?"

Curtis smiled, hoping to disarm and defuse. "Yeah," he said. "I mean other than that."

JD cracked a smile but he wouldn't give Curtis any more than that. "Listen," Curtis said. "Let me just remind you of something. If we keep the emotions in check, we can maybe use this situation to our advantage. You follow me?" JD acknowledged with his eyes. "Feel free to rattle his cage. But let's keep it to where he still wants to work for you. I'm gonna try to drive him into our corner. Best case, he stays and feels like he owes you."

"Yeah," JD said, "I get it. Now how 'bout you shut up and let's get on with this?" He was walking back towards the shop when Curtis stopped him.

"One more thing." Curtis held out the key to the old flower shop that JD had given him. "We need to make this quick so you can get to the real estate office and turn these in right away. Ask Jackie to give you a receipt." JD took the key and clipped it onto his retractable key ring that hung from his belt loop, an old janitor's device that had never gone out of style for a certain class of greaser.

"Cool. Thanks. I'll be ready to get outta here anyway. Clear my head and all that. Plus," he said with a certain glint in his eye, "I got errands to run."

Curtis retrieved his EverReady and a couple cans of seltzer from the trunk and made his way into the shop. The Headbangers Ball-style lettering of the window of the shop was not quite complete, but it already looked pretty good. The sounds of Motorhead assaulted his ears as Curtis entered, and he walked right to the laptop at the back of the shop to shut it off, in part to assert some control over the situation and in part because he was still hungover. And he hated Motorhead.

Angel looked up with an expectant expression, but Curtis ignored him and assessed the room instead. It smelled like Pine-Sol, and all the random shit had been organized into defined little areas of the shop. There was a seating area at the front that reminded Curtis of a stage set for a community theater production, and then in the middle, the position of prestige where a black faux-leather tattoo chair stood on its silver pedestal. And at the rear of the space, a piercing area behind the room divider with the minimalist faces that looked like Chinese characters. It still didn't look like a nice tattoo studio, but at least now you could tell what it aspired to be.

Curtis took all this in and within a few seconds he understood that Angel wanted to make up for what he'd done. You didn't clean with Pine-Sol if you were just putting on a show. But that's exactly what Curtis was doing in this moment. He called to JD, standing at the front of the shop, to lock the door. Then walked over to the seating area and repositioned the chairs so Angel would sit, isolated, right across from him. JD would sit off to the side as a kind of observer.

Curtis took his time opening his laptop and getting himself settled, hoping the extra time would make Angel nervous. He checked the location of the steroids from the RFID: package one in the old flower shop, and package two still in the trunk of the Mazda, where they belonged. He tunneled into his *Tattoos and Tans* folder, opened a blank notebook file in case he wanted to make any notes, and then started a recording app.

JD watched all this in silence, intuitively understanding that Curtis was trying to build a sense of anxiety for his little impromptu interrogation that was about to take place. Angel had stopped scribbling at whatever he was working on and was leaning against the wall, head down but his eyes on Curtis. For his purpose, Curtis was watching the clock at the corner of his laptop, just waiting for sixty more seconds of silence to tick by. Once it did, he counted another twenty for good measure and then looked up at Angel, who was waiting. "Okay, come sit," he said, and looked down at his computer. After Angel had slumped in his chair, JD silently took his seat.

"Do you know who I am?" Curtis asked Angel, his polite tone laced with aggression.

"Yeah. You JD's boy. From D.C."

"And do you know what I do?"

Angel wasn't sure how to answer. He pulled at the knees of his baggy pants, then said, "Shit, I don't know . . . government, I guess."

"That's right," Curtis said. "I deal with intelligence. With secrets. Of all kinds. But the main thing I work on is drugs. International drug rings. Cartels. Ecstasy. Fentanyl. Human growth hormones. Steroids. That kind of stuff. I work with the DEA a lot." He held Angel's eyes for a couple seconds, then moved on to the real business, letting his prepared little preamble just hang in the air for Angel to interpret however he would.

Curt pivoted to a more upbeat, friendlier tone. "Okay, so we're gonna do this in two parts. First, you tell us all the facts surrounding this package of steroids in the old flower shop on 2nd Street: where they came from, who knows they're there, when you touched them, who told you to handle them, and where they're going. Just the facts. No lies, no half-truths."

"Wait," Angel said, glancing at JD, a plea in his eyes. "I came here to come clean man. To make it right! But I ain't trying to get arrested or anything." Curtis held up a hand, smiling in a friendly way.

"No, Angel. Listen, man. You're not gonna get arrested. You're on our side. At least, I *think* you are. I met with my contact at EPD this morning, and the detective doesn't even know your name. And it's gonna stay that way." Angel's pupils dilated in a slo-mo explosion that ended with a tear pooled in the corner of his eye, threatening to fall. "The only name they need to know," Curtis said, "is the name they already know. Lenny Prichard."

He looked at JD, then back to Angel. "Tell us everything. No more secrets between the three of us. And then you're on our side." He paused for effect. "How it works out in terms of you here at this shop, learning the tattoo trade, working for JD. Well, that's between the two of you." Curtis thought JD might jump in then. When he stayed silent, Curtis continued. "But in terms of the law, if you lay it all out right here and now—no more secrets—then you're one hundred percent in the clear. I'll see to that."

Angel was still sitting slumped in the chair like a tranquilized animal when his phone started making noise. He looked up at Curtis and then pulled it from his pocket to glance at the screen. "Speak of the muthafuckin' white devil," Angel said. Then he held the phone up for Curtis to read. JD came in close to see.

Hey, Pancho. Swing by Tans this afternoon. I need you to get my truck washed.

"That reminds me of the second thing we're gonna do," Curtis said.

"Who the fuck is Pancho?" JD asked.

"JD's gonna go run his errands," Curtis continued, "and while he's gone I want you to give me the full background on everything you know about Lenny."

"That's what that whitey Lenny calls me . . . man, can you believe that?" Angel replied to JD.

". . . the people he hangs out with—everyone," Curtis finished his thought. " . . . his cousin Jackie who runs the real estate business. Everything."

Angel's whole disposition changed at the mention of Jackie. He got animated. "Jackie's not involved in any of the drug shit! She's just a regular chick. A businesswoman. She's classy, man!" Curtis realized he'd hit a nerve.

"Okay, yeah. I get it. That's why I need you to explain it all to me." JD was pulling a cigarette from the pack in the pocket of his pearl-snap shirt.

"Yeah, man," JD said, glancing at Angel. "Jackie's the shit. Hey, you know I fucked her, right?" Curtis just put his head down, frustrated. He looked up at JD.

"Don't you have somewhere to be?"

Ten minutes later JD pulled out of Old East in his van with a lot on his mind. He turned east on 190, towards Eunice Memorial Hospital. If he didn't get anything else accomplished today, he at least needed to get his sharps disposal certification letter signed. Once he got the van up to fifty for the short drive to the hospital, just inside city limits, he fished a small, empty baggie from his front pocket and worked the inside of it with his finger. There was barely enough residue to numb his gums, but it was all he had, and it would have to do. For now. He pushed the bag inside out and gave it a couple licks before flicking it out the open window.

Curtis could be a real fucking show-off, but he had to give the man credit. That line of bullshit he fed Angel worked pretty damn good. And though JD didn't like being reduced to some kind of sidekick in his own place, he had to at least admit he was happy to have Curtis as an ally in all this. Even if he felt a little embarrassed to have summoned him to Louisiana in the first place.

Just before he left the shop, Angel told him and Curtis how Lenny had told Angel to pull the steroids out of the shop the day after JD had showed up to confront him in the tanning salon. Which wasn't surprising to JD. He knew damn well Angel wouldn't just up and do something like that on his own.

But what *was* surprising—no, frustrating—was that Angel couldn't really say for sure what Lenny was all ate up about. Angel actually seemed to think it had something to do with Sadie. That it wasn't really about the 'roids hidden in the shop, but somehow about Sadie. That was Angel's impression, anyway. It didn't make any sense to JD. As far as he knew, Sadie had never even met the dude. Eunice was a small town, sure, but Sadie had been a public school girl. She didn't run in the same circles. He'd have to ask her about it.

But right now his biggest concern, now that Lenny's steroids were back in the old flower shop and he was ready to return the keys and get his three-hundred-dollar security deposit back, was Curtis. It was already clear to JD that he was in full-on war mode, on the hunt for Lenny now. And JD could appreciate that on some level, knowing that at least in part it came from a place of loyalty, Curtis still worried about some minor run-in with the Houston cops a decade back. But the thing was, Curtis was gonna get on a plane and go back to D.C. at some point. And Lenny would still be in Eunice.

If Curtis had some kind of crazy fucking aspiration to see Lenny Prichard in jail for any length of time or like, humbled in some real sense to the point where he'd just decide to turn the other fucking cheek, well, JD knew better. And Curtis should know better, too. But JD knew his friend well enough to see him getting carried away. It was only a matter of time before he bit off more than he could chew.

He wasn't worried about Angel. Hell, he liked Angel, and JD saw enough of himself in the younger man to take a Christian view of the whole thing. The dude had made a mistake, but he'd seen the error of his ways and had tried to make it right. For JD, it was really that simple. He'd been tattooing for more than a dozen years, and during that time he'd met hundreds of people—artists, managers, piercers, salespeople, hangers-on—and one thing they all had in common was they had all pretty much fucked up in some major way at least once in their lives. That was just a part of the tattoo racket; people had checkered histories.

If you started getting up on your high horse every time somebody fucked up, you'd be up there all by yourself. But if you helped people through their problems, you usually ended up with a good and loyal friend, or at least someone you could call on when you found yourself in a tough spot of your own.

Besides, Angel was practically working for free and JD needed all the help he could get.

When he got to the hospital, JD spent some time in the parking lot working his phone, checking in with various people he still knew and some others he'd just met. He was gonna need to score. He told himself it was necessary to push through all he had to do, with hopefully a little left to celebrate with Curtis if they could manage to gently back out of this situation.

Word had already gotten around town that JD was opening a shop, and it was amazing how many backroom doors that was opening. People he didn't know were starting to reach out to him, his status as hometown hero returning to bring tattoos to Eunice already on the rise. He'd always been able to cross the strict tribal lines of Eunice society. Black, white, skinhead, biker, rednecks, even rich folks with something to lose. JD had a way with them all. Asking around for the availability of a quick score, he told himself he was also spreading the word about the grand opening of his shop a week from Friday. But JD was experienced enough to recognize this rationale as something William Burroughs, one of his personal heroes, had called "junkie logic." It was just another lie you told during the process of getting high.

Getting the signature on his sharps disposal letter was refreshingly easy. It seemed like the hospital staff was mostly women, and JD has always had a certain charm that worked its way through his somewhat frightening exterior. He called everyone over a certain age sweetheart or sweetie, and that worked well for him. With younger females, tactics were different but his odds of winning them over were just as high. Fifteen minutes after he walked in, JD had the necessary signature and stamps on his letter—the lady had even given him a file protector from her desk to keep the letter in—and he was on his way back into town.

His next stop was the Sun-*N*-Y realty office. In the parking lot, he sent some text messages, then locked the van and went inside the small office attached to the Sun-*N*-Sports complex that dominated that part of Highway 190. It was thankfully devoid of customers and didn't look like Jackie was expecting any because she was leaning back in her chair with her Doc Martens on the corner of the desk, reading *A Confederacy of Dunces* and listening to KRVS: *Radio Acadie* out of Lafayette. She was vaguely businesslike in gray pants, suspenders, and a blazer over her black Pine Leaf Boys tee shirt. JD took in all this in a casual way. The thing that really jumped out at him was the sly way she slipped off her reading glasses when he walked in.

"Hey, Jackie," he said, waiting for her to adjust to the fact of him standing there. "I got two important questions for you." He stood there in front of her desk—she with her feet still propped up on the corner, nonchalant, him holding up the key to the old flower shop.

"I was hoping you'd stop by before five," she said. "Did you get everything outta there alright?" JD paused for a second, not totally convinced she wasn't making some veiled reference to the steroids in the ceiling.

"Yeah, I got all my tattoo equipment out of there, if that's what you mean. But I have to tell you, Jackie, I'm still disappointed we couldn't make that location work. It would've been perfect."

She brought her feet down from the desk and took a deep breath, looking up at JD with sympathetic eyes. "Oh, honey, I'm sorry to say, that would never have worked out. I think I owe you an apology because I shoulda known better." She paused, and JD gave her a quizzical look. "Call it wishful thinking on my part, okay? The idea of a body art shop right there on 2nd Street. Man, that's something I've been fantasizing about since back when I still wore safety pins as accessories." She gave him a big smile then. She reached out for the key, and JD dropped it into her hand. "You had questions?" she asked.

"Yeah," JD said, giving her a certain look he reserved for a certain type of woman in a certain kind of situation. "Question one. Since this has been a royal pain in my ass, not to mention set my grand opening back a week, can you please give me my deposit back?"

Jackie smiled up at him. "Of course! It's the least I can do." JD had half expected her to start doing the paperwork and such right then, but she just stayed still, arms folded on the desk and looking up at him. "What's the second question?"

He paused for effect. "It's not exactly business-related. But I have to ask—and I hope you won't take offense because high school and the decade that followed are kind of a blur for me. Anyway . . . did we get together one night? Maybe after a show at the community center?"

Jackie narrowed her eyes in a way that might have been flirtatious or might have meant she was seething with anger. "JD Dugas! If you tell me you don't remember you damn sure won't get that deposit back!"

"I knew we did!" JD said, his gusto betraying his poor

recollection. But then the memory actually did start to come back to him, triggered somehow by her tone of voice.

"We went back to my parents' house. Out back? The pool, right?"

"Yeah, the pool! You didn't have a bathing suit." Jackie said, still looking up at him, laughing. After a few seconds she broke eye contact and reached down to open her desk drawer. "I assume a check is okay?"

"A check is okay, but cash is better," JD said, admiring the shape of her as she leaned over, remembering now that she hadn't worn a suit either that night.

With JD out running his errands, Angel seemed to be opening up more, but there was still something guarded about his answers that Curtis didn't like. Angel had told him what he needed to know, but he hadn't opened up like Curtis had hoped. Maybe he'd been too heavy-handed in the opening stages of his interrogation, and that was why Angel was talking to him in that way you talk to authority figures who act like they want to be your friend. But it didn't matter. Angel didn't need to like him. In fact, it might be better if he was a little bit worried about Curtis.

When Angel pulled his phone from his pocket for the second time, clearly bothered by whatever he saw, Curtis jumped on the opportunity. "That's not Lenny again, is it?"

Angel nodded, then continued working on a design he'd been doing on his left hand with a ballpoint pen for the last ten minutes.

"Do you usually answer him right away?" Curtis asked.

"If I wanna get paid I do," Angel said.

"Yeah, I hear you," Curtis said, thinking. "Then you need to answer him now. We don't want him thinking anything's different."

Angel studied Curtis for a few seconds, then asked, "What are you telling me, bruh? I still gotta go wash the dude's truck?"

Curtis smiled, not just to let Angel know he had a plan, but because the thought of getting the best of Lenny Prichard seemed like more of a possibility now than it ever had.

"Yeah," Curtis said. "That's what I'm telling you. Cause if you don't go pick up Lenny's truck, then I can't make duplicates of his keys. And if I can't do that, well, then we can't execute the rest of the plan."

Angel was looking at Curtis like he'd been speaking another language. "What you mean, execute? And what plan?"

Curtis just smiled. "One step at a time. Now, why don't you put on some music? I gotta think for a minute."

Angel paused for a beat, then dropped the ballpoint pen, shook his head, and got up to move towards the laptop at the back of the shop.

"Wait a sec," Curtis said. "Let me see those messages again."

Angel handed over his phone. "You're not gonna reply?" Angel asked, worried.

"No, no," Curtis said. "You're gonna do that. I just want to study them for a minute." He turned his eyes to the phone as Angel turned his back to tend to the music.

Curtis navigated to the phone settings. Within a couple seconds, he'd taken a screen capture of the phone's IP address, and as Angel stood at the laptop queuing up music, Curtis opened Angel's email, pasted the image, and sent it to himself. It only took a few more seconds to delete the sent message. After that, he turned on the location sharing just as Angel turned back towards him, some kind of heavy drum and bass thing with a Latin vibe now growing louder.

As Angel sat back down, Curtis was at his laptop looking up the number to Ace Auto, the shop that Tac had recommended. "Respond to Lenny's text," he said. "Say you'll be there soon but don't give a time." Then Curtis used his flip phone to call the automotive store, plugging one ear with his finger against the music, Angel eyeing him curiously as he typed out his text to Lenny. He hit send and then listened to Curtis as he spoke in a clipped tone that struck Angel as kind of phony, but pretty slick too.

"Howdy. Y'all got car batteries? Uh-huh. How 'bout a key-cutting machine, you got one of those? Good. I gotta be in Lake Charles with a duplicate set in a couple hours, so I'm in a hurry. Okay. What time y'all close?"

When Curtis hung up, Angel said, "We just gonna steal the man's keys? What for?" Curtis got the impression Angel was asking to be convinced, once and for all. They had been through his relationship with Lenny already, and Curtis thought he'd done a thorough job of pointing out the various ways Lenny had used him to insulate himself from danger.

Angel understood his loyalty had been misplaced. But there was something still tugging at either his conscience or his sense of self-preservation. Curtis couldn't put his finger on it, but he thought it might have something to do with Angel's particular sense of integrity. In Angel's mind, the unabashed way Lenny went about making his money was, if not honorable, then at least deserving of a kind of respect for the simple fact that he didn't sugarcoat his crimes, and he never apologized.

"Lenny spies on girls in his tanning salon, right?" Curtis asked. Angel nodded. "And Jackie says he doesn't appreciate her?" He nodded, which was good because Curtis felt like that one was pretty weak. He continued. "And he treats you like shit?" Angel nodded. "And he had you taking all kinds of risks, moving packages around?" Angel just stared, unwilling to confirm what he'd come out and said thirty minutes prior. Not that it mattered much. Curt had audio of the whole conversation. "And you said he even uses Lefty to do deals for him?"

"That I can't say for sure," Angel said. "But I think he might, from the way I heard them talk."

"You know Lefty's real name?

"Nah. Sorry." Angel's phone beeped, and he held it up for Curtis after he'd read it.

"Tell him you'll be there in twenty minutes," Curtis said. "So listen, the point I'm making is Lenny doesn't have a problem using the people around him to get what he wants and to keep himself safe. If he'll put his *friend* at risk, and he can't be bothered to say a kind thing about his cousin, then trust me, he wouldn't think twice about hanging you out to dry."

Angel pulled a generic pack of cigarettes from his front pocket and shook one out, his attention on the smokes, looking down. "Yeah, I get it," he said, thinking better of lighting up and tucking the cigarette behind his ear instead. "But, no offense or anything Curtis, but I don't think you're understanding me. I'm down, bruh. I'm down with JD. In fact, I got a sweet idea to get my cousin Slim to paint an advertisement on that old Astro van he has. I mean, look around. I wanna make this shit work and all about being JD's apprentice, even if I can't make no money for a while. And I feel bad you had to come down and get involved." Angel looked up at Curtis then and held his eyes. "So I'll do this one thing with the keys or whatever. But once I return that man's truck, I'm gonna tell him what I have to say, man-to-man, and after that I'm out. I'm not about playing no cops and robbers shit with Lenny Prichard."

Curtis thought he was done and so started to lurch into another speech about how he understood, but Angel silenced him with a hand. "I'm not finished. You might not realize this 'cause you live in D.C. and all, but I'm telling you now, Lenny Prichard is not a dude you wanna be fucking with. You can trust *me* on that."

Curtis was still stinging from the way Angel threw his line back at him when Angel broke the silence to ask, "So what you need me to do?"

"Pick up his truck. Drive it to Ace Auto on your way to the car wash. Give me the other keys on the ring—I don't need the truck key—and then stop on your way back to pick 'em up." Curtis handed him a prepaid Visa card and with a short list from his pocket notebook folded against it. "And after you're done, if you don't mind, go to Walmart and pick up that stuff for me.

Get whatever else you need for the light box and keep the rest. There's two hundred on that." Angel gave him a wry smile and Curtis understood at once that he must kill with the ladies.

"This is like the shittiest bribe I ever seen, man."

Curtis reached down into his EverReady and opened a discrete Velcro compartment, fishing out a hundred-dollar bill. "You're right," he said, folding it once and handing the bill over to Angel. "I appreciate everything you're doing. Thank you for the information."

Jackie called out as he walked out of the office with his three hundred dollars. JD stopped with his hand on the door.

"Hey! Not to sound like an old lady checking up on him or anything, but how's Angel working out?"

JD thought it was cute the way she asked it, and he couldn't resist taking in the vision of her leaning against the front of her desk. Jackie was incredible. She was at least three years older than him and here she was managing to look sexy as hell and exactly her age at the same time.

"Well, he has great taste in the ladies, I can tell you that much."

"A cheap line, but I'll take it," Jackie said.

"In all seriousness, he's good. I can't stand that fucking gangsta rap he plays."

"They don't really call it gangsta rap anymore. Just an FYI." Jackie said, smiling.

"Good to know. Thanks." JD pulled the door open, his mind

mostly on his rendezvous—now that he had the cash—with a dealer he knew at Cecil's Bar. "But yeah, he can draw and he has a good attitude. I don't know why he was ever mixed up with all that shady stuff your cousin Lenny has going on, but that's another story, I guess." JD gave her a smile to soften the blow of his little jab, but Jackie's face was not what he was expecting. Her mouth fell open for an instant and then resolved into a tight gritting of teeth.

"What shady stuff?"

Episode Five
Keys to the Kingdom

———— ✻ ————

Curtis and Angel manage to make duplicates of Lenny's master keys. Lenny continues to pursue Sadie. JD makes a dramatic gesture to show he's in control and ready for a new beginning. On hearing that Angel has been doing Lenny's dirty work, Jackie has it out with Lenny.

> "Please! I am not in the mood for a dialect story!" (Ignatius Reilly)
> — John Kennedy Toole, *A Confederacy of Dunces*

T he building that was Sun-*N*-Tans wasn't anything special, but it did the job and Lenny liked that it was new. He'd been able to set it up exactly how he wanted. You walked into a good-size reception area that had not just all the tanning lotions and goggles and such, for people who didn't want to use the free ones the state made him provide, but also machines for snacks and sodas, passive income that always made him at least a hundred bucks a month. There was a unisex bathroom with a "no dumping" sign on the wall and then the tanning studios, numbers one, two, and three.

His office was at the very end of the hallway and the door

pretty much stayed shut, unless he saw from the appointment schedule somebody good was coming, and then he'd make sure she was in studio three and his office door would stay open, at least until the girl went inside, hopefully not before they exchanged a few words. His office had a deadbolt. He told himself it was for the inevitable occasion when his sexual fantasy would come true and one of these girls would walk into his office and it would be on. But there had been times when the fantasy stayed in his imagination and he needed the dead bolt just the same.

It wasn't fancy, just a raised metal building about the size of a standard double-wide trailer, but it didn't need to be, especially since he was basically the only game in town. Technically, there was one other place, a little piddly-ass shack in the wrong part of town, but it was barely hanging on now. In fact, it was to the point where the dude who owned the place called Lenny every month, it seemed like, to see if he wanted to buy the one tanning bed he had left. Not that he ever would.

He'd had to take out a loan with St. Landry Bank to pay for the new construction, but it was worth it. The land already belonged to Uncle Ely, and he co-signed for Lenny too, so he ended up not having to take any money out of his pocket. He saved a shitload on permits too, again thanks to Uncle Ely. And since he contracted the construction to Lefty, naturally they both made out pretty good on the deal.

Lefty was as good a general contractor as they came, and when he was doing his own thing, it was one hundred percent by the book. But Sun-*N*-Tans wasn't somebody's house. It was just a tin building where people were gonna pay to lay naked under some UV lights that Lenny got a great deal on. So they maybe cut some corners in places where it wasn't gonna hurt anybody. But at the end of the day everybody did shit like that. Where they went the extra mile, and it was in situations like this where it really paid to have lifelong friends like Lefty, was with the video surveillance lines they ran to each one of the tanning studios. Not too many people knew about that.

Sun-*N*-Tans was two years old at this point, and Lenny was proud of the business, proud of its success. And that success gave him a sense of confidence as a businessman that he didn't have when he first started, because the whole thing had been his idea. He was the one that recognized the market potential. He was the one that got the best deal on the tanning beds, that came up with the name, came up with the money, that oversaw the construction of the building. All of it was his idea, his plan, his decision-making.

And that wasn't just vanity talking. That was fact. He made a few thousand in profit every month, rain or shine, and that wasn't bullshit. It was cold hard cash. He had hard-earned praise from Uncle Ely too. A couple times the old man had even joked to his friends around the table at Rudy's, with Lenny sitting right there, about how his nephew had perfected the art of pulling in "that trashy dollar" that Eunice seemed to be flush with these days.

So it stung him that much more this morning when Uncle Ely had brought him back to that same table at Rudy's to tell him in no uncertain terms what a clusterfuck the 2nd Street property was. Of course he'd heard about it. Lenny wasn't surprised about that. And neither was he surprised that Uncle Ely didn't like the idea of a tattoo shop opening for business downtown. He seemed to consider it a personal affront to decency and tradition.

"You bring in tattoos now, then what's next?" Uncle Ely had asked him, totally rhetorically, hamming it up a little for the other old men at the table, but still clearly pissed. "A titty bar? Devil worshipers? A-rabs?" Lenny wasn't sure if he should object, knowing his uncle was well aware of how crazy he sounded. But he couldn't resist.

"We already have Mexicans downtown," he said. "*Cajun Customs*—right next door. They're doing fine."

Uncle Ely jumped on that, his voice climbing in the crowded little cafe. "That's exactly my point! It's already bad enough!" The matronly waitress, making the rounds with the coffee pot, leaned over to top off Uncle Ely's cup and eased right into the conversation.

"I like Slim and them. They do real good work. My nephew just got them to paint like a sunset scene on the tailgate of his truck? Like with cypress trees and ducks and all? It's beautiful."

Uncle Ely gave her an exasperated look. "Thank you, Rhonda," he said, ". . . for the coffee." If she understood that he was telling her to butt out she didn't show it.

"And I think they're Puerto Rican. Catholic, too. Same Jesus, just, you know, browner."

Lenny had been about to mention how Slim from *Cajun Customs* had actually painted the beach scene on the side of the Sun-*N*-Tans building that everybody recognized, but he kept his mouth shut. The conversation might have been sort of comical up to now, but Lenny had understood Uncle Ely was coming to his main point, and it damn sure wasn't gonna be a laughing matter. It was the point that had Lenny sitting in his office later, blasting Metallica from his computer, just stewing with anger.

"Since when does Jackie Guidry run your business for you?" Uncle Ely had asked, and the way his eyes penetrated Lenny's, nothing else needed to be said. Lenny understood at that moment the whole debacle with 2nd Street was his fault. His fault because he had left the decision-making to Jackie. Uncle Ely was testing him in that moment, challenging him.

He knew better than to quibble. Jackie had rented the damn space to JD without even checking with him, but that didn't matter. Not anymore. The point Uncle Ely was making, without saying another word about it, was that if Lenny was running the business right, Jackie would never in her wildest dreams think about renting anything to anybody without checking with him first. Much less a prime location like 2nd Street. That's what it meant to be in charge, to be a man. To be a Prichard man.

If he'd left Rudy's full of humble pie, it had dissolved into anger and irritation in the pit of his stomach by the afternoon. He sat in his office, cycling through the ways he would cut Jackie down to size. Goddamn, but she had fucked up! And she knew it, too! He knew she did. Always so quick to align with the freaks. She heard tattoo shop and she just jumped at it! It was so like Jackie. And then of course she saw an opening to get Pancho in there and that was it. She was so damn eager to find him a job she totally abandoned her sense of professionalism. Not to mention loyalty to the company, and to Lenny especially.

There. That was how he was gonna say it to her: abandoned her sense of professionalism and loyalty to the company. That was good. But speaking of Pancho, where the fuck was he?

Lenny checked his phone and saw the reply to his text that must've come in when he'd cranked up "Nothing Else Matters" (he'd always loved that song). He picked up the landline and dialed the Sun-*N*-Tans main number and waited until Britney picked it up at the reception desk.

A minute later, she knocked on his office door and he greeted her by saying, "It took you long enough." He pulled the keys from his pocket by the blue St. Eds lanyard and kind of flipped it to her. She'd been an athlete—looked good in a bikini, too, they all did—but she wasn't the sharpest. How sharp could she be, after all, when she ran the IT for the business, but she didn't know about his cameras? "Give these to Pancho when he comes by in a few minutes."

"Who's Pancho?" she wanted to know. Lenny held out two twenty-dollar bills he'd paper clipped together, giving her a look that had her shrinking towards the door even as she reached out to grab the cash.

"Some people call him Angel," he said.

Tac had been sitting at his desk for the better part of two hours, doing what he thought of as causal research. He was reading through printouts of information on the civil history of one Curtis T. Laroux. It was frustrating how little was there, but the fragments of text that *were* on the page more or less jived with what he knew about Curtis and what little he'd volunteered this morning. He had dates: U.S. Air Force, 2006–2012, Department of Defense, 2012–present, with just the word "civilian" to describe his role in the DoD. There were a handful of known associates, mostly in the D.C. area, and his mom and brother in Eunice. The list of previous addresses was extensive compared to the rest of the report, but it still didn't offer Tac any particularly useful insights. California, Texas, Georgia, Maryland, a couple in D.C. That was it.

His searches online didn't yield much more than the state and federal databases did. Curtis appeared to be one of the few people Tac had run across who didn't live half his life on social media. No Facebook, no Twitter. None of that shit. This fact was less intriguing than it might've been because Tac was also one of those people. The only information he could find about Curtis was stuff he already knew. Curtis in a Eunice High baseball uniform, reaching for a ball. Curtis and his mom and brother listed as surviving members of the Laroux family in his dad's obituary.

Maybe he was going about this the wrong way. For one, they just needed to talk. He pulled out his phone right there and texted Curtis. Second, he realized he didn't need the man's bio. If he wanted to know why Laroux was in town, he just needed to triangulate his connection to JD Dugas and Lenny Prichard. Last and most importantly, Tac reminded himself that he had other shit to do. It wasn't a case. It was curiosity. The fact that he was trying to stalk Curtis online said it all. His wife would probably say he had a man-crush at dinner when he told her all about it.

And he wasn't too proud to acknowledge there might be some degree of truth to that. He had dreamed of shipping out as a Marine since he was old enough to shoot a gun, and the fact that it all evaporated over the course of a ten-minute bathroom brawl was a tough pill to swallow. The lump in his throat was still there years later. But whatever that was—jealousy, loss, missed opportunity—it wasn't an emotion that was motivating him now. It was the Prichard family.

There were certain moves that anyone with any kind of career ambition just didn't make. In the EPD, fucking with the Prichard family was one of those moves. It was a small town, and you could talk about justice being blind 'till you were blue in the face, but the fact was there were certain families in town that wrote the checks that found their way into the most important institutions in town. Tac had actually spent a lot of time thinking about it, and his conclusion was that there was an uncomfortable but necessary equilibrium in Eunice.

You couldn't say the town was dying. That wasn't true. But it wasn't healthy either; it wasn't growing. What it did was stay the same, perpetuate itself. In order to do that—to maintain that balance so the decay didn't take hold and bring everyone down—rich people who liked things more or less the way they were had to write checks. Ely Prichard was one of those men, and Lenny Prichard was the next generation.

Anyway, he was bored and his eyes hurt. He told himself it was just the computer, but he suspected it might be time for reading glasses. He took his gun out of his desk drawer, put on his coat, and signed for a mobile data terminal from the comms locker, where they kept the little bit of technical equipment the EPD had . There was a Monster energy drink and a pack of sunflower seeds at the 7-Eleven with his name on it. And while he was out, he might just swing by some of the properties Lenny Prichard owned. Just for the hell of it. He'd gone to the trouble of making a little list.

Jackie flipped the sign on the door to the closed position and went back to sit quietly at her desk, working hard to keep her anger in check. She turned the radio off and tried sitting there in absolute silence with her eyes closed, but every few seconds she couldn't help but slam her fists on the desk, waves of anger reverberating through her body. She could feel it in her stomach as a kind of adrenaline that almost made her sick, it was so strong. It was hard for her because she couldn't stay focused on just one of them. Lenny and Angel were both at fault.

But it was harder to blame Angel. Christ! He was barely twenty-two. People always made the joke about being too pretty to go to jail. Well, that was Angel. A tear fell as she sat there, thinking about it. It's not that he was innocent——not like that, anyway. But there was a naive kind of purity to the way he leaned into life, something to do with a sense of fate, maybe, or narcissism or just plain old arrogance of youth that carried him into situations and experiences by the seat of his pants. And most of the time it worked out. But Jackie knew from experience that sometimes people followed their bliss right into the grave.

JD wouldn't say any more about it, of course, once he realized he'd put his foot in his mouth. He'd just made his exit and maybe she could've pressed him, but the whole thing caught her flat-footed. So she couldn't play it cool and maybe extract some details from him. Anyway, the details didn't matter that much. What mattered was Lenny was using Angel, and whatever it was exactly Lenny had him doing, it damn sure wasn't legal. Angel was only good at three things—music, drawing, and fucking—so unless both Angel and Lenny were in the closet or Lenny had some kind of newfound appreciation for the arts, which was even less likely, they were up to no good.

She was no fool. Lenny might have been a businessman,

and he was, she had to give him that. He had a good sense of what would work in Eunice, and he found ways to make money that others might not. But he wasn't *just* a businessman, that's for sure. He took care to shield Jackie from whatever he was up to, and to be honest, she wasn't totally sure if she appreciated that or if she was maybe sort of insulted by it, but she always knew there was more going on than just the tanning shop and the real estate business. She kept the books for both businesses, and the amount of cash coming in just didn't reconcile with Lenny's lifestyle.

She texted Angel, and he hit her right back, like usual, but he said he couldn't talk because he was taking care of some important business for the shop, and she didn't push it. The surge of adrenaline seemed to be tapering off, but her stomach was still in knots. She sat there for a few more minutes and it suddenly occurred to her that Angel might have been lying. Was he really doing something so important for JD? And how could that be if JD had just been here in her office? Maybe he was hiding something. Or maybe JD had already warned him. Of course he had! Why wouldn't he? They were both cut from the same cloth. Jackie knew that.

She was furious again. How dare Angel lie to her. And after everything she'd done for him! She stood up and tried to remember where her keys were. He wasn't gonna get off that easy. Eunice wasn't a big town; she'd just go find him and then they would see what was true and what wasn't. It was that simple. She found the keys laying under her book and marched to get in her Celica she'd had since high school, when she stopped cold in the middle of the little office. And just stood there. *What the fuck are you doing, Jackie?* she said aloud.

What had she told JD? She wasn't trying to act like an old lady, but that was exactly what she was doing now. No. She wouldn't do it. She needed to get a fucking grip. No way she was gonna go driving around town trying to hunt down her boyfriend. That was crazy making. It sounded like one of those terrible country songs people around Eunice couldn't get enough of. She wouldn't do it. So she stood there for a while, trying to think.

And then it hit her. Angel would come to her in due time. He always did. But right now, she would go see Lenny. And she knew exactly where he was.

Outside it had grown cold and overcast, the barometer dropping and the mild morning giving way to storm clouds and a cold north wind. The rain started just before she reached the Celica, and it was falling hard by the time she got to the door. With her blazer pulled up over her head, she managed to get the key in the lock—no remote keyless entry for her, this was the 1983 GTS that her mother had bought, knowing she'd give it to Jackie on her high school graduation. And Jackie was careful here as always, rain or no rain, not to scratch the metallic blue paint that still looked good.

She fell into the bucket seat of her baby and cranked it to get the engine warm and the defroster going. The Cult was blasting "Wild Flower," an alright soundtrack for now as she sat low in the car and the steady rain leveled off a little. She worked the clutch and backed out of her spot, long used to looking through the rear window grill that gave the car its distinctive badass look but damn sure didn't make it any easier to see. And when she put it in first, she used her finger to dial up the volume a few notches to feel the groove from the custom Pioneer system, with the amp under the hood powering an array of speakers that still sounded better than anything else on the road.

Sun-*N*-Tans was barely a mile from the realty office, but Jackie almost never went inside during business hours. Lenny had never come right out and said it, but it was clear he didn't like her being there. Which she thought was weird, but it was also fine by her. She hated the place, had always associated tanning salons with the kind of jocks and cheerleaders and buttoned-up, khaki-wearing crowd she'd gone out of her way to reject since she was fifteen years old. But of course, it wasn't that simple for her. For one thing, this damn tanning shop paid the bills. And for another, and this was the real kicker, many of her family members and people she cared about not only benefited from the business, but they actually *liked* this kind of shit.

The building itself was a tan color and the whole street-facing side of it was filled with this cheesy sort of beach sunset scene. It was like a mural, except it was an advertisement. There were silhouettes of people tanning in the sun, frolicking in the water, playing volleyball, shit like that. It was a cliché thing, and it always made Jackie think of David Lee Roth singing how he wished they could all be California girls. It looked particularly sad drenched in rain.

Even from the turn lane on Highway 190, she could see Lenny's truck wasn't there. Which was surprising. She pulled into the gravel lot anyway, if for no other reason than to cruise through and come out at the rear exit onto 9th Street and just go home from there. Somewhere beneath her anger, she could tell her stomach wasn't right, and she was already thinking after this she'd just go on home for the day. Lenny parked towards the back of the building, and even though he always backed into the spot, that new truck was so big you couldn't miss it from the road. It was definitely not there. But then she saw the little blue car parked next to the empty space. A Ford Focus. Angel's car.

Suddenly she was furious all over again. She pulled up right behind it, and there was no mistaking the car. It was Angel's alright. The frog lights of her Celica illuminated the new "Black Jack Tattoo" sticker in black and silver centered on the back bumper. That lying son of a bitch! Everything around her receded out of focus—Concrete Blonde on the stereo, rain pattering the roof of her car, the wipers beating back and forth across the windshield—and the only thing she saw now was Angel. He was in there, and she was gonna get some answers. In a quick series of movements, Jackie killed the wipers, the lights, and the engine. And then she was marching through the rain, unflinching, to the front steps of the building.

Lenny saw her come in, and even though he couldn't see her face from the angle of the camera, he knew right away it was Jackie. She stood at the entrance in rolled-up pants and those boots people used to wear, shaking out that thick brown hair with the blue streak and he could tell she was pissed just by the way her shoulders were all tight.

An instant later, she was marching down the hall towards his office. He'd been ready to tell her off, so it should have been good that she was suddenly here, but somehow this was all wrong. She knew better than to come, but an instant later she was standing in front of his desk—no knock, no nothing—and he was still trying to pause his Metalica when she started asking "Where's Angel?" like she owned the fucking place.

"Angel?" he said, still focused on turning off the music and was slow to translate Pancho's actual name in his head. He was still coming to grips with the situation.

"Angel! Goddamn it. Where's Angel? His car's here. Where is he?"

Lenny wasn't focused on the question. Instead, he was thinking about how fucking irritating it was that people he didn't like were suddenly busting in his office demanding shit from him. Why did this keep happening?

He found himself struggling to cap his anger at the appropriate level. It felt like a situation where maybe putting his fist through the wall or even dragging Jackie out by her hair wouldn't necessarily be that far out of bounds. There was an animal rage brewing in him like a drug that was coming on strong, ready to take over. And it was probably no coincidence that whatever part of his brain that was still in control of his reason saw this because, in reality, it was a residual effect of the growth hormone he'd sampled for a time. It was weird the way it stayed with you even after you got clean.

She didn't know it, because she was wrapped up in her own adrenaline-fueled anger, but it was this more rational part of Lenny's brain that had kept oversight of him as his primal self threatened to emerge. These few synapses saved Jackie, in that moment, from a few life-changing seconds of violence.

Lenny didn't have any kind of strategies he could use to keep these destructive urges in check. He just kind of muscled through it. He never turned his mind towards this question about himself, of why these extreme bouts of boiling rage that sought violence emerged every so often. Lenny simply forced himself not to think about it. On some level, he understood something would happen someday, but beyond that, it never occurred to him that there were remedies available to treat his psychological condition. He just did his best to live with it.

"He's washing my truck," he heard himself say, and he looked at Jackie for the first time then. She seemed to understand, looking at his eyes, that there was a line somewhere close that she couldn't cross. That moment of intuition helped Jackie keep her cool, to avoid giving in to emotion and letting herself lose control. Which was unlikely, but certainly possible in this moment.

"So," she asked, her voice returned to a normal register. "What are you doing with Angel? He works for you?"

"That's a strong word," Lenny said, noticing that the door was still open. He glanced at his computer monitor and saw Britney wasn't at her desk. So he raised his voice and said "Britney, close the door!" and watched as she took a couple steps forward, out of the shadows of the hallway, and pulled the door closed. On the computer screen, he watched her take a few steps down the hallway, hesitate, then go back to her desk. "But yeah, he does little jobs for me here and there." He finished the thought.

"This is bullshit! You're using that boy!" Jackie said, her anger welling up again.

Lenny gave her a measured look. "Talk about the pot calling the kettle black. You really wanna talk about using him?"

"Oh, give me a break," Jackie said. "It's a totally different thing." She hated the way she sounded, suddenly defensive. "And anyway, I don't like having to find this stuff out from other people."

That got Lenny's attention. "Wait, what you mean, other people?"

"It doesn't matter," Jackie said.

"Oh, it matters," Lenny said, his irritation spiking again. "If Pancho didn't tell you, who the fuck did?"

"I don't like you taking advantage of Angel . . . and stop calling him Pancho!"

"Jesus, Jackie! It's not like you're married to him! He can handle himself. Besides, it's not all like you think. He's washing my truck, for God's sake! What's so fucking dangerous about that?" Lenny paused, getting a hold of himself. "Anyway, if he didn't tell you, who did?"

Jackie paused for a second. "So, JD Dugas came by to bring back the keys to 2nd Street, and I cleared him."

"You gave him the deposit back?" Lenny barked.

"I had to. We totally screwed him on that place."

"We?" Lenny said. "By the time I'd even heard about it, you'd already given him the damn keys!"

"But you're the one who decided to kick him out! And for no reason!" Jackie's voice was climbing again.

"That's because we don't want a fucking tattoo shop on 2nd Street! Are you crazy!" Jackie started to speak, but he didn't give her a chance. "And if you would have just checked with me, like you're supposed to, we never would've had this problem!" He looked at her for a beat. "This is *your* fault, Jackie. *I* own the place. *I* make the decisions!"

"Then who's 'we,'" Jackie asked.

"No. *I* make the decisions," Lenny repeated.

"You said 'we don't want a tattoo shop on 2nd Street.' So who's we?" Jackie couldn't help but smile now, grinding salt in the wound.

Lenny just looked at her. "You don't give the keys to nobody until you talk to me. It's that simple."

Jackie stopped her pacing and sat down then. There was fucking with Lenny, and then there was fucking with Uncle Ely, and those were two very different things. She was tired of fighting. Besides, she was suddenly feeling a bit woozy. Lenny swiveled in his chair and pulled a cold bottle of water from the little college fridge he kept there and offered it to her. "I'd rather have a beer," Jackie said, but when Lenny reached back and grabbed a Michelob Ultra, she changed her mind. Lenny went ahead and cracked it. He took a long swallow and for the next few minutes he and Jackie had a conversation. Lenny offered her a few more harmless details about how Angel came to work for him, and she acknowledged her part in the clusterfuck that was the 2nd Street property.

Jackie was smart. She had long since come to understand that she would never enjoy the kind of special attention Uncle Ely paid to Lenny and the other members of the Prichard side of the family, but especially Lenny. For his part, as they sat and shot the shit there in his office, Lenny more or less acknowledged that Uncle Ely hadn't been happy about hearing what happened with the 2nd Street property. He didn't have to tell Jackie how Uncle Ely assessed her own role in the debacle. She could just about imagine.

"Once a Guidry, always a Guidry," Jackie said. Which wasn't exactly fair, at least from Lenny's perspective. He'd seen his uncle embrace all kinds of folks whose last name wasn't Prichard. In Jackie's case, it was definitely true that Uncle Ely was somewhat cool on her, but honestly, that probably had more to do with the way Jackie thumbed her nose at tradition more than anything else. And as for the claim that you had to be a Prichard to rate in Uncle Ely's book, well it just wasn't true. And that was why everybody and their momma around town called him "Uncle Ely." People who didn't even know the man called him that.

He tried in his way to explain this to Jackie. Not that Uncle Ely needed Lenny or anybody else to defend him, but the truth was the truth. Jackie had fucked up. *He* had fucked up—not that he was gonna come right out and say that to her. And the truth was, Uncle Ely helped a lot of people. Lenny worked through the rest of his beer and tried to illustrate the point by telling her about Lefty.

They were Vidrines, and Lefty's real name was Troy, but everybody who played ball with him called him Lefty. By the time they were twelve years old, Lenny and Lefty had been playing baseball together for years. Lenny's dad coached every year, and since the Prichard family basically funded the league, things had a way of working out well for the Prichard kids who played. And so it came to be that Lenny's dad had the pleasure of coaching teams that were flush with talent. Troy Vidrine was one of those talented players.

He'd always been a stout kid, tall and strong, even in Tee-ball. Troy's dad had helped shape him into an even better player. The very first year of Tee-ball, already on a Prichard team but somewhat of an unknown at that point, he batted from the right side like a normal right-handed kid. But by the next year, he had learned to hit left-handed. The rumor was his dad had tied his right hand behind his back from the end of baseball season in August all through the fall and winter, until the weather got warm enough to start practicing again in March. Not for school, of course—Troy went to the public schools—but as soon as he got home, he would automatically put on the little piece of rope his dad had fixed for him to keep the arm tucked against his body, useless to him for well over twelve hours a day for those seven months.

And that wasn't all. As Troy got older, his father's training techniques kept pace with the boy's physical endurance levels. By the time they were into the pitching leagues, his old man would pitch five hundred balls to him every night of the week. No exception. Birthdays, holidays, Sundays, even on game days. Lefty could hit two home runs and two doubles in a game, which wasn't that rare for him, and still he'd be out there on the field with his dad hitting buckets and buckets of balls long into the night.

Lefty's dad worked construction, and their family got by, but that was it. He was a public school kid on free lunch. But left-handed hitters were so valuable in high school baseball. A reliable hitter like Lefty in the line-up was the difference between average and great teams.

The two boys, Lenny and Lefty, bonded. For many years, Lefty played first base, with some games as a right-handed fielder and some as a left-handed fielder—his father still experimenting with his son's ability— while Lenny played shortstop or second base. And later on when it was established that Lefty was far better on defense with his glove on his left hand, he moved to center and left field, and started playing behind Lenny because they made a strong unit that way. Lefty played left field when Lenny was at shortstop or moving to right field when Lenny played second.

Just before his freshman year at the public school, Uncle Ely helped Lefty's dad establish his own construction company, and it wasn't long before they were getting all kinds of work. Pretty soon, the company was doing a brisk business and Lefty was wearing khaki pants and a white shirt at St. Eds. From the first day he showed up at school, Lenny and Lefty were thick as thieves. And two years later, they went on to win the first of their two consecutive state baseball championships.

Uncle Ely had everything to do with that. And the thing is it wasn't just like this with the Vidrines. There were two or three other new families at St. Eds every year, public school families with sons who were great ballplayers. And that was just one way Uncle Ely helped the school and the families. Even the community. The man was a pillar, a legend at this point. It was why people just called him "Uncle Ely," whatever their relation to him. He was everyone's benefactor.

Jackie was bored as shit by the time Lenny finally got done talking about his best friend Troy and how it had all worked out so well. She wasn't the least bit interested in baseball or state championships or who played where on the field. All she wanted to do now was get out of there before Angel got back with Lenny's truck. She was all argued out, and plus her stomach was still feeling weird. She got up and tucked the empty water bottle into her back pocket, knowing full well Lenny wouldn't have a recycle container in the building.

Lenny had said, "I'll catch you later. Feel better." Maybe the most compassionate thing he'd said to her in weeks. Jackie counted it as a win. Even though she definitely didn't feel good about anything at this moment. He didn't get up, of course (not that she expected him to), and Britney showed no signs of acknowledging her as she made her way down the hallway. But when she realized she was going to throw up and lunged for the bathroom door a few steps away, grasping at the doorknob and slamming the door behind her, Britney couldn't help but notice.

Jackie didn't have time to decide if she felt better afterward. She wasn't sure what was going on, but the one she did know was she didn't want to linger in the bathroom waiting around for another potential round. She damn sure didn't want to cross paths with Angel at this moment. She felt Britney's eyes on her as she emerged from the bathroom, but she stayed focused on the front door, head down as she marched towards the sanctuary of her Celica and her little house a few blocks away. All she was thinking about was brushing her teeth, getting some chamomile tea, and curling up on the couch with her fleece blanket and David Bowie on the stereo.

Curtis was forced to use the Gulf Coast Mud hat to keep the rain off his glasses. He pulled it off as soon as he entered Ace Auto, the auto-parts store with the old Honda three-wheeler suspended from chains a good fifty feet in the air. He had separated the blue St. Ed's lanyard from the rest of the key ring before he'd entered the store and took a few seconds to study the keys themselves. It was a relief there weren't any dimple keys or even four-sided ones. Two were stamped with *do not duplicate*, but he wasn't too worried about that. If he needed to, he'd use the fifty-dollar bill he'd put in his front pocket.

Angel, meanwhile, was just pulling into Squeaky Kleenz car wash on Martin Luther King Drive, about a block off of Highway 190. There were two full-service car washes in town, and they both stayed afloat because they generally split the customer base. Angel was sure Squeaky's did a better job than the white one—they called it *All-American Car Wash* or some shit like that—but the real reason he came here was that they had better air fresheners and they usually rocked some old school R&B that you could jam to in the little seating area under the pavilion where they finished the cars.

Today, with the rain coming down on the tin roof like a drummer riding the cymbals, you couldn't hear shit. Which was fine by Angel. He liked the natural rhythm of the rain anyway. His only problem was it was cold as shit and the dudes who worked there thought he was crazy to be bringing his truck for a wash during a rainstorm. Until he explained to them that the truck belonged to his boss.

"He white, right?" the main guy had asked, and they both had a good laugh.

They went ahead and washed the Tundra, and Angel didn't think twice about it. That's what Lenny had told him to do and this was gonna be the last thing he did for the man anyway, so the truck was gonna get washed. And vacuumed and Armor All'd too. Besides, Curtis needed time to get those keys duped.

Angel sat there on one of three molded-plastic seats under the big pavilion. It was warm in the tiny cashier's area where they kept all the air fresheners and crowns and shit that nobody bought, but the girl who worked the register didn't like anybody loitering around in there. Outside under the tin pavilion, he was tucked in as close to the old coke machine as possible to shield himself from the cold wind. He had his hood pulled over his head and had pulled himself into his sweatshirt as best he could, checking his phone. Jackie wasn't answering his texts, which was weird. So he texted Curtis to see how much longer he was gonna be.

Curtis was loitering a few feet from the counter, laboring through a response to Tac on the flip phone and trying not to look too eager while the clerk, an older man who looked like he must've worked there for decades, worked the key-cutting machine. The patch on his work shirt said he was "Mr. Tooky," and he was on the second key. Curtis was feeding them to him one at a time, hoping to keep the process moving along and keeping track of how the keys were oriented on the ring. But the older man was on his own clock. Curt was handing over key number three when he felt the flip phone vibrate in his pocket: Angel checking in. It took him a minute, but eventually he typed out "15 minutes" and hit send.

Angel was still looking at his phone and thinking he didn't want to sit there for fifteen more minutes, freezing his ass off, when he got a text from Lenny.

Hurry up. I'm taking off early. And it's raining.

Angel wasn't sure what exactly that meant, but he didn't care. He told himself he'd give it five minutes before he replied. Curtis seemed to be pretty wound up about this whole little "operation," but it wasn't nothing but a thing as far as Angel could tell. Lenny was stuck at the tanning place with no truck, so what was he gonna do? Nothing. And if he didn't like the fact that he was washing his truck for nothing, well then he should've checked the fucking weather. That wasn't Angel's problem.

He pulled up his little notes app on his phone and started working on a rhyme he'd been messing around with the last couple days. A few minutes later, he decided to go ahead and let Curtis know Lenny was getting antsy.

Curtis felt the phone vibrate in his pocket and when he glanced down at the message, standing at the counter, it didn't help his frustration. Mr. Tooky was refusing to copy the fourth key in the set.

"Ya see. It says right there, 'Do not duplicate.'"

"Yeah, I see it," Curtis said. "But, like I explained, it's not a law. It's like a warning label. Like the tag they put on mattresses."

"Exactly," the man said. "You're not supposed to remove it." Curtis was at a loss. On some level, he thought Mr. Tooky was bullshitting him, but the look on his face was dead serious. The man was feeling righteous. Curtis was busy resigning himself to the apparent reality that he was only going to get three of the five keys when another employee, this one younger, scruffier, appeared behind the man and offered to take over. He gave Curtis a hopeful look.

Curtis took a moment to give them some space, perusing the aisle of car batteries behind him and fingering the folded fifty-dollar bill in his pocket. Every battery looked the same to him. When he glanced back towards the counter, the older man was clearing out. Curtis was optimistic when he heard the old man say "suit yourself" with a dismissive wave of his hand. The younger dude's name tag said "Dirty." Everybody around here seemed to have a nickname.

"Lemme see that key," Dirty said, and Curt approached the

counter with the fifty palmed in his right hand and slid the key over with that same hand. He let the money fall to the countertop and moved his hand slightly to expose it. Dirty made a show of looking down at the key, peering close to read the words, then he smoothly put his hand on top of the fifty just as Curtis pulled back. "Shit, bruh! It don't say nothing about cuttin' a new key. It's just one of the commandments written on there. You know, like *do not kill . . . do not fornicate . . . do not duplicate.* It's like a proverb . . . like Moses and shit! "

Curtis liked this guy Dirty. It was hard not to. He stood at the machine working it like a virtuoso, an artist and a craftsman. Stopping every so often to check the key against the light, buffing it, talking to himself in a running banter. Curtis appreciated the show, but he was in a hurry. When he leaned over the counter to impress that point on Dirty, he responded by passing him the finished fourth key. Curtis slid the last one across the counter and worked through the alphabet on the flip phone to text the word "ready" to Angel.

Already sitting in Lenny's truck with the heater going, Angel was connecting his phone to the Bluetooth to play some of his own music. He wanted to see what the factory speakers in the Tundra could do. The rain had stopped and the sun was even threatening to come out now, but it was still cold and there were puddles all around the parking lot of Squeaky Kleenz. The truck would probably be muddy by the time he got back. But the inside was clean, and it smelled good too. Angel was taking care to keep his feet on the paper mat they'd put down. Another text appeared just before he put it in drive. It was Jackie.

Hey. Swing by my place before you leave Eunice tonight.

Before he could even respond, another message appeared

from Lenny, but he didn't even bother reading it. He put it in drive and pulled out, making no effort at all to avoid the puddles. Fuck Lenny. He cranked up the volume and enjoyed the ride.

Curtis was sitting in his car in the gravel lot around the back of Ace Auto when Angel arrived. He pulled up next to him in the Tundra and Curtis walked around the passenger side to open the door. He passed over the original set of keys and the lanyard and then went around to the rear passenger door of Lenny's truck and started fooling around under the seat. Angel didn't know what the fuck he was doing, and he didn't want to know.

"All right," Curtis said. "I'm gonna go back inside and get a battery for my car. Can you still go get that stuff at Walmart after you drop the truck off?"

Angel said, "Yeah, I gotcha covered, boss" and immediately regretted saying it that way, like he was some kinda errand boy.

"I need to add one thing to the list. It's for the library later." Curtis said. "Can you get me a Trapper Keeper?"

Angel screwed up his face. "What the fuck's a Trapper Keeper? And did you say the library?"

JD had been back at the shop for at least thirty minutes, during which time he'd cut two big lines from the sixteenth of cocaine he'd bought at Cecil's Bar, snorting them on the back of the commode. He told himself he had a lot of work to do, but the shop was pretty clean already, thanks to Angel, and he had a hard time deciding what he needed to do next. So he decided to go get some beer.

When he came back from the drive-through at the Daiquiri Hut, JD worked through the first couple of beers and imagined his little tattoo shop, clean now but a long way from ideal, exactly the way he wanted it. He could see it all: the customer lounge area, paint on the walls, merchandise in the case that would separate the tattoo area from where the customers would hang. He grabbed his sketchbook and did three pages in quick succession, showing the room from different angles, focusing on certain parts. Raw as he was this morning, he'd woken up with a perfect vision of the shop in his head. The drawings didn't take him long because the images were already with him. It was just a matter of transcribing what he saw.

Drawing it was easy but finding the money to make it happen was another thing entirely. He'd be lucky if he could finish raising the thousand bucks for the inspector without asking his brother, or maybe Curtis or somebody else to make up the difference. He knew it was expensive opening a place, but still he'd been surprised at how quickly everything added up.

With all the excitement over the last week, he'd neglected to place his inventory order. He had five-hundred-something dollars' worth of basics sitting in his cart on the website that he absolutely needed by next Friday. It was another expense in the back of his mind when he was talking to his brother this morning, but he couldn't bring himself to mention it. He told himself he still had time, which he did. But not much.

JD took another pull from his beer and tried to stay positive. He would make it happen. And really it was just a cash-flow problem. The cash wasn't flowing because he wasn't tattooing. Aside from the one job he'd done for Tac, the cop, at his house, he hadn't made any money since he got to Eunice. Fuck it, he thought. He'd find a way to make it work. The first priority was to make sure he could legally open the shop. Anything beyond that could wait.

He'd just build up slowly, one job at a time. And wasn't that the best kind of origin story anyway? The one where the hero moves back to his hometown with just a handful of greenbacks and his gear and builds something great, from scratch. That was gonna be Black Jack Tattoo. He could see himself in the perfect shop he had sketched, telling a customer as he pulled a perfect line on her hip how he'd started out with a single workstation, with folding chairs and milk crates for a waiting room.

It was the stuff of legends, and he was building it one step at a time. That was it. He repeated the phrase to himself. *One step at a time.* That sounded good. JD stared at his pride and joy, the black Snap-On tool chest that housed everything he needed to produce the baddest-ass body art east of the Sabine River. He walked to the computer and put on some Elvis. The early, real rockabilly shit. The original badass from Tupelo doing his thing at Sun Records. It always made JD feel good.

He started organizing his inks. He had enough, just with what he had in his toolbox, to last at least a couple days. He could probably cut his order down to two hundred bucks if he needed to. The phrase *two steps back* interrupted his stream of consciousness, rebounding from the walls of his psyche, coming back at him. *One step forward, two steps back.*

He worked to push his anxiety back into the box where it lived in his mind. The coke was only a hundred and fifty bucks, and half of it was for Curtis, he thought, trying to convince himself. It wasn't for him. It was for *them.* So they could stay up most of the night and go over the details of whatever plan Curtis was cooking up, to plot out the moves. Plus, the coke was the fuel JD needed to get his shit done. He would make his half last until the grand reopening. Then he would taper off. It wasn't a physical problem; it was just a money problem. But you had to spend money to make money. Dammit! Why the fuck did he buy so much!

He had a sudden urge to talk to Sadie. It was amazing how good she looked, maybe even better than in high school. And it wasn't just that time had added shape to her skinny frame. Or, it wasn't *just* that, at least. She was amazing. So at ease with everything, so quick to smile and laugh, even with her brother's death and now her mom in decline. He wanted to text her. But there was a good chance she would be sleeping and he didn't want to wake her up. The note he left would be enough. She would call when she was ready. Meanwhile, he would get his station fixed up and fill up on a dose of cool from the King.

He needed to talk to Angel, too. The man did him wrong, for sure. Call it what you will, but to his mind it was a betrayal, the way Angel moved those steroids in and out of that 2nd Street shop, yanking his chain. But JD had fucked up, too. You didn't go volunteering information like that to another man's woman. And now he at least owed Angel a heads-up. But he was busy running the key operation with Curtis, so again, he didn't want to reach out at the wrong time and fuck anything up. Same thing with Curtis. His hands were tied, so he cracked another beer and cut another line on top of the toilet.

Curtis was standing at the door with the EverReady on his back, holding a twelve-pack of fizzy water when JD emerged from the tiny bathroom. He could hear Elvis through the door—

one of the real early ones, "Mystery Train" maybe—and he admired the way JD carried himself with a similar kind of swagger as he approached. He studied JD's face. Curtis couldn't tell how wired he was because JD was cool like that, but he'd been leaning over the toilet and his pants were up, so obviously there was at least one line down.

"Shit, bubba, I thought you brought beer!" JD called over the music, grabbing the generic brand of lime seltzer Curtis had been lucky to find at Winn-Dixie. Curtis set down the EverReady in the waiting area and dove into it, pulling out a small Ziplock bag with individual blister packs of various kinds of over-the-counter pills.

"It would've been easier to find beer at the Winn-Dixie. Trust me." Curtis said, fishing out a pack of Vivarin tablets. He held them up. "Want some?" he asked, knowing damn well what JD would do next.

"Shit, bruh! You don't need *that*." JD said. "I picked us up two grams of the good shit! Lemme cut you one." Curtis avoided eye contact, grabbing the power cord from his pack and plugging it into the wall. "Maybe in a little bit, bubba," he said, eyes on his computer, disappointed he lacked the courage at that moment to say something about the blow, unwilling to walk through the opening he'd created. "I still gotta go to the library later on."

"The library? You mean the Eunice Public Library?"

"Yeah," Curtis said, smiling. "Angel's buying me a new Trapper Keeper as we speak. I'm gonna cruise over there later and let Mr. Able, the librarian I kinda met there earlier today, think I'm a grad student. You know, working on a research project. And then after that, I think I'm gonna go break into Lenny Prichard's house."

"Maaaan," JD said, drawing it out for comic effect. "Angel wouldn't know a Trapper Keeper from a—wait, what now?"

There was a particular smell to the old Crown Vic that Tac used (it had been his work car since he made detective) thanks to a scent called Black Ice and probably a decade or two of fat Eunice cops farting into the seat. It wasn't the kind of thing you wanted to smell in your house or even in your own car, but there was something about the scent of this particular car that just made him feel like a cop. It was a powerful, sort of musky smell. It was hard to explain. Stupid, really. But that didn't matter because he'd never bother trying to explain it to anyone. He wasn't crazy. The thing about Tac, he was smart, cerebral even. But unlike a lot of other smart people who tended to let their mouths get them into trouble, he understood that talk is cheap. Especially in the police force.

The Black Ice air freshener was made by the same company that made the little green trees that everybody pretty much grew up with, but the only place in town where you could get Black Ice was the Squeaky Kleenz. It was the strangest thing. You couldn't get it anywhere else. Tac knew because he had checked. All American Car Wash didn't have it. The 7-Eleven over by Eunice High School on the west side of town didn't have it. The tobacco emporium on the corner of 190 and Highway 13 didn't have it. The RaceWay didn't have it. The little tobacco store that just opened up in the Old East Shopping Center where Kluckie's Fried Chicken and Sugar Ray's Bakery was didn't have it. They all had the green trees, but not the black ones. He assumed it was a race thing.

The heavy rain earlier had cleaned the streets and the air felt fresh and cold. His Monster energy drink tasted good. He had the back windows down and there was a satisfying sound of the tires on the wet street. Tac didn't like putting the driver's side window down because it made him too easy to recognize. It was just a good safety practice. This was another one of those things he'd never bother to articulate, but if he ever did have the conversation with another cop, he'd make the point that just because you worked in a small town didn't mean you sacrificed operational security. Tac wasn't one to let his guard down.

Lenny Prichard's big Tundra, the new one with the "Sun-*N*-1" vanity plates, wasn't in the parking lot of the tanning place with the big mural when Tac drove by. So he made a block, circled around and scoped the place out again, taking note of the cars in the gravel lot. A Ford Expedition, a little Nissan he'd seen around, and a blue Ford Focus in the back that probably belonged to somebody who worked there. There were a handful of cars parked out front of the Sun-*N*-Sports compound when he drove by, and for a moment he thought about going inside to browse around, but he was already starting to feel silly about what he was up to. Which was nothing. He was just driving around.

He *did* want to cruise by the 2nd Street property before he went back to the station, so he took a right into the little downtown area. He slowed to a crawl once he crossed Walnut Street, glancing west towards Rudy's Cafe and Cajun Customs, with that ugly-ass warehouse glommed onto the original brick storefront like an afterthought. On his left, there was a new fancy coffee place and despite the cold, there were people sitting at the wrought iron tables they must've wiped down after the rain. The old flower shop that Lenny had supposedly rented to JD was next to the Liberty. Tac stopped and watched it for maybe sixty seconds, until he noticed a little black SUV—a KIA, it looked like—start to meander down the winding street, coming up behind him.

Lenny's place was out off of Highway 13. From the map, it looked like there was a pretty long driveway to the residence, maybe a quarter mile or so, but he'd at least go as far as the main road and see what he could see. But that was for later. He turned east on 190 thinking he'd make his way to the Old East to check out JD's new tattoo shop. Curtis wanted him to stop in the evening, so they could talk and maybe have a few beers.

Squeaky Kleenz was set back off the road about a block, and he was almost past the turn when he decided to swing by and get another Black Ice air freshener. The empty parking lot was filled with a network of little puddles that looked to Tac like a cratered-out bomb site in miniature. He pulled up outside the little storefront they had and he wasn't disappointed that the young, attractive girl with the braids was working the register today. She smelled and shined of cocoa butter.

"Hey Officer Tac, how ya doing?" she asked, not quite flirting, but way friendlier than most customers got. "You here for your Black Ice or you want a wash too?"

"Actually Patience, it's *Detective* Tac," he was saying, and it was something of a minor miracle he even noticed the big black Toyota Tundra splashing through the parking lot, but he did and he turned just in time to read the rear plate as the truck pulled onto the highway. He extracted a five-dollar bill from his wallet and put it on the counter.

"Say, Patience. Who was that in the black Tundra? Was it Lenny Prichard?"

"Lenny Prichard? Shit. That don't sound like any of our regulars," the clerk said. She paused for a moment, then continued when she realized from Tac's look that she hadn't actually answered his question. "What's his name. I think he go by Angel. Yeah, Angel." Tac was inclined to get in the Crown Vic and follow, but he had a pretty good idea what was going on, so he hung in a little longer with Patience.

"Do you think maybe you could check? See if you have his last name?" Tac's boyish looks and his blue eyes did their work on Patience.

"Anything for you, *Detective* Tac." And when she turned to push through the swinging door behind her into the car wash bay, Tac only felt slightly creepy for admiring the cut of her jeans as she sauntered away. She returned less than a minute later and, once she got back to the counter, paused for a beat before she spoke to Tac in an officious, playful voice "I'm sorry Officer—I mean *Detective* Tac—but we don't know Angel's last name. He don't come in here that much." Patience twirled a braid around her finger, "I wish I could do more for you," she said, the unspoken end of her sentence redolent with sexual tension, real or not.

Tac took the Black Ice from her hand, forced himself to offer a simple thank you, and made his way to the Crown Vic. He thought of the blue Ford Focus parked in the back of Sun-*N*-Tans. Somebody was washing Lenny's truck for him. The next image that popped into his mind was the tires splashing through the parking lot and then he thought about the Black Ice. Maybe Lenny Prichard liked the smell of Black Ice too. Maybe he should've asked Patience that question.

He decided to take Park Avenue to Sun-*N*-Tans since it ran parallel to Highway 190 and that way he could come up from behind the building and easily stake out the parking lot. When he pulled the Crown Vic to the side of the little street with a good view of a parking lot a block away, he thought maybe it would have been better to just follow the guy. But then he wouldn't have been able to use his field glasses. Which he pulled from a little black canvas bag and trained on the Ford Focus that was still in the lot. He noticed the "Black Jack Tattoo" sticker on the bumper right away.

Curtis had spent about forty minutes methodically walking JD through everything that had happened that morning, punctuating his account with his analysis of various pieces and asking questions of JD to make sure he understood everything in context. JD grew increasingly agitated as he came to understand the full scope of what Curtis had in mind. His frequent trips to the bathroom didn't help matters.

"I appreciate the imagination, bubba," JD had said. "But I can't be starting feuds with anybody, much less that asshole!" Curtis, the analyst, had heard enough people claim that Lenny Prichard was dangerous to realize there was risk here. But Curtis, the operator with the chip on his shoulder, didn't understand why everyone seemed to dance around this dude. He tried to walk the line.

"Yes, I get it," he'd said, maybe too defensively. "The Prichard family's connected. I understand, believe me. I mean, shit, at least three people have already told me that and I've only been here twenty-four hours. And anyway, I felt it for myself this morning. I swear everybody in Rudy's went silent when I mentioned the name. It was like time stopped."

"Well, there you go!" JD had said, triumphant, as if the discussion were over. They were silent for a moment, JD clearly ready to move on.

"But . . . fuck it," Curtis said finally. "He's just a man. He's not even a man. He's a little boy."

"Goddammit, Laroux!" JD railed. "It's over! I'm in the clear. I have a shop to open!"

"Right!" Curtis stood up. "You have to open the first tattoo shop in the history of Eunice. You *have* to do that." He looked around. "And brother, you have a shitload of work to do. You have a fucking mountain to climb. Paperwork. Supplies. Furniture. Advertising. You have to train an apprentice . . ." Curtis pointed to the window. "You have to finish the sign."

"Okay, stop," JD said. "You're starting to depress me."

"I'm trying to make you angry," Curtis said, edging closer. "You're trying to do a historic thing, a righteous thing, and your back is to the fucking wall. And what does this motherfucker Prichard do? He tries to cut your legs out from under you?" What had started as affected anger had become real, full-fledged vitriol. Curtis ground his teeth, his knuckles gone white. "Listen to what I'm telling you. *Fuck, - No.* He *will not* get away with it."

JD laughed in the way some people do when they're surprised by a sudden outburst of emotion. Curtis, meanwhile, was breathing deeply, resolved.

"I hear you, bruh," JD said. "And I appreciate it. But we

don't want to mess with this dude." Curtis pulled the duplicate keys from his pocket and started fingering them. He put them away and sat back down at his computer, pulling up the map layers he'd already added with the probable locations the keys went with, and with Lenny's truck, now pinging nicely with the new RFID tracker.

"You got it wrong," Curtis said, staring up at JD. "It's not us that need to be afraid. Lenny's hanging out there, sawing on the wrong side of the branch and he doesn't even know it." JD started to interrupt but Curtis held him off. "No, listen for one minute, cause I'm almost done selling you on this and I'm ready to lay out the plan, and after that I have one important question to ask you."

"Jesus Christ, Laroux!" JD erupted again. "Since when did you go all Rambo?"

Curtis pressed ahead. "Lenny doesn't know I'm in town. And he doesn't have a clue what I do—neither do you, by the way. So we have the element of surprise. We also have a second package of steroids that *nobody else* knows is in play. We have RFID trackers on both boxes of steroids." He turned the laptop towards JD so he could see the map layers with the blinking lights. He pointed to a dot labeled "Pkg. 1" still sitting in the shop at 2nd Street. "And you see this one, right here in the parking lot"—he pointed to Pkg. 2 on the screen— "the second one's in the trunk of my car.'" Curtis looked up at JD. His expression was hard to read.

Curtis activated the two additional layers on his map. "And here, see this one. That's Angel. Looks like he's at Walmart now. And this one . . .do you recognize this spot, where the 'LP' is?" JD bent over and squinted at the screen. "That's

Lenny's truck, parked behind his lame-ass tanning salon where he spies on girls."

"Wait. So what are we looking at?" JD asked.

"I put another tracker in his truck. It's like the other ones. My friend in New Orleans made it; he's a genius. Totally fucking crazy, but a genius. He's like you, except with electronics instead of ink." Curtis smiled, continued. "It has extra battery power and a strong ass signal. It'll be active for probably four days. Maybe more. So, we have live tracking on both the packages of steroids, and we have live tracking on Lenny's whereabouts. We also have the ear of local law enforcement—Tac's coming over later, by the way. And now, we have the keys to at least his house, the tanning salon, and the real estate office."

JD stared at him for a long moment, at a loss for words.

"I have *all* the cards," Curtis said, waiting for that to sink in. "*And* I have a plan," he continued, "that protects you. Remember, you turned in the keys to 2nd Street and the steroids are there. You're in the clear. What I want you to do now is call Lenny. To bury the hatchet. Tell him you turned over the keys to Jackie, the place is spic and span, with everything there. It's too bad the location didn't work out, but no hard feelings." JD was suddenly animated again, preparing to protest. "And then I want you to offer him a free tattoo, or at least a discount."

"You have *got* to be fucking kidding me!"

"Relax," Curtis said. "No way he's gonna take you up on it. I'm pretty sure he hates your guts. But you offer it to him and he gets the feeling he won. You don't have to kiss his ass or anything. Just give him the sense that you wanna make sure everything's cool. No hard feelings. And he'll perceive that as victory."

After a long pause, JD spoke. "Is that the thing you wanted to ask me?" Curtis summoned his strength, kept his eyes locked on his friend.

"No," he said, pointing to the bathroom. "What I want to ask you is this. Go in there and do one more line, if you need it. And then lock the rest of it up. Somewhere, anywhere. Until all this shit is said and done."

JD's eyes narrowed and Curtis could see a flash of anger pass over him. "You're seriously gonna go all intervention on me now, in this moment? I got this shit for you!"

Curtis was suddenly exhausted. He had an impulse to pull another Red Bull from the EverReady.

"It's not about you, bubba. It's about me," he said. "I'm trampling over all kinds of ethics and security rules here."

"What are you talking about, Laroux?" JD barked. Curtis leveled his gaze.

"I'm talking about my career. My oath. I'm a sworn government officer, but I been breaking rules left and right since we first talked two weeks ago. Accessed a DEA database—enough to get me fired. Bought illegal drugs on the internet—fired, and jailed. Probably bought a stolen car, planted illegal surveillance equipment, and I haven't even gotten to the breaking and entering yet!

So, I guess what I'm trying to say is, you know, 'buy the ticket, take the ride' . . . I'm down. I *want* to do this for you, not just for you, but for me. But we've got to be doing this for good reasons. I need to stay on the right side of my conscience. And I can't afford any more peaks and valleys . . . *and* I need you, bubba. Let's do this right."

"Let me get this straight," JD said. "I gotta stop doing the blow I bought for you so you can keep your conscience clean?"

Curtis smiled. "You always had a way with words," he said. JD didn't say anything more, and Curtis was still having trouble reading him. He was fishing the baggie from his front pocket. You could tell from the residue on the inside of the bag how much JD had already used. He tossed it on the keyboard of Curtis's laptop. "Here, take it."

Curtis just looked at it. An instant later JD said "No, you know what? Fuck it." grabbing up the bag and walking to the bathroom. He flipped open the lid with his boot, opened the baggie, dipped his pinkie in it, and brought a trace amount to his tongue, then he emptied the cocaine into the toilet. Curtis watched as he unzipped his pants, whipped out his dick, and took a long, beer-fueled piss. After, he reached over to flush the toilet.

Curtis took all this with a mix of skepticism, awe, and humor. Much later, when he replayed this moment in his head, the thing that stood out the most was that JD never once looked at him. To Curtis, JD had the look of a man lost in the ritual of praying. Whether it was absolution or strength or something else JD was trying to conjure was an open question.

The sound of a ringing telephone broke the spell. Curtis had not even noticed the molded plastic phone cradled in its base on the floor at the back of the shop, another relic of the past. JD had been stepping out of the bathroom when the sound erupted near him and he jumped like it might've been a wild animal. On the second ring, JD glanced at Curtis, still sitting at his computer at the far end of the shop, and tried out a wry smile. "Look at that! Our first customer!" He picked up the receiver and with more gusto and sweetness than Curtis might've thought possible said "Black Jack Tattoo. Can I help you?" An instant later he was beaming.

"Sadie? Hey! Shit girl, I didn't even think you had this number!"

Curtis tried to get back to his work, even though he was tired as fuck. There was gonna have to be some kind of power nap in his near future. Maybe he should've just done a line after all, before JD flushed the coke.

He'd told JD he had a plan, which really was a pretty generous characterization. What he had was an outcome he wanted to achieve. That and pieces and parts he had to work with. How to put it all together was still an open question. He sat back in the uncomfortable folding chair and began to map things out, brainstorming. Lenny. Two packages. Keys to five possible locations. A police officer. Angel. The library. The library! He needed to get his camera in place right away. He texted Angel from the laptop to ask him to hurry.

JD hung up the phone, his whole disposition elevated by the call. "She wants me to go have dinner with her and her mom," he said, beaming. "This is God rewarding me. I can feel it."

"Yes," Curtis said. "I've heard that he rewards the righteous."

"What do you know about righteous?" JD said. "You fucking criminal."

Episode Six
Holding all the Cards

━━━━━ ❀ ━━━━━

With real-time intelligence in place and the element of surprise in his favor, Curtis is ready to go on the offensive, but JD isn't so sure. And as Sadie gets more involved, emotions run high.

"You'd be surprised at the kind of trouble you can find in Eunice . . . if you just know where to look." — Mr. Able

Angel left a ten and a five on the seat of Lenny's truck when he parked it at Sun-*N*-Tans next to his shitty little Ford Focus that technically belonged to his sister. It was a silly matter of pride, but he wasn't about to take anything extra from Lenny. When he pulled open the door to the trailer and went right instead of left, Britney called to him from the reception desk.

"I need to check if he wants to see you!" she called to his back as he walked down the hall. Angel didn't hear her. He was in his pre-stage mode, in the zone and focusing on the first thirty seconds of his performance, knowing from experience, plus what Jackie told him, that if he could get the opening lines right, the rest would flow naturally. He knocked at the closed door to Lenny's office—he wasn't just gonna bust in the man's office—but he didn't really wait for permission before he opened the door a crack and said, "Lenny, I need to holla at you." Lenny looked up and Angel was just glad the dude wasn't in there jerking off or something.

Lenny was already drinking beer, which Angel wasn't sure was a good sign or not. He waved Angel in, and Angel held the keys out by the blue lanyard and for Lenny to grab them.

"You mind if I sit?" Angel asked, again not exactly waiting for permission. Lenny paused for a beat to consider the question, ever the big man behind his desk. Even though Angel was already sitting.

"A lotta good it did me to wash it," Lenny said. Angel thought about saying something smart, but instead, he resisted.

"Yeah, to tell the truth I think it already has some mud on it from the drive over." He just let that hang in the air for a second.

"You want a beer?" Lenny asked. He was acting weird. Nice, even. Angel thought about it.

"No, but I'd take a water if you got it," he said. He was genuinely surprised when Lenny swiveled around in his chair and came up with a bottle of water from the little fridge he kept behind his desk. Angel cracked it and drank half of it down, reveling in the small pleasure of having the man wait for him. As he screwed the cap on the flimsy plastic bottle, he was about to start saying his piece when Lenny beat him to the punch.

"Your girlfriend was just here," he said. Angel didn't quite know what to make of that.

"Who you mean, Jackie?" he asked. Lenny gave him a

strange look. Protective. Offended. Something.

"Yeah, Jackie. Who else?" Lenny said, and there was a little grit in his voice. Angel pushed some air through his teeth and looked around the office.

"Shit, bruh. I don't know if I'd call her a girlfriend. That don't sound like the right word for a woman like Jackie. She was here?"

"Yeah. Looking for you."

"Why?"

"I guess your new *padna* JD Dugas said something to her about how you work for me." Lennie said, even keel. Angel sat there and took the charge. It stung, but he tried not to show it. Jackie was gonna be pissed. What was JD doing talking to Jackie? Then he remembered Curtis saying how he should go turn in the keys at the real estate office and get a receipt and stuff, giving too many instructions the way he liked to do. Probably Jackie tricked JD into saying something. She was crafty that way. That or maybe it was retribution. Which didn't seem like JD.

Lenny seemed to be watching Angel for some kind of reaction that wasn't gonna come. Angel glanced down at the design on his hand he'd been scribbling with a ballpoint pen that afternoon while Curtis talked at him, and he realized two things at once. When he got back to the shop he'd ask JD to ink the design on him permanently, maybe let Angel pull a couple lines himself, just to get the feel. The second thing was the way Lenny's tone changed at the mention of JD. It was like a key change in a song. The conversation was moving in a new direction now, and that was good, 'cause that's where Angel needed to go anyway.

"Yeah, so, speaking of. I went ahead and put that package back at 2nd Street. It's all there, just like before." Angel fished the single key from his pocket and placed it on Lenny's desk. Then he sat back and glanced up at Lenny, just a glance, before turning his attention back to the design on his hand instead. No need to poke the bear. Lenny's hands came down on his desk, two sledgehammers making the key jump, and Angel couldn't help but flinch. "Shit!," he protested. "Yeah, bruh, I needed to put it back! I couldn't be driving around with that shit in my trunk."

"Who told you to do that?" Lenny demanded. He wasn't yelling, exactly.

"Nobody," Angel said, holding his ground. "Just like nobody told me to pull the stuff outta there in the first place. I just did what I thought had to be done." Angel took a quick mental picture of Lenny's face before he looked back down at his hand, and when he studied the image in his mind it made him very nervous. A kind of chill came over him. It was time to get out of there. "So, I just wanted to come by and let you know where it's at." He hesitated. "And to say thanks, you know. For throwing some work my way over the last however long it's been."

Lenny stood up from his desk and Angel reflexively pushed back in his chair and stood up too. But the little surge of anger had spiked and receded. Lenny pivoted to grab another Michelob Ultra from the little fridge and there was definitely no offering one to Angel now. He twisted the top and took a few big gulps while Angel lurched forward with what he had to say. "I got a little saved up now, so I'm gonna go learn to do tattoos.

At Black Jack's, you know. Jackie hooked me up."

"So, you're quitting? To go work with the greaseball JD Dugas?" It wasn't a question, the way Lenny phrased it.

"He's actually a real good dude," Angel said. "The man's from the heart. He's gonna give people Lafayette quality tattoos at Eunice prices." Lenny just laughed, sarcastic, and Angel was a little embarrassed at how eager he sounded. Anyway, he was done. There was just one more step, and he'd maybe spent more time thinking about this than he needed to. "Anyway," Angel said, and extended his arm for a fist bump. A traditional handshake was somehow too respectful to a man who didn't deserve it, he'd decided. "I just wanted to say thanks, you know. I appreciate you." Lenny stared at Angel's outstretched fist for an instant, then he looked up and Angel had the feeling there was something trapped inside of Lenny when he brought his hand up and barely made contact, like the man couldn't trust himself to use the right amount of force.

The dude in the baggy pants driving the Ford Focus emerged from Sun-*N*-Tans maybe ten minutes after Tac started his stakeout. He was thankful for the Steiner ShadowQuest binoculars his old lady had bought him for Christmas. It would've been hard to lock in on the kid's face with the shit the EPD issued. He was wearing a flat brim ball cap with a hoodie pulled over it, but Tac got a good look as the guy paused halfway across the gravel lot to light a cigarette. He was dark. Mexican maybe, or black. Tac picked up a tattoo on the left hand, right in the webbing between thumb and forefinger.

He'd already run the plates. The car was registered to Isabel Martinez Ocasio-Castille, who it felt like had twelve more names after that. She lived in Opelousas, and Tac guessed she would probably end up being the sister. She was too young to be his mom. He hadn't had time to look up Angel Martinez, Ocasio, or Castille, which, if Patience at the car wash was right, was this dude's name. There was time for all that later. For now, he just wanted to get a look at the guy running errands for Lenny Prichard. Tac's first impression was that something was definitely wrong with this picture.

The Eunice that he'd grown up in was unabashedly racist. There was a natural, self-segregation that happened, at least among blacks and whites. You went to separate churches, lived in separate parts of town, lived separate lives. Hell, even in school where everybody was thrown together, people kept to their own—in the cafeteria, voting for class president, whatever. Back in the day, there was no way in hell a guy like Ely Prichard would've been turning over the keys to his Cadillac to a Mexican dude to drive away with. Shit like that just didn't happen. But here you had his nephew doing exactly that.

So okay, Tac played the devil's advocate in his head. Lenny's a different animal. He doesn't see color. He's enlightened, modern. Tac sat with that idea while he watched the kid—he was maybe twenty-five—stop halfway to his car to light a cigarette. There was a certain swagger to him, Tac could see. He was a good-looking kid, actually. Had a bone structure his wife would almost certainly notice.

Tac followed him to Walmart and sat in the parking lot and, while the kid was inside, did some research on his mobile data unit that he hadn't had time to do earlier, taking notes. Patience had been right; the dude's name was Angel. He made a mental note to tell her thanks next time he was at the car wash, and he couldn't help but dwell on the image of her braids sweeping across her back, a few inches above her curvy ass. Aside from a misdemeanor for shoplifting when he was eighteen, Angel's record was clean. There was a mugshot with the records, but Tac didn't really need it. He never really forgot a face. The haircuts changed. The cheeks and the neck grew fatter and softer with age, but the core of the eyes and nose and mouth never changed, and that's what Tac saw. He'd been training himself since junior high.

It was around five that afternoon when Curtis walked back into the Eunice Public Library, his new zippered D-ring binder tucked under his arm and the EverReady on his back. He regretted that the damn pack was so bulky. It didn't look quite right in the library (unless you were gonna be camping on the roof) but there was nothing to be done about it. Curtis needed the laptop and he liked having the variety of emergency essential tools—the pistol among them—just in case. Though if it turned out he needed the gun here, he was definitely doing something wrong.

The binder was more than a prop; it contained all the tools and materials he would need to mount his camera on the brick exterior of the library. The place was even quieter than it had been that morning. The information desk was off to the left, but he decided to make a circuit through the stacks on the right side first. He strolled through, casual. Just some college student getting the feel for the place. Aside from a young mother and her son hunched over a book, the place was empty.

Curtis was making his way towards the stairs to recon the second level when Mr. Able rounded the corner. He smiled when he saw Curtis standing at the foot of the stairs. "You made it!" the old volunteer called out, maybe a bit too loud.

"Just barely," Curtis replied. "I didn't want to miss the chance to do a little research while I'm in town." He watched Mr. Able do a quick deliberation on where he wanted to take the discussion next. Curtis sensed he was more interested in his personal circumstances than any research project, but the elder man stayed on point. Sort of.

"So, what are you interested in?" he asked, and Curtis felt sure he'd made a point of phrasing the question in an open-ended way.

"Well, for starters, that statue out front is intriguing. So, Eunice was the wife of the man who founded the town, right? She was C.C. Duson's wife?" Mr. Able smiled. He was a spry old man, probably pushing eighty. Well-dressed, bright-eyed, and eager for conversation. Even at the end of the day.

"Oh, that's a *good* story," he said, touching Curtis on the elbow and gently moving him towards the tiny elevator, just past the base of the stairs. He pressed the button and waited for the ding and the doors to open before he continued. Curtis felt like he was back in the little bathroom across the street at the old flower shop. He couldn't help but worry about getting stuck in the tiny, upright coffin of the elevator. Scanning for the safety information, he noted with concern that the maximum weight capacity was just five hundred pounds. Jesus, he thought. That's just two average-sized Cajuns.

Mr. Able continued. "You see, C.C. Duson, as you say, is the businessman who founded Eunice. Him and his brother, actually. Well, C.C. was married to his first wife, but he fell in love with a local woman named Eunice and they began a *torrid* affair. Now, mind you, this would have been right around the turn of the century. I don't know precisely how they met, but I'm sure it was quite a scandal." He gave Curtis a conspiratorial look. When they arrived at the second floor and stepped off the elevator, Mr. Able continued his oral report.

"The Duson brothers had already incorporated the town of Crowley, and Eunice was their next project to the north." Curtis nodded along, familiar with the limited details Mr. Able was offering in part because he'd read the Wikipedia article on Eunice that afternoon at the tattoo shop, and because he'd heard the story growing up. Mr. Able had read the same article, it sounded like. "Well, C.C. decided to *divorce* his first wife, *marry* his mistress, Eunice, and *name* the town after her!" Mr. Able laughed, tickled by the scandal. "So, our town is named after the *other* woman! You can only imagine how such a thing was received back then."

There was a definite homosexual undercurrent to the way Mr. Able carried himself, and Curtis admired the man's courage for it. Whether he was actually gay or not, all you needed to do was land a bit on the feminine side in a town like Eunice and that was enough to make life very complicated. To actually be a gay man, or worse, to be a gay kid in Eunice, was a herculean task. It must have been tough.

"Can I ask, Mr. Able, what profession did you retire from?" Curtis asked.

"I was a florist. For 45 years, if you can believe it." Mr. Able said with pride.

"Wow! What an achievement," Curtis said. "You weren't in

the shop across the street, by any chance? I understand it used to be a flower shop."

"It was indeed. Floyd's Flowers. A wonderful little shop. Great location, too. But no, I wasn't there. And I didn't own anything. I'm just an old itinerant florist." He smiled broadly at Curtis. "I worked in Opelousas, Rayne, Kinder, and I finished my career here at the Eunice Flower Shop over on Laurel."

"And you're a volunteer here now?"

"Well, you gotta stay busy somehow." Mr. Able smiled again, indulging perhaps in a moment of nostalgia. "Well, here we are. Why don't you find a table and I'll pull a few things for you. Then you can tell me more about your project."

Curtis took the table nearest the window and put his binder with the tools on the table. Then he pulled out the flip phone, shielding it with his body, typed 666 and hit send on the prearranged code to JD. A minute later, as Mr. Able was still looking through the stacks on the second floor, Curtis heard the first distant ring of the telephone from the information desk downstairs. It was JD calling to ask if the library carried popular DVDs and what their policy on borrowing them was. JD could ask questions on the subject for hours if he needed to, but they'd agreed on a ten-minute minimum. Curtis checked his watch as Mr. Able rode the elevator to the first floor to take the call.

He didn't waste time getting to work. Curt pulled a pair of latex gloves from his pocket, put them on, and unzipped the binder. The tools for this operation were simple: a big-ass tube of Gorilla brand epoxy, a rag, some duct tape, and one of Jacque's flexible cameras with on-board power and transmitter. He opened the window quickly and, after checking for activity in the library and the street, poked his head out to eyeball the exact spot on his right where he would mount the camera. The brick exterior was damp to the touch, but it would have to do. He wiped at the area for a couple seconds with the rag then tucked it in his back pocket. He was already into his third minute.

The epoxy was in a syringe-type applicator, and he'd already prepped it in the Mazda, so it was just a matter of leaning out the window and pressing out a big glob of it on the wall. When he was done, he dropped the applicator in the zip binder and spent ten seconds watching and listening inside the library. He couldn't hear Mr. Able talking on the phone, but it was a library after all.

He didn't like turning his back to the interior of the library, but the next step was critical. Jacque had given him two of these little Wi-Fi cameras. They were simple devices: a bulb-like camera lens on the front with a hard plastic shell, a flexible shaft, and a heavy-duty spring clip on the end. The guts of the thing were encased in the plastic shell behind the bulb. He had to point the camera so it centered on the door of the old flower shop but hopefully kept the corner of 2nd and Park Avenue in view. Shooting from the hip, he aimed the rounded front of the little camera and smushed the spring clip into the goop on the wall.

The epoxy instructions said to apply pressure for five minutes, but he probably didn't have that much time. He removed his left hand from the camera, holding it just with his right, and checked his watch. Six minutes had elapsed. Still facing out the window, he got his left hand in position again on the base of the camera and slid his right hand away so he could turn his body to face the inside of the library. He heard the phone ring downstairs, and it seemed like it got louder with each successive ring. An instant later the flip phone in his pocket was vibrating, but the damn thing was on his left side so he couldn't reach around to get into it with his right. The latex glove he was wearing made it near impossible.

He tried not to panic, but it was difficult not to. He was totally exposed and awkward-looking in that moment, his back to the open window with his left hand outside, straining to apply pressure while he reached around with his gloved right hand to fish the phone out of his pocket. He heard the elevator *ding* just then, and all Curtis could do was count *one, two, three* for a couple extra seconds of pressure on the camera before he released it just as Mr. Able came into view. He forced himself to smile as he sank into the nearest chair at the table, conscious of his latex-gloved hands and doing his best to keep them low, out of sight as Mr. Able approached.

He worked the gloves off under the table. Mr. Able didn't seem to notice. He just leaned over the table to tell Curtis how some people could just go on and on like everybody in the world was just waiting around to tell them if they had *The Walking Dead* on DVD, and if it was Blu-ray and how many seasons did they have? Mr. Able noticed the open window then, and he quickly walked over to pull it shut. As he was doing so it must have occurred to him that Curtis opened it because he stopped and asked "Sorry, did you want this open?"

JD, meanwhile, was leaning against the porch railing at Sadie's place, a cigarette clenched between his teeth and both thumbs working his phone.

Sorry, bubba. I couldn't keep the old coot on the phone. He's squirrely. Hope it was enough. Call me when you can.

Sadie had gone inside to check on her mom and JD was enjoying the first little bit of privacy he'd had since driving over before dinner. The street was quiet, clean. It was twilight, and there was a fresh coldness in the air, like the town had been sanitized. At least it felt that way for him. There was something medicinal about the evening. Sadie's call was like divine intervention, or at least damn good luck. But whatever it was, he was here with her now.

With a belly full of rice and gravy with smothered okra and two cold glasses of milk, his body seemed to have already absorbed the remainder of the coke in his system and he was actually feeling good. Which was surprising. No doubt it had everything to do with Sadie, and on some level, it seemed like she understood he was maybe going through something, because there was something extra gentle in how she'd treated him this afternoon. And that was okay. He realized he was more than happy and more than *ready* to leave the speed behind if it meant he could have Sadie instead. Still, he was conscious of what was left in the baggie he'd palmed earlier when he was making a show of dumping it all out for Curtis. He hadn't used any of it.

Maybe Sadie really was the antidote to the chemical dependency he'd been nursing. He'd never put it that way with her, of course, because she was more than some kind of distraction. This was no casual thing for JD. Sadie had been his first love, and the connection they'd established back then still had not eroded. It had just been—suspended. She was still amazing, and though they both had more than a decade of separate experiences under their belts, neither had really changed in any of the fundamental ways that mattered.

As he stood on the porch looking out at the glistening streetscape, JD realized that he totally believed in fate. It was no accident Sadie was back in town. It was no accident she'd decided to call this afternoon, at that moment. He needed her— wanted her to—for sure. But she was vulnerable too. It was heavy shit she was going through now with her mom, all alone. Especially after Remi was killed, and maybe this wasn't luck or karma or whatever bringing them together; maybe it was God, capital G.

It finally occurred to JD in that moment that it wasn't about how Sadie could help him. Maybe this moment was *his* opportunity to be there for Sadie. He was still chewing on this revelation, there in the quiet of the porch, when he felt her arms slip around him from behind. He felt her rest her head against his back, and something about the way she stood there in silence, holding that pose, told him that she was ready to give their relationship another try. They stayed like that for a long moment, silent, just holding on to each other.

At some point later—it might have been five or fifteen minutes, JD had been unwilling to move and break the spell—a white delivery van pulled up to the house. Sadie squeezed him harder when the middle-aged man in dark jeans and a button-up shirt came around the back of the van with a big bouquet of flowers. "What's this?" she said in a tone that JD knew was trouble, because it was clear she thought they were from him. He hoped they were for her mom, but a sinking feeling in his stomach told him otherwise.

Mr. Able seemed to be of two minds, Curtis thought. He was paying more attention to Curtis than necessary—that much was clear. Exactly why was probably open for debate, but Curtis had a clear sense the older man figured he was gay too. Which was totally fine. It wouldn't have been the first time somebody made that assumption.

Or maybe Mr. Able was just kind of bored. That was *definitely* a possibility. Curtis had literally observed just two other patrons in the library. It could've just been good customer service. But whatever the reason for the extra support and attention he was showering on Curtis, it was also getting close to closing time and Mr. Able was clearly anxious to get out of there on time.

There were two stacks of books on the table now, which was impressive considering Curtis had barely elaborated on his supposed thesis, just offering up something vague about learning the "origin stories" of small South Louisiana towns. He'd added "especially along the railroad" for no other reason than it popped into his head at that moment. Curt had pulled a couple of the books from the stack more or less at random and positioned them around the laptop, which he'd pulled out of his EverReady to sync with the camera outside.

Mr. Able appeared and was loitering near the table just as the camera feed came up on the screen and Curtis casually toggled to the notes document he'd started, a simple list of the names of the books on the table. He had typed them up when he first sat down. He was no super-spy, either in real life or on this Louisiana excursion, but if he did have any superpower at all, it might be the ability to type fast. It wasn't really necessary because it was fifteen minutes to six and Mr. Able was clearly more focused on getting out of there than anything else. The elder man politely cleared his throat.

"I hate to interrupt you," he said, and Curtis was already gathering up his things before Mr. Able finished his sentence.

"It's closing time. I understand." Curtis said. He extended his hand and put his second hand on top when they shook. "You've been a big help, Mr. Able. Thank you. Should I reshelve these books before I go?"

"Oh, no," Mr. Able was quick to dissuade him. Curtis assumed because any reshelving at this point would only delay his closing. "Shelbie can do that in the morning." Curtis would've liked to get another peek at the camera outside, to make sure it was holding, but he didn't have a chance. He rode the tiny elevator down with Mr. Able, who locked the library door behind Curt.

When he got back to the Mazda in the little parking lot behind the Liberty Theater for the second time that Wednesday, Curtis realized how tired he was. Running on fumes was the expression, and that was about right. He was still upright thanks to adrenaline, the remnants of this morning's etouffee and eggs, a few handfuls of pecans and raisins, and a shitload of caffeine in multiple forms.

At work, during a crisis or something, he could keep himself alert and productive for at least twenty-four hours, but that was under "normal" conditions. This was a different thing. He couldn't control his food. He couldn't do push-ups on the hour. He probably wasn't drinking enough water. And to top it off, engaging with all these new people was exhausting. In that moment, he again thought of how he could've used the coke JD had flushed after all.

He lowered the front windows of the Mazda to let the cold air energize him as he drove. Once he got to Park Avenue, heading over to Pearl Street, where he'd grown up just a couple blocks from the cluster of ball fields that dominated his childhood, Curtis punched up JD on the flip phone.

"What's up, bubba? You in jail yet?" JD asked. There was a layer of irritation or maybe worry underneath JD's joke. Curtis could hear that something was off, but he pressed ahead.

"No. I'm all clear. The video's set up. I'll show you back at the shop. What time you gonna be there?"

"Shit, bubba." JD protested. "I wasn't planning on going back tonight. I was gonna just hang here with Sadie on the swing." JD looked up at her from the other end of the porch, where he'd moved as a matter of courtesy because he was well aware that when he and Curtis started talking their voices climbed the ladder until they were both practically yelling. Yeah, I was just gonna hang and, you know, profess my love to her."

"Nice," Curtis said. "Well, I hope that cheesy ass line worked for you, bubba. I'm not on speaker, am I?"

"Fuck no," JD said, ignoring the dubious look Sadie was giving him from the swing.

"Seriously," Curtis said. "We really do need to rendezvous back at the shop. For one thing, there's something Angel wants to lay on you."

"Fuck." JD interrupted. "I forgot to tell him I spilled the beans with his old lady."

"I don't think he's too worried about that. He had an idea for a cool way to advertise the shop that he wants to ask you about."

"Oh, shit. That's all I need. What is it?"

"I think he wants to have somebody paint your van. The dude that has that custom shop next on Walnut? Anyway, it doesn't matter. But I *do* think you want to keep him close, at least for a while."

Curtis was cruising slowly around the block that people in Eunice just called "The Ballpark": four baseball diamonds inside a city block in a nice section of town. Curtis had grown up a few blocks over, in a little wooden house on the working-class block of Pearl Street. "Anyway, Tac's gonna swing by later, and I think it would be good if we both talk to him together. He doesn't trust me."

"Because you're a criminal," JD said.

"Says the pot to the kettle. Anyway, so there's that."

"Listen, bubba. You don't want me talking to Tac, because I'm about ready to come clean on all this shit. I shoulda went to the cops in the first place, but I didn't and look where it got me. You're running around pretending to be Jason Bourne and I got a traitor for an apprentice. I got a grand opening next week, and I'm pretty much flat broke. This whole thing's a fucking mess."

Curtis didn't know what to say. There was nothing he *could* say. He parked a couple doors down from the house on Pearl Street and killed the engine. He switched the phone off speaker and held it to his ear, still eyeing his childhood home. The porch light was on. "You there?" JD asked.

"Yeah, I'm here. I just stopped at Pearl Street."

"Oh, shit," JD said. "You going in?"

"Nah. I can't. I'm in New Orleans, remember?"

"Fuck that bubba! Just walk up to that house and give your momma a hug. Now that's a fucking order!"

"And what about Bobby?" Curtis asked, knowing full well he wasn't going to the house.

"Kick him in the nuts," JD said without hesitation.

"And the other thing is, I need you to call Lenny," Curtis said, happy to change the subject. "Tonight. Angel has his number."

"Oh, I got his number," JD said. "It was on the fucking card that came with the flowers he sent to Sadie not twenty minutes ago!" He wanted to look over at her but he couldn't; his jealousy had enraged him and he knew she wouldn't like it. Curtis was busy expressing his surprise on the other end, but JD wasn't listening anymore. His voice lowered to a growl. "If you think I'm gonna go play nice with this muthafucka—"

"So, Lenny's into Sadie?" Curtis said, framing the obvious in the form of a question and forgetting for an instant that JD was still involved in the discussion. The connections in his mind were starting to form. "Ah, that's why he's fucking with you!" he said. It started to make sense.

"Apparently," JD said, and Curtis could hear Sadie then telling JD to put the phone on speaker.

"Hey, Curtis?" she said. "It's Sadie. Since I'm right here and all."

"Yeah, of course," Curtis said. "So, Lenny sent you flowers? Was it the first time?"

"Yeah. First time he sent flowers. But he's been trying to talk to me for a couple weeks. He started stalking me on Facebook, and then we had coffee before I realized he was a creep."

"You didn't know he was a creep?" JD cut in.

"I never knew any of those private school kids," Sadie said, maybe a little defensively.

"Yeah, well," Curtis said. "For what it's worth I can definitely attest to him being a creep." So, listen Sadie, I feel like I got this under control, but I need JD to call Lenny and make nice. About the thing with that certain box of items in the shop on 2nd Street? I'm sure he told you?"

"Okay, enough of this shit." JD cut in. "If you're not gonna go see your momma then just come over here so the three of us can talk this out. Let's just stop talking on the phone like a bunch of fucking teenagers."

"He has a point," Sadie said.

Back at the shop, Angel had the light box, such as it was, mostly assembled. He had originally envisioned something much more substantial, but he didn't have the time or the tools to find plexiglass and start cutting wood and drilling into the cinder block wall to mount it. So he'd done the next best thing. He finished securing the light to the inside of the clear plastic tote he'd found at Walmart with a couple of zip ties, then he worked the cord through the hole he'd made with his knife and lighter. It looked like what it was: just a shallow plastic container, like the kind rich people use to store their winter clothes, with a light inside. But it worked. He had found these foam blocks back deep in the sewing section that fit perfectly inside the container in a way that braced the lid so it didn't give at all. The thing was actually pretty fucking tight . . . for twenty-bucks worth of plastic, foam, and tape. When he was done, he squatted over the box on the floor and tried tracing a piece of flash he'd pulled from one of JD's binders. *Ugly but functional . . . just like ya momma* he said to the empty room and laughed.

Functional, but not funky, he said out loud. So he decided to take it outside and use some of the window paint to dress it up a bit. With his earbuds in and his hood up, he busted out some of the darker paint colors that JD liked but Angel knew wouldn't contrast enough on the window and he used those to give the box some style. It was mostly black and blue, but with some deep swirls of purple and shit and also some little pinhole size gaps of negative space that would probably look cool with light escaping from it. Angel worked quickly, just having fun and enjoying the frictionless way the paint felt with the brush against the plastic. It kind of looked like a Van Gogh. When he was finished, he left it on a milk crate to dry, snapped a picture, and sent it to Jackie.

He knew she was gonna be pissed about his—what would you call it, association?—with Lenny, but at the same time he had the feeling that really she'd be more disappointed than anything. He knew she didn't like her cousin, and so she didn't like the idea of Angel associating with the dude. Especially for any off-the-record stuff. And why should she? Dude was a first-class asshole. But anyway, Jackie wasn't the type of lady to just go flying off the handle about stuff. At least not anymore.

Though obviously he didn't know her back in the day, like when she was just wild and raging against everything—pissed off, the way she told the stories, because she felt trapped in Eunice where nothing interesting ever happened. Why she decided to stay was still kind of a mystery to Angel. Same as it was with JD. Why either one of them would hang around Eunice just baffled him.

No way he wasn't gonna play it that way. This whole state was gonna be just a memory to him in another year. Angel wasn't one to make big plans and shit, but no way was he gonna stick around for too long. He would at least go to Houston. Maybe head back to San Juan and stay with some cousins for a while. There were always plenty of parties and tourists around, ways to make money. But all that was for later. Right now, the thing to do was what he always did. Take it one day at a time and have as much fun as possible along the way. And really, he had always found ways to keep himself entertained and in the company of good times and foxy females. You just had to know where to look, how to be, and who to stay away from.

And right now, thinking about it, things didn't look too bad. He was free of Lenny. He had Jackie. And he had JD to learn from. It kind of just hit him all at once . . . this shit could work! He looked around the clean but sparse shell of a tattoo shop and imagined himself as JD's second. How long would it take him to start doing simple jobs? A month? Two? He could handle that. And he had no problem making himself useful until then. There were all kinds of shit he could do. Hell, he was already doing it!

He knew he should wait to talk to JD first, but he couldn't help himself. He took out his phone and found the number for

Cajun Customs. His cousin Slim owned the place. Well, they weren't really cousins, but both their people were from Puerto Rico and that was cousin enough for them. In a town like Eunice where every Coonass cracker seemed to be related, where you didn't fit in with the whites but at least they didn't treat you like you were black, every hombre was a cousin. It didn't matter if you were from Mexico or Puerto Rico or the Dominican Republic or fucking Peru. If your momma spoke Spanish, then you were a cousin.

Eventually, he got Slim on the phone and it didn't take long for Angel to remind him who he was and establish that he was now at Black Jack Tattoo, which was about to open up in the Old East Shopping Center. That piqued Slim's interest for sure. He was saying "Yeah, bruh. So my boss got this old Astro van, like from the nineties and shit," when a text from JD came in.

Me and Curtis r coming back. u at the shop? I gotta tell u something about Jackie.

Sadie came to the door of the nice little wood frame house with the open porch before Curtis had a chance to knock, and he was confused for a moment because he did recognize her, but his memory of her wasn't distant at all. He had seen her recently.

"Wait," she said, standing in the door. "Were you over by the statue this morning?" It clicked for Curtis then.

"Yeah, I was. And you came running by? Around the statue?" She smiled in an easy way, and Curtis had a flash of intuition that told him she had somehow noticed him checking her out, or maybe she just made that assumption. Standing in the doorway in jeans and a tight black sweater, he was sure she understood the primitive carnal tension between the sexes better than most. Better than he did, at least. In a whisper, Sadie asked him to wait and Curtis summoned every ounce of discipline he could muster to look elsewhere as she walked away.

JD emerged from the house with the look of a new man, but Curtis could see there was something simmering underneath. He was thankful they had a moment to themselves before Sadie came out of the house with a bottle of red wine and three small jelly jars. JD was wearing what looked like new khaki pants and a gray old-school thermal shirt. "It's Sadie's brother's stuff," he said, leaning into Curtis and whispering, "He died in the war." And then in response to the unspoken question, Curtis asked with a raised eyebrow, another whisper. "No, bruh. I just needed a shower so she put my clothes to wash for me." He handed Curtis the little card that had come with the flowers.

Curtis was leaning against the porch railing reading the card when Sadie appeared with the wine. She noticed the card in his hand. JD was sitting on the swing, which didn't face the road but instead looked down the length of the porch. Sadie set the bottle and the glasses on a three-legged stool by the door and sat back on the swing with an exaggerated, luxurious stretch.

"You pour the wine," she said to JD. "I deserve to be pampered," quoting from the card Curtis held in his hand.

Curtis looked down at the card again. He spoke the second line aloud. "Let's go on a real date soon." It was signed "Lenny," with a 337 phone number written underneath. JD had slowly extracted himself from the porch swing, and Sadie put a socked foot on his backside to give him a gentle push. Curtis was watching JD carefully, but trying not to let on. He could see that JD was struggling with exactly where to land with this Lenny thing. Before the flowers had shown up on Sadie's door, he'd been ready to let sleeping dogs lie. Now, not so much. But how did Sadie feel about it?

Curtis watched as JD took up Sadie's glass of wine from the little stool and did half-genuflect in front of her as he presented it, to which she replied, "Thank you, now rub my feet."

He shot back just as quick, "Fuuuuuck no," going back to the stool to grab the remaining two glasses and handing Curtis one. He sat back on the swing and without a word grabbed up Sadie's socked feet and started massaging them. Curtis took a courtesy sip of the wine and set it down on the porch railing. He was searching for a roundabout way to ask JD how much Sadie knew when she spoke up.

"So, Curtis. What are we gonna do about Lenny? JD said you have a plan?" He glanced at JD then and the imperceptible nod he got in return told him to speak freely in front of Sadie. Curt took a deep breath and cast his eyes just above Sadie's head, towards the dark shape of the azaleas beyond the porch, and told himself *you can trust Sadie,* saying her name in his head as a kind of official indoctrination. Curtis took his wine off the railing, grabbed the stool and positioned it right in front of the swing, and poured the wine from his glass into JD's.

"Okay," he said. "Here's how I'm thinking we need to try and manage Lenny. Let me lay that out for you and if it makes sense to you, I can lay out the full extent of the plan. At least as much as I have. But before we do anything, I need to get my computer and log into your Wi-Fi so I can watch the 2nd Street shop. And we need to move quickly through this so me and JD can get back to the shop and meet up with Tac."

"Can't you just use your phone?" Sadie asked as Curtis moved towards the steps to get his EverReady out of the Mazda.

"He left his phone in New Orleans," JD said.

"*Mais, la*! What'd you do that for?" Sadie wanted to know.

Lenny was out at his property in the country, standing on the cement slab that would be his house someday, pinging golf balls into the adjacent field with his favorite aluminum baseball bat. He was standing on what would be the living room, and it was perfect for hitting balls because it was nice and open and there wasn't too much rebar sticking up out of the cement. There was a certain technique to doing it right: start with the bat on your right shoulder, toss the ball out in front of you with your left, let it bounce as you rock back into your swing, then connect with the ball at the apex. And when you got it all together and connected just right, it was the most satisfying feeling in the world. To an ex-ball player, at least. But he couldn't see them land anymore, a good five hundred feet out in the pasture.

It was quiet out here, getting dark fast. He had gotten some wings to go from the sports bar in Eunice that used to be the Golden Corral, and they were still sitting in the Styrofoam container, uneaten, on top of his big red Igloo with the handle and the wheels that he used for barbeques and stuff. A six-pack of Bud Light with just one finished sat next to the wings on top of the ice chest. He didn't need ice tonight because it was like fifty degrees outside and plus these beers weren't gonna last that long anyway. Talk about hitting the spot—it was exactly what he needed right now. Those Michelob Ultras he drank in the afternoon had fewer calories, but they barely tasted like beer, and plus, that was just a chick beer he kept in the office for special occasions.

He cracked another Bud Light and took a few deep swallows, relishing that familiar effervescent sensation of cold bubbling beer rising up into his sinuses. He killed off the rest of the bottle and put it back in the carton, resisting the urge to smash it with his bat. He didn't have any problem at all hitting golf balls into the field—and there had to be hundreds of them by now sunk into the mud of the field that belonged to the Arceneauxs—but beer bottles and broken glass was something else entirely.

This place was gonna be his family homestead. Generations of Prichard kids would play around here, and yes, he had his eye on the Arceneaux property as well. If he concentrated, he could see his future son in the batting cage he would build in the spot where his trailer was now, the kid taking advice from his old man while he stood strong at the plate, waiting for the pitching machine to spit out the next ball. Lenny let out a long, satisfying belch, then reached down to grab one of the wings out of the container. It was warm, which was enough. He pulled the meat off the bone with a practiced technique and flung the remainder into the tall grass just off the slab. Then he dove in for another, since his hand was already full of sauce, and repeated the action until the container was empty except for some pale, flaccid pieces of celery that would end up in the grass.

Five minutes later, he was hunched over the hose next to the deck at the front of the trailer, rinsing off his hands in the glare of the security light. He belched again, flicked water off his hands as best he could, then mounted the wooden steps and grabbed his phone off the deck railing. Damn! He'd been hoping for a text from Sadie. She should've got the roses by now. He started to call the flower shop, but it was almost eight and they'd be closed, for sure. Plus, it would make him look desperate. And a man who sent a dozen red roses to a woman he hadn't even been to bed with wasn't desperate. That was just classy. He grabbed his keys, pulled the screen door open, and unlocked the trailer.

That familiar trailer smell met him, as always, and even though it wasn't a pleasant aroma—the new carpets he'd insisted on, probably—he'd come to associate it with home. So now he registered the smell with a sense of relief. Comfort even. His place was his sanctuary. It was no palace, but then again, it kinda was.

The first thing you saw when you walked in was a massive glass trophy case that was home to his most cherished possessions, from his first very first Tee-ball trophy to the two massive state championship trophies in blue and gold that were the centerpiece. He had at least one trophy from each year he'd played, whether it was a team trophy for winning the league or occasionally just second place, or for the all-star team, or most valuable player; he had quite a few of those. There were framed team photos, medallions, ribbons. He had an all-star jersey from Little League when they made the state semifinals and another one from high school. He had the glove that he'd used to catch the final out of state, senior year. He had batting gloves, signed balls. Everything. The lady he hired to clean the place knew better than to touch any of this shit when he wasn't in the room.

He had a couple leather, reclining movie-chairs set up in front of the 75-inch high-def television that pretty much took up the entire wall of the living room. Between that and the trophy case there wasn't much room for anything else, but what else did you need? The kitchen was just the kitchen. It stayed clean because he didn't really cook and whatever dishes he did use for cereal or beer or pizza went right into the dishwasher. He was disciplined that way.

In the extra bedroom where he kept sports gear and his shoes, all boxed up and organized, he had two gaming chairs in front of his PC with the 27-inch monitor that he used for *Call of Duty* and other games. He had to be careful about playing because once he started, it was hard to stop. He and Lefty had lost more than one weekend to gaming, sometimes even without cocaine, to the point where Lefty's old lady once had literally come to pull him out of Lenny's trailer. Lenny could still see the venom in those sharp little oriental eyes when she'd come pounding on the door, the kids in the backseat of the Honda, maybe a prop, maybe a necessity. Lenny wasn't sure, but he had his opinions.

He only had one beer left, but he did have some good tequila—about a third of a bottle of *Patrón* that Jackie had actually got him for Christmas last month—so he poured himself a healthy shot and put the last bottle of beer in the freezer. It burned going down, but he was thankful he had something strong on hand. He was feeling bloated, and the shot helped with that. It didn't help with everything else he had on his mind though.

He looked at his phone again. He should've had the flowers sent earlier. But between checking with Uncle Ely at Rudy's, and first Jackie showing up to rant and rave and then Pancho right behind her, talking all man-to-man like they were equals or some shit, he'd barely had time to even put in the order. He wondered what Sadie was doing. Lenny couldn't help but imagine her inside that cheap little house on Vine Street, the dozen roses like a ray of light in the dark interior. Sadie glistening with sweat in her sports bra, still breathing heavily from a hard run, on her way to the shower, unable to resist the urge to stop and breathe in the heady scent of the flowers, fingering the card with Lenny's name on it. An erection stirred in Lenny's pants as he imagined the scene. He decided right then he needed a shower.

Angel was about ready to bail by the time JD and Curtis got back to the shop. He had pretty much finished the lettering on the window—"Black Jack Tattoo" in black and orange gothic letters—and it looked pretty good too. He sent Jackie a picture and she texted back to say it reminded her of the Headbanger's Ball, and to asked when he was coming over. She would order a pizza if he could stop and pick it up. After the day he had, it sounded perfect.

The Old East parking lot was pretty much empty, and so he'd walked around the back of Sugar Ray's to take a couple hits from a J he'd stashed there in a Sprite bottle yesterday, and he had just got back to the shop and put on some Wu-Tang Clan when the boys showed back up. JD seemed like he might be drunk and Curtis, well, Angel had no idea. The dude might always look like that for all he knew. Anyway, Curtis didn't say anything, just sat down on the folding chair and pulled his computer outta that big-ass backpack he always carried.

Angel went to the back of the shop and turned down the music on the laptop right away because he knew JD didn't like rap, but he didn't change it. Angel wasn't gonna go that far.

"Nah. Don't turn it down. I love that shit!" JD said when he got inside, prepared to fuck with Angel in a friendly way but noticing the lightbox and getting distracted. They needed to get some kind of table or something to put it on, but for now Angel had just put it on the floor. "What's that?" JD said. "A *Light Bright*?" Angel didn't know what he meant.

"You mean Starry Night?" he asked. JD had pulled one of the three-ring binders from a milk crate in the seating area and forced open the rings to pull out a page of flash, what people in the tattoo business called their drawings. Angel went over to where he'd been sitting against the wall and tore off a piece of tracing paper and handed it to JD.

"Yeah, okay. I can see what you're saying." He gave Angel a friendly kind of smirk that suggested the bullshit was getting thick. "But it's a painted Tupperware box. Van Gogh might be a bit much, don't you think?" JD squatted down then and flicked the light on, taking a second to admire the way Angel had secured it to the container and braced the top. He placed the flash—a classic Sailor Jerry heart design—on the top of the box with the tracing paper over it and, realizing he didn't have a pencil, looked up to find Angel holding one out for him. The color image of the banded heart shown through perfectly. "This is pretty tight," he said, tracing a few lines to outline the heart, then writing in "Angel" in a quick, artful cursive. A small, prideful smile bloomed on Angel's face as he observed this.

JD handed the sheet to Angel. "Here. Give that to Jackie. You can tattoo it on her ass when you're ready."

"Yeah, no. I don't think so," Angel said, disappointed he

couldn't manage anything cooler.

JD could see his comment hadn't landed like he wanted it to, so he quickly added "Jackie's a hard woman to pin down, but if anybody could do it, you could. Say, did you talk to her today?"

"Nah," Angel said. "But I talked to Lenny. He said she went over there and kinda raised hell cause I've been working for him." Curtis looked up from his computer, interested.

"What happened?" he called from across the room. Angel shifted his focus from JD to Curtis.

"I don't know for sure 'cause I ain't talked to her yet," he said. "Lenny told me she showed up looking for me. And then she was grilling him about what I did for him. But I don't know if it went down like he said it did. He was fucking with me, I could tell."

"Yeah," JD cut in. "Jackie asked about you when I went to drop off the key to 2nd Street, and I ended up mentioning Lenny."

"She probably saw your car at the tanning place," Curtis observed. "While you were in Lenny's truck getting it washed."

"Yeah, that's pretty much what I figured too," Angel said.

"How did Lenny act when you dropped off the keys? Was he suspicious at all? Did he say anything?" Curtis wanted to know. Angel paused for a couple seconds, not really thinking about the answer so much as thinking about the question. Curtis didn't care if he'd got jammed up with Jackie; all he cared about was Lenny. But then, really, *that* was all Angel's fault. *He* was the one that started all this craziness. He turned to JD, shaking his head in sorrow.

"Say, bruh, I'm so sorry all this shit with Lenny went down the way it did. When I pulled the shit outta that 2nd Street shop, I didn't even know you yet. I damn sure didn't know he was gonna try and use it against you."

"You should've just told me right away," JD said. "Tattooing is a trust business. If you wanna stay in it, you can't play games like that."

"I know. I know. I'm gonna make it up to you, if you let me. I promise."

Curtis cut in again. "So what did Lenny say?"

"He didn't say nothing," Angel snapped back. "What could he say? He didn't like it when I told him I already put the shit back in 2nd Street, but there wasn't nothing he could do about it. I gave him back his key and tole him I was done working for him. Dat's it."

"You quit?" JD asked.

"Fuck yeah, I quit," Angel said proudly. "Told him I was gonna come over here and learn the tattoo business."

"Was he suspicious about the truck? The keys? Anything?" Curtis asked again. Angel gave Curtis a steely look.

"No, bruh. I told you, it was fine."

"I bet he *loved* that," JD said. "You quitting to come work for me."

"I'm not gonna lie," Angel said. "He talked some shit about you, but I set him straight."

"Maybe it's more to do with Sadie than with the steroids," Curtis said. That stopped Angel. He looked at JD.

"Sadie? Like, your lady?"

"He sent her a bunch of roses. Just this afternoon. Fuck, I was over there when they came!"

"Muthafucka! So, first this dude's fucking with your business. And now he's fucking with your lady?"

JD leveled his gaze on Curtis and let it settle there for a second before he turned back to Angel. "Yeah. And now I'm about to call him up and kiss his ass."

Lenny was reclined back in his chair in the living room watching *Sports Center*, drunk and drifting, when his cell phone rang. His pulse quickened when he saw the unknown number on the screen.

"Hey," he said, putting the phone on speaker and simultaneously muting the TV. "I was wondering when you'd call." He could hear music in the background, some kind of rap. And then a man's voice he didn't recognize.

"Huh? How'd you know?" JD said on the other end, Curtis and Angel listening as he held the phone out. And then, recognizing Lenny was confused, he asked, "Do you know who this is?"

"Who's this?" Lenny demanded, not listening.

JD just gave Curtis another dubious look and said, "This is JD Dugas," then waited.

"You calling about the flowers?" Lenny asked, still not

exactly sure what was going on.

"No, bruh. I'm not calling about the flowers. I'm calling . . . just to let you know there's no hard feelings. Not from my perspective." He waited a beat for Lenny to say something, and when he didn't, eager to get this over with, JD plowed on through. "It's too bad the 2nd Street shop didn't work out. I thought it woulda been a great spot. But, you know, I understand why it didn't. And so I just wanted to call and tell you that . . . it's all good, you know?" He paused again for a breath and then forced himself to continue. "We're having our grand opening next week in the new shop. It's next to Sugar Ray's Bakery. Hey, bruh, you still there?" JD stopped to ask.

Lenny cleared his throat. "Yeah, I got you."

"Anyway, we open a week from Friday. Stop by and I'll give you a good deal on a new tattoo."

"A new tattoo?"

"Oh, you don't have any?" JD said. "In that case, I tell you what, the first one's free." JD glanced at Curtis, then played his next lines like the thought had just occurred to him. "If you want, come in tomorrow night. Whatever you want. Portrait, tribal, old school, color. I'll put it on for you. And you can give me some business advice. Or something." JD gave a quick head nod towards Angel, smiled, and made a jerk-off motion.

"Yeah, maybe so," Lenny said, sitting up in his recliner but still fairly confused. "Can I ask you something?"

JD waited a beat, actually thinking about the question because he knew what was coming next. "Sure."

"So, you and Sadie. You're like, together?"

"Maaaaan, me and Sadie dated years ago. But she's not worried about me, bruh. She deserves better anyway."

"Yeah," Lenny said, thinking.

"Anyway, just let me know if you want to come by," JD said. "Take it easy," disconnecting the call before Lenny could say anything else.

Tac was back in his work car after an early dinner with his wife, still in the same clothes he wore all day. As he drove back into town from his house out in the country, he was thinking idly to himself that maybe he should've at least changed his shirt. His wife had asked if it was business or pleasure, and he had to admit he didn't know. It would be his second discussion with Curtis today, and he didn't really know what the fuck was going on. Would it just be a couple beers and a typical nostalgia bullshit session, or would it be something more interesting?

He'd taken the work car instead of his truck because he at least hoped this was more than just an impromptu high school reunion. He wasn't about to go chasing after Lenny Prichard, at least without a damn good reason and some kind of endorsement from EPD leadership, but it didn't hurt to hear what Curtis had to say. If he would tell him anything in the first place. And besides, there were plenty of criminals out there, and they weren't all connected. You could keep meat in your freezer all year long without ever killing a deer. Tac popped a handful of sunflower seeds in his mouth and cracked the window, enjoying the crisp night air and the quiet of the highway.

Ten minutes later, he pulled onto Highway 190, just outside the city limits, the dark quiet of the two lane blacktop giving way to the brightly lit divided highway that ran through Eunice and all the way into Texas, if you followed that far. He hoped JD would be at the shop too. Tac felt more comfortable with JD. Curtis was practically a stranger at this point, too far removed and too different to ever really recover anything that resembled local credibility. Tac didn't hold that against him. Shit, he envied Curtis on more than one front. But he still didn't really trust him, and that had nothing to do with the badge he carried. It was a deeper sense.

Since he was passing that way, Tac swung through the parking lot of the Regency Motel to see if he could spot that Mazda Curtis was driving. He'd started to run the plates when he first came across Curtis stalled in the median, even after he recognized him, but for some reason he never finished the scan. He told himself he didn't have to go around being suspicious of everybody, but he wasn't sure that had anything to do with it. So much of being a cop in Eunice was about where not to look. Tac accepted this truth, but he didn't like it. He couldn't help but feel like he'd grown *too* cautious in his job. He didn't like this automatic feeling of reluctance he had when it came to the Prichard family. Curtis was an entirely different thing. Anyway, he was probably overthinking things. The Mazda wasn't in the parking lot, which probably meant Curtis was already at the shop.

He stopped and grabbed some beer on the way. He started to get Abita, the amber bock they made was pretty good, at least for the first one. But then Tac decided fuck it, he wasn't gonna pander to Curtis or anybody else. If they didn't like the Coors Light they didn't have to drink it. And who knows, just because he seemed that way didn't mean Curtis was actually one of these craft beer snobs. Though Tac wouldn't bet against it.

The Old East parking lot seemed to have another big-ass pothole in it every time Tac pulled in. Maybe half the pole lights worked in the lot, and the ones that did were fading fast. Half the storefronts were boarded up, and the ones that were occupied were already closed this time of night. There were a few cars at Kluckie's, and Tac could see a couple people standing near the counter, waiting for their food. Kluckie's didn't really have the kind of atmosphere that made you want to dine in. The lights were on in the tattoo shop and he could see people on the other side of the big window sporting "Black Jack Tattoo" in bold, ornate letters that looked pretty badass. Tac couldn't help but smile. It was really happening: a tattoo shop in Eunice.

He was thinking about how cool it was that the lettering on the window was done in that same style reminiscent of the Headbanger's Ball that he'd seen on Angel Castille's car earlier today . . . *I'll be damned,* he said to himself. There was that same blue Ford Focus. Same bumper sticker. And as if on cue, the same good-looking kid, Angel Castille himself, strolled out the front door and sauntered over to his car. If he noticed Tac pulling into a spot on the other side of JD's van, he did a good job of hiding it. Tac pulled his little cop notebook from the center console and made a note. *Shit, this is getting interesting,* he thought. Then he grabbed the twelve-pack of beer and made his way inside.

Episode Seven
Skin Deep

———❋———

Sadie gets involved in Curt's plan to get over on Lenny. Sadie and JD get together. Jacque makes a surprise visit to Eunice.

"Sexy Sadie. You made a fool of everyone." — The Beatles

Despite his lack of sleep over the previous three days, Curtis woke before the sun came up that Thursday morning. He wasn't dead tired, but he wasn't quite alive either. He woke in a kind of purgatory state, operating on muscle memory. He'd messed around and drank too much beer the night before.

It was only Coors Light, but it was enough to do some damage, especially on top of the lack of sleep. His mind was sluggish, his body ached, and his stomach was sour. But if he didn't exercise he knew he would feel worse. There was nothing to do but suck it up and sweat. The bubbles in the can of seltzer he drank helped some. He put his contacts in, tied his room key into the laces of his shoes, clipped his mace to the waistband of his shorts, and headed out for a predawn run along the highway.

Picking his way in the dark among the broken bottles, clumps of grass, and litter along the shoulder of the road, he didn't have any reserve brainpower to think about the cautious conversation they'd had with Tac. JD didn't lay it all out like he'd threatened to, and Curtis was glad for that. They had drunk beer and laughed together, and that was a kind of progress in itself. In Curt's mind, it was better to play it close to the vest with Tac. It was like JD had said, whatever else he was, Tac was first and foremost a cop.

An out-and-back run along the highway was a long way from ideal for Curtis, who usually did circuits around the national mall and the Potomac river, but the place had its own kind of charm, even with the occasional truck rushing by at sixty miles an hour. By the time Curt stopped to turn around and head back towards the motel, twenty or maybe twenty-five minutes out, the sky was getting light, and traffic was picking up. It wasn't exactly a safe place to be, and he had his back to traffic now, so he picked up the pace, double-timing it back to the motel. He finished his run the way he finished every run, sucking air and in pain, except that this morning he was in the grimy parking lot of the Regency Motel, still hungover and realizing he was hungry.

There was a Conoco station less than a quarter mile from the hotel. He remembered how the familiar smell of fresh *boudin* had hit him when he stopped by yesterday morning to grab some Red Bull and water on his way to Rudy's cafe. The spicy, poached sausage of pork and rice and onion bursting with flavor was the perfect Cajun delicacy. With a cup of black coffee, it was the perfect hangover breakfast. And the best *boudin* around was usually found at random little gas stations sprinkled throughout Acadiana. Curtis wasn't sure why, but this was pretty much an undisputed fact in South Louisiana. If you wanted great gumbo, you went to your grandma's house. If you wanted killer *boudin,* look for a gas station with too many pickup trucks in the parking lot for the price of gas they're advertising.

Fifteen minutes later Curtis was back at the motel, parked in front of his room and leaning against the hood of the Mazda with a large cup of Community coffee that he hadn't sipped yet, but would surely taste like sticks. The door to his room was propped open again with the bible and the laptop was open on the floor just inside so Curtis could keep an eye on 2nd Street, even though he had help in that department now.

Outside, he had the big square of waxy butcher paper the clerk had wrapped the *boudin* in spread out on the hood, and the aroma from it rose like a cure in the chilly morning air. The smell was amazing out here in the fresh air, but he knew he would regret it later if he brought it inside his room.

He'd bought three links, way more than he needed, but he'd been in Eunice for something like thirty-six hours and hadn't had a decent meal yet. Rudy's Cafe had nothing on this gas station. He sliced the first link into bite-sized pieces with his Leatherman tool and savored it, the snap of the casing and the familiar, silky texture of the savory ground meat and rice. He made involuntary guttural noises as he shoveled in the remainder of the first link, then the second into his mouth, scooping up chunks of seasoned rice that had fallen onto the paper. He told himself he wasn't going to eat the third link right up to the point where his knife punctured the casing to slice it up, and then it was gone. Old habits came back quick.

It wasn't quite 8 a.m. when he went back into the motel room to shower and crawl right back into bed, satiated and stretched out from the run. Today was going to be crucial, and he needed to be at his absolute best. That meant eight hours of sleep, even if he needed two separate sessions to get it. There was nothing happening at this hour anyway. Luckily, the curtains were dense, because the sun was angling right at the window. The walls were thin, but he was in an end unit, and the TV coming from the adjacent room didn't bother him. Curtis needed to sleep, so he did. Two minutes of deep breathing and he was gone.

JD was sitting in his Astro with the window down, smoking a cigarette and texting back and forth with Sadie when Angel pulled up in his little Ford Focus. The muffled sounds of early Red Hot Chilli Peppers came with him, Angel rapping along note for note. JD didn't notice. He smiled the blissful, involuntary smile of a man in love as he looked down at his phone, hanging on every word Sadie offered.

"What's up, boss? You ready to do this?" Angel said as they shook hands on the sidewalk.

"You know I don't have money, right?" JD said in response, and Angel assured him it was cool.

"Slim's my cousin. I talked to him yesterday. Man, he's *psyched* to help you out!"

One of the strange things about being back in Eunice that JD was still getting used to was the new identities given to familiar old stores. On this front, *Cajun Customs* was probably the biggest mind fuck that JD had had to deal with. The large glass storefront was right next to the Queen Cinema, still the only movie theater in town and right next door to Rudy's Cafe, which seemed like it had been there when the streets were still sod. They were both Eunice institutions, but growing up, no building was more important than where he stood now, because this was

Music Central.

JD could still see the racks of records in custom-made wooden bins, cassette tapes lined up inside special anti-theft plastic racks that had to be opened with a round key, and later, CDs along the far wall in their long cardboard boxes. He could still see Todd, the walking music encyclopedia of Eunice and premier local DJ, greeting him as he entered. He could hear Cajun, blues, zydeco, rock, even punk, depending on the time of day and who was in the store at that moment.

Now, as they walked in, where the records had been, there was a wall of car stereo receivers and blinking lights, and where the tapes had been there were shiny, spinning rims of various sizes. In the area where the CDs had once been, there was an array of accessories—fuzzy dice, seat covers, special dust rags, and wax and polish and shit. Some familiar-sounding Tejano music was playing. As he stood there fighting against nostalgia, the words *"Para donde vas?"* escaped JD's lips as he sang along to the chorus from the Iguanas song, one he'd heard hundreds of times across Texas, even though they were a New Orleans band. And that was all it took to recalibrate to this new reality.

By the way Angel looked at him right then, you'd have sworn he'd turned water to wine. JD didn't notice. He was focused on a fat vato dude with plugs in his ears that came around the counter then and said "Hey, bruh. You must be JD." Angel snapped back to life, too late and totally unnecessary, voicing the introductions Slim had already started without him.

"Yeah, so JD, this is my cousin Slim," Angel said as JD was already extending his hand, Slim adjusting mid-stream to give JD the traditional shake he was expecting, but then adding a soul shake to the ritual and bringing up his free left hand to clasp him on top. Slim even leaned in for a half bro-hug, his enthusiasm overflowing. Angel was saying, "This is his place. They do rad shit with airbrush."

"Man! The first tattoo shop in Eunice." Slim said. "It's about fucking time, brother!" Slim looked out the window toward the van. "How 'bout let's check out your ride while you tell me about it, my man?" He gestured back towards the door, manic in his excitement, jabbering non-stop as they made their way to the Astro van.

Lenny was sitting in the sauna at the Eunice Health Club, not thinking about much, just trying to get clean. He had maybe got a little too drunk last night, but really it wasn't that bad. And though it was always a good idea to detox when you had the chance, that wasn't really what he was up to now. It was more a kind of preemptive purge. Cleaning the slate.

Him and Lefty had some business to discuss, in person, like always. And just like always, it was kind of their little tradition to go to Cecil's Bar and party. Not a lot. Just a few drinks, some shots, maybe a little sniff if the opportunity presented itself. Lefty's little oriental wife kept him on a pretty tight leash, and so Lenny tried to help him cut loose whenever he could. Sitting in the sauna and sweating this morning was kind of the fast before the feast. But he did need to think too.

About this phone call he got from JD, for one thing. He wished he'd had the presence of mind to record the damn thing because it was hard to remember now exactly how it went down. But anyway, he had the gist of it. JD wanted to make sure everything was cool between them. Which, on one level Lenny could respect. As a local business owner, he knew it was a good move to make. It was hard enough to make a dollar in this town, any kind of dollar. And you never knew when or who you might need a favor from. So all that made sense.

It was what JD had said about Sadie that was still fucking with him. Damn! She *still* hadn't bothered to call or even text. Lenny had woken up in his armchair thinking about that and it was still cycling through his mind. That shit was just bad manners, and he was disappointed in her for that. He came back to the call with JD, trying to focus. What was that bullshit line he'd tried to feed him? JD had said she *wasn't worried about him* or some shit like that. Even drunk Lenny had known that was bullshit. No way an ugly motherfucker like JD Dugas was gonna be so casual about a beautiful woman like that.

In his most private, introspective moments, Lenny had more than once confronted the fact that he really didn't understand women. Most times he didn't have a clue what they were thinking, and it didn't matter if it was his mom or Jackie or the chick at the drive-thru or that nosy waitress with the big hips at Rudy's. They were all pretty much a grand fucking mystery. But his lie detector was actually pretty good when it came to men, especially dudes his age. And the way JD had acted when he mentioned Sadie, plus that whole thing about *come on by for a free tattoo* or whatever. Well, that felt like bullshit to Lenny. *Don't bullshit a bullshitter*, he said to himself. That invitation JD had thrown out there was the kind of thing you did because you knew the other guy would never take you up on it. Like inviting somebody to a party when you knew they were going out of town.

Lenny put the thought aside and he found himself fantasizing about what kind of tattoo he would get. Not that he would, but he couldn't help thinking about it. In his mind, he saw himself at the annual St. Eds alumni softball game, muscles rippling in a sleeveless shirt as he stood in the batter's box with his hat backward. The image he saw on his arm was a blue jay, the St. Eds mascot, but it was way cooler, angrier, more menacing than he'd ever seen it before. For a moment, an image of him sitting in a tattoo shop like he'd seen in movies flashed in his mind . . . and vanished. Involuntarily, he glanced down at his sweaty paunch, dark red lines where his excess fat rolled onto itself, sagging against the towel at his waist. He was well past peak tattoo shape. And that made him feel bad, so he buried it deep and just sat there for a minute, sweating and trying to keep his mind clear.

And then something dawned on him. He smiled, thinking about it. He'd text Lefty and tell him to come by *Tans* early. There was another little errand they had to take care of before they went to Cecil's to blow off some steam. They had to talk about delivering the 2nd Street package anyway, and more to the point, they were overdue to get together for a few beers and maybe a sniff or three.

At Black Jack's, Angel was sitting at JD's station in the one nice customer chair they had with his left arm on the armrest. JD sat in a folding chair next to him, hunched over Angel's hand. He had prepped the top of his hand and wrist with a soapy green antibacterial spray, shaved the area with quick, expert upstrokes, and dried it with a paper towel, talking Angel through best practices for sterilization while he worked.

"I think this is literally the first tattoo I ever did before noon," JD said.

"Yeah, bruh. I'm getting the early bird special." Angel threw in, just to have something to say. He could tell JD was happy with how things went at *Cajun Customs*, which was good. Angel was happy about it too. He wasn't trying to do anything but make the shop as good as it could be, but if things started clicking with JD and he showed him more because of it, that was cool.

"More like the apprentice special, cause you're gonna do at least half of this yourself."

"Really?" Angel asked, thankful.

"What'd you think, bruh? I'm just gonna be your personal tattoo artist? It's on your left hand, so you can fill it in yourself. Plus, I got shit to do."

"Nah, it's cool," Angel said. "I was hoping you'd let me do some. And anyway, you gonna need those hands to keep texting your lady." JD just glanced up at him and smiled.

"She's coming by later to pick me up. For lunch."

"Aww yeah!" Angel said, animated.

"Stay still!" JD scolded, and when Angel settled down he asked, "So how'd it go with Jackie? Was she pissed?"

Angel sputtered air through his teeth with exaggerated nonchalance. "Nah, she was cooled out by the time I got there. Kinda emotional, maybe. But she wasn't pissed." Angel flashed back to the scene in his mind, he and Jackie sitting on the floor of her living room, eating pizza and listening to music. It was a good thing he wasn't hungry because she ate the whole thing, practically.

JD reached over and plucked up a Bic ballpoint pen from the top of his Snap-on tool chest. As he handed it to Angel, he thought of the little bit of coke he still had in the baggie. He still hadn't touched it, but he wanted to. "Here," he said, "draw the outline."

"Where?" Angel asked, suddenly confused.

"On your hand. Draw it." Angel took the pen and paused for a beat before he touched the rounded tip to his skin and started drawing. He thought of the shape like a bird transforming into a star. It was abstract, but he could see it perfectly. When he was finished, JD reapplied the antibacterial cleaner and after drying it with a paper towel, took up his machine. "Okay, so, I have a nine-tight round with a long taper in the machine. It's basically a cluster for outlining." He held up the tip of the machine close to Angel's face. "See my needle depth? That's a good place to start. What part of the skin we gotta get into?"

"The dermis," Angel answered.

"And what's that?"

"Dat's the middle layer. Not so shallow that you just scratching, not so deep that you blowing out the line."

"Right on," JD said, then dipped the tube at the tip of the machine in the plastic well of black ink he'd laid out in one of the open drawers of the toolbox. "Like I showed you before, I'm gonna start my line at a specific point and go to an end point, and keep it in motion, like we talked about. Nice and smooth." The needle touched Angel's skin as he talked and Angel found himself marveling at how relaxed he felt, and how in control JD was.

After a minute or so of staring down at his hand and appreciating the piercing, but somehow dull pain radiating from the tip of the needle, Angel realized how quiet it was. "Hey, how 'bout we put some tunes on?"

"Nope," JD said right away, and Angel was surprised at the injunction. "I wanna keep it quiet in here so you can concentrate on the feeling of it," JD said. "You're gonna have customers who wanna drink, pop pills, spread fucking numbing ointment on. They're gonna be fixated on the pain, and they're gonna have every kind of crutch you can imagine to help deal with it. Special music, fuzzy slippers, a fucking teddy bear, what have you." Angel looked up at him then, understanding this was a lesson. "You need to learn what it feels like. You gotta learn those sensations. So you can help people while you keep control. They are the customer, but you're controlling the experience." He paused. "It's just like learning what pleases a woman. If you learn what buttons to push, you can both have an amazing experience. This is the same." He broke into a laugh then. "Okay, well, it ain't *exactly* the same."

"Yeah," Angel said. "I'm picking up what you're laying down. It's just like any other, like, physical thing. It has its own, like, signature."

JD nodded and went back to his work, Angel settling in and observing everything he could. He tried to pay attention to the process and stay tuned in to the pain, which was very real and pinched like a muthafucka, to tell the truth. It was too bad it was such a small design, about the size of a Mardi Gras doubloon, 'cause it went pretty quick. JD switched to a shading cluster to fill in the design.

"Pay attention. You see this little pattern I'm using to fill it in?" JD asked. He worked the needle cluster in small, overlapping circles. "Okay, you ready?" he said after a minute.

"Yeah, gimme the gun," Angel said. JD pulled back and gave him a look Angel didn't like.

"It's not a gun. Never call it a gun."

"Sorry, boss. Machine. Lemme have the machine." Angel accepted the tool, and after a moment, applied the needle to his skin, figuring it out for himself under JD's watchful eye. At some point, Angel said to JD, "I thought you had shit to do?"

"I do," JD said. "I gotta teach you how to tattoo."

Sadie stood in the kitchen of her mom's house, organizing pills at the counter while keeping an eye on her cell phone and looking up every so often at the red roses on the counter. They looked amazing in the light that came through the window. She couldn't help but smile. It was a long time since someone sent her flowers. Much less a dozen roses! That really was special. Too bad they came from such a first-class dick like Lenny. Curtis had told her about the cameras he had in that tanning salon, and that did it for her right there. She didn't even need to hear the rest of the plan. She was in, whatever Curtis and JD needed.

Though it wasn't really JD's plan. Matter of fact, they needed to keep JD out of it as much as possible because he was the first person the cops or Lenny or whoever would look at when things started going wrong. And things were fixing to go *real* wrong. Still—and she realized it was kinda weird—but she felt like she should at least text Lenny to say thanks for the flowers. It was rude not to. But if she did, she knew damn well

Lenny would just keep pestering her. Hell, if she agreed to go out on a date with him the dude would probably show up in a limo and a tux. She smiled again at the thought, very much aware of her own sex appeal.

She looked down at the video feed on her cell phone. It showed a static image of the storefront on 2nd Street that JD had rented from Lenny but he reneged on. She was helping Curtis keep an eye on it. An old man in coveralls actually walked by while she was looking at the feed, which made her heart race because she had literally not seen a single person on the screen since Curtis downloaded the app last night. But nothing came of it. She switched over to the mapping software to check the GPS location of "PKG 1," the steroids stored in the bathroom ceiling. *Same place it was two minutes ago*, she told herself. Then she opened her messaging app to text Curtis.

Morning, sunshine! All quiet on 2nd Street. Hey, should I text Lenny to say thanks for the flowers?

It was close to noon. She closed the pillbox and set it on top of the notebook, open to the page for that day, where she kept track of her mom's diet and medications, then she went into the living room to check in on her. They'd had some quality time this morning, drinking tea and talking. It had made Sadie's day already.

Lunch was already fixed—some soup she'd made from chicken bones this morning and flavored with frozen basil and corn from the summer garden. Not that it mattered. Her mom wouldn't eat, but it made Sadie feel better that it was there if she wanted it. Or the sitter could have it. Speaking of, she would be there in twenty minutes. Sadie felt a pang of guilt about going out for the day, but it wasn't going to change her plans. Even with the guilt, the thought amused her; JD had no idea what was in store for the both of them. He just thought they were going to lunch.

She had even talked to her mom about it, and it didn't even feel weird. That was a symptom of someone dying, she guessed. In the face of it, her need for not just a good hook up, but for the promise of real love was not something to be embarrassed about. It was to be cherished. And if the timing was inconvenient, well, wasn't that the main lesson of death? You couldn't wait to live. Her mom had squeezed her hand and given her a smile, and that was all that needed to be said. She had retreated to the bedroom then to put a few things in her backpack.

It was a good fifteen minutes before the return text from Curtis came in, which kind of surprised her. She'd been walking around the house with her phone in the back pocket of her jeans because she expected him to respond right away. The dude was compulsive—she could see that plain as day. And with the way he sucked down those Red Bulls, there was no way he got more than five or six hours of sleep a night.

Thanks for the report. Yeah, it's a good idea to thank Lenny. But keep it in writing —no phone calls. He's probably gonna ask you out. If he does, don't reply. I want to talk to you (and JD) about it.

She replied to Curtis real quick then spent a few minutes composing something to Lenny that struck the right tone.

Hi. It's Sadie. Thanks for the flowers. Very nice. Just wanted to say thanks. I don't think we're compatible, but it was a nice gesture.

That should do it, she thought. Just then there was a quiet knock at the door, and she put the phone in her backpack and walked to the front of the house. After she'd got the sitter situated and kissed her mom goodbye, Sadie went into the kitchen and pulled one of the roses from the vase. At the door, she treated her mom to a mischievous smile, then made a little show of putting the rose stem between her teeth before she opened the front door and was gone.

JD had taken control of the tattoo machine to finish the work, explaining to a somewhat disappointed Angel why he'd basically insisted on changing his initial design. There was negative space—unblemished skin—in the interior that mimicked the outline of the star-bird shape of the tattoo. JD finished retracing a pretty good line Angel had done and put the machine down on the tool chest. He grabbed his phone and held it next to Angel's hand, contrasting the before picture he'd taken showing Angel's design done in pen-ink with the modified, permanent one they'd just put on.

"You see how it pops, with the negative space?" JD said. "That's because the shape from the outside is reflected in the interior." Angel made some affirmative noises. It wasn't clear if he was buying it or if he was just a little wounded because he hadn't thought of it himself. "Now, if you wanted to, you could come back with a contrasting color in the negative space to really make it pop. Or you could always just fill the rest in, but if you live with it for a couple days you're gonna be happy you didn't go with the jailhouse tat design." Angel gave him a laugh then, still looking down at his hand, and he seemed to consider it in a new light.

"Yeah. I can dig it. Looks pretty bad-ass, right?"

"Yeah, bruh. It's righteous." JD said, taking off his black latex gloves. "Okay, now let's talk aftercare. Do me a favor and grab that little drawing I did . . ."

Later, JD was standing outside, smoking a cigarette and appraising Angel's work on the window lettering when Sadie pulled up in her little champagne-colored Corolla. She killed the engine and sat there watching him for a few seconds, narrow-ass in faded jeans on a wiry frame, all electric energy and untapped potential. It was fifteen years since she'd known him sexually, and those years had given him a honed, masculine edge. They weren't teenagers anymore. Sadie noticed the slogan written in black below the big orange gothic lettering of Black Jack Tattoo. It said, "*Welcome to Your New Addiction!*"—and it might've been clever, but it was uncomfortable too, cutting way too close to the bone.

She'd given JD a valium last night, and another half—the last one he'd get from her—because he'd sworn to her when he told her about flushing the coke that he didn't need to go to rehab or anything. Not that he could afford it anyway—he was broke and he had a tattoo shop to open. But even so, he was fine. It was a crutch, for sure, but not a physical addiction, he said.

She wanted to believe him because it was clear he wanted to believe himself. And he might be right. Only time would tell. It wasn't her first experience with a man who was hooked on something—booze, pills, porn, work, weed. Memphis was full of weak dudes who fell into traps they couldn't get out of, and usually she bailed at the first signs of desperation because she knew intuitively you couldn't save somebody by jumping down in the hole with them.

But JD was a different thing. She was willing to take a chance on him, and maybe the promise of her would be enough to give him strength. Maybe there was even a potential future for both of them. But that was too heavy for this afternoon. What they both needed now was some relief, some release. Not everything in life had to be complicated and stressful and fraught with risk.

Later on, when she recounted the events of the afternoon to her mother in surprising detail, she would start by telling her about the expression on JD's face when he turned at the sound of her car door closing behind him. It was a sudden warm glow that started in his eyes and blossomed almost immediately between her legs.

The kiss she gave him standing there on the sidewalk was like an awakening. It had started innocent enough—him leaning in to thank her for the single rose, which he knew was repurposed from the dozen Lenny had sent to her house but she hoped he was smart enough to see the significance of her now bringing it to him. She could see Angel inside the shop, and she wasn't down with public displays, but when JD's lips on the cheek she offered drifted down towards her neck she didn't stop him. She arched herself towards him for a moment and then turned to find his lips with hers. When she met his eyes as the kiss resolved, it was with the promise of more. They both lingered there in each other's arms, lust mixed with something like relief and hope.

Angel was polite, but standoffish, or maybe just too deferential in a way that made her feel her age. Which didn't make sense because Sadie knew he was seeing Jackie Guidry, and Jackie was maybe two years younger than her. Sadie could see the attraction, looking at Angel. He was a beautiful boy, all the more attractive for that scruffy exterior. Come to think of it, he was like a next-generation JD. Only Puerto Rican.

She asked Angel about painting the van, not just to have something to talk about. She was genuinely interested, and as she looked around the shop it was clear JD needed all the help he could get. Angel prattled on a bit about the design JD and his cousin Slim had come up with and how awesome it was that JD could just sketch something out on the spot and how it just made perfect sense to Slim

"How much?" Sadie asked when he was finished.

"It's not like Pimp My Ride or anything," JD said "...he's just doing the door panel. We agreed that something like five hundred in skin work was fair, and maybe we can do more down the road."

"When we start making *MON-AY*" Angel hollered. Sadie could see the worry on JD's face, even as he laughed at Angel's impromptu cheer.

The shop wasn't much to look at, but Sadie made a show of pivoting on her heels to take it all in. Angel excused himself to get something out of his car. When he left JD said "He's a good dude. None too bright, but I like him." Sadie didn't say anything. She walked towards the back of the shop, admiring the room divider with silhouettes that looked like Chinese characters.

"What's back here?" she asked. JD followed.

"Well, this part's gonna be the piercing studio, eventually. I'm certified, but I'm gonna need to hire a girl like post fucking haste 'cause piercing actually brings in a lot of customers . . . plus I don't really like doing it." Sadie hopped up on the massage table.

"Really?" she said. "Why not? I imagine you get pretty close to some pretty young girls that way." The first thought that hit JD's brain was the lock on the door, because he knew that look she was giving him. He moved closer to her, standing between her legs, eye to eye, and said something designed to sound clever and sexy. She laughed and kissed him. They lingered there in the back for five minutes or more, engaged in the kind of make-out session you remember for the rest of your life. Firm, sucking kisses that went from zero to sixty in a matter of seconds and just held the needle there, both of them relishing in the feeling of another long first kiss. Angel had been kind enough to stay outside, but they both knew it wouldn't last, and anyway, they were eager for more.

At the Regency Motel, Sadie and JD fucked with abandon. It was the stuff of fantasy, except that it was real and emotional and deep. The window unit labored to cool the warm air in the tiny motel room as Sadie sat straddling JD, drenched and glistening with sweat and musk, her nipples a taut bundle of nerves. One of them was under the most exquisite pressure from JD's fingers, the other exposed to the cooling air and alive and electrically charged to the pressure of the room. His other hand caressed her face and neck and probed with his fingers in her mouth as she sucked on them with her tongue and lips. One of her own fingers was in his mouth—another point of mutual contact through which they reconnected in the most profound way.

Her toes curled in ecstasy against the sheets. She ground her pelvic bone against him in a hungry rhythmic cadence that was synched with their breath. The ripe head of his penis did its magic inside her, massaging, massaging her deeply in that special place and manner that he and only he seemed able to find. And as she glided up and down on his shaft, the thumb of his free hand found her spot and contributed its own friction in perfect unison and it was always almost too much, with each soul-shaking thrust between them, but they were both tuned to the rhythm and able to sustain the intensity of the pleasure it brought and of the promise of the new heights they would reach together.

And they rocked in that way, in that deep and sensual way, rocking and rocking against each other until their bodies, nerve by nerve and muscle by muscle, began to call them back to reality, and then as they sustained the slick, pressurized coupling of their bodies, like two marathon runners approaching the finish line in unison, they moved joyously and in perfect, paced harmony together, approaching but never hurrying, grinding and rocking and massaging and licking and sucking and devouring each other in a steadily escalating rhythm that at long last, with the greatest care reached the height of human sexual crescendo and Sadie and JD burst through the vortex of orgasm like newborn adults.

Curtis had spent the last two hours scouting properties that Lenny either owned or was connected to. He owned property, five acres south of town off of Highway 13, in the little enclave of Mowata, a community that consisted of a church, a cemetery, and a little general store that had some of the best *boudin* and cracklins around. There was a double-wide trailer set up towards the front of the property, but the commercial imagery Curtis had checked out showed the early stages of some foundation work directly behind it. He guessed Lenny had plans to build a permanent home there.

Then there was Sun-*N*-Tans, another double-wide trailer, except this one a beige-colored commercial structure set up on blocks in a gravel lot along 190, not too far from the Winn-Dixie and McDonald's, Taco Bell, Popeyes, all the franchise stuff people loved. The mural, if that's what you wanted to call it, on the street side of the building was just about as tacky as the business itself. Of all Lenny's properties, this was the one Curtis wanted to spend some quality alone time in. But he knew from Angel there were video cameras. Driving around it—he didn't want to get too close—it was impossible to tell if they were hardwired in or if it was just some wireless doorbell cameras. Neither setup was impossible to circumvent, but pretty much everything Curtis knew about defeating cameras he'd seen in movies. It was too risky.

The real estate office—Sun-*N*-Y Reality—was connected to the big, bright yellow and orange Sun-*N*-Sports building, which ran to most of the city block when you counted the parking lot. There was a lot of activity at the complex, and even though the little real estate office was at one corner with its own entrance, there was just the one way in and out and Curtis had observed actual security cameras mounted at each corner.

Lenny's mom lived just behind St. Anthony's Church in one of the truly elegant properties in Eunice, a stately white Victorian, set back on a corner lot with mature oaks, cedars, and magnolia trees. It might've been the grounds of a small museum or some kind of old money institution—a sophisticated kind of place. The Camelia Street address was just a couple blocks behind St-Eds and the vaulted interiors of St-Anthony's, all stone and marble and inspirational Catholicism. Curtis couldn't imagine Lenny growing up in this place: walking to school, drinking tea on the patio, and playing croquet or whatever activity rich people did out in the yard to pass the time.

Ely Prichard's place was a totally different thing. It favored the style that most moderately rich Eunice families went for, an oversized brick structure with columns and arches, palm trees, and even cement-cast lions guarding the entrance to an expanse of smooth, poured concrete driveway. At Ely Prichard's place, the perfect surface of the driveway fanned out at the garage to form a half-court basketball surface that Curtis could see was designed for regulation free-throws on the plexiglass hoop. The front yard was an immaculate carpet of green, and around one side there was a batting cage of aluminum fencing. An eight-foot privacy fence enclosed the backyard, and over it Curtis could see the top of the pool slide.

He'd wanted to see the two big houses in town to satisfy his curiosity more than anything. No way Curtis was gonna go sneaking around either of these places, key or no key. He was no master spy and neither was he some kind of cat burgling B and E man. But there were smart ways, safe ways, to go about this. He had a set of keys, after all, and he had a tracker in Lenny's truck. And it stood to reason that at least one of those keys opened the trailer house on Highway 13. And the good thing was it was an isolated place—easily a twenty-minute drive from the city limits. For Curtis, it was a matter of careful observation, understanding Lenny's motivations, and shaping the environment to get Lenny where he wanted. Where he didn't want him, actually. And that's where Sadie came in.

Returning from his drive around Eunice, Curtis couldn't help but notice a powder blue VW bug parked at the edge of the parking lot. It reminded him of Jacque's. He unlocked his room and left the sign on the motel door that actually still said "Do not disturb" on the handle, the Regency owners apparently not yet hip to the woke new world standard where even door signs had to water down their commands to polite little injunctions like "privacy, please." The package of steroids he'd brought from New Orleans was still where he'd left it, funny enough, tucked up in the drop ceiling of the motel room. For the couple hours he was out, at least, Curtis trusted his hiding place more than the little safe bolted to the floor in the closet.

Once he double-checked the steroids, he opened the laptop, logged into his VPN, and checked his maps. As he waited in the quiet for his credentials to validate, the sounds of not-so-distant lovemaking established itself in the room like a physical presence. *Holy shit.* Somebody was having a *damn good* time. Curtis pulled up KRVS.org, the Lafayette public radio station that was still mostly music, on his laptop in the hopes of drowning out the enthusiastic couple next door.

His map showed Lenny was at Sun-*N*-Tans, which was good news because it suggested he spent his workdays there. He had been there yesterday, and he was there again today. If he went back to work tomorrow, Friday, Curtis would be ready. Pkg. 1 was still at the old location on 2nd Street. A quick look at the camera confirmed that the feed was still working. It might have slipped just a little, but it was hard to tell. Either way, you could see the front door. And Angel had apparently not turned off his phone tracking yet, because Curtis could see his phone was at Black Jacks. He thought about calling JD, but really he needed to talk to Sadie first.

He texted her using his computer interface and sat there, stupidly staring at the chat window waiting for her reply. When it didn't come immediately, he texted JD, just to check in. And then sat there, waiting. Curtis hadn't really keyed in on the radio since he'd put it on—it was hard to prioritize over the sound of the lovemaking next door—but at that moment the familiar, sleepy voice of Francis Doyle cut through the action to grab his attention. Curtis had come to know and appreciate the unorthodox delivery Francis brought to the mix from locations across the globe.

He wasn't one to get homesick—not in the way most people mean—but after enough distance and time away from Acadiana, he'd developed a taste for that narrow slice of Lafayette culture that had one foot in the swamp and another on the kick drum of American rock and roll. Curtis found he could scratch the itch with just a single source. He'd spent more than a few hours streaming KRVS.org and enjoying the sleepy-stoned delivery of Francis as much as the records he spun on programs like the *Medicine Ball Caravan* and the longest-running reggae show in South Louisiana, *Jah Mon.*

So Curtis dug into the EverReady for his nice noise-canceling headphones and cranked KRVS while he worked. They did a better job of muting the carnal athletes next door and with some concentration, Curtis was able to focus on his plan. And if he did it right, he'd get a piece of action too, although for Curtis, it would be the sweet release of fucking Lenny Prichard over.

Sitting at his computer, he saw a new text pop up on his chat interface. It was about time either Sadie or JD responded. He clicked over and couldn't help but feel a surge of panic when he read the message from a number he didn't recognize. It was just three words.

Open your door

He rushed for the pistol in his EverReady and crept to the window. The first thing he saw when he peeped through the curtain was the powder-blue VW Bug. It was just as out of place as the voice at the door.

"Hurry up, bruh! I'm feeling conspicuous as hell standing here." Curtis opened the door with the chain still on, not quite believing Jacque was, in fact, standing in front of him. He looked like he was working for the power company or something: gray pants, gray jacket with a patch that said "Leroy," and a black baseball cap devoid of any logos at all. "Come on, nigga! Don't leave a black man exposed like this in cracker country!" Curtis unlocked the door and Jacque stepped through holding a large silver suitcase.

The sound of lovemaking from next door was impossible to ignore. Curtis shrugged his shoulders. "Thin walls," he said. "What are you doing here?"

"You know who that is, right?" Jacque asked. In that instant Curtis was thinking Jacque had flipped out, was having some kind of episode that he was about to get sucked into. As he stood there trying to grasp the fact of Jacque there in the room and whatever this question about the couple next door meant, Jacque said, "That's your boy JD. And Sadie, of course. Can't forget Sexy Sadie."

Curtis pulled his glasses from his face and rubbed at his eyes. "What?"

"That's your boy JD, and Sadie. They checked in earlier. Catching up on some afternoon delights!" Jacque set the case on the edge of the bed.

"How do you know that?" Curt asked. Jacque turned back and gave him a look.

"Fool. You using *all* my equipment. You really think I don't know what's going on?" Curtis looked over at the hard drive plugged into the little tablet on the floor.

"What exactly do you know?" Curtis was almost afraid to ask. Again, he got the knowing stare from Jacque that he was starting to find infuriating.

"Every keystroke, every text, every pin dropped, every video streamed." Curtis leaned back against the dresser. "And anyway, Sadie's car's parked around back. But there's some shit I don't know," Jacque said, unsnapping the case. "So why don't you fill me in, and whatever it is you getting ready to do, I'll be your eyes in the sky." He pulled the lid back to reveal the strangest looking drone Curtis had ever seen. As Curtis gawked at the thing—matt black, with an ominous bulbed camera lens mounted underneath—something occurred to him and he felt hope welling up.

"You didn't bring my phone, did you?"

Jacque gave him another cold stare. "I could've just gave you a new SIM card. Next time, let the master help you." Jacque said.

A̲t some point later, after the sweat had dried and left them first shivering under the covers and then huddled together and as a consequence of that, engaged in another round of lovemaking, Sadie was the first to emerge from the bed. JD had drifted off while she lay listening to the rhythm of his breathing. He woke when she moved and it wasn't until then that he realized how completely the arm she'd been laying on had fallen asleep. When he sat up in bed, it fell behind him uselessly, cocked at a comical angle that he was powerless to change. He was staring down at the useless appendage, trying to jerk it back into a more natural resting position when Sadie came back into the room, stark naked and at ease. She walked over and picked up his dead hand, letting it fall back to the bed like a stunned fish. "One," she called and picked it up again. The tingling was beginning to come on strong and JD winced with anticipation of it. "Two!" Sadie grabbed his hand and held it aloft again. "Three! And . . . he's out!"

Sadie checked her phone, curious about the time more than anything. "Uh. The boss texted. I better hit him back," she said. "And, of course, three messages from the creep."

"Goddammit," JD said. "Who you mean, boss?" he continued, ambling over towards the shower with his dead arm.

"Curtis. I think he wants me to meet Lenny somewhere."

JD stopped where he was, anger flashed across his eyes but his attempt to gesture with the dead arm was comical and Sadie erupted in laughter.

"Dude! I broke you, huh?"

"Talk about," JD said. "Now gimme my phone, please, so I

can tell Curtis to knock this shit off."

"Don't be like that. It's a good idea. That way we know where Lenny is and Curtis can do his thing." Sadie reached into the front pocket of his jeans on the floor and plucked out JD's phone.

"There's got to be a better way," he said, taking the phone from her with his good arm and attempting to unlock it. He handed it back to Sadie when he couldn't manage. "Never mind. I'm gonna shower, see if I can wake up my broken arm."

Sadie was staring intently at his phone. "What's your code?"

"One-one-one-one," JD said. "Why?"

" 'Cause it looks like you got a text from Lenny," she said.

That stopped JD. "Fuck. What does it say?"

Sadie read it to him. "'Hey, bruh. I'm thinking I wanna take you up on that offer. What are you doing this afternoon?'"

JD stood there for a second, taking it in. He flexed the fingers in his hand, bringing them back to life and very much enjoying the sight of Sadie standing there naked, his phone in her hand. "Tell him, yeah, no. Today's out. I'm busy making ravenous love to the woman you're infatuated with. How's that?"

"Alright," Sadie said. "You can take a shower, and I may or may not go in there to wash your back and see how deep those scratches are. And then we'll call Curtis."

When Sadie pulled up in front of Black Jack Tattoo for the second time that day, it seemed like everything had changed.

She was feeling satisfied, no doubt about that, but a whole other kind of anxiety had seemed to well up and carry not just her, but JD and Curtis along in the swell. It wasn't fear, exactly. It was just a sense that everything was moving now, and there was nothing she could do to stop it.

Curtis thought he had a good idea of how it would play out, and they had a contingency plan, but she knew perfectly well you couldn't predict what people would do—not exactly. Sadie saw it time and again at the hospital. The patient doesn't react to the medicine the way he's supposed to, or the doctor prescribes something different than you expect, or something takes longer to heal, or less time to heal, or somebody goes fucking crazy in the waiting room. You just can't plan for people.

Lenny was due to arrive at the shop in barely forty-five minutes, and none of them knew what to expect. The creep had done what none of them expected, apparently coming in for a free tattoo. So on top of it all, the mother fucker was cheap. JD had asked him what he was looking to get, but Lenny was coy. But they had agreed on a time, and that was enough. It was almost too good to be true, really. Which they all recognized probably meant that's exactly what this was, but no matter what kind of shit Lenny might be up to, if he was here, it meant he couldn't be at home. And for JD, that meant Sadie could stay out of it all and that was enough for him. So they'd decided to go for it, like it or not. She got outvoted.

Her biggest worry was for JD's safety. It was that simple. She didn't know Lenny Prichard from Adam—had never associated with the St. Eds crowd—but she knew the type. Guys like him could be dangerous. She hated the idea of JD all alone in the shop with Lenny. He had dismissed it when she brought it up, of course. Typical guy. And she'd done her best to rebuild any of his pride she might've bruised, even though it wasn't about that at all. She knew better than most that JD Dugas was no candy ass. The man was a hundred and fifty pounds of braided steel, and he never backed away from conflict. That's just what growing up with older brothers in the country did for you. And that was *exactly* what she was worried about.

She was thankful at least Angel would be there, even though from the look of him, he wouldn't be much help if it came to a fight. And that was if his very presence in the shop didn't fuel the damn fire. *Damn!* She had a bad feeling about it all, but it was too late to do anything other than play her part, and that included supporting her man as best she could. She turned off the ignition and brought her leg up onto the seat so she could turn and face JD, then leaned in for a kiss she hoped conveyed everything she was feeling.

JD was not happy about any of this shit, and the way Sadie had kissed him in her car didn't exactly improve his mood. It was like she thought it was the last kiss they'd ever have, and yeah—it was amazing—but damn! The fact that she was nervous just made him more nervous, and he didn't get nervous! *Goddammit, Curtis!* It was all his fault. He had to get cute with this whole thing. Talking about burying the hatchet and all kinds of nonsense.

Angel looked up from what he was doing when JD walked in and said, "*There* he is! *Dat's* the man right *there!*" JD ignored him, marched past him, and stood in front of his workstation, assessing his inks.

"Okay, so Lenny's coming over. Apparently, he's ready to

pop his tattoo cherry. So I think it's better if you get outta here."

Angel responded with a blank look, unable to comprehend the words JD had just spoken. "Wait. What?"

"Look," JD said, working hard to keep his cool. "I offered to give him his first tat, and he decided to take me up on it. Never mind that it was a totally hollow offer and the last thing in the fucking world I wanna be doing today is seeing Lenny Prichard, much less putting some fucked barb wire armband or Tasmanian devil or whatever the fuck he's gonna want. But that's what's gonna happen. And he's coming in like thirty minutes, and I have to get ready. So you gotta go."

Angel stood up. "Damn. That sucks," he said, understanding now that this was no time to be fucking around. He started moving about the shop, gathering up his stuff. Phone, earbuds, lighter, ballpoint pen, cigarettes, scrap paper he'd been scribbling lyrics on.

"Don't forget your aftercare stuff," JD said. "And follow the damn instructions! I can't have an employee with a shitty-looking tat because he was too lazy to follow instructions." Angel just heard the word "employee," and it made him proud. He gave JD a quick nod.

"Yeah, yeah, boss. I got it. But hey, listen though. Maybe I should stick around? It sounds to me like that man's up to something."

JD actually smiled. "And what? You gonna protect me?"

It was Angel's turn to laugh. "You know I'm a lover, not a brawler. But you know, I could still back you up, just in case."

"Listen, bruh," JD said. "The day I need a skinny ass Puerto

Rican to fight my battles is the day they put me in the ground."

Angel automatically fell into comedy mode. "Why you gotta make it racial?" he said, arms outstretched in mock indignation.

"Yeah, you're right." JD came back. "It's not 'cause you're Puerto Rican or Honduran or whatever. It ain't even because you're twenty-five and I know damn well you can't fight. The real reason is I got enough shit on my mind and I don't have time to worry about you, too." He paused for a second and leveled his gaze at Angel. "So for my sake, you gotta get the fuck out. Okay?" Angel offered an outstretched hand and it was a clap of solidarity when their hands met.

"All right. I got you." Angel consented. "But where's your man Curtis?"

At that moment Curtis was in the Mazda, swallowing a fist full of nootropics with a sixteen-ounce Red Bull. He was nervous and he felt unprepared. Though he wasn't. Curtis had many flaws, but lack of preparation wasn't one of them. And anyway, he had Jacque backing him up now. He was parked at the far end of the Winn-Dixie parking lot, in the no-man's-land area next to Highway 190 where the high school kids held car washes on the weekends and lost long haul truckers sometimes parked to sleep. He powered down the window of the Mazda and listened for the drone that he knew was somewhere overhead, but he couldn't hear it.

He was a good quarter mile from Sun-*N*-Tans and had a clear view. He could see Lenny's big-ass black truck from here. Soon he would need to stage himself out on Highway 13, close to Lenny's trailer, but for now he wanted to have eyes on the

Toyota Tundra while he walked through the plan in his head.

Curtis was rummaging through the EverReady for the walkie-talkie Jacque had given him when the commercial truck pulled into the gravel parking lot. He noticed it as soon as he looked up. A white, four-door Ford F150, it looked like, with a rack on top and a bright orange water cooler just barely visible in the bed. It was dirty, lived-in. The truck was unremarkable except for the logo on the front door panel. Curtis couldn't totally make it out, and he was tempted to pull out his binoculars real quick, but he couldn't risk it. What he could see was two baseball bats crossed in an X pattern. He was probably looking at the truck Troy Vidrine drove, the man Lenny called Lefty, at least according to Angel, who Lenny apparently called Pancho. He liked his nicknames. Lefty, Pancho . . . *Hmm. Pancho and Lefty*, he thought.

Curtis recognized his mind was poised to veer off on a country music tangent and recentered himself with a focused breath. SouthPaw Construction had actually been started by Troy's father—his name escaped Curtis and again he resisted the urge to waste energy pursuing an irrelevant first name at this moment—but it was Troy who expanded the business beyond Eunice and branded it with the crossed baseball bats. The logo came up pretty quick in the half-hour's worth of research Curtis had done in the motel.

As he laboriously typed out the words "comms check" on the flip phone, he cursed his stupidity yet again for leaving his smartphone in New Orleans. He spoke into the walkie: "Blackbird, you see the construction truck that just pulled in November?" The N in November stood for the third letter in Tans. The tattoo shop was Tango, the T for Tat. Curtis read the text message from Sadie that came back right away while he listened to Jacque on the walkie say, "Copy that. I see it."

In place at home. Lenny still at Tans. Everything else is quiet. Are you at Winn-Dixie?

Sadie was seeing Pkg. 2 in the trunk of the Mazda. This was good; she was paying close attention. Curtis typed a Y in the chat to confirm. A few seconds later JD responded to the thread.

I'm ready here. What u think he's gonna want? My money's on a dildo w/ a snake rapped around it

A few seconds later the door to Sun-*N*-Tans opened and a tall, muscular dude in a flannel shirt and a ball cap emerged. Lenny came out a second later, stopping in the doorway and speaking to someone still inside. It looked like he had a beer in his hand. Meanwhile the tall guy—he carried himself like a construction worker—had opened the rear passenger's side door of his truck and was rummaging inside. It had to be Troy. Curtis looked down to locate his notebook, his analyst instincts overriding the operational priority, and when he looked back he saw a glint of sunlight reflecting from something that might have been in Troy's hand when he climbed into the cab of Lenny's truck. Curtis watched them leave as a sinking feeling settled in his stomach.

On the walkie, he said, "Stay with LP's truck. It looks like TV is with him. I'm guessing they're on their way to Tango."

Jacque came back on the walkie-talkie. "Copy that. Now get your ass where you need to be. In and out. Don't fuck around."

Curt called Sadie and cranked the Mazda as it rang. She was not going to like what he had to say.

"Lenny has someone with him," he said when she answered. "I'm pretty sure it's Troy Vidrine. The guy they call Lefty."

"Fuck! What the fuck?"

"It doesn't change anything. Just give JD a heads-up."

"A heads-up? That two dudes are heading over to fuck him up?" Sadie was still technically cool, but she was losing it quick.

"The plan stays the same," Curtis said, and he felt just a little guilty for the way he said it. "JD knows the distress signal. Tell him to use it if he needs it." He was tempted to tell her about Jacque, watching from a couple thousand feet above, but he was on strict orders not to.

"Goddammit!" she protested.

"I'm on my way to deliver package two. Stick to the plan," was all Curt could think to say.

JD was sitting in the one nice customer chair at his station, listening to the Doors live, just waiting and trying to stay cool. It was crazy how quick his world swung from calm to chaos. Barely twenty-four hours ago he'd scored some of the best blow he had in a while at Cecil's Bar, and hours later all but two precious bumps of it was down the toilet. Curtis had dropped everything to come down and help him sort out a case of some missing steroids, and now there were two boxes of the damn stuff floating around Eunice. Angel was a traitor, but now he was a loyal apprentice. He was renting from Lenny Prichard, then he wasn't. Lenny was after Sadie and now here he was giving the man free tattoos. Everything was fucked up, and all he wanted right now was to jam his key in the baggie he'd palmed while Curtis was watching, thinking he'd flushed it, and do a quick bump to help him through whatever was fixing to happen. But he resisted, for now.

He wasn't worried about whoever Lenny might be bringing with him. Sadie seemed to think it was time to call in the fucking SWAT team, but he had calmed her down. She knew better than most that some people were weird about needles and blood and stuff, and you couldn't typecast those people. Lenny might just be bringing the dude 'cause he was nervous about the tattoo. Tough didn't have anything to do with it. Squeamish was squeamish. So a lot of them brought moral support; it was just another crutch, like he'd been telling Angel earlier in the day. Was that even today? Too much was happening at once. What he needed to do was get the shop open and start making some fucking money.

That might be his biggest beef with Curtis and his bright ideas about calling Lenny. Shit, a lot of times in Texas he was making close to three-hundred an hour on some pieces! And here he was in Eunice, in a shop with his own name on it, working for free like some kind of fucking street busker. Like this was amateur hour or something. Giving it away to Slim. Giving it away to Lenny! Hell, he'd only charged Tac like half of what he should've. All these friend discounts were gonna have to stop, and soon.

JD was all about symbolism, and at that moment it wasn't lost on him that the Doors kicked into the blues number "Money" from their *Live in New York* album, Jim Morrison coming back from the dead to sing "I want some money." Simple as that. JD loved how the line just hung out there, unfinished. Like you didn't need to say anything more than that. He knew pretty much every recording of the Doors ever released, so maybe it was a subliminal thing. Maybe his mind had picked the song without him knowing.

The song ended and while the band was retuning you could hear all those kids from 1970 calling out "Light My Fire"! That's all they wanted, just play the hits, the shit they heard on the radio. JD got up to restart the album. It was actually a cool song, especially the way they stretched it out in concert, but there was something about those fucking brats demanding Morrison give them what they wanted that he just couldn't stomach. That could've been Lenny in the audience.

When he turned from the computer he noticed the rose, barely visible against the black of the massage table. And something about the angle of the way it rested on the table, near the head of it, that caused his imagination to superimpose a half-naked Sadie lying there. She was wearing her faded jeans, unzipped, and her black lacy bra, as she brought the rose to her nose for a sniff. It was the expression he saw on her face that caused him to reach for his sketchbook. Her look wasn't seductive or coy or any of that cliche shit. It was just natural, the way he saw her there. She was more interested in the rose than anything. The way she breathed it in, she didn't have a care in the world.

They were doing "Five to One" by the time he got her face exactly right, and Morrison was singing "one in five, no one here gets out alive" when he heard the sound of something hard rapping on the glass up front. JD looked up to see this big lumberjack-looking motherfucker tapping on the glass with a baseball bat, and Lenny was at the door with his hands cupped to his eyes, looking inside. He heard Lenny say "there he is" to the dude with the bat and then he called out over the music.

"JD Dugas! I see you in there! Open up!"

Episode Eight
Take the Money and Run

JD's encounter with Lenny at the tattoo shop doesn't go as expected. Curtis steps across another ethical line and Sadie struggles to keep their plan (and herself) from falling to pieces.

"If I had a nickel for every jock that tried to intimidate me. Well, I'd have a lot of fucking nickels, I'll tell you that much!"
— JD

Curtis had too much on his mind to worry about JD. He could take care of himself, and anyway, there was no benefit to worrying. Actions shaped outcomes. Nail-biting did not. So as he made his way past LSUE on the outskirts of town and hooked left onto Tiger Lane, a two-mile stretch of road that connected to Highway 13 south of town, he called Tac. Outside of abandoning the plan to double back to the tattoo shop, it was the only move Curtis had available to him. Tac picked up on the second ring.

"Detective Youngblood."

"Hey Tac, it's Curtis . . . but you already knew that, right?"

"Yeah, of course," Tac said.

"Okay. I'm gonna assume you're in the office so you didn't want to say my name. Anyway, listen man. I need to ask you to do something for me. Like, right this minute. It relates to what we were talking about last night?"

"Yeah, I'm tracking. What's up?"

"So, I think it's possible our friend Lenny might be headed over to Black Jack's with less than noble intentions."

"Lack of nobility ain't against the law. You know that."

"Look, Tac. Please don't feed me that shit right now. Lenny and I think Troy Vidrine are headed over there now and I have a bad feeling about it. Can you go check it out?"

"Yeah, I know that name. You want me to dispatch somebody?"

"No!" Curtis barked. "Look. It's complicated. We can't have black-and-whites rolling up there. Lenny had an appointment for a tattoo this afternoon. It's just that . . . like I said, Vidrine's with him and I think maybe there's gonna be trouble."

"So this is your move?" Tac asked.

"It's not a move, Tac! I'm just concerned, okay? Can you drive by? Maybe just scope it out from a distance? We both know JD don't need a babysitter, but I'm worried, man."

"There's something you're not telling me."

"There's all kinds of shit I'm not telling you! But none of that has anything to do with what I'm asking you now. Right now, I'm concerned about JD's safety. It's that simple."

"And where are *you*?"

"I can't get there in time," Curtis said.

"Yeah, that's not an answer," Tac came back. "But I get it. I'll swing by."

"Thanks, man. And try to be discrete if you can."

"Okay, now you're pushing it," Tac said and hung up.

In the walkie, Curtis reported to Jacque. "You should see an unmarked car, a black Crown Vic, somewhere in the vicinity. That's my friend in blue, checking up. I asked him to watch the action, in case there's trouble."

"Copy that," Jacque said. "Now stop meddling and do your job."

JD glared at the dude in the window and he stopped tapping with the bat. Lenny stood at the door wearing creased jeans and a button-up shirt, still dressed exactly like he did in high school, JD figured. He gave a sort of half-wave when JD looked at him, and JD dropped the unfinished sketch on the nice customer chair on his way to the door. The only emotions he felt were dread and irritation. He knew he was supposed to call Sadie and leave the line open so she could listen in for the emergency word or whatever, but fuck that. He turned the latch on the door and pushed it open for Lenny, then looked towards the jock in the flannel.

"You break it, you bought it," JD said evenly. After a moment, the tall man spoke.

"It wouldn't take much." It wasn't clear to JD if he was talking about the breaking or the buying.

"JD, this is my man Lefty," Lenny said with the slightest head nod in Troy's direction.

JD let him know with eyes that he wasn't impressed. "What's with the bat?" he asked, still standing in the door.

"I never leave home without it," Troy said.

"Well, ain't you just a cryptic motherfucker?" JD said, deciding pretty much in that moment he didn't like this guy at all.

"He's not much of a talker," Lenny said. "That's what I like about him. You shoulda seen him in the batter's box though. Lefty's a *beast!*" JD watched the dude they called Lefty smile involuntarily. He looked towards JD.

"I finished with a 550 slugging percentage." JD just stared at him for a second, waiting for the punchline.

"I guess that's good?" he asked when it was clear none was coming.

Lenny laughed. "Yeah, that's pretty good," he said. "Can we go inside?"

They stood in the little waiting area—four metal folding chairs and a handful of black milk crates with tattoo magazines and three-ring binders of flash, all ringed around a low, stout table of planed-down pallet boards a friend in Texas had made for JD. Lenny stood there taking it all in. Troy sat down and put a boot on the table, giving it a not-so-gentle push to check its stability. When the table didn't give, he put his foot down and peered underneath to inspect the construction.

"So what are you looking to get?" JD asked. Lenny paused,

and JD found it odd that he appeared to be thinking about the question, maybe for the first time.

"I'm not really for sure," Lenny said.

"You don't know what you want?" It was hard to believe, but Lenny just gave him a noncommittal look. When he didn't offer anything more, JD walked over to one of the crates and plucked up his personal portfolio, a black binder covered in stickers from other shops he'd worked at. It contained a decade of his best work. He handed it to Lenny. "This is all my work. The highlights, at least. If you see something that strikes you, I can draw up something custom."

Lenny sat down and opened the book on the table, leaning over to flip through the pages. "So, this is like, the menu?" Lenny asked, and again JD was suspicious. Since when were dudes this ignorant of how tattoos work?

"Nah. It's not a menu. I wouldn't put the same exact design on you. That's not fair to the people in that book. Or to you, for that matter. What you want is something original. Something that's your signature." JD stood there for a few seconds, thinking. "Are you looking to get something today?"

Lenny shrugged. "Maybe." He looked up from the book and nodded towards the lumberjack. "*He* wants one though."

"Yeah," Troy said, standing up. "I wanna get one. When Lenny said you were giving out free tattoos, I said fuck yeah!".

"Oh, I think you heard it wrong," JD said. "I told your man here I'd give him his first one for free. But that offer's non transferable."

"Pretty big fucking word," Troy said. JD just held his eyes.

Thousands of hours spent in bars, tattoo parlors, and drug dens had given JD a clinical ability to differentiate truly dangerous men from what they used to call in high school the posers. The lumberjack was in the latter class.

"But I'll cut you a good deal, bruh. That's my whole business model. Lafayette quality tattoos at Eunice prices. So what are you looking to get?"

"I heard that somewhere," Lenny said. JD ignored him.

Troy brought the bat up to within about six inches of JD's face and held it there, right on the line between implied and implicit threat. "You see that logo?" he asked.

"What, *Louisville Slugger*"? JD asked, reaching up with one hand and gently pulling it down and away from his face, making a bit of a show of finding the right distance to study the oval-shaped logo. The lumberjack let go of the bat.

"Yeah. I was thinking maybe on my arm?"

"You might think about right here on your chest," JD said, creating the oval shape with his fingers and imprinting them on the upper part of Troy's pec. "You'll wear it better there, trust me. Like a badge."

"Yeah, I like that. Just like my nametag on my work shirts."

"He's gonna have to ask his old lady first," Lenny chimed in.

"Oh yeah?" JD asked, ignoring Lenny. "Where do you work?"

"She's oriental," Lenny said, to no one in particular.

"I got my own construction company," Troy said proudly. He reached around and pulled out his wallet—JD still holding the bat—to extract a business card. He held it out for JD to see the criss-crossed baseball bats embossed in blue, with the words "SouthPaw Construction" written in awkward block letters, the geometry of the two ideas on the card at odds. JD squinted at the card and frowned to show his disapproval.

"I hope you're a better carpenter than you are a designer," he said, handing the bat back to Troy. He grabbed his sketchbook from the nice customer chair and flipped to a clean page. In thirty seconds or so, he'd sketched a new logo that mimicked the oval-shaped design of the Louisville Slugger one, incorporating the criss-crossed bats, with "SouthPaw Construction" lettered in a style that matched the baseball bat. "It should look more like this."

Lefty took the sketchbook and marveled at what JD had done.

"So, JD. What's the deal with you and Sadie?" Lenny asked. That got JD's attention. He leveled his gaze at Lenny and labored to control his emotions.

"Aw, shit!" Troy exclaimed. "That's the fucking shit!" He looked at JD with something like awe, then turned to Lenny, still sitting on the folding chair watching the exchange, and thrusted the sketchbook at him. "Check this out."

Lenny was reluctant to accept the sketchbook, his question about Sadie still hanging in the air. Just then the sound of the landline ringing at the back of the shop cut through the Doors doing "Roadhouse Blues" and all three of them turned. JD walked over to answer it. He wasn't surprised it was Sadie.

"You didn't call me!" was the first thing she said, no greeting, no preamble whatsoever. Aware of Lenny's eyes on him from the front of the shop, JD did his best to mask the identity of the caller—he even thought about calling out "Hey, mom" or some such shit—but he wouldn't stoop that low.

He reached over to the computer and inched up the volume. As Lenny studied him, JD casually pivoted to turn his back towards them. And so he didn't see Lenny turn to the previous page where he'd done the sketch of Sadie lying on the massage table. In fact, he had no way of knowing how long they had been gone. He only knew that when he turned around the shop was empty, and when he walked to the front to peer out the window, Lenny's truck wasn't in the parking lot. His sketchbook lay on the coffee table, but both sketches—the one he did for Troy and the one of Sadie—had been torn from the book.

Tac watched much of this unfold like a silent movie through his binoculars from across the parking lot. Or maybe a play. It was already dark, and so they stood out like players lit up on a stage, performing behind the glass. Tac didn't need the dialogue. He could pretty much tell what was happening. For most of it at least. But things had gotten a little cloudy towards the end. The guy in the flannel shirt Tac knew it was Troy Vidrine—a known associate and local business owner—well, he seemed to soften.

That in and of itself didn't surprise Tac. He knew from first-hand experience how JD could disarm you in his way. It wasn't charisma, exactly. Not like movie-star shit. It was just a certain quality he had. Maybe it was just what the guy did for a living.

But that couldn't be. Tac had a handful of tattoos, and he couldn't remember a single thing about any of the other guys who'd put them on him. Anyway, what you called it didn't matter, the point was JD seemed to have an effect on Vidrine. And if you're Lenny and he's the guy you're bringing in for the muscle, to intimidate, well, he could see how it would piss Lenny off to no end to have the guy end up practically tongue kissing JD before it was all said and done.

Maybe that was why they booked all of a sudden. Lenny just deciding fuck it and getting out of there. Maybe. Except that it almost looked like they were *sneaking* out. He took another couple minutes to sit there in the car and watch JD while he breathed in the Black Ice cop smell of the Crown Vic and hopefully let it help him think clearly. He still needed to swing by Squeaky's to thank Patience for identifying Angel, and instantly he could see her behind the counter, smiling, that beautiful skin. Tac recognized the tangent and recentered himself. He took a deep breath and watched JD return from the sidewalk where he'd gone out to presumably look for Lenny's truck, long gone now.

With his ShadowQuest binoculars Tac could've probably read their lips, if he knew how. But he didn't need the binoculars or the words to understand. He caught himself wondering if maybe there was online training for reading lips and then came back to what he was supposed to be doing. JD was pacing around the brightly lit shop working his cell phone with his thumbs. He didn't look calm, but then Tac thought of Troy Vidrine putting that bat in JD's face, and considering the way that went down, JD seemed pretty chill. If Tac was in his shoes, he wasn't sure he would have that kind of composure.

When JD heard the rap at the window from Tac's ring he didn't flinch, but his blood pressure spiked and he wielded around ready to do some damage. Enough was enough. But then he saw Tac standing there in his cop casuals—cargo pants, boots, and a shirt his old lady might've picked out—and his anger morphed into suspicion. He'd already texted Sadie to put her on notice that Lenny had taken off, so there was nothing else he could do. Curtis was on his own. There was nothing to do but open the door and see what Tac had to say.

"Don't tell me you were in the neighborhood," JD said when he opened the door.

"What neighborhood? There's like, two stores open here. A chicken joint and a tattoo parlor."

"Yeah, sounds like the start of a bad joke." JD stepped back to let him in the shop, then extended a hand. They shook in the traditional style.

Tac cut to the chase. "So what was that all about?"

"How much did you see?" JD wanted to know.

"Well, I got here right about the time Troy Vidrine was putting that baseball bat in your face." JD's eyes gave nothing away, and Tac had to admire his cop defense instincts.

"So that's who that was?" JD said. "That'll have to go in my report back to Curtis."

"Well, I can save you the trouble. Curtis called me. Said those dudes were coming over."

"And what, asked you to come play big brother?" *Dammit, Curtis!* JD thought.

"He said it different than that. I think he was just concerned" Tac said. "Where is Curtis anyway?"

JD recognized he was fishing. No way he was gonna bite. He leveled his gaze at Tac.

"That's hard to say, bruh."

"So what's the deal with Lenny? Are you guys buddy-buddy now?"

"Let's walk outside while I smoke a cigarette," JD said. It was nice out. The cold air felt good on his face. He pulled a smoke from the soft pack in his shirt pocket and he could smell Sadie on his fingers when he put it to his mouth. "I don't know for sure what Lenny's deal is. Maybe his only problem is he needs to get laid. That and he hangs out with a low class of people."

Tac wasn't sure what to say to that, so he stayed quiet.

"I can understand the need to get laid. The problem is," JD continued, "it's Sadie he's trying to fuck."

"And don't forget the low class of people." Tac jumped in. "Like that kid, Angel. Right? You stole him from Lenny. And now he's, what, your apprentice?"

JD gave Tac a look. Why didn't he ask about Angel last night, when they were having their heart-to-heart?

"Well first, I didn't steal Angel. And anyway, the more time I spend with him the more I think he might be righteous after all. He just, you know, maybe got mixed up with the wrong crowd." JD smiled and dragged on his cigarette, proud of how he turned that around.

"I did a little homework on Angel," Tac said. "He's not as crime-prone as he might appear to be."

"Shit, bruh, you just figuring that out? Angel ain't any more a gangsta than I'm a steroid-kingpin. That's all image, bubba." JD said. "If you're looking for kingpins, it's the dude who just left here. But you already know that. My question is, when're you gonna stop worrying about Curt's little piddly-ass secrets and start asking the right questions about Lenny?"

Tac shook his head in a friendly way.

"It's like I told your boy last night. I like to do my police work myself. And I already know what Lenny's into. Shit, we had a case against him two years ago and they wouldn't let me charge him."

JD considered that for a second. "But it wasn't nothing like the kind of weight we told you about last night, was it?" Tac stayed silent, making it clear the answer to JD's question was no. "At some point," JD continued, "somebody's gonna come get that shit from 2nd Street. All you gotta do is be ready to follow it." JD finished his cigarette and flicked it out into the parking lot.

"It's not that simple," Tac said, unsure of the words coming out of his mouth. "I need probable cause. All that."

"You'll figure that out," JD said. "You're not gonna let twenty-thousand dollars' worth of high-test steroids get loose into the community. That's against your oath. And anyway, I know you better than that."

Tac stood silent, taking his cue from JD and giving away nothing.

"Listen," JD said. "I didn't want to say this in front of Curtis last night because the mother- fucker's already too big for his britches. But he knows what's up. If he tells you something or shows you something, it'll be ironclad. You can trust *me* on that. The dude's not gonna feed you bad information. Now, you might have to work some magic to make it *usable*, but the info will be solid. Now lemme see that arm. Is it all healed?"

Curtis had edged the Mazda over the cattle guard at the entrance to the property and driven down a quarter-mile track of loose gravel cut through a field to arrive at Lenny's homestead. The trailer and the surrounding property appeared to be empty, but he'd just sat in the car watching for a good five minutes to be sure. He was parked a little ways from Lenny's trailer, outside the glow of the security light, still waiting when the first text from JD came in.

They left! The MF took a sketch I did of Sadie and hauled ass!

A few minutes later a text from Sadie came in.

I see him moving down Laurel.

And then another one.

He stopped.

Curtis had got out of the Mazda, which he'd backed in a little off to the side of the long-ass gravel driveway that led right up to the front door of the trailer. He had tripped the security light above the front door when he pulled up. It stayed on long enough to worry him, so Curtis walked quickly up to the deck and flipped the switch at the base of it to turn it off.

Back in the Mazda, he checked in with Jacque. "Where are the boys?"

"Looks like they stopped for a drink," Jacque came back on the walkie.

"Do your thing. I'm gonna swing over and cover you from the top." He called Sadie real quick and she confirmed Lenny's truck was at Cecil's Bar.

"Text me as soon as it moves," Curtis said, feeling like an idiot. He pulled a clean blue bandana from his back pocket and tied it across his nose, train robber style, pulled on a watch cap, then fixed his headlamp on top of it. Before he went outside, he took five deep breaths that felt like forever, then checked his watch and grabbed his walkie-talkie. He would give himself fifteen minutes. No more.

From studying the overhead imagery, he knew exactly where the main electrical meter that fed the house was located. It was dark out here in the country; the headlamp was an absolute necessity. But as he made his way around the back of the trailer to the meter, he was struck by how quiet it was out there. The silence was absolute: the sounds of his footsteps in the grass, wind. That was it.

At the meter, he switched on his headlamp and used his Leatherman tool to unscrew the heavy glass front cover of the meter, put the screws in his pocket, then worked the tool in the little slot beneath the dial to flip the main switch, just like in the videos he'd watched. The power was off now. Or, it should be, at least. He would know soon enough. He put the glass back in place, without the screws, and walked around to the front of the trailer.

By the time he retrieved the EverReady from the trunk and clipped the 9-millimeter in the holster to his belt, five minutes had already passed. And he was getting nervous. *Get in and get out*, he told himself. He shouldered the pack and pulled the flip phone out of his pocket to double-check on any new texts he might've missed. He typed the letter "e" to let JD and Sadie know he was entering the residence, then he closed the phone without noticing the battery was almost out. There would be no "x" to indicate he was free and clear of the property.

He'd pulled on latex gloves at the door to the trailer, then pulled the screen door back and put his ear to the inner door to listen for a dog or anything unusual. All he needed was some little yapper nipping at his heels once he got in there. Or worse, some Doberman frothing at the mouth. But it was quiet, so he tried the first of the five keys he had. Then he tried the second, and the third. By the time he tried the fourth key, he was sweating, and his heart was pounding when he tried the last key on the ring and it still didn't fit. He took a deep breath and started again, and this time the second key slid roughly into place when he applied some pressure.

He pushed open the door and stood there on the threshold, listening, and as he did, something interesting happened. The swell of panic he'd been working to keep down suddenly flattened out, neutralized by something that might have been adrenaline or might have come from some darker place that he couldn't articulate. He didn't have time to think about it because there was work to do. Much later, when it seemed he had nothing but time to think about all this, Curt would identify this moment, standing there on the threshold of breaking into Lenny's place, as the moment of no return. *Slow is smooth and smooth is fast*, he told himself. *Get in, get out.*

He reached over and flipped the light switch to confirm the power was off. Plenty of wireless cameras still worked without an internet connection, and just as many had battery back-ups. But a lot of them didn't, and even some that advertised those features didn't really deliver on the promise. Either way, Curtis figured a power outage tipped the odds in his favor. It was a point Sadie and JD had split on when he'd laid it out for them at the motel.

He started scanning the room from where he stood, from the top down. He checked the corners for cameras or wires or speakers, quartered off the rest of the room, and scanned it as carefully as he could. There were two small speakers at the back of the room, but they looked like surround sound speakers, and not the smart variety. The subwoofer and soundbar under the TV were just as harmless. People these days seemed to have their whole lives wired up, but it looked like Lenny hadn't yet embraced the internet of everything.

Still, he had to be careful. *Slow is smooth and smooth is fast.* "Hey, Alexa!" he called out. And when he didn't hear anything, tried again. "Hey, Google!" and again waited. His last shout was just for him. "Hey, Lenny," he called to the empty room. "Fuck you!"

Curtis stepped into a living room that was like a jock's wet dream. He stood there gawking at a massive trophy case against the opposite wall. It was a monstrosity of glass and gold with a menagerie of trophies and ribbons and baseball paraphernalia inside it. Curtis walked over to get a closer look. At the center of the case were two blue, gold, and mahogany trophies in the shape of Louisiana that he recognized as state championship awards. Each was about two feet tall with various ribbons hanging off it.

There was a baseball adorned with signatures in a worn glove that was positioned just so in front of the trophies. Above the two marquee trophies there was a small glass shelf with a little velvet pillow and a big-ass championship ring with a blue stone in the middle. Up close with his headlamp shining down on the case, the real surprise to Curtis was how clean the damn thing was. There wasn't a spec of dust in the entire case, and it was a monumental thing. There were probably a hundred different artifacts in it. Shirts, framed pictures, baseballs. Even a bat and a helmet, for Christ's sakes!

Curtis quickly scanned the rest of the room. There were two black leather reclining chairs, the kind with built-in cup holders and media ports and shit like that. And they faced a television that took up the entirety of the wall it hung on. There was nothing else in the living room.

He didn't go in the kitchen, but from what he could see of it in the beam of his headlamp, it was neater than average. Canisters of coffee and cereal and rice in a neat row on the counter. The coffee maker and rice pot on the counter shiny and set just so. No clutter whatsoever. There were a few papers attached to the side of the fridge with magnets, but otherwise Curtis didn't see anything that looked interesting to him.

There was a hallway that led from the living room to the back of the trailer. It was maybe fifteen feet long, with two doors off to the left and one at the very end of the hall. He went to the end first and opened the door to the master bedroom. He had to laugh when he saw the waterbed. "Fucking classy" Curtis said aloud, pressing down on the corner and watching the expanse of the thing undulate under the dark comforter. He noted the closet against the far wall—he would come back if he had time—but for now he didn't linger. He needed to prioritize.

He opened the bathroom door only long enough to confirm it was the bathroom then quickly moved to the second bedroom, which turned out to be the most promising. Lenny had it set up as a little office. Or maybe game room was a better description. The main feature of the small room was a big TV monitor on a low table connected to a gaming system. The shelves under the monitor were full of cartridge cases. Curtis focused his headlight beam on them; alphabetized by sport, it looked like. Auto Racing, Baseball, Basketball, Football. There were two of those low gaming chairs with the speakers built-in positioned across from the monitor.

There were three large, black rubber totes with locking lids stacked in the corner, a set of golf clubs, a motorcycle helmet, and a laundry basket filled with NCAA footballs. Curtis opened the storage tote on top and saw it was full of what looked like promotional tee shirts. He lifted it down and opened the second one. It was more of the same. Tee shirts, shorts, socks. Curtis pulled that one aside and opened the bottom one. It was full of old baseball uniforms. Curtis recognized some of them from his own youth, and he smiled despite himself. It was pretty cool that he'd preserved this stuff.

He almost felt guilty for putting the steroids there, but it was too perfect. No way Lenny was digging into this bin on a regular basis. And plus, he needed to get out of there. So he set the EverReady on the floor and pulled the box of steroids from it. It was about the size of a shoebox. It wasn't too hard to work it into the bottom of the bin without messing up the folded uniforms too much. Within thirty seconds or so he had everything arranged on top and it looked more or less undisturbed.

When he was done, he checked his watch and saw that his fifteen minutes were up by three minutes plus. He reached into his pocket then to check the flip phone for new messages, but it was dead. A fresh wave of panic rose up in his chest and flashed hot on his neck and head.

Cecil's Bar was loud, smoky, and known to get rowdy sometimes, especially on the weekends. That's what made it cool. Old man Cecil Brown had opened the place far enough back in the history of Eunice that all the old regulars who used to drink there had already died off. Old Man Cecil was in the grave too, but his son—they called him Teetsie, an ironic nickname he'd picked up as a fat kid growing up— had been running the place at least since JD and Curtis and Lenny were drinking age, part of the last generation of Louisiana citizens to be legal at eighteen. At some point Teetsie had gotten into rap, and ever since then he'd taken to calling himself Teet-C. Teet-C was a good three-hundred-fifty pounds of butter beans, Crown Royal, and crawfish, and he ran Cecil's like it was his own personal fiefdom. Which wasn't far from the truth.

The square cinder block building would've been big for its time, and judging from the black-and-white pictures nailed to the interior walls, not much had changed. A bar ran along the length of the building to the right of the entrance, with bathrooms and a tiny little kitchen back behind it. The main area was divided into two sections. The front half was well lit and big enough for two coin-operated pool tables, and even when there weren't games going on, a lot of patrons never made it any further down the bar. The back section mostly stayed dark, but on weekends it came alive.

There were plenty of comfortable, safe places around Eunice to go out and hear traditional Cajun music. Cecil's on a Saturday was a different thing. The bandstand in the corner was just high enough to be a tripping hazard and barely wide enough to hold a drum kit, but somehow a handful of regular Cajun bands with sometimes up to six players made it work. At least a couple weekends a month a certain class of people from Eunice and the surrounding little towns would crowd into Cecil's to hear bands like The Bayou Brawlers, The Tell-You-Whats, or The Gone Pecans and spend a couple hours jitterbugging their asses off. There was never a cover charge at Cecil's. Instead, a hat was passed around and the band received whatever ended up in it: crumpled bills, phone numbers, condoms, pills, and all kinds of contraband.

Sometimes fights broke out. Sometimes there was lewd behavior, but whatever or whoever was going down, people dealt with it more or less the same. If it was a fight, whether it happened in the bar or spilled out into the parking lot, they formed a tight circle and watched, shielding the combatants from the EPD, who kept a close eye on the weekend crowd. On the other end of the spectrum, sometimes couples got carried away, and when that happened, most people had the common decency to turn away, but there was still a natural tendency to protect the individuals from outside scrutiny. Cecil's was a kind of protected space, a refuge, in that way. What a certain rougher type of bar used to be, except in the case of Cecil's, it still was.

There was no sign, but it was understood that cell phones never came out at Cecil's. On those occasions when someone violated the rule, either by mistake or temptation, they'd be lucky to walk out with the phone intact. Teet-C was known to throw them in the deep fryer and come back with the phone in a little basket with a couple french fries on top, or drop it right in his styrofoam cup of Crown and Coke and keep it in there while he sipped at his drink all night long.

But weekdays at Cecil's were a good bit different. Tamer, quieter. They were days ordered by routine and familiar faces. Teet-C would show up around noon with his lunch—maybe a shrimp po'boy, dressed, or a footlong chili dog from the Sonic, or a plate lunch from Rudy's—and sit up high in his captain's chair next to the little drive-through cut-out at the far end of the bar, watching TV and smoking out the window. Around happy hour, he'd fix himself a big Crown and Coke and migrate down to the other end of the bar, where the pool tables and the women, when there were any, tended to congregate.

There weren't really regulars at Cecil's. He got semi-regulars instead, people who moved in cycles. Some of them worked offshore, out in the Gulf of Mexico, or maybe on a rig off the coast of Africa or South America. Some of them were farmers, harvesting crawfish, soybeans, rice, sweet potatoes. They came in for a few weeks to spend their money and time between seasons. Sometimes people skipped town or went to jail. And there were still others, like Lenny, who came but never stayed long, and only on weekdays. Those were the people who knew the C in Teet-C did not stand for Cecil.

If Teet-C knew you—not knew *of* you, but actually *knew* you—who your daddy was, what you did for a living, where you went to high school, who your cousins were, if he really *knew* you, and if you asked no more than once a month, he would sell you up to two grams of good cocaine at roughly twice the going street value. He jacked it up that way to discourage people. He considered it a safety measure.

It was unclear why Teet-C took this calculated risk, but he'd been doing it for years and it seemed to be working for him. What he sold individually to the small handful of individuals who met his criteria was just a small piece of a regular shipment he received about once a month from Houston and passed on to the same dude from Opelousas he'd been selling it to for ten years.

The only thing Lenny found strange about the connection was how easily it seemed to fall into his lap. And that was almost literally what happened, maybe six months after he'd opened up Sun-*N*-Tans. In fact, he almost thought he was being set up at first. He was sitting there drunk one early Thursday evening, talking about driving back to his lonely ass trailer while Teet-C played solitaire at the bar and some cowboys played pool, and they got to talking. First about baseball, then about family. It turned out old Cecil Brown used to run with his Uncle Ely back in the day, and Teet-C got reverential all of a sudden. The next thing Lenny knew he was sliding a to-go cup of ice water across the bar with some coke folded in the napkin.

It had become a kind of tradition for Lenny and Lefty to meet at Cecil's every so often for a couple quick beers before they lit out to Lenny's place with usually just a gram—nothing crazy—to hit golf balls into the field and play Xbox. Lenny told himself he did it for Troy. The dude's wife was overbearing, and whether he knew it or not, he needed to cut loose. There was some truth to that, but it damn sure wasn't that simple. For one thing, Troy worshiped his wife, Thao, in a way that Lenny and others would never understand and Troy himself would never fully express to his friends. It was uncool to do so, even if your old lady wasn't Vietnamese. First-generation Vietnamese-American, technically, not that any of the assholes he hung around could ever appreciate the difference. And besides, Lenny was usually the one hoovering up the blow like there was no tomorrow.

But on this night, with Lenny seething from the portrait of Sadie he still had in his hands and couldn't help but keep coming back to (and yes, somewhere in his semiconscious he was already planning what he'd do with that drawing once he was alone). Well, they both needed the drinks. The problem was Thao had texted Troy almost as soon as the first round of Bud and tequila had hit the bar in front of them. Lenny wasn't even warmed up yet and Troy was already making noise about how he needed to get back, especially if Lenny still needed him to run that errand in the morning. Which he knew damn well Lenny did. "What do you think the key's for?" Lenny had asked, maybe with too sharp a tongue.

It was just a couple minutes later when Troy checked his phone, even though Lenny didn't hear anything, and said he really had to go. But they'd come to Cecil's in Lenny's truck, so Lefty would just have to wait at least until Lenny finished his second round. And Troy had decided, fuck it, since he was sitting there, he'd go ahead and have another round too.

Sadie watched the map as the indicator started moving again. By the time she got finished sending her text to Curtis and JD, Lenny's truck had stopped again. He was back at the tanning place, and she was hopeful he would at least go in for a few minutes, but the truck was on the move pretty much right away. And within a minute he was going past Eunice High, on the outskirts of town, probably to hit Maple to connect from there to Highway 13. Fuck! She sent a series of texts.

Lenny's on the move again! I think he might be going home!

Please tell me U R out!

Do you copy?

She was calling Curtis when JD's text fell on deaf ears, just like hers.

Get outta there, bubba!

The phone went right to a nondescript voicemail, and Sadie didn't bother. For an instant, she even thought about getting in her car and flagging Lenny down, but it was already too late by the time it occurred to her. He was already on Highway 13 and the speed limit was 55. He could be at his house in fifteen minutes, easy. Less than ten if he hauled ass. And then he stopped, right there on Highway 13, and Sadie felt a building sense of relief, cautious, but hopeful. Maybe he was turning around. She waited for the icon to reverse itself, but after a minute or so it started moving again, in the same direction.

But she could call! Yes! She'd call him, distract him somehow! No. She couldn't do it. Couldn't bring herself to do it. And anyway, what was she gonna do? Invite him to come over? That was going too far. She called JD.

"Just call him!" Sadie demanded.

"And say what?"

"Anything! We have to try!" She didn't know why Curtis

wasn't answering, but it damn sure wasn't a good sign and her intuition was telling her the situation was fucked up. JD didn't like it.

"Either one of us calls that man and he immediately knows something's up," he said.

"You called him last night! Just call and ask him why he left."

He didn't like it, but JD gave it a try. The call went straight to voicemail, which didn't surprise him. He thought about texting, but a damn text message wasn't gonna convince the dude to turn around. He called Sadie back and told her the truth, which was that Curtis was on his own. All they could do was hope, pray, and keep sending the messages in case his phone came back on.

Curtis ran to the window to look outside, but he didn't feel relief when he saw nothing but darkness. He stood there for fifteen seconds maybe, enough for one big deep breath. The sound of the walkie-talkie in his pocket coming to life made him jump. "Move your ass! Repeat. Move your ass!" Curt rushed back towards the living room, then pushed the walkie to talk.

"How much time?"

"No time," Jacque said, his voice still level.

"I need two minutes," Curt said, as if Jacque had the power to grant his wish.

"The man is on his way. Repeat. Get-the-fuck-out." Curtis ran back into the extra room and opened the closet door. It was like a Jenga stack of shoeboxes in two colors. Orange Nikes and Black Adidas. They were stacked practically to the ceiling in four rows. He backed up as far as he could to capture the entire tower of boxes in the beam of his headlamp and stood there studying it for a few seconds. There was something about the way they were organized. It wasn't immediately clear there was any pattern at all; it just looked like four big-ass stacks of shoe boxes. But there was something to them. Three of the stacks started with Nikes. The other was a black Adidas box. The orange columns had four blacks at the very bottom, but the black columns had only three orange boxes at the bottom.

He noticed the very last box in the third orange column. It should have been black like the others, but it was a Nike box. He reached down and grabbed the box with both hands, pulled it out in one quick motion. The whole column fell in a uniform stack. He opened the box and he was only half surprised it wasn't an old pair of shoes but a gallon-size Ziplock bag with six fat rolls of bills rubber-banded together.

His hands began to operate independent of his brain, and long before he had a chance to second guess the act he was already committing, he had removed about twenty percent of the first of the rolls, which was about the width of a soup can and seemed to be mostly twenties. Later on, when he reflected on this moment of greed, he finally understood that this was, if not a rock bottom, then at least an all-time low. He would reflect not just on the depths he had sunk to, but also how invigorated and alive he'd felt in that moment. He wasn't sure he liked what it said about him.

When the mind and body are focused and powered by adrenaline, it's amazing what a person can accomplish inside of sixty seconds. Curtis had jammed the six fistfuls of money into the EverReady and rebuilt the tower in reverse, trusting by feel that he was lining them up as carefully as they had been. Fifteen seconds later he was at the door, pulling it closed behind him and working his latex-gloved hand inside his pants pocket for the key ring. And then his nerves kicked back in. He remembered which key on the ring fit the lock, but try as he might he couldn't get the damn thing to work. It wasn't until he forced himself into a deep breath that he didn't have time for that the key finally, reluctantly, fell into place.

He sprinted around the back of the house to the electric meter, his bandana loose around his neck now. His adrenaline was too much for that kind of precaution in this moment. He had to tear off the latex glove with his teeth to free his fingers enough to grab the tiny screws at the bottom of his pocket. When he brought his Leatherman tool up to pull out the screwdriver and work it into the little slot, his hands were shaking. He drew another deep breath and that seemed to make all the difference.

The walkie-talkie in his pocket came to life again. "You got maybe two minutes. I better see that car start moving in ten seconds!"

In retrospect, he should have left the glass unsecured. It could have stayed that way for months, probably, set in place without the screws, and it would've been fine. But he was committed, working at the screws there in the dark behind the trailer, with Lenny so close he could almost hear the faint sound of the tires of his Tundra on the highway. He got two screws in the meter and decided that would have to do. He sprinted back to the Mazda.

And as he opened the car door, he heard it—the low drone of heavy tires on asphalt—and then he saw it—lights in the distance, approaching fast from the left. It was a long, *long* way to the end of the driveway for Curt. Practically a quarter mile of hard gravel baked into the dirt lane. Curtis was in the car, windows down, listening and sitting forward because the pistol had shifted on his belt and it was practically behind him, when he realized there was no way he would make it. He was fucked.

In a matter of seconds he would come face-to-face with Lenny on the gravel driveway, his own property, and there would be no way out. The gun would come into play then and whatever the outcome, they would both be fucked. The droning bass of the tires on the highway began to slow then as Lenny closed in on the last hundred meters or so to the driveway.

Curtis was out of options. He heard the sound of Jacque's voice then. "Drive to your left! Cut across the driveway and kill the lights!" He cut the wheel hard to the left and the Mazda bottomed out hard on the little ditch that ran parallel to the driveway, but he made it through. The back tires fell into the channel with a thud and bounced out the other side and he was in the field now, lights out and windows down, accelerating *slow is smooth and smooth is fast* away from the driveway entrance. And he was exposed. He was *totally* exposed.

But he wasn't in the line of sight and now he was at least fifty meters from the entrance and he was close to the fence that defined the property. It was just a simple wire fence, the kind you electrified to keep the cows from crossing, but on the other side of it, between Curtis and the highway, was a ten-foot ditch that might as well have been a moat. He took his foot off the accelerator and let the car coast, aware enough in that moment to keep his foot off the brake as he rolled up close to the fence, just as Lenny passed in front of him on the highway, a ten-meter target if he wanted to take his shot then and there.

Two ships passing in the night. The phrase came to Curtis as he registered the fact that Lenny never glanced to his right as he passed. It was hard to know what he would have seen if he had. This was the country. They didn't have street lights here and the moon was just an inconsequential thing that night. Curtis drew the pistol then, maybe because he actually felt a sense of relief that he wouldn't need it at that point, or maybe because it was digging into his back. He watched Lenny tear-ass down the gravel driveway, accelerating to maybe 45 or 50, which was fine by Curtis, and then hitting the brakes hard when he got close to the trailer. Hard as hell—initiating a slide that probably went a couple car lengths by the time it was over.

The car was still running. Curtis put his hand on the ignition. New battery or not, he didn't want to risk the car not starting again. Maybe he'd fucked something up going through the ditch. He watched the brake light on the back of the Tundra for what seemed like minutes, Lenny's foot still on the brake. He turned the car off, hoping he hadn't made a fatal mistake. He watched in the rearview mirror of the Mazda as the interior light in Lenny's truck came on as Lenny emerged from the truck.

He was strolling up to the front door when Curtis realized he failed to turn the security light back on. A few seconds later Lenny discovered the same thing. Curtis watched breathlessly as the silhouetted figure at the front door waved his hand in front of the light several times before eventually reaching over to activate the switch. Curtis had grown paranoid that he'd fucked up the power some kind of way, so he was relieved, to some extent, when the light came on in the trailer when Lenny stepped inside.

Curtis inhaled and turned the key. He only exhaled once the car started. He didn't waste any time getting out of there. When he was safely on the road heading back towards Eunice, Jacque came on the walkie.

"I don't know if you're crazy or stupid or both. But one thing's for sure. You a lucky muthafucka."

"I heard sometimes it's better to be lucky than good," Curt said.

"Well, that settles it then. You stupid." After a pause, Jacque came back. "I'm out. Bring my walkie back with you. When you wake up tomorrow, just drive your ass out of town. Do not pass go, do *not* collect two hundred dollars. Just get the fuck out. You hear?"

"Copy that," Curtis said. "Out here."

"Out here." Jacque's voice came through one more time. "Crazy ass muthafucka."

Lenny was riding high, and it didn't have anything to do with the sixteenth he had in his pocket. Lefty wouldn't even take a bump before he got in his own trunk to go back to that little mail-order bride he had at home, and that irritated him. But, whatever. That just meant there was more for him. But anyway it wasn't the coke that was making him feel good, even though he'd pulled over to the shoulder on 13 to do a couple big bumps from the tip of the folding knife he kept in the glove box, and that damn sure got him going: two big piles of that shit, one in each nostril. But no, it wasn't the cocaine making him feel accomplished and invincible. That was just a coincidence.

He was feeling good because he'd had a revelation right there in the parking lot of Sun-*N*-Tans as he watched Lefty walk back to his own truck. The poor bastard was slinking back to his wife and kids, emasculated. And then there was JD Dugas. So hung up on Sadie Lee he's sitting there alone in his crappy ass tattoo shop drawing sketches of her! And you *know* a woman like that wasn't gonna be with a dude like him. Not long-term anyway. And the fact that JD Dugas actually thought Lenny was gonna let him put a tattoo on him was hilarious. There was no fucking way! Lenny had to laugh when JD called him—like they had anything to talk about.

Shit, even Pancho (no, be nice and call him Angel) was pussy-whipped. Lenny could just tell, and if you really needed proof, you could just look at how Jackie had stormed into the office to defend him. What was *that* all about anyway? It was pathetic, that's what it was. Maybe if he'd called him Angel instead of Pancho he wouldn't have quit.

Lenny had banished the thought from his mind as soon as it registered. Nothing was gonna bring him down tonight, because he was free. That's what separated him from those other dudes, or anyone else for that matter. He was free. He could do whatever the fuck he wanted, cause he had money, he had talent. And tonight he had some blow and a fifth of tequila. It was on! Time to celebrate his freedom.

He was jamming to some "Welcome to the Jungle" when he got to his trailer and couldn't help but come screaming down the gravel driveway—and fuck the car wash, cause he could get his truck washed every day if he wanted to—and he just hit the brakes when he got close to the trailer, where the gravel was thicker, enough to lock up his seat belt against his chest and he wasn't gonna lie, it kinda surprised him how hard it bit, but it was fucking cool the way the truck just slid in home like an in-the-park homerun just as Axl went, "It's gonna bring you down." And then his ears were ringing like a motherfucker.

It was hard not to get frustrated with the damn security light. It never came on, even when he waved his hand in front of the damn thing. But after he got in the trailer and he went to the kitchen for the tequila and saw the clock on the microwave was blinking twelve, then it made sense. The power had gone out. Which, he might've worried about if he wasn't feeling so jacked.

He had the TV on SportsCenter and he was in the kitchen getting a plate for the blow and ice for his Patrón—and there wasn't any lime, which kind of sucked, but fuck it, he would manage—when a text came in from Lefty. His phone was there on the counter next to the drawing of Sadie Lee.

I left my bat in your truck. And save me some of that shit!

Lenny typed something crude in response and then turned the phone over. He wasn't gonna start chatting back and forth like a little bitch. And anyway, if Lefty really wanted to hang out, he shouldn't have gone home. He bent over to do a line, then grabbed his glass of good tequila and went outside to get the bat. When he opened the rear door to get it there was a flat, round object on the floor under the seat. It was about the size of a Mardi Gras doubloon, only fatter. He didn't know what the fuck it was, but when he picked it up he knew it wasn't good, and the very first name that popped into his head was Pancho.

Episode Nine
Dominoes in Motion
—————— ✦ ——————

Curtis debriefs JD and Sadie on his close call at Lenny's place. Lenny melts down. And Lefty makes a routine pickup that turns out to be anything but ordinary.

"Curtis came down a hero, and two days later he's a felon."
— JD

While Lenny was alone in his trailer, spiraling in a funnel of booze, blow, loneliness and suspicion, Troy Vidrine was at the dinner table enjoying a late meal with his wife, Thao. And even though a part of him would have liked to cut loose with Lenny, he was already over it, and things were definitely looking up in the Vidrine house. He was probably even gonna get laid.

The girls were showered and ready for bed; he'd already kissed them goodnight, and they were playing quietly in the bedroom they shared. Thao had showered too, but there was something extra in the scent of her tonight, and Troy couldn't help but notice the sexy lingerie she wore under the silk robe wrapped tight around her. She ladled soup into his bowl and pressed her breasts against his back as she leaned in. He took a long swallow of beer and let the stress of the day melt away, breathing deeply with the techniques Thao had taught him. Her presence always soothed him. And on nights like tonight, it was more than that.

Troy Vidrine did not have a typical Cajun home life. Thao saw to that. She had her rules, and they were ironclad. It had taken some getting used to, but there was a sense of peace and order to his home that Troy wouldn't trade for anything. It was quiet, clean, joyful, supportive. Troy and his crew may have built the place, but it was Thao's house, and as soon as Troy had learned to yield to her ways, things had clicked into place for the both of them. At this point, seven years into their marriage, it seemed like his entire life was propped up on Thao's rules, which seemed too simple to have such a profound effect.

You took your shoes off at the door. You showered every night before bed. Meals were a time for communion with family. And home was a refuge from a noisy world. Television was fine for specific times and occasions, but it didn't just stay, vomiting out noise into the house. Music was welcome, but the volume and genre had to fit the occasion. And cell phones mostly stayed off. They were useful for emergencies, but it was unhealthy and rude to be staring at one of those tiny screens when you were in Thao's house. Breaking the cell phone rule was a cardinal sin.

And it didn't matter how you came to have your phone in your hand, whether you pulled it from your pocket in an idle moment or someone called or texted you and curiosity got the best of you. It didn't matter. If you wanted to sleep in *her* bed or enjoy *her* attention and support, you honored the cell phone rule.

Troy had taken pretty quick to everything but the phone thing. He'd been a slow learner on that front, until finally he got tired of being rebuked when it inevitably went off at the wrong moment and he just started leaving the damn thing in the truck overnight. There was a landline for emergencies anyway. Hell, he was still listed in the phone book for that matter.

It was all *so* worth it. No question in Troy's mind, especially when you held it all up against the anger and the authority and, well, these days you'd call it downright abuse of his childhood. There wasn't anything like tranquility in his old man's house. Tranquility was for pussies. It might have been quiet in their house, but it damn sure wasn't peaceful.

He didn't blame his dad. He really didn't. Troy would not have been the ballplayer he was without him. And if he hadn't been good enough, St. Eds wouldn't have recruited him. And if they hadn't, well, then his dad would've never started SouthPaw Construction, thanks to seed money from Uncle Ely and the boosters, with an eye towards giving his son something to fall back on if baseball didn't work out. So no, Troy couldn't blame him.

But still, he was a slow learner. His first and only year of organized ball after high school, at Pearl River Community College, just across the state line in Mississippi, had been an absolute disaster. He'd rolled across the Pearl River on the other side of Slidell in his little truck with his gear in the back and his bride of barely three days next to him, and things just went from bad to worse.

The girl—her name was Candy, if you could believe that—wasn't any more prepared for marriage than he was, and within a matter of weeks, they were having exactly the kinds of knock-down, drag-out fights he'd grown up witnessing. Less than a year later, it was all over, just like that, and he would have considered it a blessing if it wasn't for the fact that his baseball career was evaporating at the same time.

The chaos in his personal life affected his performance on the field, and he rarely went to class or cracked a book, so by the time the first spring rolled around he was ineligible to play. So much for his meteoric rise through JUKO ball, up through the minors and into The Show. The dream became a nightmare in barely ten months. It all just fell apart. He returned to Eunice and started working with his old man again, and a year after that he officially took over SouthPaw Construction. But there was a silver lining.

People always liked to say everything happens for a reason, and he'd always thought that idea was bullshit, right up until the day he married Thao, two-and-half years after he got back from Pearl River. They had met on the day he walked into the little office at the apartment building just off campus where he dragged his ass into on his very last day in town. He was there to plead with the lady that ran the place to have mercy on him and give him his deposit back, even though he was breaking the lease and there was at least one fist-sized hole in the drywall. But her English was almost nonexistent and Troy got frustrated and walked out, pissed off at the world.

And that's when Thao showed up. She'd called after him on the sidewalk with this weird accent, half slow Mississippi drawl and half whatever he thought she was at the time. And damn was she pretty! She was wearing shorts and flip-flops and a tee shirt too big for her and no makeup, and so it took him a second to register her beauty, and another few to register her age. He walked back into the office with her and she translated for her mother. When he walked out thirty minutes later with her email address and the promise from her mom that she'd take a look at the apartment and send him anything left over from the repairs, he was no longer mad at the world.

Back in Eunice, he still had a few wild years in him, though, and it was during that period where he fell into a certain rhythm with Lenny that more or less persisted to this day. It wasn't complicated. They got together every now and then to drink, reminisce, play softball, start shit in bars—whatever they could do to have some fun. In those early days, they were both still licking their wounds from unsuccessful attempts to make baseball and life work outside of Eunice. They fell into some bad patterns, and some of those habits hardened like crawfish mounds on a hot day, even as the months wore on and they both eventually found their way to a lifestyle that looked something like maturity.

Troy meanwhile had fallen into an email relationship with Thao. It kept going even after he got the check from Thao's mom for twenty-five dollars and twenty cents—something they still laughed about to this day—and at some point he took a weekend trip back to Mississippi to visit. Things accelerated from there and the more Troy dialed into how being with Thao made him feel, the more he wanted a life with her, damn whatever cultural differences there might be. Their first daughter was born before their first wedding anniversary.

It had been a long time since Troy needed the extra money he got for delivering the occasional package of steroids for Lenny, but he couldn't just stop doing it. After everything the Prichard family had done for him, he couldn't do that to Lenny.

To tell the truth, he didn't really think about it anymore. That's how harmless and routine the whole thing had become. It wasn't any more stressful than picking up donuts for the crew. All it was was some medicine some athletes used to gain an edge. No big deal.

Thao didn't know anything about it, of course, and she didn't need to. Really, it should have been that simple. It wasn't exactly, but it was close. She did the books for the business, for one, and so he had to get creative to explain the extra cash. Which he did—a simple, sparse explanation of an under the table cash payment—and he felt bad about it the first time. But it got easier. And after a while, he didn't even need a story to go with it; he just handed her the cash and she deposited it. For sure, she understood the source of the money wasn't totally legal, but he had the sense she'd probably be more bothered if he whipped out his phone at dinner.

He always kept a few thousand back, of course. The good thing about living with three girls was there were plenty of places around the house that were pretty much his domain. He had a nice shop in the back, and he didn't get in there as much as he liked, but he had a fridge and a radio and even a window unit to keep it cool. And Thao was good about making sure nobody fucked with his stuff or bothered him when he was in there chilling. She would shit if she knew how much he had stashed in there, but he'd have to be dead for her or anyone to go digging around.

After dinner, when the house was quiet and he finished his shower while Thao waited for him, stretched out on the bed, he felt a familiar contented feeling. It was more than the promise of sex. It was the two perfect little girls sleeping in the next room. It was financial security and a dozen other elements along those lines that added up to satisfaction, pure and simple. Troy emerged from the shower that night already satiated with life. It would be his last such night for a very long time.

Curtis, JD, and Sadie were sitting on the porch of her mom's house with nothing but a candle for light because Curtis was feeling paranoid, and by the time he reached the end of his story they were all on edge. JD was quietly seething, which Curtis tried not to take personally.

"Well, I guess sometimes it's better to be lucky than good," Sadie had said, more an effort to lighten the mood than anything. It had the opposite effect on JD.

"What about being stupid?" he said, glaring at Curtis. "Where does that fall on the continuum, bubba?"

"What are you mad for?" Sadie cut in. "He got away! It worked, dude. Relax." She grabbed his arm to try to soothe him.

"He's mad because I couldn't leave well enough alone," Curt said. "He thinks it was over when he turned in the keys to 2nd Street and asking him to kiss up to Lenny was like pouring salt in his wounded pride." He looked up at JD. "And to make matters worse, I somehow managed to drag you into all this." He looked at Sadie, then back at JD. "How'm I doing, bubba? That about right?"

"Fuck you, Laroux."

Curtis didn't say anything right away, but he couldn't hold JD's eyes. He looked at Sadie instead. "Hey, can you maybe go get me a Ziplock bag? Like, a gallon-size one if you can, or bigger." She frowned and looked like she wanted to ask why but she never did. When she had quietly closed the door behind her, Curtis said simply, "I'm sorry." He didn't have a clue why he should be, but it seemed like the thing JD needed to hear. And anyway, he hoped what he was about to show him would change the mood.

A few minutes later Sadie returned with a frozen handle of vodka—Smirnoff, it looked like—and she stood before them pulling shot glasses out of her coat pocket. When she had the shot glasses arrayed around the candle, she pulled a Ziplock from her back pocket and handed it to Curtis. Then she set about filling the glasses. Curtis meanwhile was rummaging around inside the EverReady with the Ziplock bag. JD was too irritated to care what he was up to, and Sadie was busy pouring shots. She handed Curtis his and he held it, waiting and feeling some of it spill over the edge onto his fingers. JD took his and Sadie stood then with her own.

"What should we toast to?" Curtis asked.

"How 'bout to not being in jail tonight?" Sadie said, and all three of them repeated the phrase and drained their glasses. Curtis asked for another right away. He was still wired as fuck.

Sadie poured a second round for all of them, but this time they didn't toast. JD lit a cigarette and let his shot sit there on the floor by the candle, and Sadie sat back on the swing next to him with hers and took a small sip. Curtis finished getting all the bills into the Ziplock and organized into a stack. He finished the second shot, put the glass down next to where he sat, and used his flashlight to double-check he'd found all the bills he'd stuffed into the EverReady. He looked up.

"There's one more thing," he said, and held out the bag, full of bills. Maybe ten seconds elapsed. It was hard to gauge either of their reactions in the dark, but Curtis was reassured when Sadie took the bag and JD started cursing in a tone that Curtis recognized as not so much pissed as generally irritated with the situation. "I came across some cash when I was there, so I skimmed a little. Maybe twenty percent. I don't think he's gonna miss it. Not for a little while, at least."

The silence that ensued lasted longer than Curtis was expecting. The moment started with a very serious vibe, but then the silence extended a bit and they could each feel the tone of the thing changing. Eventually, Sadie laughed, just a little. But it was enough to be contagious. Curtis was next, a burst of laughter that threatened to really get away from him, on the cusp the kind of laughter you experience only once or twice in life, the kind of absurd, stomach-aching, eye-watering laughter that almost makes you question your sanity. JD, ever cool, started with a chuckle that he wasn't ready to give in to yet. And then an instant later they were all roiling with it, hands over mouths, shoulders wracking, trying not to be too loud because there were neighbors and Sadie's mom and it was late.

"Seriously, Laroux," JD said, once he could speak, wiping tears from the corner of his eyes. "You *crazy-ass motherfucker.* I'm not sure about this. Somebody's gonna come looking for this money."

"It's sixteen thousand something," Sadie cut in. "Close to seventeen, I think."

"You see? That's a lotta fucking money, bubba!" JD said, and he was definitely not laughing now.

"That's why you have to be smart with it. Which is why I suggest. . . ." Curtis stopped himself right there. "So, I gave this some thought in the car on my way over here, once I'd calmed down enough to think at all, and I can tell you what I think if you want."

"Shit." JD interrupted. "Like there's any way in hell somebody's gonna stop you from saying what you wanna say. Just spit it out, bubba."

"My suggestion is, let Sadie take this money. Make her your new silent partner in the shop."

"Ooo! I can buy furniture! That place is a fucking dump!" She squeezed JD's arm. "Sorry baby, but it reminds me of the cafeteria in elementary school."

"There you go. Get the shop fixed up. But within reason. Don't go all reality TV makeover with the place. And don't spend *any* of this in Eunice. Keep it out of town and anonymous. Maybe make a trip to Houston or something."

"There's a glass case I been wanting to get for the front. To put jewelry and tee shirts and stickers and shit in. What do you call it? A display case."

"We can make the shop of your dreams," Sadie said. "The one you told me about." JD was nodding his head, warming to the idea.

"Great. Just keep the spending plausible. You borrowed some money from Sadie or your brother, or you're taking on some debt. Whatever. But try to make it to where it's so gradual nobody even asks. But if they *do* ask, you have an explanation ready. Curtis dropped his voice and looked at Sadie. "And later on. When, um, the inevitable happens with your mom, nobody will question the cash."

"People will assume it's insurance money," she said.

"Exactly. But the source of the money won't even be an issue if you don't go overboard. And if anybody does ask—"

"That's a dick thing to say, Laroux." JD spat. "Anyway, I'm still worried. *When* he notices the missing dough, he'll wonder if I had something to do with it."

"But he was at *your* shop today," Sadie said. "Talk about a good alibi."

"Exactly," Curtis said. "And he doesn't even know I'm in town. And plus, it'll be weeks or maybe months before he notices that money's missing. But even if for some reason he discovers it soon, it won't be you he's suspicious of—"

"It'll be Angel." Sadie finished his sentence. "He'll suspect Angel. He'll remember Angel took his keys to wash his truck."

"And then Angel will buckle under the pressure and we'll all be fucked." JD said. Curtis was quiet for a few beats.

"I don't know that Angel will be too credible if it comes to that," he said. "But even if the business with the keys comes out and Lenny believes it all, *you* weren't there. It's still on Angel."

Angel was sitting in the passenger's seat of Jackie's bad-ass little Celica, rapping in his head over a remix of this New Order tune she had turned him on to. They were on their way to *Nose to the Grindstone* for open mic night. It was almost 10 p.m.— the tail end of the open mic—but that was perfect because Angel liked to be last if he could. The owner was cool about saving him a spot. Tonight was kinda special 'cause the lyrics were all about Jackie. And the music was fucking dope. It sounded great in her car, and that shit was gonna be bigger than life when the DJ cranked it in the coffee house. As soon as he had heard it in Jackie's house, he knew he could put a rhyme on top.

It wasn't Shakespeare or some shit like that, but he had a feeling she would be into it. And anyway, the words probably didn't even matter much. Just the fact that he was doing a song for her. She knew something was up too because he wouldn't let her hear it in the car. But that just made it better, built up the anticipation and shit. She'd just leaned over and cranked the system, with that amp she had under the hood pumping all four of those six-by-nines. That car was like their own personal spaceship, with Jackie at the wheel looking fine as ever in a man's shirt, unbuttoned halfway and rocking perfect tits that just demanded attention. Goddamn this woman was fine! Angel was in heaven!

He looked over and grinned, showing white teeth and feeling the beat, and she reached over and put her hand on his leg. It was like she was warming him up, not just for the show but for later on. Angel was glad she was in a better mood. Last night, she'd been acting all weird, even after he'd apologized for not telling her about working with Lenny and he'd done all his groveling and promising and shit.

She made him do his "penance," going down on her for like a half hour it seemed like, judging from the music, on the couch in her living room, and that was all good, for sure. He loved that shit. But he could tell something was wrong because she barely let him put his condom on before she climbed on top, like he liked, so he could look at her. The way she screamed out at the end he knew for damn sure he'd done his job, but then she got all sulky and shit after, so he didn't know what was going on.

Angel was just happy it was all good now. Today was turning out to be pretty great; shit was improving on all fronts. Things were cool with JD. It didn't seem like he was pissed about those 'roids at 2nd Street, now that Angel had put 'em back and Jackie returned his deposit. It even seemed like JD was starting to maybe trust him a little bit, which was righteous. The tat on his hand looked cool as hell, the way JD designed it. All Angel wanted to do now was learn to tattoo so he could make a little money and maybe move down the road a piece in like maybe a year or so. Houston, if possible, but maybe just Lafayette or even Lake Charles. Just keep on moving forward, like a man.

Curtis had watched JD's full shot glass for a good five minutes before he finally reached over and grabbed it up.

"I just want half of it," he said, and knocked the whole thing back. He looked at Sadie and grinned. "My half was on the bottom." She laughed. JD didn't. He had probably heard that line a hundred times.

"Where is Angel tonight, anyway?" Sadie asked, then pulled out her phone a few seconds later. "Wait, lemme check."

"Some kinda open mic night," JD said. "He raps. Plays guitar a little bit too, I think."

"Is he on YouTube?" Sadie asked, still studying her phone. "You ain't famous yet if you don't have a YouTube channel. Yeah, it looks like he's in Opelousas. On South Street. Say, this thing is handy. Can you tap JD's phone so I can keep track of him?"

Curtis didn't bite. And he wasn't the least bit interested in what Angel was up to. "Can you check on Lenny? Is his truck still at the trailer?" It was good he'd given Sadie access to the live map that showed the trackers and the video feed from the library. She did a good job of staying on top of it, and since he'd left his phone in New Orleans, like a dumb ass . . . While she worked the phone, Sadie looked up at Curtis for a moment.

"Would Lenny recognize you if he saw you?"

"Maybe," Curtis said, thinking about it. "Probably. We were never friends, but we played together all the way through high school. Well, against each other." They were silent again for a moment. "Why do you ask?"

"Well," Sadie hesitated for the briefest moment. "I don't know. It just seems like it's kinda personal for you."

"What's personal?"

"Lenny. The way you're going after him."

"No shit," JD chimed in. "Laroux's having the time of his life all of a sudden."

"Stop it," Sadie said, frowning at her phone. Curtis couldn't help but notice the change in her expression.

"What's wrong?" he asked. Sadie kept her head down, refreshing the screen, hoping with a growing sense of alarm that the blinking icon would appear again.

"It's gone," she said. "Lenny's truck. It's like it disappeared. It's not on the map anymore. See?" She got off the swing and held the phone up for Curtis. The tracker was offline. He took the phone from her, studied the screen for a few seconds, then checked the other feeds. Lenny was somewhere, for sure, but where that was or what he knew was anybody's guess.

Curtis felt a hot flash on the back of his neck and his forehead, and before he could complete a single deep breath JD was off the swing and gathering up the vodka and the glasses.

"Let's get inside," he said, and it wasn't a suggestion.

"Yeah, good idea." Curtis offered, zipping up the EverReady. He stood up and scanned down the block in both directions just as JD snubbed the candle between his fingers. It was quiet, colder now than it had been all of a sudden. "Where you sleeping?" he asked JD.

"Right here," JD said.

"Good," Curtis checked his watch. Sadie slipped her arm into JD's while they stood there. "I'll be up early. Before it gets light, for sure."

"You sticking around tomorrow?" JD asked.

Curtis shook his head, unsure. "Maybe not. I don't know. I need to think."

"The GPS could've just run out of batteries, right?" Sadie asked.

"It's possible, but the other trackers are still working. They should go for three days, maybe more." Curtis looked towards both of them. He could barely see their faces, but he didn't need to.

"So that means he found it," Sadie said.

"That or he drove his truck in the bayou," JD said. "Either way we need to get inside."

At first Lenny had dropped the thing in the toilet and proceeded to piss on it, then just before he went to flush, he realized how stupid that was. Talk about adding insult to injury. Luckily, he had some rubber gloves under the sink. So he fished it out and after that he spent a frustrating thirty minutes trying to get into the damn thing.

It was hard to tell, but if he got his eyeball right up close to it, he could sort of see a seam. He'd do a line and a shot, then try again, prying at the thing with a succession of smaller and smaller screwdrivers, and it was only a matter of time before it slipped and cut the fuck out his hand. He ended up with a gash in the meaty part of his palm that stung like a motherfucker. Once he got some gauze wrapped around his hand and did another couple shots and one more rail to help with the pain, he ended up just smashing it to pieces with a hammer, right there on the kitchen counter.

His countertop came out worse for the wear—two round hammer-size depressions in the laminate where he'd missed—but at that point, he didn't give a fuck. He set up another round for himself after it was in pieces, realizing that he'd gained absolutely nothing from the act of smashing it. The fragments of hard plastic and smashed circuits and wires didn't mean shit to him. He'd never gone in for that nerd shit. But you didn't have to be some kind of CSI expert to know this was bad. Somebody was fucking with him. That much he knew. The only question was who, and *that* question *was* one he could answer.

His first impulse was to get in his truck and drive to Pancho's house, and maybe stop by Tans on his way to get his pistol. But he thought better of it. For one, he didn't know where the little fucker lived. And second, well, he couldn't remember what was second. He was a little drunk by then. Not sloppy drunk, because of the coke, but not in a condition to go driving around town. So he did another line and tried to ignore the fact that the baggie was at least half-empty now. Then he refreshed his drink and went outside with the big Maglight he kept under the sink.

He needed to inspect his truck. He checked under the seats, the glove box, and all the other little compartments and shit they put in new vehicles these days. He even got on his back and studied the undercarriage for a while. Everything looked normal, as far as he could tell at least. But the situation was anything but. Frustrated he couldn't do anything about it, at least not now, he retreated inside and sat in his leather recliner in front of SportsCenter and switched to water for a while, because he couldn't afford to get sloppy drunk. He cut back on the lines too, thinning them out not because he realized he was getting too high, which might have been true, but more practically because he would run out if he wasn't careful.

It had to be that little bastard Pancho. He did something. Lenny was sure of it. He should have known something was up by the way he came into his office all cool and shit, like he was in control of the situation instead of Lenny. Goddammit! What was he up to? That was the thing that was fucking with Lenny. First of all, he didn't really know what this round metallic thing was. And second, well, shit, second wasn't important. Maybe if he could figure out what it was it would help him understand whatever kind of shit Pancho was trying to pull. Whatever it was, he damn sure wasn't gonna get away with it.

Lenny started searching online for information that might help, but he didn't really know where to start. He typed "round metal object" and got results on flying saucers and a bunch of stuff about, like, these special coins people in the military carry around with them to commemorate their squads and stuff. Like state championship rings, except not as cool. And not even a little helpful.

But eventually he got on the trail of the right keywords—Google was almost smarter than he was, it seemed like—and he hit on GPS trackers. He should've known that's what it was, but he was fucked up and on top of that, it just seemed too sophisticated for Pancho. He was more the type of dude to key your truck or maybe slash your tire. It didn't make sense, but whatever. He'd squeeze the truth out of Pancho soon enough.

A couple hours later, and it must've been three or four in the morning by then, he started to worry about his package at 2nd Street. One thing probably didn't have anything to do with the other, but still, his mind kept coming back to those 'roids. Pancho knew about it. Shit, he was the one that put 'em there! Maybe it was all connected. Hopefully, it wasn't.

He started texting Lefty then, at first just cautioning him to keep his eyes open, whatever the fuck that meant, and then following up with text after text, first saying to just call him when he got up, and eventually telling Lefty to stand down, at least until he could figure out what was going on. Around five or so, Lenny even called him, figuring if Lefty wasn't up yet he'd be up soon. But he got nothing, and the more he thought about *that*, the more it infuriated him. Here he was trying to maybe save him from a dangerous situation and Lefty was just gonna ignore him? It was probably that little chink wife of his.

The bitch was probably hiding his phone or telling him not to answer or something.

Lenny was sober by then. Or, at least he'd stopped drinking tequila. The empty bottle was in the sink. He'd rinsed it out because the smell of the liquor was making him sick. So he made a pot of coffee. It was just starting to get light outside anyway; he figured he might as well. He'd turned over the empty baggie of coke and shook out all the residue into his coffee cup, then put a little water in the bag and went ahead and drank that, not so much because he needed it, but needed to clean the bag and there was no point in letting it go to waste. He wasn't high. He was just alert, and ready. So ready he had already written his text to Pancho. All he had to do was send it, and then they would see who the fucking smart guy was.

Angel didn't usually get up before ten. Not if he could help it anyway. But his phone was making noise and he needed to take a piss, so he willed himself to open his eyes and sit up in bed. The house was quiet, Isabel and the girls already gone. Maybe a little bit early, looking at the time. It was always easier to move your ass on a Friday. There was coffee in the air, thanks to Isabel. He checked his phone, hoping it was Jackie, and when he saw it was Lenny something more than disappointment came over him. He turned the phone over on the bed without reading it and walked to the bathroom. It was way too fucking early in the morning for Lenny fucking Prichard.

As he stood in front of the toilet waiting for his dick to go down, he thought of last night. Which didn't help much at all with the erection problem. Jackie was all over him in the Celica after the show. *All* over him, to the point where it seemed like she wanted to do it right there in the backseat in the parking lot. He was down, for sure, but he didn't have a condom with him and things kinda got awkward after that.

He had been riding the high from his performance and so everything was still kind of surreal. The whole sequence of events was like a movie in his head. He started to play through it in his mind while he flushed the toilet and then turned on the shower. The tattoo stung a little when he put his hand in the water, already so accustomed to the design he forgot it was there. He remembered his aftercare stuff was in the car and made a mental note to go get it as soon as he got dressed. JD gave him a whole speech about "don't neglect your aftercare. Say it with me now. . ." so he needed to make sure he was straight before he went into the shop.

Which reminded him, he needed to ask JD about getting some real practice. He had asked Slim if he'd be willing to roll up his sleeve, but he said no. That was kind of fucked up, but Slim already had a couple free sessions with JD coming up, assuming the van came out good, so Angel couldn't hold it against him. It still bothered him a little bit though, seeing how they were cousins. Well, not *actually* cousins, but shit, bruh, two Puerto Ricans in Eunice *had* to be cousins, even if Angel technically lived in Opelousas.

Speaking of, he needed to holla at Slim to see what was up with the van. Angel hoped it was gonna look as cool in real life as it did already in his mind. But even if it didn't, that was okay. It just had to be righteous enough for JD to like it. If he didn't like it . . . shit, Angel didn't even want to think about that. It all needed to work out because Angel was the one that set the whole thing up.

And on a deeper level, it was kind of weird but Angel had a whole like, *vision* of a bad-ass version of Black Jack Tattoo in his head. Him and JD working side by side, the place all pimped out with furniture and like, plants and music and people hanging out. Maybe even a fish tank, a saltwater one. He could see the whole thing in his mind, and he could even *feel* the vibe of the place. And it wasn't like a selfish trip he was on. The scene he saw made him feel good because it was JD's success story. He was just there to support it, and that was cool.

Something occurred to him just then. What he'd do, he'd find out from JD what else they needed to get before the grand reopening next week, and he'd take some of his money—he could do three hundred, probably—and he'd just go buy it, whatever they needed. Yeah, that's exactly what he'd do! Today, right away. He could go to Lafayette, Lake Charles, whatever it took. Maybe even stop at a couple other tattoo shops while he's there. Drop off some stickers maybe, or just go in and scope some other places out to get some ideas.

Suddenly, he was full of energy, and he just naturally started spitting his "Jackie-Rhyme" from last night.

J, A . . . C *to the* K *to the* I *to the* E

Jackie Jackie baby

you straight up rock me

and your mind, it drives me crazy

it's like a maze to me

I'm spinning and spinning to infinity

the way you excite me

it's like religious ecstasy

I heard God was dead

but you my goddess instead

and if I had to give my life for one minute in your bed

then put some thorns on my head

cause when you ride me and rope me and dope me

it feels so good to me

and I know that sounds corny

but it's true Jackie Jackie baby

you know I'm not one to trifle

but Jackie baby, I'm your disciple

and the only question

is *how high we gonna go?*

His dick was hard again before he finished the first eight bars, and he wasn't really in the habit of jerking off in the shower, but it felt like the most natural thing in the world. He just spit his rhymes and thought about Jackie in the back seat and spit his rhymes and thought about Jackie in the backseat and spit. And after he was done and dried off and he had his pants on, he walked out to the car barefoot and shirtless to get his aftercare from the car. It was only after he'd applied it, and after he'd put on his Bad Brains hoodie, feeling good, looking good, and after he'd poured some coffee in his favorite mug and sat down at the kitchen table did he look at his phone.

Come by Tans this morning when you get this. I got

something for you.

Troy was the first one up in the Vidrine house, as usual. He never was a morning person. He'd just learned to make the best of it. And Thao had somehow programmed herself to still be dead asleep but nudge him out of bed at the same time, sometimes just before the alarm actually rang. He had no idea how she did that shit, but he was thankful anyway.

He had slept hard, and even though he had popped awake at the alarm, he knew the day was gonna be rough because he was operating on at least a two-hour deficit. Which probably meant the afternoon was gonna drag ass. But then again, it *was* Friday and he *was* the boss, so maybe, fuck it, he'd just take the afternoon off and come home and take a nap. Maybe even see if he could talk Thao into a quick one.

His morning routine was efficient. The coffee pot was programmed for ten to six, and by the time he padded into the kitchen in his socked feet, it was just a matter of pouring it into his thermos and grabbing his food for the day. Thao made these amazing *bahn mi* sandwiches that he usually ate for lunch, and of all the little things she did for him, the way she set aside his lunch everyday ranked way up there. Always in the same spot in the fridge, a quarter piece of a sandwich—just enough to keep him focused without dragging ass in a bread-induced food coma—some fruit, washed and cut up, nuts, and something sweet, a peppermint candy or a piece of dark chocolate, sometimes with a little heart or something drawn on the wrapper.

Troy got everything into his little Playmate cooler and took that and his thermos into the little mudroom and sat on the bench to put on his boots. It was a good ten degrees colder in there. That was enough to tell him it was gonna be a cold morning. So he put on his insulated flannel jacket that hung by the door and made his way out , his boots making noise in the light frost on the grass as he walked across the yard.

He cranked the heat and the defrost in the truck, and while he waited for the windshield to clear, he poured himself a shot of coffee from the thermos. It was nice to just sit there for a minute or two, not quiet, exactly, with the sound of the defroster blasting warm air on the glass, but quiet enough. And still, nothing really moving at this hour. He knew from experience this might be his only moment of peace for the whole day, so he sat quietly with his shot of coffee. It was cool enough to drink right about the time the windshield was clear enough to drive.

He was backing out of the driveway before he thought to check his phone sitting in the little cubby below the radio. It didn't respond when he clicked it, so he put the truck in park and found his charger under the armrest. Once he had it connected, he dropped the phone back in the little cubby and continued on his way. Within a few minutes, he came into Eunice, picking up Highway 190 on the east side of town, near the hospital. It was still early, barely six thirty, and the streets were fairly quiet.

When he hit Highway 13 in town, he was just a couple blocks from the old flower shop on 2nd Street. But instead of going straight there, he took the extra precaution of making the block a few times, taking his time as he circled the place in expanding circles. It wasn't just quiet in downtown Eunice at this hour. It was dead. He made a last loop, driving slow in front of Cajun Customs, the Queen Cinema, and Rudy's Cafe before turning right on 2nd Street. At the end of the block, he parked in front of the shop and stepped out onto the sidewalk. The library across the street was closed and quiet. There were a few cars in the parking lot at City Hall on the other side of Park Avenue.

Troy didn't waste any time. He used the key Lenny had given him to enter the shop and once inside, he marched straight to the bathroom, then climbed up on the sink and lifted the ceiling tile to get the package. The whole process took maybe fifteen seconds, and then he was locking the door and walking out of the shop with a US Mail Priority box under his arm, scanning the empty street as he crossed to his truck, which he hadn't bothered to lock. It was that simple. He put the box on the floorboard in the backseat and made his way out of town.

Curtis had been up for about an hour, doing burpees in his room, drinking water from the tap, and trying to overcome his hangover by sheer force of will. He had the laptop open at the foot of his hospital-cornered bed and KRVS going on the clock radio. It was good to hear Cajun French, even in a passive form, and somehow straining to comprehend the dialect seemed to be helping his head. He was thinking how he needed to find an excuse to come back to Eunice sometime soon, to visit with his mom, maybe even make some kind of peace with Bobby, hear some great local music, and just appreciate the riches of South Louisiana, when he noticed a familiar construction truck on the video feed.

Instantly he was crouched in front of the computer taking screenshots of the streaming video and squinting at the somewhat grainy picture to read the license plate on the truck at the same time. Seconds later a man appeared, the same lanky dude from yesterday, and he had the box of steroids under his arm. Curtis was pretty sure he'd been quick enough with the keystrokes to get at least one shot of the guy—it had to be Troy Vidrine—before he got in the truck.

He grabbed the flip phone from the charger by the bedside and found Tac's personal cell in the contacts. While it rang, he switched the map viewer on the laptop and he could see Pkg. 1 on the move now, heading down Park Avenue. The phone rang at least four times before it went to voicemail and just then a text came in from Sadie.

Pkg. 1 on the move!

Curtis opened the text interface on the computer and typed an alert to Tac. When he toggled back to the map, he could see Troy by the Circle Park, not far from Sadie's house. Maybe he was going to Sun-*N*-Tans. If so, they would maybe have some time. He felt relief when his phone rang, but it wasn't Tac. He put it on speakerphone and laid it on the bed so he could work the computer.

"He's moving!" Sadie said in a yelled whisper.

"I know. Tac's not picking up." Curtis was looking through the clipboard of screenshots he'd captured on the computer, hoping for something useful. "Any thoughts on where he's going?"

"Shit! No." Sadie barked. "I don't know. He just turned south on 7th street." Curtis found a decent screenshot that showed the license plate of the truck, "S-PAW-1."

"He's probably not going to the tanning shop then. Maybe he's going to Lenny's place in the country." Curtis could hear

JD, muffled and groggy, in the background, followed by the sound of a slamming door, then heavy breathing.

"I'm gonna follow him," Sadie said. She was already out the door of her mom's house, setting the phone down on the porch for a second to get into her shoes. Curtis heard "Fuck!, I forgot my license!" and then more scratching sounds as she put the phone down again. He barked into the phone.

"No! Sadie! Stay where you are!" But she either ignored him or didn't hear. The call from Tac came in just then, and he might've screamed into the phone when Tac came on. "It's Vidrine!" Curtis said. "He's on the move with the steroids from 2nd Street."

Jackie was in the bathroom of her house throwing up. She didn't know what she was gonna do. For now, all she really wanted was to not be staring at the inside of the fucking toilet bowl. It was disgusting, no matter how clean you thought you were. Just the thought of it was almost enough to make her go another round. She pulled her head back and stared up at the ceiling, the sharp, acidic residue of vomit scorching her nose and throat, and just waited. She waited for a long moment, breathing through her open mouth because it was less disgusting than inhaling through her nose.

And once she was convinced that was the last of it, she slowly pushed herself up from the toilet and stepped over into the tub to take a shower. She turned the water on and stood naked at the back of the tub with her eyes closed, waiting for the water to warm. Then she reached over to grab her toothbrush and toothpaste off the counter and started the process of clearing her mouth and nose and throat. She needed to pee but resisted the urge. The test kit was on the counter, ready whenever she was. But she wasn't sure exactly when that would be.

To know was to accept the responsibility, and she still wasn't sure if she was ready for that. She was getting older, and fast. She'd been back in Eunice since not long after she finished college fifteen years ago, and every year since then, she swore it would be her last one in town. But along the way, she had somehow gotten comfortable and the thought of moving just sort of faded into the background. You could actually carve out a pretty nice existence around Eunice if you knew how to play it.

She took weekend trips, to New Orleans, Houston, sometimes even up to Memphis or Nashville or over to Austin. But whatever the town, her M.O. was pretty much the same: get a nice room in a big hotel downtown, eat something she couldn't get back in Eunice, like sushi or pad thai or bibimbap, check out a local band, then hit a club that hopefully stayed open after hours and dance her ass off until her legs gave out or she met somebody interesting. She didn't always take a man back to the hotel. It had to feel right.

Those long weekend trips anchored her year, gave her something special to look forward to, but there was plenty of fun to be had around Eunice too. You just had to know where to look. In fact, some of the most interesting music and art in the whole country was happening right there.

There had been a revival going on for the last decade or more, driven by local kids steeped in the traditions of the Cajun and zydeco music they heard in restaurants and local festivals, but not enslaved to them. She'd never liked the traditional music growing up, but there was a vibe—she thought of it as a punk rock kind of spirit—that groups like the Red Stick Ramblers, the Pine Leaf Boys, Feufollet, the Lost Bayou Ramblers, the Revelers, and dozens of others had. Their shows could be orgasmic.

Of course, it wasn't all sweaty concerts and fucking. There were simple pleasures, too. Sleeping with the windows open in winter, satsumas in spring, midnight skinny dipping at her mom's house in the summer. She had a couple girlfriends too, and they helped to keep her sane. They were married, but they'd been able to maintain an identity that was more than wife and mother, and that was no small achievement.

She would be the first to admit it wasn't the life she had planned for herself. But she had made it work, in a way. The thing was, it worked for *her*. Raising a kid here in Eunice was another thing entirely. And raising a kid with *Angel*, of all people. Well, that was just laughable. That wasn't even a serious question. Angel was a kid himself, and even though she loved him—in a way, though she would never in a million years say that to him—there was just no way.

She allowed herself to cry in the shower after she'd finished brushing her teeth and had tossed the toothbrush and toothpaste into the sink to get them out of the way. And then stood there with her hands over her face for a long while, quietly sobbing. She felt alone. *Was* alone. Angry—with herself mostly. Lost.

When the hot water started to run out, the change in temperature was what brought her back into the present. She lifted her head to the cooling water and just let it hit her. Then she put her head down again and let the water run off the back of her head, pushing her hair down in a wall in front of her while the cold water went down her back. And she remained there for a while before she thrust her head back, all traces of heat gone, and let the water run across her taut breasts, her nipples like .22-caliber shells. She turned off the water, then reached over to grab the test strip.

Angel turned his phone face down on the table and started doodling on the back of some random pieces of mail on the kitchen table. As a kid, he'd heard someone say that "Idle hands are the devil's workshop" and the phrase had always stuck with him. So he tended to draw, especially when he was nervous, or confused, or even happy, hoping to ward off evil spirits.

Something didn't feel right about this text from Lenny. "I got something for you." That was the kind of thing you said to a dude you wanted to fight. It was sneaky, designed to put a man on edge because he didn't know exactly what it meant. It was almost as unnerving as hearing that somebody around town was "looking for you." There was a direct threat in a statement like that. The threat in Lenny's statement was just below the surface, but it was still there.

Motherfucker knew something. Angel could just feel it. He didn't know what to do. He had some options, he guessed, but none of them included just folding. Whatever it was Lenny wanted, he damn sure wasn't gonna run from it. That just wasn't the kind of shit a grown-ass man would do. Especially not Angel. Especially not now. Pretty soon he was gonna be the Angel that worked at Black Jack Tattoo, apprentice to JD Dugas, the dude that brought tattoos to Eunice. He needed to carry that weight like a man, and he was determined to do exactly that.

He started to text JD, but it was still pretty early. And anyway, he wasn't sure what he would say to him. He texted Jackie just because he needed a little love, even though she wasn't one to get all sentimental and shit, especially on the phone. He didn't write anything special, just that he was thinking about her and how last night had been hella fun, but he barely had a chance to put the phone down and refill his cup before she was calling him.

Sadie was driving way too fast past Eunice Elementary, checking her phone every two seconds to chart Troy's progress on the map and then screeching to a stop at Maple Avenue. The good news was he appeared to be poking along. The bad news was she had no idea what she would do if she caught up with him. But for the time being she pushed that problem out of her head, reflexively relying on her nursing instincts. It was just like emergency triage. First things first: catch up with him.

Troy was turning right from Maple onto Highway 13, heading south out of town. Maybe he was going to Lenny's. Or somewhere else. There was no way to know. She started to follow him but she balked and found herself cutting the wheel hard to the right, her plan to pick up Tiger Lane a couple miles south of Highway 13 and haul ass down that stretch of road to flank his ass coming into her mind after her body had reacted to the decision. "Cut him off at the pass!" she said to herself in the car, swept up in the adrenaline of it. She pushed the button to call Curtis and dropped the phone on the front seat, all about driving now.

She got up to almost eighty in her little Corolla before she came into the big sweeping curve that skirted the LSUE campus, just before Tiger Lane, and she backed off just a little there, but the road was banked and she handled it just fine at around seventy. A truck coming in the opposite direction on the curve passed and the violence of the rushing air as it went by would've been scary if she hadn't been so jacked. Curtis answered as she slowed to fifty to take the left turn onto Tiger Lane and then pressed her foot all the way to the floor, two miles of two-lane highway between here and Highway 13. There was an awful stalling sensation before the little Toyota responded with a high tortured whine that pinned her back against the seat.

She was approaching a hundred miles an hour a few seconds later and Curtis was shouting at her through the phone. But her attention was on the van in front of her that was probably doing fifty or so but might as well have been standing still. She had already pulled into the left lane. Clearing the van was not a problem.

It was the railroad tracks just up ahead that was the problem. Highway 13 had been laid parallel to them way back when, the mode of transportation changing but the route the same, which in most cases around here where the land was flat as a pancake was a straight line connecting point A to point B. Fifty yards beyond the tracks was the stop sign where Tiger Lane met Highway 13, and if she'd had the time to glance at the map on her phone, Sadie would've seen that she had time.

But everything was happening at once, the van, the look of horror on the driver's face, the tracks, Curtis yelling, the double yellow lines under the car, the stop sign beyond the tracks. She took her foot off the gas, instinct telling her she was moving way too fast to hit the brakes. But as the tracks came up on her at an ungodly pace—the stuff of nightmares—her foot went to the brake and she tried to feather it as best she could but she still climbed the incline of the tracks at eighty and there was a sickening silence when she went airborne.

Her foot came off the brake in the air and that's what saved her. The front tires hit first but the impact was manageable. The speed she was carrying was still the problem; her hands stayed at ten and two and when the car started to fishtail, she thought she had it. And at first she did, but she overcorrected on the first wash-out. The second one, when the rear end of the Corolla whipped back to the left, was too much to handle. An instant later, the seatbelt was pinning her back and she was a teenager again experiencing the Tilt-A-Whirl for the first time. It was a sickening, high-velocity spin.

Her hands were still gripping the wheel when the car finally came to a stop. She was facing the wrong way in the road. The sound of Curt's voice was somewhere in the backseat, and the car was still running. She wasn't sure if she had beaten Troy Vidrine to the intersection.

The van had come around her and the driver—some kind of delivery guy in a work uniform—was slowly navigating onto Highway 13, rubbernecking but not ready to stop for the crazy white girl who'd just jumped the tracks. But he was so occupied with Sadie and keeping his distance that he crept into the intersection and Troy Vidrine in his SouthPaw Construction truck had to hit his horn and slam on the brakes to avoid hitting the van.

Troy was half out of his truck on the shoulder of the road barking at the van driver, who was giving him the finger out the open window as he pulled away, when Tac Youngblood pulled up behind him in his Crown Vic.

Episode Ten
Suntan Showdown

❦

Tac applies pressure to Troy. Lenny lures Angel to Sun-N-Tans and gets a larger audience than he was expecting.

"If I hadn't seen it with my own eyes, I wouldn't have believed it. Shit, I *did* see it and I *still* don't believe it!" — JD

Lenny was in his truck, hauling ass towards Lefty's place with Metallica cranked up loud. He'd been calling and texting the son of a bitch for the last two hours and the longer it went the more it freaked him out. Even as he slowed on the highway to turn into the long gravel driveway, he could see plain as day that Lefty wasn't there. But he was angry and agitated and so he couldn't help but lay on the horn after he'd stopped in the gravel driveway, creating long, powerful blasts from under the hood of the Tundra that could wake the dead.

And it wasn't long before his chink wife came out and stood in the doorway flailing her arms around and telling him to be quiet, as if he gave a fuck. All that did was piss him off more, so he jammed the truck in reverse and when he dropped it in drive he was in the yard and he just let it roar and didn't even give her the courtesy of checking the rearview to see where the mud and gravel were landing, but he could hear it kicking up against the truck like a goddamn hailstorm.

He came sliding up onto the highway and he almost lost control but he was too pissed off to slip up. Instead, he just powered through it and the wheels caught and he was literally burning rubber for the first ten yards or more on his way back into town. His brain ratcheted back enough to ease off the accelerator as he came into the winding twenty-five-mile an hour limit of 2nd Street. You couldn't go much faster than that anyway, the way it curved.

There were cars down the block at Rudy's to his right, but he didn't see Uncle Ely's car. Not that he would've stopped anyway. But otherwise, downtown Eunice was quiet, and the shop at 2nd Street didn't look any different. Even in this cranked-up state he knew he couldn't go in, but still, he slowed down and studied the place as he glided by, the big truck reflecting back at him from the windows. It didn't do him any good. It was just an empty shop. There was no way to tell if Lefty had been there or not.

So he did the only thing he could do. He turned right on Park Avenue and started making his way to Sun-*N*-Tans. He had beer in the little fridge in his office there. And his pistol. He would wait for Pancho to show up, and somehow he knew the little fucker would. He was too stupid not to.

Tac didn't recognize the good-looking brunette in jeans and unlaced shoes standing in the door of the little Corolla. Not at first, at least. But as he approached the vehicle he could actually hear, just faintly, a familiar voice coming from somewhere inside her car. It was Curtis. Which was weird because Curtis had been texting and calling him over the last ten minutes.

Then things started to fall into place. He stopped a few feet from her vehicle and pivoted back to where Troy Vidrine was parked on the shoulder. The man had gotten back in his truck and he was looking like he was fixing to leave. Tac heard the big truck crank and that was all he needed. He took a couple quick steps to stand in front of the vehicle and held up his hand.

"Stop!" And just stood there for a few beats, locked eye to eye on Vidrine, the same dude Lenny had brought with him to Black Jack's. The asshole with the bat. "Turn off the vehicle!" Tac commanded, and when Troy broke eye contact to kill the ignition, Tac already felt like he had him. "Get out of the vehicle! Keep your hands in plain sight." Tac saw his expression change then. He pressed further, all about maximizing this dude's anxiety now. Pure and simple. "Put your hands on the hood." Vidrine complied and protested at the same time.

"Wait, what's going on, man? I just stopped to help that lady."

"You were attempting to leave the scene of an accident," Tac said with real authority. He brought his right boot between Vidrine's legs and forced them wide, then patted him down, more rough than thorough. When he was done, he stepped back and let Vidrine turn around, but Tac didn't say anything for a long while. He just stared with his practiced cop look. "Let me see your driver's license."

Troy reached into his back pocket and pulled out his wallet, a hefty brown leather thing worn smooth from years of use. Thao was always trying to get him to use the new one she gave him two Christmases ago, but he was a creature of habit. He fished the license out from the clear sleeve he kept it in and there behind it, protected, was the little family portrait of him and Thao and the girls, from that same Christmas. She'd insisted on the damn picture of all of them in front of the tree, and he remembered how proud she'd been of figuring out the timer on the camera with the new tripod, running back to take her place next to him, giddy like a damn schoolgirl, and how her smile had just lit him up for the picture. He handed the license over to the officer, who wasn't in uniform, and all of a sudden that fact—plain clothes—registered with him and his heart rate went into the stratosphere. He realized he was in real trouble.

Tac looked at the license to confirm it was Troy Vidrine. He noticed the address. "Oh, shit. We don't live too far from each other," he said, genuinely surprised but using this new information for effect. Then, in a calculated move, Tac looked towards Sadie, standing in the open door of her car with the phone to ear, quietly narrating the scene to Curtis, and called out to ask if she was okay. Troy looked on behind a mask of swelling fear as Tac called out "Okay, then. You can go. Be careful." And with that, Sadie was getting in her car, which seemed to be no worse for the wear, and slowly drove away.

Tac walked back towards Troy's truck and peered inside, scanning first the front of the cab and then moving to the back seat. The white and red and blue Priority mailbox was on the floorboard in the back, pushed about halfway under the seat. Tac resisted the impulse to pull out his phone to check the faint markings he could see on the box against the picture Curtis had sent him. There was no need anyway. It was the same box. There was no question in his mind about that. The only unknown was whether Troy would consent to a search, and he was feeling pretty optimistic on that front.

"Where you taking that box?" he asked, looking up at Vidrine, and his face betrayed everything. The man knew he was fucked. He was still standing there with his wallet in his hand, staring down at what looked like a picture. Tac stepped closer to him to get a better look and Vidrine said exactly what he was expecting—"What box?"—barely able to choke the words out, so far from conviction or confidence that Tac didn't even bother to say, "That box of steroids you have in the back. The one you picked up for Lenny Prichard," like he'd planned.

Instead, he just gave him a few more seconds of the cop look, the one that saw right through all the bullshit, half priest, half executioner. And then leaned in next to him to look at the picture. Vidrine actually held up the wallet so Tac could get a better look. Tac took the wallet from his hand, curious if Vidrine would let go of it. There was resistance, but he let Tac take it, and he held it up at eye level, taking his time with the picture. "Wow. What a beautiful family. My wife always says mixed people are more attractive. You know?"

Troy nodded, not trusting his voice. Tac was watching his right eye twitch involuntarily, and his hands were no better. Tac offered the wallet and just held on to it for a second with the lightest touch possible, and through the shared object between them he could feel the vibrations from Troy's hand. Tac held his eyes and just waited.

The sound of Troy's cell phone ringing in the truck interrupted the silence. Tac smiled at him. "Let's see who that is," he said and stepped into the open door of Troy's truck and reached in to pick up the phone, still attached to the charger in the console. He glanced at it then held it up for Troy, who stood back a little from the door, conflicted about whether he wanted to be in the truck or as far away from it as possible. "L.P. That's Lenny, right? How 'bout we let that one go to voicemail?" Tac said and dropped the phone back in the console. "You can call him back in a few minutes. But first I want to make sure you understand the two roads in front of you. You following me?"

"Hey, I don't know what you're talking about, man." Troy croaked out. "I just stopped 'cause that woman almost crashed." He pushed the brim of his Astros cap back and rubbed at his forehead.

"Now I gotta tell you, Troy," Tac said with calculated folksiness he knew wasn't believable. That was the point. "I don't like it when people insult my intelligence. But I'm gonna let that slide because I know you're nervous, and you should be because transporting illegal drugs is a felony." Tac paused to hold his eyes. "And now you're caught. I *got* you. And I will arrest your ass here and now for possession with intent to distribute and you will *not* go home to that beautiful wife and those beautiful kids." Troy seemed to diminish as Tac spoke. A tiny sound emerged from his chest. "But you're a local business owner, so the judge will probably allow bail and your wife—what's her name?"

"What?"

"Your wife."

"It's Thao."

"Thao. That's nice. Vietnamese, right?" Troy nodded. "Thao will probably be able to bail you out. But she might have to put your house up for collateral. And meanwhile, of course, your business. Well, it's not gonna be good for business, I can tell you that. You might have to bring someone else in to run it for you, while you're in jail and in court. And then if you're convicted—and I'm saying *if* but the drugs are right there in your truck so it's pretty much a slam dunk—then you're gonna go to prison for, what? I'd say probably in the range of five years. Maybe a little less, depending on the judge and how much money you spend on your lawyer. And speaking of money, now you're talking money for bail, money for the lawyer," Tac ticked them off on his hand, "and you're *losing* money with your business *every day that goes by*."

Tac put his hand on Troy's shoulder. It was a move he would never in a million years expect to do, but it felt right in that moment. "And meanwhile where's Lenny Prichard? You think he's coming forward to own up to his role in this? Fuck no, bruh! Now he might, he *might* help you out with some money. But no amount of money is gonna keep you together with your family. You'll be an inmate." Another indiscernible sound came from Troy. His face had drained of color. Tac drove it home. "And trust me, prison will break you. I'm not even gonna tell you what happens to soft white dudes like you in there. Or maybe you think you're hard. Well, trust me on this. You are not hard, and you will find this out your very first night in prison. But it will be too late." Tac stood there waiting and watching. Vidrine's eyes were on his boots. "Look at that picture one more time, 'cause it's Friday and you won't even stand before the judge until Monday, earliest. And a weekend in the Eunice jail is *as good* as it's gonna get."

Eventually, Troy croaked out the question Tac was waiting for. "Is there another way?" Tac could see the surrender in his eyes.

"Yes. There's another way. We can do it my way. Here, sit down." Tac stepped aside and motioned for Troy to sit in the driver's seat of his truck. "And with my way, you go home tonight. But only if you do exactly what I say. Exactly." Just then Troy's phone rang again. Tac said "Lemme see" and when he saw it was his wife he said, "Hand me that box and you can answer it." Troy's face melted into a puddle of tears and he reached behind the seat to grab the box with one hand and pass it to Tac. "Go ahead. Talk to your wife." Tac said, accepting the box, and when he saw Troy hit the speaker button, said "No. I don't need to hear. Just talk to your lady. Tell her you're gonna be home tonight."

Tac opened the rear door of the truck and sat directly behind Troy with the box. He used his phone to take a series of pictures of the vials all lined up inside it. And then, as Troy listened to his wife and grew more animated in the front seat, Tac quietly searched for the GPS tracker he knew was hidden somewhere inside. He couldn't help but smile when he found it. Meanwhile, the mood in the front seat was far less buoyant. Troy Vidrine seemed to have gone from scared and desperate to royally pissed off. Tac would have to see if he could use that.

Curtis walked into the Eunice Public Library just after a lady he'd never seen before opened it up. He'd been sitting by the statue of the original Eunice for maybe a minute, waiting. He was relieved it wasn't Mr. Able on duty again today. It would make his task that much easier. He'd come to retrieve the camera mounted outside the second-floor window.

He could see the woman—late fifties, a gray cardigan, short gray hair with reading glasses poised on her head—off to the left, moving around the main information desk. He made his way to the stairs as quietly as possible and took them two at the time to the second floor. Right now, he wasn't that concerned about being stealthy. If slow is smooth and smooth is fast, he was fine just skipping ahead to the fast part.

Curtis was at the window within a few seconds, and after a few more he'd opened it and was peering out onto the street. A black economy car, a Kia maybe—he wasn't sure—drifted by below the window. But he wasn't concerned about cars, only pedestrians. And as his eyes tracked the black car out of sight to his left, towards where the statue of Eunice was, he saw someone on foot. It was Mr. Able, just now stopping to open the glass door of the library directly below Curtis.

This was not what he needed. His trip to the library to take down the camera was extraneous in the first place. He'd only stopped because it was just a few blocks from Sadie's place and he figured all things being equal, it was better if no one ever discovered the random wireless camera mounted in such a haphazard way on the side of the library. Especially once word got out about the bust Tac must be making right now. He didn't have time to be fucking around, so he reached out and grabbed the thing by the base and pulled hard, and it gave, but it didn't come off. The epoxy was holding.

He reached for the Leatherman at his belt, flipped open the serrated knife, and went to work at the base of the camera. And now fear started to grip him. He didn't even need to be here, but he'd been impulsive, just couldn't resist the urge, and so now he was leaning out the window of the library in broad daylight, sweating while he sawed at a camera he'd put there in the first place and if anybody saw him . . . but, it seemed to be working. Once he sawed through the first bit of epoxy between the base of the camera and the wall he could feel it coming loose. And once he had enough room he was able to get the knife in there and pry the rest of it off.

As he pulled the camera back into the library he could hear bits of the wall raining down on the sidewalk below. He dropped the camera with half the wall still attached, it seemed like, at his feet. It was there framed against a square of blue industrial carpet, little bits of red brick all around it like some kind of abstract painting.

Curtis looked up to watch the stairs while he put the knife away. Then he used his foot to break off as much of the brick still attached to the base of the camera as he could. It fit somewhat awkwardly, but he was able to get the camera into his back pocket and more or less concealed under his jacket and the tail of his shirt.

Mr. Able was waiting for the little elevator when Curtis got to the base of the stairs. The old man lit up when he saw Curtis, and for some reason that made Curt feel horrible in that moment. The smile he offered Mr. Able was forced. Curtis wasn't ready with a lie.

"I was just . . . I just forgot something," he said. But something about Mr. Able's expression told him the man wasn't expecting an explanation. He was just happy to see Curtis.

"Oh. Okay. You're all set then? Are you leaving town?"

"Yeah. I think I've done all the "research" that I can," Curtis said. In that moment, it occurred to him he could probably ask this man just about anything.

"Good. Good. Well, if there's anything I can ever help you

with—"

Curtis interrupted him. "Well, since you offered." He double-checked no one was within earshot. "What do you know about Ely Prichard? It seems like he—" Mr. Able's eyes had gone wide like something had spooked him. "What is it?" Curtis asked, confused, and maybe a little worried.

Now it was Mr. Able's turn to look around. "Wherever your research takes you, I strongly advise you, *don't* write about Ely Prichard. Or anybody with that name." He put a gentle hand on Curt's elbow. "He's a vindictive man. Dangerous, too." Curtis wasn't sure what they were talking about.

"Really?" was all he said.

"Yes." Mr. Able kept his hand at his elbow and came in a little closer. "He controls a lot of businesses around here. And they don't all keep regular hours, if you know what I mean."

"No, I don't think I do. Like, criminal kinda stuff?" Curtis asked in a whisper. Mr. Able just held his eyes for a moment, then looked around again.

"Just please listen to me," he said. "Because I can tell you're a nice boy but you're young and—no offense dear—but maybe a little naive. Just like I was, a long time ago. But Ely is different than us in that regard. So you stay *away* from him, okay?"

"I'm sorry, Mr. Able but I'm not . . . actually, I'm straight." The words just popped out of his mouth, a symptom of stress, maybe, but hardly a logical response to Mr. Able's words. That was when the discussion went from strange to stranger.

"Well then, you would be the odd man out between the

three of us." Mr. Able said, and then seemed to wait patiently for Curtis to catch up. It took a moment.

"Oh! I see." Curtis said a little too loud. "And that's, how you know him, I guess. It didn't end well between you, I guess?"

"He killed my business. Practically ran me out of town. Threatened far worse if I ever breathed a word of it. It's one of the best-kept secrets in town."

And you just blurted it out to me, Curtis said to himself. "So, why are you telling me this?" he asked. Mr. Able looked hurt, and again Curtis felt bad about how he was bumbling through this. At the same time, he suddenly felt a powerful impulse to hurry up and get out of town. He glanced at his watch.

"Because I don't want to see you or anyone else get hurt for asking the wrong question to the wrong person." Curtis reached into his back pocket for his notebook and flipped it to a blank page before offering it to Mr. Able.

"Would you mind giving me your number? In case I have other questions?" Mr. Able paused, and Curtis was surprised he seemed to be considering the question.

"No," he said, gently pushing the notebook back at Curtis. "More questions will only lead to trouble. Now go on, get out of here." It took Curtis a second to recover. Once he did, he simply extended his hand and they shook.

"Thanks," he said, and left.

Angel was driving west on Highway 190 in his Ford Focus, just beyond the Eunice city limits, feeling nervous. He had some drum and bass on, just loud enough to where he could talk to himself or spit some lyrics without hearing his own words. Shit with Jackie was getting weird, and even though he tried not to sweat it he couldn't help but replay their conversation on a loop in his head.

"We might have to stop seeing each other." She had said outta nowhere.

"Why's that?" he had said, thinking she was fucking with him.

"Because we're having too much fun." And when he heard *that* he was sure she was fucking with him.

"So why stop?"

"Because it's getting more complicated." She'd said.

"Complicated? I thought you said we was having fun?"

"It's the fun that's complicating things."

"Fun's complicated?"

"Almost always," she had said, like that was supposed to be obvious or some shit.

"What, you didn't like my rap?" he'd asked her, and that got a laugh. That classic Jackie laugh she had where it was like she didn't have a care in the world for at least as long as she was laughing. And then she had just started telling him how, no, she actually really dug his lyrics, especially the like, religious imagery or whatever and then she went into this long thing about religious symbols in music and how the Beatles had got in trouble for saying they were bigger than Jesus even though that's not really what they said.

When he got into town and passed by the Old East Shopping Center, he pulled in even though it was way too early for JD to be at the shop. Really, it was the window that pulled him in. The way it said "Black Jack Tattoo" in that orange and black old-school type lettering, it just grabbed you. He couldn't help but whip out his phone and take a couple pictures.

He sent one of the selfies—far enough back to where it wasn't just his face, but you could see the whole sign in the frame—to Jackie and then it occurred to him to send one to JD too, so he did. He was kinda surprised when JD hit him back right away, at first wanting to know what he was doing there so early, and then coming back with another to tell him the sign looked bad-ass.

Angel said he had to cruise over to Tans to see what Lenny wanted, and then maybe they could, he had started to type out *rendezvous,* but no matter how he wrote the word it looked wrong, so bad that the autocorrect didn't pick it up so he just wrote *meet back here later.*

Negative. DON'T go meet LP or anyone! Hang tight.

Which didn't make a lot of sense to Angel. It was barely nine o'clock. But whatever, if JD wanted him to wait, he didn't mind. Any excuse to put it off was good with him.

OK. What's going on?

JD came back right away and said to just wait, that he'd tell Angel when he got there. Angel put the phone back in his pocket and at that moment the smell of sweet baked goods just seemed to hit him all of a sudden. Sugar Ray's! He was walking towards the bakery before the anticipated pleasure of it fully registered in his brain. Maybe they had coffee, too. Coffee and a donut. Nothing in the world sounded better than that right about now.

He was dumping sugar in his cup from one of those old-school dispensers when he felt his phone going off in his pocket. But he took his time, enjoying the smell of the place and the friendly vibe of it. And it was obviously black-owned, which was righteous. He could've done without the gospel music they had going, but whatever. He picked up his small white box of half a dozen glazed and his coffee and called out "alright" to the dude behind the counter and leaned against the glass door to push it open.

At the door to Black Jack's, Angel put his coffee cup on the ground and then carefully set the box of donuts on top of it, not wanting his food touching the ground. Inside, he put the donuts down on one of the milk crates in the reception area and walked with his coffee to put a funky R&B playlist on, Frank Ocean singing about being "Lost" in the thrill of it all behind an infectious beat that always made Angel move.

After a while, sitting down on one of the uncomfortable-ass folding chairs back in the waiting area, he used his fingernail to cut through the little piece of masking tape the dude at the counter had used to seal the box, he guessed not realizing Angel was literally gonna walk like thirty feet maybe to the new tattoo shop. He didn't look at his phone till he'd taken his first bite, and it tasted so fucking good even Lenny Prichard couldn't spoil it.

Seriously. Get over here ASAP. I got your severance.

Angel looked up the word, just to be sure, and then he texted back the same two letters he'd sent in response to the first text from Lenny. *OK.* Just okay. No promises. No, *you got it* or *be right there,* or any of that shit. He'd be there when he got there. But right now he was enjoying his donut and, noticing the blank canvas of the top of the donut box, he found the nearest pen and started drawing on it. What he'd do, he'd just leave the donuts here for JD when he showed up. He'd even leave the music going, just to kind of fuck with him, while he went to see what Lenny wanted real quick. The box of donuts would be his note.

He pulled the three hundred he'd brought from his stash at home and tucked it under the box and drew an arrow to it, but then he realized his drawing on the box was weak, lost in the sea of white on the box. You couldn't even see it from a few feet away, so he grabbed a Sharpie and spent maybe five minutes really pimping out the box with stick figures in motion and in silhouette and did some quick graffiti lettering and stuff. It was cool. He had some MC Escher type stuff going on with the side of the box, one figure on top pulling another one from below, both figures mirror images of each other, to where you couldn't tell if the guy on the bottom was pulling the guy on top down, or if it was the other way around.

When he was finished, he positioned the box right where JD would notice it first thing, then he locked the door behind him and strolled out to his car, sipping at the bottom, sugary part of his coffee, the best part. Hopefully, he could come back with some extra cash and they could spend the day really taking the shop to the next level. It was gonna be cool as fuck!

Lenny called out, "It's about fucking time" to his empty office when Lefty finally returned his call. He put the phone to his ear and started talking. "Please tell me you didn't go to 2nd Street?"

Troy was sitting there in his truck, with Tac, sitting next to him with the windows up to mask the road noise. The cop was holding his phone up near his mouth, and the cop's phone was on the dashboard recording the whole thing.

"Yeah, of course I went to 2nd Street. I'm on my way to Jennings like we talked about." The pause that ensued was longer than normal.

"Really? So everything was cool?"

"Yeah, everything was cool. Why wouldn't it be?" Troy asked.

"Cause somebody's fucking with me." Lenny came back. "It must be that little fucking wetback Pancho. But he's gonna get his, trust me. I'm gonna kill that muthafucka when I see him." Troy just kept quiet, and Lenny lurched forward into the silence. "I got worried it had something to do with 2nd Street, so I tried calling your ass all fucking morning! Where the fuck were you? I had to go to your goddamn house!"

"You went to my house?" Troy already knew the answer. He knew exactly what had gone down at his house, and that was what changed everything. Thao had sent him a picture of the front door and the side of the house—mud and rocks and shit everywhere—and told him how she barely managed to close the glass door before the rocks started hitting it. One of the pictures showed the point of impact on the glass, like when a rock hits your windshield at sixty miles an hour. And that was what did it. That rock could've hit his wife, and that's *all* he could think about now.

"Yeah. But you already left. And your fucking cell phone must be broken or something! I was freaking out!" Tac could see Troy's temper swelling and he motioned for him to keep cool, thinking to himself that later on if he needed some extra incentive all he had to do was promise Troy five minutes alone with Lenny.

"Anyway," Troy said, desperate to move on because if Lenny said one single thing about his wife he was gonna lose his shit for sure. "Where you wanna meet? I gotta go to the job site after I drop off the shit at the gym in Jennings, but I can be back at like four."

"I'm thinking Hooters in Lafayette," Lenny said.

"No. I can't do that. I'll just bring the money to your house. Or to Tans if you want."

"Goddamn, bruh! That woman has you fucking whipped! When we gonna party?"

"Soon," Troy said, swallowing the bitter pill of the words just to get this shit over with. "But not tonight."

"Alright. Whatever. But just so you know, I finished all the shit I got for us last night." Troy looked up at the cop but his eyes revealed nothing.

"Yeah, whatever. It's all good," he said weakly. "So, four? Your house?"

"Fine," Lenny said and disconnected without another word. Tac made sure Troy's phone was disconnected, then he reached over and stopped the recording on his phone.

"Good job," he said. "Now here's what we're gonna do. Me and you are gonna drive to the police station in Crowley—that's eighteen miles straight up the road—and when we get there, a whole lot more people are gonna get involved." Troy's face took on a pained look. He'd been hoping, beyond reason but hoping still that the cop would just take the package and let him go about his business.

Tac registered this in Troy's expression and continued in the cop-tone he'd been cultivating for years. "You're not out of the woods yet. Not by a long shot. When we get to Crowley, I'm gonna take your statement, and then I'm gonna coordinate with the police in Jennings and they're gonna be there when you bring this in." He waited to make sure Troy had absorbed everything he'd said so far. "And as soon as you get the money, everybody's gonna get arrested. *Everybody* will get arrested, that means you, too. But I'm gonna take you into custody and take you back to Eunice." Again, Tac waited, giving Troy time to process it all. "*If* you do everything exactly like I tell you, you will sleep in your own bed tonight. But *only* if you do everything I say. Do you understand?"

"Yeah." Troy croaked.

"If I tell you to answer a question 'yes' and you say 'yeah, but,' you stay in jail. If I tell you to walk ten steps and scratch your right ear and you take nine steps, you stay in jail. You follow me?"

Troy silently nodded his head, leaving it there against his chest as he gave into despair and the tears began to flow. There was no stopping it. Tac was happy to see his new informant in such a vulnerable state. It would give him the greatest chance of success with what he had planned for the rest of the day. He absolutely had to make arrests in Jennings and make this case a multi-parish operation. They might even be able to bring the state police into it. And if that happened, the chances of

Prichard slipping out from under this shrank considerably.

Sadie had been back just long enough to stop shaking. JD was standing at the door of the house when she turned in, watching, and by the time she killed the engine, he was opening the car door and pulling her into a hug. She was shaking like a wet dog, and he told her so in between kisses and praise about how brave—no, how bad-ass she was.

As freaked out as he was when she left the house—he had like fifteen seconds to stop her, and for the first ten of those he was still buck naked and dreaming—she was a hero now. They'd have to wait for the details to come out and keep their mouths totally and completely shut, but no matter how you sliced it, Tac showing up when he did was fucking beautiful. And it wouldn't have happened if it weren't for Sadie.

"Not that I had any idea how I was *actually* gonna stop the dude once I caught up to him." Sadie interrupted JD's praise to point out.

But JD's main concern was still Lenny. And when Angel had texted just before Sadie got back to say he was going to see Lenny. Well, JD's gut went sideways on him. Something was up for sure. He told Angel to stay put.

It might be paranoid or whatever, but he didn't want to say anything to Angel on the phone, or even face-to-face for that matter. Not because he didn't trust Angel, but because of Jackie. She was Lenny's cousin and it didn't matter how cool she was, Lenny was her blood, not to mention her boss. Of course, until Sadie came rolling in, he couldn't do shit because he was watching her mom, and anyway, his van was still with Slim at Cajun Customs.

Curtis showed up not two minutes after Sadie did and JD, standing there smoking his first cigarette of the day, could tell right away he was leaving town. It was just something about the casual way he sauntered up to the house, like he was already checked out. Well, JD was ready to check him back in right quick. They needed to get Angel situated before Curtis hauled ass and left the mess for JD to clean up.

Sadie had put on some coffee and she brought Curtis a cup when she saw him at the door with JD. So they sat at the kitchen table and Sadie told them both how it went down. Her mom was sitting in her chair in the living room with her lukewarm tea, and Sadie briefly wondered how much of it all she was getting. But she didn't dwell on it. Anyway, her mom had probably liked her time with JD this morning. He always called her *sweetie* or *honey* or *dear* or some such thing, and Sadie knew how she liked to be flattered.

"I musta jumped three feet in the air!" she was saying, already past the factual account and into color commentary now. "When I landed. It was like one of them fair rides, just *spinning*! But the crazy thing was I could hear Curtis barking in the phone the whole time!" She slipped into an impression of him, entertaining both of them. " 'Sadie! What's going on? Whatchyou see' "?

JD was working his leg under the table, bouncing on the ball of his foot. It wasn't much, but Curtis picked up on it.

"Lenny texted Angel and said to come see him," JD said, and the chemistry at the table changed. Sadie's eyes shifted into a kind of squint, the kind you don't want to be on the receiving end of. "I told him to keep his ass at the shop, so don't worry," he assured Sadie. Curtis sipped his coffee while Sadie snatched up her phone and JD kept talking. "But I'm thinking maybe me and Curtis will go check him out. Tell him to keep his distance from Lenny for a while. Like maybe forever." He didn't even get a chuckle from Sadie, who was directing that determined squint at her phone. She stood up so suddenly the kitchen chair fell backward with a sound like the crack of a bat.

And suddenly they were all standing. She thrust her hand out with the phone so JD and Curtis could see. "Well, he's not at the shop. I think he's at the tanning place." JD was already moving towards the door, cursing to himself, and when he looked up and saw Curtis still rooted to the floor, unhurried, the bark that erupted from JD made Sadie's mom jump and Curtis spill coffee on the table as he attempted to put his cup down and get himself in motion all at once.

JD was holding the door open, his jaw locked in a mix of determination and anger. Sadie was trying to dial Angel's number, spinning around the kitchen in a sudden coil of nerves. "Wait!" Curtis said, and stopped. Even Sadie's mom looked up at him. "He has cameras. We don't know how many. We'll be on tape." The look that JD gave him then could've cut class.

"Well then don't steal anything this time!" he barked. "Let's go."

When Angel didn't pick up, Sadie looked up the number for Sun-*N*-Tans and called the reception desk. She had never met Britney whatever her last name was that picked up the phone, but she wasn't gonna let that stop her. Everybody in Eunice was connected in some kinda way. It was just a matter of announcing your last name and linking yourself to someone else with that last name. It was funny how people worked; all you needed was one thing in common, whether it was the combination of letters that made up your name, or the highway you lived off of, or even where you went to school when there was literally only two options, and ninety-nine percent of people went to option one.

"That dirty little prick!" Britney spat when Sadie told her about the cameras. She didn't have time to hang with Britney on the phone. But before she let her go, she told Britney there might be some trouble that involved the cops and if they found those cameras they'd want to see the videos—all of them. It took Britney maybe two seconds to understand. "Don't worry about it, girl," Britney said. "I know exactly what to do."

While she was on the phone she walked over to the living room to kiss her mom and help her recline in the chair, and then she walked next door to the neighbor's to see if Ms. Alma wouldn't mind coming over for a little bit. It was kind of an emergency, she said.

Curtis had popped the trunk of the Mazda and retrieved the 9-millimeter from the false cavity of the spare tire, checking the action and holstering it on his hip before he walked around to the driver's seat. JD was impatient, halfway through a cigarette he had lit while Curtis stood there fucking around in the trunk. "Slow is smooth, and smooth is fast," Curtis said to him.

"Fuck you. Fast is fast! Let's go!"

They were on Park Avenue and Curtis thought about the library camera. It still had juice in it.

"Hey, you see that camera on the floorboard? That's the one from the library. It's still on."

JD had picked it up and was examining the bits of red brick

still stuck to the base of it. "You just ripped this off the wall?"

"Yeah. That's why I was late." "Okay. When this is all said and done we need to have a talk. You need to like, take up skydiving or some shit, bubba." Curtis looked over at him and flashed a wicked smile.

"That sounds fucking boring," he said. "So, the camera. See if you can maybe fit it in your front pocket or even down the front of your pants, and like work the front part of the camera out so—"

"Yeah, I get it," JD said, his seat belt off and already experimenting with the little camera. "Just get us there. I have a feeling Angel's fixing to get ambushed."

Curtis muttered some expletives, then started fishing his bandana out of his back pocket. "I think you're right. That tracker didn't just stop working. He must've found it." He started tying the folded bandana across his nose.

"What are you doing?"

"The cameras," Curtis said.

"Jesus H. Christ, Laroux! Forget about the element of surprise! Lenny's gonna see you. He thinks Angel planted a fucking tracking device in his truck! You think it's gonna go smoother if you roll in there like a fucking bank robber?" Curtis pulled the bandana down around his neck, and it wasn't lost on JD that he didn't actually take the thing off. "Look. We just need to get Angel out of there. We don't need any heroics. Don't pull out that piece unless you have to."

"You want me to leave it?"

"Fuck, no," JD said. "Just let me do the talking."

Lenny was sitting at his desk with the busted guts of the tracker laid out on a sheet of paper in front of him, drinking his third beer of the morning. Britney had knocked and then strode in with Angel right behind her. "He's here to see you," she said, and reached down to take his laptop off the desk, but Lenny reached up and clamped his hand on it in midair. And then Angel was hovering in the doorway looking all meek and shit, so he let it go and gave Britney an evil look, just to let her know what was what. "I have to update your antivirus!" she said, scurrying out of the office.

Angel hung back, just trying to assess, but that didn't take long. One look at Lenny and he knew he'd fucked up by coming. The dude was cranked up on something.

"Sit down, bruh," Lenny commanded. "I wanna talk to you about something." Angel didn't have much choice but to comply. He stepped to one of the two chairs on the other side of the desk and pulled the closest one back about a foot, closer to the door, and sat down. Lenny gave a nod toward the door. "Close the door." But Angel stood his ground.

"Nah, I'm good," he said, and then kept silent. He was determined not to antagonize the man.

The nerve of this fucker! Lenny couldn't believe he had the balls to defy him. But it wouldn't matter. He was gonna get his answers, one way or another. He was one hundred percent prepared to choke it out of him. In fact, he'd been fantasizing— no, planning—how it would go down. First, he'd come around the desk and sit at the edge of it. Then catch him by the throat and bring him right to the floor.

"Tell me about this," Lenny said, gesturing with a nod to the broken electronics on the sheet of paper. Angel leaned forward to scope out the mess on the paper. Jagged pieces of broken plastic, a little circuit board that had been folded in half, some other mangled shit he didn't recognize.

"Looks like some broken shit to me," Angel said, giving Lenny the same kind of look he'd give a cop that was trying to sweat him. Like, *this is what you called me here for? Some broken shit?*

"Well, it wasn't broke when you put it in my truck. So tell me what it's for before I beat your ass." The way Angel knew he was serious was he didn't raise his voice. He started to push back from his chair, but Lenny reached into his desk drawer and pulled out a big fucking chrome pistol. Clank. It sounded like a fucking pipe wrench hitting the desk. "Sit the fuck down!" And now Lenny *was* yelling, and there was only one way this was gonna go.

Angel had both hands on the arms of the chair, ready to bolt outta there if he had to or fight if he couldn't. He glanced behind him to double-check the door was still open and there was JD standing there, like an apparition. He was sure he was hallucinating until Lenny stood up with the pistol and started yelling, "What the fuck you doing here?"

JD had been taking slow, quiet steps down the hallway, but once the yelling started he made himself visible, standing in the doorway with a calculated expression on his face.

"Hey, what's up boys?" he said, ever cool. Curtis stood a few feet behind him. He couldn't see Angel from there, but when Lenny came around with the revolver he reached for the pistol at his hip and then paused. Lenny was holding the big chrome revolver like a baseball, his hand wrapped around the trigger guard. The man didn't want to kill anybody. He was posturing. Curtis put his hand on the hilt of the gun and stood still, ready.

Lenny turned at the sound of JD's voice and it took him a long time to grasp the reality that someone else had entered the room. He stuttered out a string of expletives and half-formed phrases that resolved to "What the fuck?," and then came around the right side of his desk to keep both JD and Angel in his sights. Angel was out of his chair and had moved towards the wall near the door, automatically moving away from the gun. JD stepped further into the room and slid to his right to shield Angel from view.

"I'm just here to pick up my man Angel. I need him for something." At that, Lenny raised the gun and Curtis could see he was holding it by the grip now. It didn't matter that his finger wasn't on the trigger. Curtis slid the pistol from the holster and slowly raised it to center mass, sliding right as he did to maximize his angle away from JD and Angel.

Lenny didn't notice the movement to his right because he was busy losing his shit and screaming. "Pancho! Pancho! His name is Pancho! And he's a fucking liar!" his voice breaking up as he punctuated the air with every syllable. JD's hands went up automatically.

"Okay, okay. Just cool out. Do me a favor and lower that gun. I know you don't wanna shoot nobody." JD glanced up at Curtis in the hallway in that moment and when he did, Lenny looked over too. Again, he seemed to reject the reality of someone new standing there. Curtis couldn't see the recognition blossom in his lockjawed face because he was watching Lenny's hands, only his hands, his finger still outside the trigger guard.

"You. You! Laroux!" Lenny screamed. "You couldn't hit for shit!" his brain making connections. Curtis watched the pistol bob at the end of his arm, but when it came to rest it was still trained on JD. He and Angel had moved deeper into the room, almost against the back wall of the office now. Curtis became aware of the sound of thumping footsteps then. He noticed JD suddenly animate to his right.

"Sadie! Stay back!" And suddenly, she was standing next to Curtis off his left shoulder. Curtis still had his eyes trained on Lenny's trigger finger, but he could feel Sadie's look as she assessed first him, ready to fire two rounds into Lenny at ten feet, then Lenny standing in front of his own desk, the pistol growing heavy in his arm. She stepped into the room.

"Lenny, what are you doing?" she demanded. "You need to put that gun down." Lenny was still staring at Curtis while he pointed the gun at JD and Angel.

"What the fuck is he doing here? You put the gun down muthafucka!" Lenny screamed at Curtis.

To his shock, Sadie said flatly "Curtis. Put your gun down." And then she moved closer to Lenny, in his line of sight so Curtis had no choice but to lower the pistol. He stepped further into the room and as he did so made eye contact with JD, motioning left. Angel was still tucked behind him and together they made a fat target. "You look all fucked up," Sadie said to Lenny. "How long you been up? A day? Two?"

"Whatchyou put in my truck?" Lenny screamed again at Angel, his voice breaking up. Sadie had maneuvered behind Lenny and was standing on his left side now. Curtis holstered the pistol—there was no safe angle to fire from with Sadie on the other side of Lenny. He stepped closer as Lenny gestured with the revolver. He could see JD was sliding ever so slightly to his right, and just as Angel spoke up, Curtis saw Sadie pull the mace from the back pocket of her jeans.

"He's the one that put that shit in your truck," Angel said evenly, pointing to Curtis. Everything seemed to happen at once then. Lenny turned his head towards Curtis and as he did Sadie reached around and blasted him with the mace. Curtis closed the distance and latched onto the gun, still in Lenny's grip, with both hands. The gun went off. JD moved to his right, and as he did, the .45-caliber slug from Lenny's revolver struck Angel dead center and he fell back against the wall. The violence of the sound and the impact and the acrid smell of gunpowder made the world stand still in that instant. But in the next, chaos erupted.

Lenny screamed like a wild animal as Curtis broke his trigger finger back against itself with a soft pop and the gun fell on the desk as Curtis slipped behind him to pin him face to the floor in a naked choke. He screamed and bucked and Curtis rode him for a few seconds while he sorted out his legs to hook Lenny into submission. There were more screams, the first from Sadie as she realized what had happened and leapt over the desk to get to Angel, and then a new voice, primal and awful, as Jackie rushed into the room.

Jackie made a habit of driving by Sun-*N*-Tans on her way to the office to see if Lenny was at work yet. She knew something was up as soon as the building came into sight. There were way too many cars there for this early, parked at weird angles. And then she saw Angel's little Ford Focus. In the next instant, she saw Britney standing by the road with her phone to her ear and that sent a wave of something unfamiliar through her.

She pulled in and was out of the Celica walking towards the open door of the building when the sound of the gunshot changed everything. In the days and years after this event, she would replay her view from the hallway in her mind and it would forever seem like a haunted house scene somebody might do in their backyard. Unreal and almost comical in its absurdity. Angel was slumped over at the base of the wall and it was the position of his body that told her he was dead. The recognition of it hit her like a sound wave. She saw him there dead, but it took a few seconds to register. Angel was dead. And even while the fact of it resonated in her head, she couldn't believe it.

She ran forward and it was like it was just the two of them there. She fell at his side and grabbed him. "Angel. Angel!" And then her brain registered the hot and the wet. His Bad Brains sweatshirt was soaked and heavy, and it took her a long time to understand it was his blood. The blood belonged in his body but here it was soaked into his sweatshirt and he was dead and it didn't make sense because she had talked to him this morning.

She didn't think about the baby at first. That didn't come until later, when people she didn't know started pulling at her, gibberish coming from their mouths in sensible tones. She started to wake from the nightmare of this haunted house scene then, except that the waking up just made everything worse. It was all too real. Policemen and paramedics and people clawing at her. They were clawing as if some emergency was still in motion, but Angel was dead. He was dead and he stayed dead no matter how much she pleaded and held his face in her hands. He stayed dead. The cold blood was proof of that. He was a mess and his beautiful face had gone all slack, his eyes cast down looking at something he could no longer see and it was awful. He was gone. Dead and gone. And here she was. Alone.

That was when she thought about the baby inside her. Not a baby, not exactly. She had refused to think of it in those terms. She couldn't allow it. She had refused to tell Angel, and now he was dead but—and she hated herself when the thought first occurred to her—a part of him was still alive.

JD and Sadie would both say the tone of Jackie's cries changed then, and it was Sadie who was finally able to help her detach from the body so the paramedics and the cops could do what they needed to. Jackie would not remember how long she stayed there clinging to Angel, or the horrible acrid smells and the cold congealing blood. She would only recall the awful moment when she remembered she was pregnant and how evil and conflicted she felt when she pleaded with a god she didn't believe in to take the baby and give her back her Angel.

It was just after sundown before anyone approached Lenny in the holding cell. A couple hours before, somebody had yelled at him to shut the fuck up, but that was it. He had been screaming for his uncle, calling out "Ely Prichard," and then yelling out his phone number. His eyes still stung like a motherfucker, and he could tell his face was all puffy because he could literally see the fat part of his eye encroaching in his field of view. His finger throbbed in the splint they had put on it, but the real pain was the softball-sized knot in his back where Curtis Laroux, of all people, had driven his knee into his back. At least he thought it was Laroux, even though that didn't make any sense at all.

But nothing made sense, least of all the fact that Pancho was dead. He still couldn't bring himself to accept what he had done. It wasn't that he didn't remember. He remembered, but he couldn't see it. In his mind, he couldn't see it. And that had everything to do with that bitch Sadie Lee. She had set him up, that much was clear.

He had been sitting on the cement slab with his head back and his eyes closed trying to imagine what his uncle was doing right that second when a cop he vaguely recognized appeared at the door with a bottle of water. He motioned for Lenny to approach.

"Here," he said, discreetly offering him a matchbox. Lenny took it absently and palmed the matchbox. He accepted the bottle of water the cop put through the bars. "Don't take 'em both at once. Space it out. You're gonna spend the night, at least."

He slid the matchbox open and found two tic-tac-shaped pills. He cracked the bottle and swallowed the first one, not yet sure what he was taking but still looking to his wrist, a reflex, to check the time on the watch they had taken from him. Sometime later he noticed he couldn't feel the knot in his back or the throbbing in his finger. In fact, he felt fine. Not good, but numb, and that was good enough. His only problem was he had killed a man, and now he was in jail.

Curtis, JD, and Sadie had given their statements, first at the scene and then later on at the police station. They were remarkably consistent.

Sadie had told the officer at the scene "Well, Lenny shot Angel, and then I maced him. And that's when Curtis grabbed hold of the gun and wrestled him to the ground. Then, him and JD held him until y'all got here."

When they asked JD, he said "Thank God Sadie came in when she did, 'cause if she hadn't maced him we might all be dead. Angel was standing right next to me when Lenny shot him. And then Curtis was able to take the gun from him while he was blinded."

"Sadie was a hero," Curtis told the investigator back at the station. "We were all shocked when he fired the gun and hit Angel, but Sadie stayed cool. She maced him before he could get another shot off. I saw the opening and I got my hands on the gun to secure it. If it wasn't for Sadie, there's no telling how bad it would've been."

There was no mention of a second gun. They'd probably waited five full minutes for the first police officers to arrive. It was more than enough time for Curtis to slip out to the Mazda and stow the pistol, the camera from JD's pocket, and the fragments of the broken tracker while JD maintained the hold on Lenny, who'd gone quiet and contemplative, his mouth open and his eyes resigned like a fish out of water.

It was almost midnight when Curtis pulled the Mazda into a parking spot at a Marriott just off of I-10, outside Lafayette. The Eunice police had his statement and his contact information, and though he'd downplayed it, his status as a federal employee seemed to factor into the sergeant agreeing he should return home. He used his regular credit card at the front desk. There was no masking his whereabouts now.

Pretty soon everyone would know he was in Eunice and the questions would probably come thick and fast. The Eunice police were nothing compared to the hardened intelligence officers in his chain of command. He would have to report the incident within forty-eight hours, and there would be questions from the security element. That much was certain.

He felt dirty and drained. The bottle of whiskey and the bucket of ice didn't help in the way he had hoped. His burger and fries from room service went untouched. He tried to watch the video from the camera in JD's pocket, knowing full well what it would show, but he was too drunk to see at that point. Maybe it was for the best. No one could ever know the footage existed, and that was just one more lie Curtis would have to maintain for the rest of his life.

The next day he pulled up in front of Jacque's house in the Mazda and just sat there for a few minutes. He wanted to give Jacque time, but he needed time himself. To decide how much he wanted to share, for one thing. To decide how he would tell it, for another.

Eventually, he unlatched the front gate and made the potentially dangerous walk across the little yard to the electrified porch. When he stepped onto it, some small part of him thought it might be a good way to go if it turned out to be his last. But it wasn't. All that happened was Jacque opened the door after about sixty seconds and stood there appraising Curtis.

"You don't look so good, my man," he said, standing in the doorway in a white tee shirt pulled taut over his belly. He stepped aside and as Curtis slid by him, he said "That town fucked you up, huh?"

Epilogue

The grand opening of Black Jack Tattoo was like a small carnival—the kind of party the carnies might throw for themselves after they closed down the fair. Sadie had talked to some of the other owners in the Old East Shopping Center—Sugar Ray's Bakery, Krispy Kajun—and Tee-Bug at the Daiquiri Hut down the road. They all joined in the party.

The Astro van was the centerpiece of everything. It was parked in front of the shop like a magazine centerfold. Slim had outdone himself. The side panel he'd done before the news of Angel's death was impressive, but it wasn't nothing compared to what he finished with after a couple extra days.

The van was a showpiece now. Not just a rolling, badass advertisement for Black Jack's, but a tribute to Angel. His name and his dates were scripted into the artwork on the hood and the main side panel, but the more Sadie and JD studied the van, the more subtle little references to Angel they found.

Slim made some noise about accepting the extra cash JD offered him, but eventually he took the money. The whole crew from Cajun Customs had shown up for the grand opening with a tricked-out car of their own, an Oldsmobile in metallic-flecked green with a sound system that could wake the dead. The little face-painting booth they set up for the kids was popular, and it didn't take long for Slim and JD to recognize the natural alliance between their businesses.

Tee-Bug from the Daiquiri Hut had set up a little table of his own, mixing up virgin drinks for the kids and the cops and directing all others to the frozen handle of vodka he had stashed in the bed of his truck.

Sadie had tried to get Jackie to come out, but it was still so raw. They had only just buried Angel, and for her it was tragically complicated. Her family was unsympathetic, and his family was suspicious. She turned inward because there was no other place to turn. Her unborn child already carried an impossible weight.

The shop itself was a vision, like something graceful and real plucked from an alternate reality where the entire city of Eunice was as vibrant and alive. The walls were angles of black and gray, broken on both sides with gaping rectangles of mirror that reflected back on themselves to give the place a funhouse vibe, magnifying everything.

There were low slung couches and armchairs arranged around the sturdy little coffee table that had been with JD since Texas. The entirety of the waiting area was framed by a glass case separating it from the working part of the room. Black Jack's tee shirts in black, stickers, and beer koozies were interspersed inside among the studs and rings and other piercing paraphernalia made of stainless steel, silicone, fake bone. All kinds of shit.

Beyond the case, there was still just the one nice customer chair that anchored JD's station. Which would do fine for now. They'd barely spoken about it, but Sadie understood JD wasn't even ready to hear the word apprentice. So it was just the one, black vinyl and chrome, a classic thing that would still be working in another twenty or thirty years, at least.

His station was a kind of cathedral to the art of tattoos. Beyond the black and gray and chrome toolbox positioned against the wall like the alpha male of cabinetry, a set of paneled mirrors on hinges created a kaleidoscope of views of whoever was sitting in the chair, making that person the center of the universe. Colored bottles of ink were arranged like the stepped notes of a pipe organ, beautiful and powerful not just in their potential, but even as still life, just sitting there in front of the mirror. The white donut box Angel had drawn on was splayed out flat and framed on the wall. The money that Angel had left, three hundred-dollar bills, were fanned out on display in the bottom part of the frame. JD figured he'd do some good in Angel's memory with that money someday, but wasn't ready.

The little piercing studio beyond the room divider with the clever silhouettes in the panels somehow felt like an entirely different place. It was unclear exactly how JD and Sadie pulled this off, but when you stepped beyond the panel it was like you were in a special hangout spot that materialized out of nowhere. It was just a few plants, a little rug, and some well-placed art. It didn't hurt that the massage table was comfortable.

Sadie had found a table to elevate Angel's little light box he had made. JD had already used it a few times. He'd sat in the shop by himself the other day, listening to the same reggaeton playlist Angel had put on the morning he died, and putting that same design on his own hand. And every now and then, he'd make a comment out loud to mock the music, hating it and laughing at the practical joke Angel was making from the grave.

It was a cool tattoo shop. It was certified by the state. It looked and felt amazing. The doors were open. JD had done it. No, Sadie and Angel and Curtis, and even Tac and Jackie and Slim. Hell, even Troy Vidrine, they had all done it. Black Jack Tattoo was open in Eunice, Louisiana. But the costs had been more than anyone expected, and the thing that JD and Sadie barely understood on the bittersweet day of the grand opening was that they had not even begun to pay the full price. The other shoe was yet to fall, and when it did, it would be backed by the full force of Ely Prichard and the enterprise he had spent a lifetime building. If anyone in Eunice thought this was over, they had another fucking thing coming. And the first salvo of the coming war was aimed right at JD Dugas and his trashy little tattoo shop.

CREDITS

Written by Jason P. Reed

Artwork by Toby Frey

Copyedited by Marie J. Coreil

A New Bayou Books Publication

SPECIAL THANKS

Susanna Huang, Wil the Thrill Rougeau, Kevin Shumate, Elizabeth Roderick, Shelbie Cormier, Nicholas Rougeau, and Marie J. Coreil

About the Author

Jason Reed grew up in South-Louisiana and was educated at the University of South-Western Louisiana. He has served as a Peace Corps volunteer (in Mongolia), a U.S. Air Force officer, and other roles in the public sector. *Tattoos and Tans* is his first published novel. He started New Bayou Books to spark a revolution in Louisiana literature. Go to NewBayouBooks.com to learn more.

Made in the USA
Monee, IL
30 April 2022